SERENADE

By Stephen Mizell

Copyright ©2024 Line By Lion Publications
www.pixelandpen.studio
ISBN 9781948807807
Cover Design by Pace Leggent
Editing by Dani J. Caile and Priscilla Van Der Weele-Smith

For more information, email www.linebylionpublications.com

LINE BY LION
PUBLICATIONS

I wrote this book for my wife, the composer of my life's song and my son who sets the tempo.

I dedicate it to my friend Chelsea; I miss talking books with you.

Prelude

Alma, Nebraska

IN the deepest hours of night, when the sun had faded into fond memory, darkness claimed the Nebraskan town of Alma. Standing in contrast was the bridge, harshly illuminated by street lamps that fought a losing battle to reach the other side. It was a white mark on a chalkboard; thick emptiness, its destination. There had been a lake here, a reason for such a bridge, but it had given its last drops in an evaporated exhalation, leaving behind old, gnarled trees. They crawled up the embankment, trying desperately to reach the bridge and escape the pursuant emptiness.

From this darkness, from this empty nothing, came the hum of a motorcycle, joined by a voice, singing softly. Notes wove through the now musical tones of the motorcycle's passage, turning into a melody unheard by the sleeping town's ears, yet heard by all. Residents of the sleeping town moved reflexively in their sleep and smiled. Those who were awake found themselves mouthing words they didn't know to a song they'd never heard before.

The motorcycle, its driver, and the song came rolling into Alma at three that morning. Following close behind, in the settling dust, came death.

Verse 1

Omaha, Nebraska

DARK hair tendrils tentatively brushed the surface of the table, spreading out like roots searching for water, as Elizabeth allowed her head to sink toward the wooden surface. She could feel the thirty-four years of her life pushing down on her shoulders. She heard the muffled sounds of her son playing in the basement, knowing she should probably check on him. Five-year-olds were tiny tornadoes when parental eyes were not on them. Instead, she closed her parental eyes and allowed her head to finish its journey to the table.

Elizabeth had decided to revisit her favorite pastime of going through all her recent life choices, followed by the life choices that had led her to those life choices, and so on and so forth into oblivion, when her phone began to sing her an old song.

"So, tell me what you want, what you really, really want. I'll tell you what I want, what I really, really want."

Suddenly, the thirty-four-pound weight was gone. She was no longer in her mid-thirties, alone in her kitchen, but a sixteen-year-old at her homecoming dance with her best friend. With an insane need to chase that nostalgic high, she snatched her phone and accepted the call.

"Bex!" she nearly shouted. Due to her morose state of mind prior to the phone ringing, she'd slightly overcompensated when given the slightest opportunity to change it. She took a deep breath to try to regulate her emotions into a more even zone.

"Beth? Hey. Yes, it's me. If that loud noise was a question. How are you? Oh, shit. Sorry, I . . ." Rebecca's voice trailed off, taking with it Elizabeth's joy. "Sorry."

Elizabeth sighed. That was the worst part of Facebook: everyone knew everything. It was impossible to quietly end a marriage these days. Her vow to never again add a relationship status was retrospective and unhelpful now.

"Honestly, I'm not great, but I am pretty good, and that is better than okay." Elizabeth was pretty sure that was a line from one of the books she'd read on divorce after Jason had moved out, but it sounded good and felt honest. "What about you? How's Kansas?" Yep, nothing says "oldest friend in the world" like asking about the state where they live.

"It's, um, flat, I guess?"

They fell into silence, neither knowing what to say next to move forward. The conversation was barely two sentences deep and it was already ruined by Elizabeth's divorce.

Elizabeth hated this aspect of her life. Normal conversations were always tainted by the roadblock that was her divorce. Once mentioned, the entire interaction derailed. She hated Jason all over again. It's amazing how reasons to hate someone can spiral out like a crack in the ice. First the heartbreak. *Crack.* Then the lost friends. *Splinter.* Now the broken conversations. *Splash.* When he'd left, he'd packed his underwear, toothbrush, and everything normal about life.

She latched onto the last thing said, using it as a pivot point back into lighter conversation. "How dare you body shame my home state? I will have you know many men prefer a flat terrain over the mountains of Colorado or the hills of—"

Elizabeth could not, for the life of her, think of a famously hilly state. "—California?"

Then they were laughing and safely off thin ice, back onto solid ground.

"Jesus, you are weird. I have missed that. But most importantly, I miss you. Will you be my maid of honor?"

The casualness with which Rebecca asked almost made Elizabeth miss the implication of the question.

Almost.

She shrieked a sound somewhere between a pterodactyl and a police siren that caused a concerned Wyatt to run up from the basement to check on her.

"I'm fine, buddy, sorry. Just really happy."

He gave her a quizzical look.

"I heard some really good news. On the phone."

Wyatt got the message and disappeared back downstairs to the game he'd left. Elizabeth took a moment to appreciate her son's concern before returning her concentration to the phone call. "Congratulations. That is amazing and of course I will be the maid of honor."

Similarly prehistoric noises came from the other side of Elizabeth's phone.

"Do you have a date in mind? I was thinking about taking Wyatt to Disneyland after he turned six, because when I was a kid, I went when I was six, and I remember enjoying it and thinking that six might be the perfect age for that type of theme park magic." She realized she was rambling due to the excitement overload and stopped to take a breath.

"When does Wyatt turn six?"

"Next January."

"Then you have nothing to worry about. Because we plan on getting married this July."

Elizabeth's mouth dropped. She looked at the calendar on the wall to remind herself of the month she already knew it was. "It's April. That is barely three months away. What could have possessed you to do that?"

"Possession isn't far off."

It took Elizabeth's mind a second to put the pieces together.

"You're pregnant?"

"Let's just say two things were confirmed last night: who I am going to marry and when we are going to start a family. But you know how vain I am. I want to look good in my wedding dress, dammit, and I don't want to wait. So, yeah, I have a crazy plan to get married this summer, and you already agreed to be my maid of honor so you can't back out now."

"Please, I'm a teacher. Summer weddings are the easiest for me to attend."

"I'm glad to hear you say that, because I'm going to need all the help I can get to make sure this thing happens. I need your elementary teacher crafting skills, your weird focus on organization, and, to be honest, all of that was a lame way of saying I need you. Please come join me for the summer."

"Join you for the summer? Like, more than the week before? I can't live in Wichita for the summer, Bex. The longest I could hope to keep Wyatt happy in a hotel room is maybe an extended weekend if the hotel has a pool."

"Beth, I'm getting married back home in Alma."

Elizabeth saw her summer plans come together like a well-designed puzzle. "Wyatt and I can stay at my dad's in Norton. It's only a thirty-minute drive. That's nothing. We used to make that drive basically every day when we were kids. I'll have to check with my dad, but I don't see any reason why he couldn't watch Wyatt here and there while I help out."

"Is that a 'yes'?"

"Unequivocally."

"So, is that a 'yes'?"

"Yes, it's a 'yes.' Get a dictionary. It's a 'yes.'"

Pterodactyl siren noises recommenced.

Verse 2

Alma, Nebraska

THE man stepped into the bar, chiming the small bell.

When the bartender looked up, she quickly registered that not only was this a new customer, but a new face. That was rare as this dive wasn't located along the highway like some of the others. Not that she was complaining. Two in the afternoon was an extremely slow time for her and she'd been in a half-doze.

She clocked the stranger at about six feet with short brown hair, a decent body, and a shadow on his face that looked intentional. He wore a plain white tee and faded blue jeans.

He took a moment to survey the bar, taking in the two older gentlemen in the back booth nursing their beers. He walked toward her, his blue eyes meeting her brown. His eyes were gorgeous.

"What can I get for you, handsome?" This was a normal intro that she used on most men, but the eyes had taken her by surprise, so it was more sincere than usual.

"First, a name. Then, something local."

Six simple words, but they took her breath away.

He smiled and she was afraid to reply. What his eyes had started his voice had enhanced, transforming his simple smile into a masculine Mona Lisa's. She told herself that her twitterpation was from the fact that she didn't see many new faces in the bar. That was all. She steadied herself.

"Thunderhead is something local, but it's a dollar more than the normal stuff. You can have the name for free, though. It's Sally." Thankfully, this phrase came out with a practiced ease that put her nerves back in order. This new face had caught her off guard, but she'd been bartending for years and was a professional. "There is also Boulevard. It comes from Missouri, which is pretty close, and the locals like it. So, I guess that makes it kinda local, right?"

"Sally."

Her breath caught as her name passed his lips.

"A Thunderhead sounds great," he continued. "Wow, that is not something I thought I'd ever say as my main mode of transportation only has two wheels and no roof." He smiled at his wit as he leaned forward to pull a thick, worn, leather wallet from his back pocket. "What about food, Sally? Got any of that around?"

"We have a lunch menu, but we stop serving in thirty minutes. Hopefully, you can speed read or Frank will do unspeakable things to your meal."

He looked up from the wallet he'd been spinning on the counter with mild shock.

"I'm pulling your leg. There is no one named Frank. I make the sandwiches. The rest of it, though, is all true." She winked, setting down the menu in front of him. "Also, you don't need to show me your ID. I'm pretty good at guessing ages. Even have my own booth at the local fair."

She immediately regretted the decision as she still didn't know his name and had passed up the opportunity to learn it without asking.

With practiced hands, she rolled a tumbler up her forearm to her inner elbow and bounced it back into her hand to fill at the tap. She realized, self-consciously and with a tinge of annoyance, that his eyes, those brilliant blue eyes, had been on the menu the entire time she'd been filling his drink. She looked over at the two men in the back. Their eyes had not been on lunch menus. They'd been watching the sad show with keen interest.

"I don't know if that little show was for me or not," the stranger said, his eyes never leaving the menu, "but it was impressive. I will take the turkey sandwich." The menu went down, and his eyes were once again on her.

Her face was scarlet; she didn't need the mirror on the back of the bar to tell her that. It felt like when she splurged at her hairdresser and got the facial as well. His little smile grew. It looked so comfortable on his face.

"Yep," she said in a show of pure professionalism as she swiped the menu away from him, fleeing to the safety of the kitchen, heart pounding.

The whole situation was so bizarre. She reminded herself that the reason she was acting this way was because he was someone new and that was rare in Alma. She managed to get herself under control and went to work building a turkey sandwich.

When she returned to the bar, the stranger was no longer on his stool. She quickly located him with the two men in the back corner. They were laughing together. She prayed it had nothing to do with her fancy glass juggling. This little doubt, this little bit of fear that she was being made fun of, was enough to cut through the weird daze she'd been feeling. Memories of high school and other tables with laughter from long ago flowed through her mind and her face became set. She strolled over to the table. "Here is your sandwich. I promise Frank did not spit in it."

"Thank you, Sally, but I thought you said there was no one back there named Frank." Smiling, he took the plate from her hands, setting it next to his beer on the table. The other two men smiled with him.

Jesus, his smile was contagious.

"Oh, he's not in the kitchen. He's up here," Sally said, tapping the side of her head. Lowering her voice, she threw in as much gravel as she could: "I was gonna spit, but Sally pointed out you'd chosen a cold sandwich to be nice."

The two old men looked at the stranger, waiting to see if he would laugh, as if they understood on some level that this joke wasn't meant for them. They didn't have to wait long as a few little giggles gave way to a musical laugh. It caught like fire to flint, forcing them all to join in his merriment.

She'd not known that laughter could be musical until her own laughter joined in harmony.

As if a dial slowly turned, the laughter began to fade, and the stranger wiped at his eyes with the napkin still wrapped around the fork/knife combo. "Well, then, Sally," he said airily as his breath tried to get itself under control, "I guess you are the hero of my lunch. Protecting it from those who seek to do it harm. For this, I am eternally in your debt."

The old men looked at her attentively, probably hoping to see the scarlet return to her cheeks. But they were out of luck. She was too distracted by how he spoke, almost like a kid playing knights and dragons, and by how much she found herself wanting to play along.

"Your food's safety is my only reward." In one motion, she pulled the small dish towel from her apron belt, threw it around her shoulder as a makeshift cape, and spun heroically, leaving their table to return to the bar. She was followed by their applause.

She was happy to be facing away from them as her face grew warm.

Verse 3

Norton, Kansas

IN a living room, on a side table, next to a very worn, very loved recliner, a cell phone began to chirp.

Harold set the newspaper on his lap, took off his glasses, and rubbed his eyes. He'd wasted too much time perusing the meaningless pages of today's news and had only just got to the important part: sports. He picked up the flip phone, looked at the outside screen, and realized he was no longer wearing his glasses.

"Crumbs."

He decided to risk answering. Knowing his luck, it would be a telemarketer wanting to sell him life insurance. After hitting a certain age, the Red Cross gives up asking for blood and passes the baton to life insurance salesmen. He hit the button and held the phone up to his ear.

"Dad, is this a bad time?"

"That depends. Do you know who won the KU-Missouri game?"

"Of course. I would never call without the basics. KU won. Was there any doubt? I don't remember the score, but I can ask Alexa if you want."

"Nah, I trust you." He reclined the chair and got comfortable. "How are you? How's Wyatt?"

"He's good. Twice the size he was last time you saw him." Elizabeth skipped nimbly past his inquiry into her wellbeing.

He closed his eyes, not sure if he was grateful or disappointed that she didn't want to talk about it. He often felt regret that he was unable to be an emotional anchor for her. Her mom had always held that place while she was alive. It was not a mantle he'd been able to take up. He was raised on the farm, raised to believe that tears were a waste of moisture. Raised to believe that hugs should be short, to the point, and as stiff as possible.

Even when his grandson was born, while there was obvious love, he didn't have the slightest idea how to show it and too often passed on the opportunity to hold the boy. When he did, as pictures would prove, he looked terrified. Judith had been better; she'd taken to grandmothering like a fish to swimming.

Harold often found himself thinking about how better off everyone would have been if he'd gone to the store that day. If he'd been the one coming home with the groceries. Then maybe his daughter would have had someone to call during her divorce. Then maybe she could have gotten a real hug.

"I guess I'll take your word for that as his mother barely sends pictures."

He knew all this small talk was leading to something. She usually called with questions about her car, or plumbing, or other "dad" inquiries. These were always followed with a curt "Thank you, love you, bye." He should probably get that embroidered for his wall.

"So, what's broken this time?"

Another difference between his late wife and himself was that he didn't have much time for small talk. While Judith would spend hours on the phone, trying to suck up every last detail of Elizabeth and Wyatt's life, he wasn't good at it. Instead, he favored quick, focused calls. *Thank you, love you, bye.*

"What? Oh, nothing like that. Remember Rebecca? My old friend from school?"

Of course, he did. He uh-huh'd his remembrance.

She continued, "Well, she is getting married this summer in Alma and I am going to be the maid of honor. Which is extremely exciting. I was hoping that Wyatt and I could stay at home and make trips there as needed."

"Of course, you can." Spending a little time with his daughter and grandson sounded quite nice actually. "When is the wedding?"

"Well, that's the thing. The wedding is in July, but she wants me there all summer to catch up and help with the planning. So, I will be needing a place to stay for most of the summer. That's still okay, right? Wyatt has been dying to see you more."

He paused to let the new information settle over him. It'd been a long time since he'd entertained anyone for longer than a night. Without Judith, the concept was paralyzing.

"Of course," he repeated. "I'll make up a couple of rooms for you and Wyatt and it will be like old times. You always did love bringing boys home."

"Har har har, Dad. I'll let you know the details as soon as I know them. Thank you, love you, bye."

And she was gone.

He sat in his chair, holding the phone to his ear for a long time. Slowly, he flipped it shut and set it on the side table to be forgotten again.

"Well, shit."

Verse 4

Alma, Nebraska

THE three men sat in the back booth, sipping their warming beers.

"So, young man, what do you do?"

Gary had been coming to this bar with his best friend, Jacob, for years. Their skin had permanent tans from their long years farming, which served to emphasize the impressively thick white hair on their heads. Long years had taken their wives and sent their families away to seek better things than Alma could offer. Those same years had cemented their relationship through repetition and custom.

Now this peculiar man with the sharp blue eyes sat at their customary table, during their customary afternoon beer, after flirting with their customary bartender.

"I'm a singer." The stranger took a bite of his sandwich. He chewed for a while, making a comically thoughtful face before turning to the bar. "This sandwich may be the best sandwich I have ever eaten."

Sally smirked.

"I'm serious," he continued, "this turkey's death was not in vain. It can feel peace, knowing its body was served up as a delicious sandwich and not ground into dog food."

He giggled at this, and Gary pondered on how young this man was.

After another exaggerated bite, the stranger said, "Iv omwy id code be serbed wid anoda bea," speaking around the glob of sandwich still in his mouth.

"That is disgusting," Sally scolded. "Didn't your mother teach you not to talk with your mouth full?"

As soon as the words left her mouth, his eyes lost all their light. His smile stayed, but it was altered, broken in some unknowable way. He swallowed the bite. It went down hard.

"I'm—" Sally started.

"You're all too right," he replied, saving her from finding a reply. "That was not very polite, and I apologize."

The light was coming back to his eyes, but some of the mirth was gone. The eyes had a guarded look to them now.

"Delicious sandwiches have a way of making me forget my manners. They also have a way of making me very thirsty. A round of Thunderhead for the table, Super Sally."

Gary and Jacob protested simultaneously.

"I insist." He turned back toward them. "You see, my fine gentlemen, this has now become a business meeting. I have told you what I do for a living, but not where I do it. This, sadly, is because there is nowhere to do it at the moment. So, I was hoping you fine young men could help me out with that."

Gary had a fleeting memory of an old movie he enjoyed called *The Music Man*, remembering how scripted the lines had felt even within the movie. The conman selling his pitch in a little song. That is what this conversation felt like: scripted lines.

"Not much in the line of singing jobs 'round here," Jacob said, looking to Gary for confirmation.

Gary took the cue, still thinking of the musical, and nodded his agreement. Sally brought new beers to the table and distributed them. The men smiled up at her appreciatively as she cleared away the empty glasses. Gary, who only ever got the cheapest beer he could, sipped the honey wheat beer and worried afterward if he would ever be able to return to the other.

"There are always weddings during the summer that need music," Jacob offered, "but usually they go with DJs. There's one being thrown together pretty quickly that you might be able to grab a role in."

Gary sipped his beer and decided that regular beer was not only acceptable, but better. All this fancy flavoring got in the way of a perfectly good beer. However, he would never complain openly about a free beer on principle.

"Sounds like my kind of shindig. What kind of crowd would that pull in?"

The two men looked at each other and smiled.

"What's so funny?"

"The girl getting married is well known in Alma," Gary said. "Her father has done very well for himself, and in a town of middle-class farming families, he kinda stands above them all. So, if he is a king, then she's the princess." He shrugged to show that he didn't quite have the words to describe it; royalty was a good comparison. "The family has ties to just about everything here, so when it was announced she was getting married in Alma, it was kind of understood that the whole town was invited."

"So how do I get in contact with —?"

Before he could finish that thought, the front door banged open.

Verse 5

Omaha, Nebraska

ELIZABETH took a deep breath, looked at the phone on the counter, and continued to dread her next phone call. Her dread came more from knowing how her ex-husband would react. For once, she wished he was a little less predictable.

She turned her gaze from the intimidating chunk of machinery sitting on the island and looked out the sliding door that led to the backyard. Wyatt was hunkered down with his little shovel, digging for toys in his sandbox with the concentration of an archeologist unearthing the world's most complete set of T-Rex fossils. She smiled, feeling a wave of love crash over her.

A wave that carried her from love to fury as soon as she looked back at the phone.

She was ready now and snatched it up, hitting the first number on her speed dial. She hated that she had to keep his number on her phone at all.

With each ring, her emotions changed. *Ring*. Her fury morphed to anxiety. *Ring*. Deep sorrow. *Ring*. That brought her back around to fury in time for him to pick up.

"Yellow."

Always with the "yellow" like it was so fucking witty, like he was the first fucking person to fucking think of that.

"Good morning, Jason," she said with false calm.

Throughout the divorce, this was a skill she'd mastered.

No matter how upset she was, she was never going to give him the delight of seeing or hearing it.

"El?"

Like he didn't know who she was when she called.

"What do I owe the pleasure of a phone call from my beautiful—?"

"I assume your new girlfriend isn't in the room if you are throwing around terms like 'beautiful,'" she said, effectively cutting off his jovial tone. She allowed a smile to crease her troubled lips. As much as she'd been dreading this call, any time she could claim the moral high ground made her feel a little better.

"El," he said, the fun gone from his voice, "we don't have to have an arduous relationship."

That was another thing that drove her crazy. He always used words that he thought made him sound smart. Why say "arduous" when he could say "difficult"? She knew it was because he felt that by sounding more intelligent his points were more valid.

"I'm going to be gone for the summer and thought you should know." Why dance around the point with infuriating small talk? "I'm going to stay with my dad in Norton for a couple of months to help Rebecca plan her wedding."

She held her breath. Now came the reply, the reason she'd not wanted to make this phone call.

"Rebecca? Your old friend from high school? That's great. Sounds like fun." He paused. When he continued, she could hear the hesitance. "You were planning on taking Wyatt, I assume?"

She let out enough breath to reply. "Would that be a problem?"

This was a bomb; the fuse was lit. His reply could destroy what little emotion she held for him after everything that had happened.

"Nope, no problem at all." His relief was unmistakable. "Send me pictures when you can and let me know when you get back and I can take him for ice cream or something."

There it was. His complete lack of caring. This once she'd wanted him to fight her over taking his son away for so long. Deep down, however, she'd known he wouldn't. Hell, it was the reason he'd left her after all.

"You're sure? I mean, it's a long time. I could maybe bring him back up for one of the weekends or something like that." Giving him an out. Always trying to lead him to where she wanted him to get on his own. Where he should get on his own.

"No." Now there was wariness to his voice. He had always known when she was trying to manipulate him. "If I know wedding planning, weekends will probably be the busiest days, and a five-hour drive here and five-hour drive back will be a waste of your time."

In other terms, his son's presence would be a waste of his time. His precious weekend would have to be spent actually being a father. Of course, because she was the one out of town, he could easily pin the reason on her rather than take any responsibility.

"It's closer to four hours," she said lamely.

Her emotions in regard to this phone call were extremely hard to figure out. She was angry at him for not caring about his son, but grateful she didn't have to drive back and see him. She was sad for Wyatt because of his absentee father, but happy he'd get to spend so much time with his grandfather. In any case, the decision had been made and there was no reason to keep pushing a locked door. "I will send you pictures every day and call you at least once a week to let you talk to him."

"That sounds great. And if, for some reason, I can't answer the phone when you call, have Wyatt leave me a voicemail. That way I can listen to him when I get the chance."

"Some reason" was probably his new girlfriend. Elizabeth thought about the young and attractive new woman sharing her ex-husband's bed. She hated that she was made to feel old in her mid-thirties. Elizabeth ran a finger up and down a light pink stretch mark peeking out from under her shirt, one of the many party favors she took home from the hospital after giving birth.

"Thank you for being so understanding."

Hopefully, he didn't hear the exacerbation in her voice. Wyatt was growing up fatherless. Jason was a glorified babysitter who watched him occasionally. She wondered for the millionth time about how this affected Wyatt. Did he recognize that his dad didn't want him? Hell, for all she knew, Jason didn't even love Wyatt. The genetic disposition to love and protect one's own offspring could be vacant in his DNA. Wouldn't that biological abnormality have been nice to know before they sealed the deal?

She sighed again. "I will definitely have him call, leave voicemails, Facetime, and in all other ways I can think of to spend time with you despite being away."

"Sounds great," he said distractedly. "Look, I gotta go, tell the kid I love him." Then the connection was cut.

She sat there with the phone to her ear, lost in her own thoughts, "The Kid" echoing around her like a cry in a deserted canyon.

Jason started calling him "The Kid" when Wyatt was a toddler. At first, she thought it was a cute little nickname. However, as the days turned into months, it dawned on her that she'd not heard him say "Wyatt" in quite some time. She finally confronted him about it, again assuming it would be nothing. It had been like pulling a stop out of the bottom of the barrel. That was the conversation that had led to the separation that inevitably led to their divorce.

"Fucking prick," she said, finally removing the lifeless phone from her ear.

"Fucking prick," echoed Wyatt from the other side of the sliding door.

Verse 6

Alma, Nebraska

ALL three men turned to look at the silhouette of the newcomer in the doorway. He was an intimidating statue, cast in ebony stone. The men stared at him as they let their eyes adjust to the outside world until his features began to fade into view.

Sally, on the other hand, had no reason to look. She returned to polishing her glass.

It had been such a good day too. She looked toward the new guy sitting with her regulars. He'd been so sweet and charming, and now, he was about to learn about the worst aspects of her life. That certainly didn't seem fair.

"Sally." The voice from the door was harsh, deep, and unpleasant. It was in direct contrast to the soft, melodious voice of the stranger. "Sally, you bitch."

"Jack," she said calmly. "Why are you at my place of work, saying such terrible things, in front of such decent people?"

The door slammed shut as he stepped in and looked around, seeing the table of men. He sniffed dismissively toward them, rounding back toward Sally.

"I don't care if the King of England is in this shit hole." He advanced toward the bar.

The new guy stood, but Sally shot him a glance that made him hesitate.

Jack saw this and turned back to the previously dismissed table. "Fuck you looking at?" he growled.

"Honestly," the young man said, "something that fixed my perspective of this town. Up to this point I'd almost come to believe there existed a town with only good souls in it — possibly the first I'd ever visited. I see that I was wrong. I feel better that my worldview can remain unchanged. The world is evil. Wherever goodness abides, darkness will come along shortly to taint it."

Jack stared at him as if he'd spoken in a foreign language.

In fact, they all shared similar looks as the man strolled gracefully to the bar to join Jack and Sally.

Sally's stunned expression changed to one of trepidation bordering on fear. If the stranger was looking for a fight, he'd picked the wrong guy with whom to find it.

"Are you one of those gays?" Jack asked, looking more perplexed than angry.

Sally coughed out a laugh, covering her mouth. She couldn't help it.

"Look, I ain't into any of that stuff, so go sit back down, 'cause I don't want to get in trouble for a hate crime or nothing."

Sally was no longer laughing. "I'm fine," she said softly.

The stranger turned those piercing eyes on her with an inquisitive look.

"I'm sure," she said as if answering his eyes.

He looked back at Jack who was mercifully quiet, probably trying to decide if this one-sided conversation taking place in front of him should make him angry or not.

"As you wish. Good day, good sir."

With that, the stranger strolled back to his two new friends, turned his chair so he could continue to see the happenings at the bar, and sat.

Luckily, Jack continued a little more subdued after the strange confrontation. "Look, Sally, I need that money, like yesterday."

She looked down and instinctively found another glass to polish. Keeping her hands busy kept her calm.

"I have given you two extra weeks. If anything, it is your fault that I had to come to your place of work." Jack gestured to the nearly empty bar, lingering on the back table. "None of this had to happen if you'd paid when you were supposed to."

"As I said when I called you last week," Sally said softly, in hopes that her customers wouldn't overhear, "it will be toward the end of the month. I have worked through the math and will be able to pay you back in full. You acted like it wasn't that big of a deal."

Jack smiled mirthlessly. "It wouldn't have been a big deal," he said loudly, "if you had paid when you were supposed to." The smile vanished entirely from his face. "You have until tomorrow evening."

Her mouth fell open. She began to protest, but he was halfway across the room before she could even muster a groan. He turned as he went to look directly at the young man sitting with the old men in the back.

"Word to the wise: We don't much care for your kind in this part of the country."

Then, in a bath of sunlight, he was out the door, leaving the bar in stunned silence.

Sally looked at the back table. As those blue eyes turned toward her, she fled to the kitchen, not wanting to be seen by anyone, especially that blue gaze.

The three men sat in silence as Sally disappeared into the back.

Slowly, the young man turned back to Gary and Jacob. "Gentlemen, you have been the dream precluding that nightmare." He slipped the worn wallet from his pocket, removed five twenties, and laid them on the table. "These should cover your two current drinks, everything I purchased, and a second round with a tip to boot." Before he returned the wallet, he removed a card. "And if you could be so kind as to get this card and a recommendation to the lovely bride-to-be's family, I would be much obliged." He stood, pushed in his chair, and turned toward the door.

"Should be able to do that." Gary appeared unphased by the interaction he'd witnessed. The man reached down, moved his empty glass, and picked up the napkin that had been under it. "Are ya lookin' for work before then? Might be able to find somethin' for you. Probably not singing, but somethin'."

The stranger found a capped pen in one of his pockets and wrote something within the ring of condensation on the napkin. He turned toward the empty bar where Sally had been standing moments ago. "I might hit you up on that," he said distractedly as he made his way to the bar. He gently laid down the napkin, stood looking at it for a second, then looked back at the men he'd left. "For now, I think I may have stumbled upon a job." He nodded at them. "Have a wonderful rest of the day and please find that card a home for me."

With that, he walked out of the bar, momentarily blinding the men as he left. The sound of a motorcycle started then faded with distance, confirming his departure.

Gary turned toward Jacob, the card still in his hand. He looked at it for the first time, seeing the beautiful flowing type.

"Samuel Serenade." He chuckled, passing the card to Jacob.

"Must be a stage name," Jacob replied, smiling. "I like it. I like him." He looked at his glass, downed the last frothy bit, then looked at the twenties on the table. "Sally?" he called toward the kitchen door. "Honey, it's safe to come out. He's gone."

Her very red face peeked through the door's window. "Glared" would probably be more appropriate.

Jacob raised first his empty glass then the cash. "Compliments of Mr. Serenade." He looked at Gary and they both began to laugh, drawing Sally out with the sound.

Verse 7

Norton, Kansas

HAROLD finished making up the guest bed, turned, and sat on the freshly smoothed cover. He sighed.

"Oh Judy."

His spoken words broke the long-held silence of the terminally lonely. Then the comfort of talking to her took over as it so often did these days. "Judy, I miss ya love."

He stood, turned, and smoothed out the bed cover, erasing the indentation of his rear with a swipe of his hand. "Sorry," he said softly, "I know you always hate it when I do that."

He placed his hands on his hips and stretched out his back, reveling in the popping sounds it made as he leaned backward. When did his back get so old? Probably the same time as the rest of him, he supposed.

"I never hated you sitting on the bed. It was when you farted on the freshly made ones that made me so upset, ya old stinker." Judy's voice, so real in his head, pulled up the wrinkled corners of his mouth.

"Had to mark my territory, didn't I?"

After the back popping, he felt happily spry and almost sauntered out the door of the guest bedroom. His eyes ran over the nearly pristinely clean basement, realizing it had been a while since he'd stepped further into the basement than the laundry room at the base of the stairs. He had no need.

Now he did. Preparing the house for his daughter and her son, his grandson. Just the two of them as she too had recently become spouseless.

"Is that what you are? Spouseless?" Judith asked.

Did she sound hurt? Only because he wanted her to.

He made his way upstairs, wondering if there was enough coffee in the pot to reheat or if he would have to make a new pot.

"You know reheating cold coffee is gross, right?"

"I am not going to waste perfectly good coffee. It is what microwaves were made for," he told the empty kitchen at the top of the stairs.

As Harold poured the remains of that morning's coffee into a mug, he began to softly cry.

Verse 8

Alma, Nebraska

JACK pulled a beer from the fridge and walked down the hall to the living room. On the way, he stopped at the door to Boomer's room.

His son was playing with LEGOs; building something spectacular, he had no doubt. *Kid is a whip, God knows where he got that from.*

Looking at Boomer brought back some of the annoyance from earlier that day. Jack hated that he had to show up at Sally's work to get her to listen to him. Money was tight ever since his hours had been slashed at work and their son wasn't going to pay for himself.

He thought back to their last phone call when she accused him of being a leach. "Why not sell any of your expensive guns?" she'd asked. It was just like her to shove his hobbies down his throat instead of fessing up to the fact that she was a shitty mom.

How shitty? Shitty enough that the judge had seen fit to give full custody to Jack, thank God.

He moved on from Boomer's door and began to sing a little song under his breath. There were no words, just a melody. He wasn't even sure where he'd heard it. Maybe from a dream? Could you compose music in your sleep? He supposed you could.

He walked past his favorite chair in the living room and sat his beer on the coaster on the side table. The coaster was kind of pointless since the side table was already covered with rings, due to his ex-wife's lack of manners.

Dammit. He was thinking about Sally again. This time, in his mind's eye, he saw two blue eyes.

He continued to softly sing as he walked away from his beer and chair.

Who was that guy from the bar? A new boyfriend? He certainly had stood up for her fast enough. It was probably just some guy unaware of the situation, thinking he could be a hero. He couldn't have been her boyfriend anyway. Hadn't he said he was gay? He could have been that gay type who like both.

Jack disregarded this thought. He would have known if Sally had a new boyfriend. He still had plenty of friends who frequented that specific bar. No, that guy was probably just a random fag with a big mouth and a love of drama. All those types loved the drama.

His singing had grown loud enough to be considered talking volume as he turned the corner and headed downstairs to his man cave.

Many things had changed for the better since Sally's departure, but by far, one of his favorite changes had been the man cave. While they were married, he'd always wanted one. A place he could get away, drink a beer, and watch sports or hunting on TV without having her hovering over his shoulder. Instead, this room had been a craft room that infuriatingly was never used.

His guns or, as he called them, his "pride and joys," had been safely locked in their case in the non-insulated garage. He knew that the case kept out any moisture or dust, but it wasn't like it was air conditioned. Extreme heat, which in a Nebraska summer could get up there, cannot be great for machinery like guns.

He began to really put some sound behind his song now as he looked at his new gun case. The glass front gleamed, allowing him to see the guns through his own reflection. As if he was one with the guns. The two shotguns, the rifle with the questionably legal sight, the pistol with the unquestionably illegal silencer, the pistol small enough to fit in his sock, and all the extra clips already loaded.

As he allowed his song to wash over him, he thought of Boomer. What a great kid he was. He understood the rules in regard to Daddy's guns. They were off limits—unless Daddy took him to the range, of course. But, in the house, they were to be locked up at all times. His faith that Boomer would never attempt to get out the guns was the only reason he left bullets in the clips at all.

Sally would never understand. Guns were a mystery that she had no desire to figure out. He'd offered to take her to the range hundreds of times. An olive branch. Maybe some common ground would be found. She not only turned him down, she did so with real venom, turning his hobby into something bad. Trying to take one of the few things he loved in life and taint it.

"What a bitch."

The words flowed into the song he was now belting at the top of his voice.

Verse 9

Alma, Nebraska

IN his room, Boomer finally noticed that something was happening and turned toward his door. He set down his toys and got up. What on earth was his dad doing? He'd never in his life heard his dad sing. Even on his birthdays, his dad would speak the words to *Happy Birthday*.

"Dad?" he shouted as he hiked up his pajama bottoms and walked out his bedroom door.

Despite shouting, his voice didn't come close to cutting through the melody flowing from the basement. Boomer smiled, shocked to find that his dad had a beautiful voice. The way he shifted between a heavy bass to a softer baritone began to pull tears from his eyes. There was an ecstasy mixed into the notes. He was hearing beauty, something he hadn't known was possible. His dad's voice became a roller coaster as he swung low into the deepest bass Boomer had heard yet before sliding up into a tenor. He held that note for a few beats.

All of a sudden, there was a crashing sound.

Boomer flung his hands to his ears and screamed.

As he lowered his hands, the silence fell upon him like a heavy blanket.

No, that wasn't right. It was like the time he swam to the bottom of the twelve-foot marker at the pool. The weight of the water had forced the air out of him until he began to believe he would never make it back to the surface. That was what this felt like: Twelve feet of water crushing him in silence.

The song was over. Cutting through the silence, a motorcycle started outside the living room window. The sound lasted only a few seconds before disappearing into the distance. The silence flooded back in as Boomer made his way down the stairs.

"Dad?"

The silence answered him the only way it knew how.

Verse 10

Omaha, Nebraska

JASON stood in front of the mirror in his new bathroom. Everything in his life was new. Even the towel around his waist was purchased only a month ago.

New was better, right?

He looked at his body and saw something else new: his gut. He thought back to when he'd been thin and had a full head of hair.

New wasn't always better, he decided.

Sighing, he picked his cell phone up and saw the picture message icon. With a swipe of his thumb, he was looking at his son sitting in his car seat.

"Off to Grandpa's," read the text underneath.

"New *is* better," he said to the mirror version of himself with as much confidence as he could muster. The chubbier, balder version of himself on the other side stared back. The eyes were sad, as if they knew something Jason did not.

"What did you say?" called Stacy from the living room.

Stacy was new as well.

He thought about El. He remembered her as she was in college when she'd been new. He frowned out at himself from behind the mirror.

Stacy popped her head in the door. The mirror changed expressions before she could see.

"Sorry, Babe, lost in thought."

She stood in the door, wearing only her pants, holding her bra in one hand, the other hand planted on her hip. Her breasts were taut like three-dimensional bullseyes. He turned away from the judgmental mirror and took her in his arms. He kissed her neck, and she giggled like the young woman she was. She pushed him away, the bra pressing against his abdomen.

"I have to get to work, you old letcher." She laughed as she turned away.

In doing so, she missed the look of pain that washed over his face before fading away. She would have been shocked by it, but the mirror would have understood. Her playful jest had confirmed what the mirror had been trying to explain all morning.

As Jason followed her out the bathroom door, he spared a final look at the old letcher standing behind the glass. He didn't like what he saw.

Verse 11

Omaha, Nebraska

ELIZABETH snuck a peak at the rearview mirror; Wyatt soared one of his action figures over his head. He'd only been allowed two and this black ninja had found enough favor to be granted one of the coveted spots. This was not because Elizabeth was a mean mom or because there was not enough room; it was because on previous trips, many honored veterans went MIA and never made it home to their action figure families. Two was an easy number to keep eyes on. No soldier left behind and all that.

Her phone dinged twice. She'd sent the picture of Wyatt in his car seat to three people: Rebecca, her dad, and his dad. She had received two positive replies. It would not take a detective to figure out who had not replied.

"How goes the battle back there?" Elizabeth asked from the front seat.

"This is the bad guy," he explained to his mom, holding up the action figure in his hand. "He's a fucking prick." His eyes danced with excitement.

Her eyes grew wide in the mirror, then slanted accusingly, then softened as she let out a sigh. "Wyatt, you know that's a bad word. Both of them actually. I know that Mommy said it, but it wasn't right then, and it isn't right now."

"I know, Mom, I'm sorry."

Elizabeth's heart broke a little at his use of "Mom" instead of "Mommy." It was what he said when he was being serious. He'd been more and more serious recently. Forced unceremoniously into a serious situation no kids should have to deal with. She hoped that this time away and, more specifically, this time with his grandpa would do him good. He needed a strong male role model now that Jason was pretty much out of the picture. Her dad was the best male role model she'd ever known.

She'd been doing her best to fill in that gap herself. She'd learned the nuances of action figure play, which was shockingly similar to doll play. Instead of kissing and trying on clothes, however, they were punching and trying on weapons. The punching aspect rarely happened though, because the bulk of the play was in setting up the battles. She would walk a character over to the table and set him on it with a look to Wyatt who would either approve or disapprove, based on the strategy that specific figure would employ in this battle. Over time, she learned most of their strategies, and had even had some arguments with Wyatt about whether the sofa cushion was an adequate staging area for the black ninja or if he would be better off hiding under the recliner.

On average the battle would be forgotten by the time the setup was complete, which was fine with her. The fighting part was hard with two people. It ended up more or less being an awkward fist bump scenario of ramming each other's figures against each other.

She looked in the rearview mirror again and smiled. Obviously, she was overreacting, but regardless, she was excited for Wyatt to spend some quality time with his grandpa. This would also free her up to be something other than a mom for once. There wasn't a lot of "co" in this co-parenting and she'd been "Mommy" significantly more than Elizabeth recently. She was excited to meet herself again.

"Mommy?" Wyatt pulled her train back onto the track. She raised her eyebrows in the mirror so he would know she'd heard him. "Does Grandpa have any cool toys?"

Ah yes, the deep concerns of the five-year-old boy. Here she was chasing down what-ifs in her head as if the world was ending on her pitiful life and he was concerned with the potential activities he could look forward to in Norton. She went to answer then had to pause.

Did her dad have any toys? There had been her toys back when she was a kid living at home, but would they have kept them? Even so, were they toys a boy would enjoy playing with? Wyatt wasn't what you would call masculine, but he definitely favored the toys marketed toward his gender-specific demographic. She remembered having a PlayStation and a Nintendo back when she lived at the house. Maybe they were still there, put away in the combination laundry/storage room in the basement.

"I'm sure he has something exciting for you to play with." Could you read doubt in someone's face? She could swear that was the very emotion she saw on his face when she gave that nonspecific reply. She thought about mentioning the Nintendo or PlayStation but didn't want to get his hopes up in case they'd sold them. "He does own a large farm, full of machinery that I used to crawl around on back when I was your age."

This brought the reaction she'd hoped to see: A look of wondering fascination.

Age had dulled her imagination, but she knew the potentials an old farm held. The giant combines could serve as Wyatt's Don Quixote windmills. Monsters from a mechanical realm, hell bent on destroying the sleepy town of Norton. Just thinking about it made her almost wish there was no wedding so she could join him on his quests without distraction. Two explorers guided by the wise old wizard. A small laugh worked its way into her mouth at an image of her dad in a cape and pointed hat.

She looked in the mirror and saw Wyatt smiling back as they continued toward Norton, the land of possibilities.

Verse 12

Alma, Nebraska

GARY and Jacob sat at their usual spot at their usual time. Jacob drank his usual, "whatever the cheapest is" beer. Gary, on the other hand, had a Thunderhead Honey Wheat, having decided that one a week along with his other beers wouldn't hurt his wallet much, but would do wonders for his contentment.

All at once, the room was lit with the dazzling outside light; silhouetted in it was the young man with whom they'd recently become acquainted.

"Mr. Serenade, as I live and breathe," Jacob said smiling.

"Please. 'Samuel' will do me just fine. I take it you read my business card, but did you pass it on?"

He settled into the seat he'd occupied the day before and turned to the bar for Sally. Instead, there was an older man behind the bar.

"Must not be Sally's shift," he said as he turned back to the two men.

They looked at him, then at each other, then back at him, stress lines deepening their already wrinkled faces.

"I guess you wouldn't have heard, not being from around here." Gary said.

He again looked toward Jacob, who seemed enthralled with his beer, the coward.

"Sally will probably be off the clock for the foreseeable future. Her ex-husband, that pleasant young man you met yesterday, killed himself last night."

Samuel's eyes widened and his eyebrows raised in shock.

"And while some may not see that as a great loss, he was the father of her child, with full custody."

Gary noticed something. The look he'd originally believed to be shock changed into real shock. He wondered what the first look could have been if not legitimate, but he let that pass and continued. "So now, Sally will take custody of her kid and will have to figure out how to be a real mom, something she never wanted nor knows anything about, I reckon."

"That's a reach," Jacob cut in, cowardice or not. "I think it is presumptuous of you to narrate her feelings toward her child like some book. She obviously loves Boomer and will probably step up and be a great mother."

Gary sighed and gave a noncommittal shrug as if to say "I don't believe it but it isn't worth fighting over."

Jacob continued, "All we know is that the original custody hearing that led to Jack having full custody was not so much about her lifestyle choices, but rather her desire to not be a mother. Whereas Jack wanted nothing more than to be a father. Does that mean that Sally won't be a great mother now that she has to be? I guess only time will tell, but I like her spirit and see a good future for them." He sipped his beer contentedly, watching to see if Gary would disagree or not.

Gary sipped his own beer, set it down, and nodded, closing the discussion between the two of them and passing it effectively over to Samuel.

Samuel sat contemplatively for a short time before his thoughts were interrupted by the new bartender.

"Hello, what can I get for ya today?"

Samuel pointed at Gary's beer. The man nodded and strode away.

"That is heartbreaking to say the least. Suicide? That doesn't seem to make sense. Why would he be looking for money yesterday if he wasn't planning on sticking around to get it?"

The two men shrugged simultaneously. In other circumstances, the action might have been comical.

"Why do they assume it was suicide? How could they have ruled out all the other options?"

His beer arrived and Samuel handed the bartender a hundred. "I'll open a tab." The bartender took the cash and hurried away. Clearly, he wanted no part in the discussion he'd walked up to.

"A self-inflicted gunshot wound to the face is hardly cause for an investigation. Not to mention that Boomer, his son, witnessed the whole thing," Gary said, shaking his head to show his dismay at the young boy's plight. "As you saw yesterday, the man had some anger issues. Who is to say there weren't other issues? The man loved his kid. You would think that would give him a reason to live, but sometimes the love of a child is not enough to sway those who have made up their mind that death is better than life."

He looked at Jacob who was giving him an odd look.

"What?" he asked defensively.

"Nothin', just surprised by how wise an old fool like yourself can sound," Jacob replied.

Samuel smiled for the first time since hearing the news and the tension at the table seemed to recede a little.

"Suffice it to say, your bartender-flirting days may be put on pause indefinitely as I am pretty sure she was the only female bartender hired at this fine establishment."

Samuel let out a little laugh followed by an exaggerated sigh. "Whatever will I do to fill the time?" he said wistfully. "Would it be improper to go see her and, I don't know, pay my respects?"

"I think it would be pertinent to wait for a bit. She will be receiving enough comfort from those who knew Jack and, more importantly, know her son." Gary finished off his beer and signaled to the man behind the counter for another. "Things are complicated as it is. The last thing she needs is the man she was flirting with at the bar to show up in front of her kid, trying to show affection."

"Now hold on, that isn't what I was intending," Samuel came back, looking shocked by the insinuation.

"I know, I know, calm your overly energetic pants," Jacob said as if he was the one who'd insinuated it and not Gary. "What he is trying to say, young man, is that Sally will not know how to process meeting you in this particular setting and could see it as something more than it is." He gave a shrug to indicate that he couldn't say one way or the other. "It's probably best to not risk her taking it the wrong way and having unneeded stress right now." Samuel nodded and the topic of Sally's complicated life came to a close.

Verse 13

Cherokee, Iowa

SLEEK and black, the car rolled up to the bar and grill at the edge of town and came to a stop in the dirt parking lot. The door opened and a man dressed in a black suit stepped out. He had close cut black hair and wore thin, square glasses. In a Google search for "Wall Street businessman," the first pictures would bear a shocking resemblance to this man.

He strode toward the door, his shiny, perfectly polished shoes puffing dust as he went. There were motorcycles parked in front of the small building and old beat-up trucks. To say he stood out would be an understatement. His suit looked like it had been ironed, steamed, ironed again, then not worn until he'd already exited the vehicle. He opened the door and walked into the low light of the afternoon bar scene.

The woman behind the bar looked old from living a hard life on the back of a motorcycle and smoking the majority of it. Her skin was tanned leather pulled over a skeleton, and her hair looked like it had been bleached, not by chemicals but the sun. A lit cigarette hung from her mouth. She had another tucked behind her ear. The room smelled like old beer, and cigarette smoke had seasoned the hard wood floors and the walls like a cast iron skillet.

The man dimly wondered how legal it was to smoke in any building these days, but figured it wasn't his place to ask nor was it pertinent to his visit.

He looked around at those seated at the tables and saw that they all bore a similar appearance to the bartender. He assumed it was either from long days in the fields or long days on their bikes. He could find out if he wanted, but again, it was not pertinent.

He continued his progress to the bar. All eyes followed him. The music was always turned down during the day for the casual afternoon conversation that usually filled the air. That conversation had dried up, however, and it felt like the bar itself was holding its breath, waiting for this newcomer to do something stupid. To do something worthy of retaliation like serve their beloved bartender papers.

He reached the bar, pulled a chair back enough to slide between the seat and the bar. "Gin and tonic," he said, louder than was maybe called for, but he wanted the room to hear it.

As soon as he'd settled, the conversations began to start back up, if a little less boisterously than before. For now, the threat had lessened, but he knew they were still thinking about him, cautiously stealing glances every few minutes.

"Startin' a tab?" the bartender asked, giving him an obviously appraising look. "Ya don't look like y'ar."

Despite trying to keep his face as emotionless as possible, the way she said "you are," like a pirate, almost caused a smile to break his otherwise placid countenance. She poured the gin and tonic and slid it across the counter over to him. He hated gin and tonic, but he lifted it and took an appreciative sip as if he drank them every night as a hobby.

"Thank you and no, I will not be starting a tab, this will be the only drink for me. I still have many miles to go and needed a refreshment." He paused here. "And hopefully a little information."

He saw her eyes pull together in an accusatory way. That look said she'd known he wasn't here for the beverage alone and she'd been right.

"I would like to ask you about Valentine's Day," he said. With that, the room fell silent again—well as far as everyone else in the room was concerned. "Would you be willing to tell me about it?" He took another sip of the wretched drink that he ordered for its appearance more than its flavor.

"Why y'askin' me? I wasn't even there."

Out of the corner of his eye, he saw someone stand from their chair, possibly to use the restroom, possibly to ask him to leave. He knew it was the latter and decided that he probably had all he needed, but he wanted to push a little more. Hopefully, it wouldn't cost him his suit; it was expensive and the only one he had.

"Bartenders tend to know more about their town than the average Joe." He thought about his reason for being here, which inevitably led him back to thinking about his old partner who had no issue with getting people to talk.

"If you know that something happened on Valentine's Day, then you probably know as much as I do. Basically, there was a ritualistic suicide party or somethin' behind the high school. Buncha people went out there and offed themselves in the name of who knows what. It was like that Kool-Aid thing a while back but bloodier." The bartender was getting upset, which upset the man who'd stood and was walking toward the bar, puffing up his already impressive chest and shoulders.

With that last push, he'd finally gotten enough information to feel like this had been a fruitful stop. He stood, set down a twenty-dollar bill and his card. "If you can think of anything else, please don't hesitate to call me."

She wouldn't call and he didn't need her to. He turned to look at the man who was now standing close enough to be a threat and nodded at him. With a quick turn, he faced the door and didn't divert his gaze as he started that direction.

The man heard the bartender pick the card up and cough a laugh. "Gideon Glimpse? That has to be a fake name, right?" They didn't even lower their voices as they passed his card back and forth.

"Private Investigator, eh? Just don't offer up your credit card number or anything to him."

She snatched the card and threw it in the trash behind the bar. "What do ya think, I'm stupid?"

The man exited the bar, briskly made his way to the car, and lowered himself carefully into the seat. With one last act of theater, he pulled a small notebook from the glove compartment, made sure it was visible to any bar patron still watching and jotted a note. With that final act done, he dropped the car into gear and pulled out of the dusty parking lot back onto the road. There was more work to be done.

Verse 14

Alma, Nebraska

ELIZABETH pulled her car into the Pump n' Pantry and got out. She was less than an hour away from home.

Well, from her parents' house. Strange how she still thought of it as home despite not living there for years. Was it possible to have more than one home? Home is where the heart is, so they say, so can a heart be in more than one location? She didn't know and was in no mood for deep thoughts like this anyway.

Wyatt had gotten fussy about an hour ago, which warranted this needless stop. Elizabeth recollected listening to long Stephen King novels on her drives instead of Baby Shark five hundred times with Wyatt as a backup singer. God, what she would give for a shape-shifting killer clown right about now.

"Wyatt? Honey? Ready to go to the bathroom, stretch your legs a little bit?"

She looked in, saw the sleeping boy in his car seat, and let her head thunk loudly on the car door. Of course, by the time she complied to the kid's demands, he fell asleep. She stood there, head on the door, letting all the bad words flow from her mind instead of toward her child.

"Are you okay?" came a voice from behind her.

All the curse words she'd been releasing internally came gushing out in a rush as she jumped forward, hitting her head for real against the door.

"I am so sorry," came the voice again.

She steadied herself while bent over and looked through the window. Wyatt had not stirred. Small favors, she guessed. She straightened and turned to address the voice that had caused her such a start.

"Hello. No apologies necessary. I was lost in thought and you helped me find my way back. So, I guess I should be thanking you." Holy cow, that had been an amazing response. She puffed up with odd pride for her witty reply then fully took in the man.

In short, he was beautiful. She wondered if she'd ever thought of a man with that word and doubted it. Yet, that was the word for this one. It wasn't that he was strikingly muscular or anything like that. He was beautiful. It was the eyes, she decided. Strikingly blue. This observation took her back to the Stephen King novels she would listen to. Wasn't there a character with eyes like that? The Gunslinger? She didn't remember his name or if he ever had a name other than "Gunslinger," but she remembered his eyes being strikingly blue. "Bombardier eyes."

In horror, she realized that the last part had slipped out. That amazing response before had completely been destroyed.

"I have never met a bombardier, but I will assume that was a compliment. Also, you are welcome, I guess, for showing you the way back from your thoughts."

Dammit. And a returned great response. It was an understatement to say she was flustered, but she would save this weird interaction and come out on top. She didn't know why it was so important that she looked good to this stranger, but dang it, she needed a win. After being left by her husband, she wasn't going to let the first flirty interaction with another man go down like this.

"Are you going to kiss my mom? Dad doesn't kiss her anymore."

Was there a color darker than red that an embarrassed face can turn? If so, her face was turning that color, and she could feel it like a sunburn. Wyatt had unstrapped himself and was staring out the window at the blue-eyed stranger. His innocent face was placid and held no shame. If there was any comfort in this situation, the man, who she now noticed was standing next to an impressive motorcycle, was also embarrassed by the question. The man, however, was quicker to find his composure and gave Wyatt a winning smile.

"Dear boy, I am not worthy of your mother's kiss. What am I but a lowly musician." He bowed in a purposefully clumsy, overexaggerated way and froze in his lowered position.

The moment began to stretch. Elizabeth was about to say something when she heard the man whisper loudly, "You have to tell me to rise." A smile cracked her lips and the embarrassment left her, taking with it the red face.

"Arise, penniless musician, your groveling will win you no favor with me."

He straightened and adjusted his clothes as he did. He smiled at them then leaned forward, taking her by surprise, causing the red to creep up her neck again. Was he going to kiss her after all?

He opened Wyatt's door and motioned for him to exit the vehicle. Wyatt obliged, clearly taken with this stranger.

"Penniless? That was a bold assumption." He reached into his pocket, dug around for a bit with a comical look of concentration, then pulled out a single penny.

Elizabeth began to wonder if he'd seen the future and knew this conversation would take place.

"Would you look at that?" He flipped the penny in the air. "Guess I'm richer than you thought." He went to hand the penny to Wyatt, thought better of it, placed the penny back in his pocket, and withdrew a larger silver coin. He placed the coin in Wyatt's hand. "You are now one hundred times richer than I am, young man. Don't spend it all in one place." The silver dollar shone in Wyatt's hand, not quite as bright as the smile on his face. Blue eyes returned to Elizabeth. "My name is Samuel."

"Nice to meet you. I am Elizabeth, and this young lord is Wyatt."

Wyatt stiffened his back to look as old and as lordly as possible in front of this new man. Elizabeth smiled, thinking about how important it is for boys to look more manly in the presence of grown men. Then she thought of his dad and how Wyatt was looking for outside outlets for this male approval and her smile faded.

Her eyes met Samuel's and he quickly looked away toward Wyatt. Had he seen her smile come and go? What conclusions could he have drawn from that?

"Nice to meet you both. I haven't seen you around town before. Granted, I am new here myself, staying at the hotel on the highway for now." He pointed toward the relatively new building next to the ice cream shop she used to visit with her parents on Saturdays when they had no other plans and drove up to meet Rebecca.

She missed spontaneous trips like that. This spontaneous summer vacation was the most unplanned thing she'd done in years. Other than her divorce, that is. That certainly hadn't been planned.

She realized that he wasn't speaking but waiting for her to respond. Had he asked a question? Not really. Rather, he'd observed that they'd not met before, which she guessed was his way of asking if she lived in town.

"We are just passing through." Then, because maybe she would like to see him again, she added, "We will be around, though. I am helping with a wedding in town."

His eyes instantly lit up. "If it's the wedding I am thinking of, I was hoping to be the singer," he stated proudly. "I was working on getting an audition earlier today. Do you know the bride well? Maybe you could put in a good word for me." He looked at her expectantly and she couldn't help but smile.

"Not only do I know her, I am the maid-of-honor. Which also means I help pick the musician. I'm leaning toward a DJ as they are more flexible. I love my Britney from the early 2000s and I'm not sure you can pull that off." She winked mischievously.

What was she? Twenty again? She certainly was flirting like she was.

"Also, how could I give a good word on your musical abilities? I haven't heard any." She paused then, gauging his response to all that. Satisfied with his lost puppy dog look, she continued, "However, I do take pity on those who have only a penny to their name. So, I will make sure that the bride-to-be knows you are hard up for cash and charming."

Charming? Sweet Jesus, kill her now. When was the rapture scheduled for again? Hopefully in the next few seconds.

"Hard Up for Cash and Charming is my band name. How did you know?"

Wyatt laughed openly, understanding that it was most certainly not his band's name.

Samuel looked down at him with a hurt look. "Do you think it's a funny name? I quite like it."

Wyatt redoubled his laughter, bent over with his hands on his knees. Elizabeth had to wonder how much of it was true humor and how much of it was to impress this interesting man.

"As do I," she cut in. "Has a midwestern feel. I bet you are a Johnny Cash cover band, aren't you?"

He gave her a puzzled expression. Then, after thinking back on the name, smiled widely.

"I do a bit of this and a bit of that, but I am not opposed to playin' some Man in Black when I feel inclined." He absentmindedly checked his watch, then, with more gusto, did a double take. "Holy cow, we have been standing here for ages. I actually had plans to meet up with someone."

Elizabeth felt a pang of jealousy.

"He probably won't mind me being late, though."

With that, the jealousy was gone, followed by a sense of shame for feeling it so strongly in the first place. She didn't know anything about this man other than that he was a singer, of which she had no evidence, and his name, again with no real evidence. He could be anyone and yet, the jealousy had been there, just the same.

On the heels of those feelings came the feeling of pleasure, however. The fact that she could feel jealousy toward anyone other than her ex meant that she was finally moving on. Even if she never saw this man again, which was unlikely as he was hoping to be a part of the wedding she was helping to plan, the fact that he got her to feel something like that made her grateful.

"Well, we won't hold you up any longer," she said. "For that matter, I remember someone complaining quite loudly about their need to use the restroom." She turned to look at her son, who looked horrified at being called out.

"Oh, you heard that through your window?" the man replied. "Sorry. When I gotta go, I get kinda loud I guess." He winked at Wyatt who laughed again, this time containing himself a little better.

He threw a leg over his motorcycle, reached back, grabbed a helmet perched on the seat behind him, and placed it snuggly on his head. "Look for my card. My full name is Samuel Serenade and I look forward to singing for you."

Her heart skipped a beat as he turned the key. Motorcycle sounds drowned out any more talk. He pushed the motorcycle out of the parking spot, walking backwards for a bit before gaining enough clearance to put it in gear and turn around. As he left the parking lot, he threw his arm back in a big wave. He hit the pavement of the highway and was out of view long before the sound was gone.

Elizabeth smiled absently. His talk of singing must have gotten in her head, because she swore she'd heard a song intertwined with the motorcycle's engine. That was obviously impossible as the engine was loud enough to drown out even loud singing, let alone the soft, sweet song she thought she'd heard.

"Okay, buddy," she said, coming out of her revelry enough to put an arm around Wyatt's shoulder and guide him toward the quick shop to use the restroom. "We only have like thirty minutes left to drive, so make this count, because we aren't stopping 'til we reach Grandpa's."

He allowed himself to be led, throwing his own arm around her waist. As she reached to open the glass door, she heard him humming to himself. She felt a chill run through her spine as she recognized the song he was humming as the song she'd heard over Samuel's bike.

"That's impossible," she exhaled, barely louder than a whisper.

"Mom?" Wyatt looked concerned. The humming had ended.

She shook her head and let it pass. It was probably a coincidence. A famous song on the radio that had played in her head as he drove away and just so happened to be on Wyatt's mind as well. She kissed the top of his head and led him through the glass door, toward the bathroom. When he was done, it wasn't too difficult to convince her to buy him a snack. Her mind was elsewhere.

They pulled back onto the road, going the opposite direction of Samuel, and drove across a long bridge.

Elizabeth felt her childhood awe of the bridge return. It made her feel like she was on another planet. The bridge felt like it went on forever, feeding into the feeling of unearthly location. Then the front tires thumped off onto the pavement on the other side, followed quickly by the back, and they were over and back on Earth once again.

As they left Alma behind on the final leg of their journey toward Norton, Elizabeth began humming that song again. It was pleasant and made her happy.

For the first time in a while, the stress of her divorce left her mind as if the song was a wind and those concerns were dried fall leaves.

Verse 15

Cherokee, Iowa

GIDEON pulled over at a rest stop a few miles outside of town. He stepped out of his car, grabbed his duffle bag, and went into the oddly pristine bathroom. Whomever had the job of upkeep in this rest stop deserved an award or a raise at the very least.

Carefully, he removed the black suit and hung it in the suit bag that was rolled up in the duffle. He needed it to remain as perfect as possible, as much as he hated wearing it. Again, he praised the cleanliness of the rest stop. Usually, when he changed in one, he had to put all his effort into making sure he didn't touch anything.

He pulled on a pair of old shorts and a simple red t-shirt with a long-faded hero's logo; instantly he felt more comfortable. Finished changing, he hefted his duffle and carefully lifted the hanging suit from the open door of the stall he was using. On his way out, he looked in the mirror, adjusted his glasses, and left the bathroom.

He sat in his car with his notebook open, unread. In fact, the only thing written down was "He was here."

He'd been pretty sure of that when he drove in. Pretty sure, because he read about the incident on one of the many news sites he followed. With so many dead, it had caught his interest as most multi-death events did. He had to weed out the ones that were actual accidents like natural disasters, car crashes, or building fires.

He thought back to when he and his partner used to work together. It was so much cleaner. This rogue bullshit had to stop. But Gideon kept finding himself one stop behind. The fact that his old partner was targeting small towns made him exceptionally hard to follow.

"Basically, there was a ritualistic suicide party or somethin' . . ."

That was what she'd said, but it had not been what she was thinking. There had been more hidden behind that sun-worn face. Not the spoken words, but the ones hiding underneath, the ones that only he could hear.

However, it was someone else he'd ended up listening to.

Everything about that visit had been designed specifically to make those in the bar trust him as little as possible. That sounded wrong, because he needed information, but nevertheless it was true.

When people feel comfortable with someone else, their minds wander, their thoughts mull around like shoppers in a mall the day after Thanksgiving. However, when someone is suspicious of someone else, their thoughts become pinpoints. They are so set on making sure they don't say the wrong thing, it is all they can think about. It fills their mind. Their thoughts stop mulling around and get in line, waiting at the door to the thought in which Gideon was interested.

If he walked in with faded jeans and a comfortable t-shirt, shoppers may have still lined up once he'd started asking pointed questions. However, when he showed up in a pressed suit and ordered a beverage that has probably not been ordered in that bar for years, if ever, instantly those shoppers stopped what they were doing. They may not have known what shop they are going to, but they were ready to line up when they found out. Then he put out a bargain sale sign. At that point the verbal part of the conversations became meaningless.

Another benefit to dressing and acting that way is it affects more than the person he is speaking to, as evidenced by the man getting up from his table. Everyone in the bar was looking at him and all their thought shoppers were lining up waiting for him to direct them.

What is better than one person's thoughts? An entire room's.

It was like doing multiple crime scene interviews all at once, collaborating their stories in real time. Not to mention, he could find someone with the right information; someone whom he never would have talked to in the first place. Like the man sitting in the back of the bar by himself.

The man had been midday drunk when Gideon walked in but, upon seeing him, he'd sat up straighter and started to focus. Once Valentine's Day had been mentioned, his thoughts froze solid. They were crystal clear as if the man had never taken a drink in his life.

And why not? The man had been there on Valentine's night, had he not?

Gideon shifted through all the thoughts that had flown around him and focused on that man's. The rest fell silent as everything focused.

His name was Donny, which was short for Donald, like the greatest president this nation had ever had, as Donny liked to tell people. Gideon rolled his eyes under closed lids.

There had been a Valentine's Day dance. Gideon watched Donny get ready. He'd bought a suit specifically for the occasion. It was pink. He stood in front of the mirror, combing his hair, hoping a certain girl would be there.

Gideon went a little deeper and got the name: Jessica.

Donny and Jessica weren't dating, but they were talking, and hopefully, the ridiculous suit would be a conversation starter tonight. As he looked in the mirror, appreciating the little curl he'd given himself, Donny began to hum.

Gideon sat up a little straighter in his chair. He knew the song. It had been used many times in his presence, but only once had he sung it himself.

Donny danced a little in his mirror, swaying to a melody he never remembered hearing. There was a weird doubling as Gideon was pulled further into his mind and he saw the man dancing with Jessica in his bedroom. However, she wasn't wearing a dress like she would be at the dance. Rather, she matched this man's attire in simple white undergarments.

Gideon always felt weird about being pulled into people's imaginations. It was kind of like being on a bad acid trip. At least this man had more class than other imaginations he'd landed in. He kept both their clothes on, as little as there were.

Donny's mind cleared and he finished getting dressed in his over-the-top pink Valentine's Day suit. Jessica would appreciate the humor. His mind began to drift again, but, luckily for Gideon, Donny understood that he didn't have time to fantasize right now. He had to get ready and get to the dance.

Donny parked in the local high school gym's parking lot, the only location in town big enough to hold events. He looked at the front door, overhung with a gaudy pink banner that matched his suit. He turned his rearview mirror to look down at his hair then further down to his tie. He adjusted it a little, took a deep breath, then stepped out of his car into the cool February air. He stepped into the foyer and was met by a smiling teenager. A volunteer, Donny assumed. The teenaged boy took his coat and pointed to the registration table where he could check in. Donny thanked him and walked over, waving at a couple of men he knew from work who were waiting outside the ladies' restroom. The man behind the desk, Nathan, knew Donny and checked him off the list before Donny said hi.

The music was already going with a live singer on stage. Donny looked in that direction and both he and Gideon recognized the man behind the mic.

Donny smiled; Gideon did not.

Verse 16

Norton, Kansas

ELIZABETH lay in the guest room bed, decompressing. A four-hour car ride isn't fun in general, but with a five-year-old who doesn't appreciate adult music, it can be downright miserable.

She sighed. Honestly, it hadn't been terrible. Wyatt was good at car rides and in general. He was a great kid. At the moment, said great kid was at the local Dairy Queen for ice cream cones, leaving Elizabeth to unpack.

Unpacking was what she'd intended to do, but while putting away Wyatt's things in her old bedroom, she'd stumbled upon her diary.

She hadn't thought about her diary for years. She wondered what kind of secrets it held, even from herself. It was like a time capsule, containing all that was important to her as a teenager. All the hopes and dreams of adulthood.

With that thought, she had set it back down. Hopes and dreams of adulthood? Did those include divorce, debt, and loneliness? How could she answer the questions and concerns her younger self would have? She'd taken the diary into the guest room where she would be staying and set it on the side table. After staring at it for a few minutes, she had decided to lay down on the bed and decompress.

Now, in retrospect, she realized that she hadn't been decompressing after a long car ride, but after a long few years. Maybe from however long it had been since she'd written the last sentence in the damn diary sitting not a foot away from her. She sighed heavily one last time and sat up. The presence of the diary felt like another person in the room. A younger, more vibrant person with questions about the future, her eyes dancing with anticipation and expectation. Did she have the heart to answer? Did she have the heart to crush that expectation and anticipation with cold reality?

She supposed if she didn't, she would never be able to leave this room. Her younger presence would haunt her like a ghost.

She opened to the very first page and read.

Hello Diary, my name is Beth, which is short for Elizabeth, I think we are going to be best friends. Shhh, don't tell Bex.

She smiled. If the rest of the diary was anything like this first page, then she had nothing to worry about.

For the most part, it was.

She skipped ahead. Not that junior high Beth wasn't entertaining, but she knew her time alone would be coming to an end shortly. She landed on a page where teenage angst and a misunderstanding of marriage had led her to write her name, followed by the last names of her crushes:

Elizabeth Leggent, Elizabeth Ables, Elizabeth Depp, Elizabeth Pitt.

She smiled at her naivety. Then a thought came to her. The consideration caused her cheeks to burn. She reached to the side table for a conveniently pseudo-sharpened pencil. She held it, willing herself to put it back on the table, followed by the diary, safely closed. Before her common sense could remind her how old she was, she quickly wrote a new entry under "Elizabeth Pitt."

Elizabeth Serenade.

She was breathing in little gasps. She could feel the weight of the crush as if she were considering asking him to the Sadie Hawkins dance.

"We're home, sweetheart."

She jumped out of the bed and fell over as her feet, unaccustomed to the guest room floor, slipped and took her to a knee.

What on Earth was she doing? She was acting like her dad had caught her in a masturbatory act with her pants around her ankles. Yet, even with the knowledge that she was overreacting, her heart was having trouble coming to that conclusion and she was still breathing rapidly. Her knee hurt from where she'd fallen. She placed every bit of focus she could gather toward that. Slowly, her breathing became less labored, and her heart rate slowed.

"You all right, honey?" Her dad stood in the doorway, looking down at her concernedly.

"Yep. I drifted off and you startled me into falling off the bed." A fitting lie, she assumed, and by the look on his face, he believed her.

"I'm sorry. Had I known you were sleeping, I would have brought in my air horn." He smiled wryly. "Wyatt had his cone dipped in fudge. I hope that's all right."

She nodded and grunted her affirmation as she used the bed to pull herself up.

"I see you found your old diary, and that you were swooning over them boys again like before." He nodded toward the book that lay unsurprisingly and mortifyingly open to the last page she'd been on. Her cheeks again lit up.

God, any more of this embarrassment and Santa might look her up to guide his sleigh come Christmas.

"Well, at least Brad Pitt is still worth swooning over," she said, straightening up.

She bent over, picked up the book, and flipped it shut just as Wyatt walked in, covered in chocolate from hairline to collar.

"Jeez, Dad, you said he got his ice cream dipped in fudge, not his face."

Wyatt found this to be one of the funniest jokes he'd ever heard. Soon, they were all laughing together.

Wiping tears from her eyes as she struggled to catch her breath for the second time in as many minutes, Elizabeth said, "How 'bout we get you cleaned up, mister, before someone snatches a picture and you lose your chance at running for the Senate?"

Wyatt chuckled confusedly, understanding that it was a joke, but not what it was about. Her father, on the other hand, who'd just got his laughing under control, lost it all over again and moved to leave the room, hoping to avoid an early death by laughter.

"Wait, Dad." Despite her joke before, she felt compelled to capture this moment; this perfect moment with the two men she loved most. She also, begrudgingly, felt compelled to share the moment with the man she hated most. She removed her phone from her back pocket and snapped two quick pictures before returning the phone. She did this with a practiced ease like a gunslinger drawing, firing, and reholstering. Mothers are good at taking quick pictures, because children are anything but static.

"Gotcha. How was it?"

"It was the best ice cream I have ever had," Wyatt exclaimed.

Elizabeth thought back to when she was young enough to consider every new thing that happened the "best ever." That TV show was the best ever. This movie is the best ever. This toy is the best one I have ever owned. She'd lived too long, however, and knew that the weeks after a "best ever" dulled into "only okay."

God, she was being both nostalgic and pessimistic today. This house was trying desperately to pull her back into her childhood, yet reality was fighting back with a grim determination. She was happy she would be in Alma for a lot of this stay. At least there, she could hopefully avoid some of the battles that would take part during this war.

Her attention returned to Wyatt and her thoughts focused back on his chocolate-covered face.

Verse 17

Cherokee, Iowa

DONNY and Gideon both looked at Samuel on stage singing an upbeat song about young love that neither of them recognized. He was beaming like a kid on Christmas morning. Donny, who'd had many meaningful talks with Samuel in the past few months, felt his heart lift that much more with thoughts of the upcoming dance. Gideon, on the other hand, felt his stomach twist, knowing that what he was looking for had finally come.

For the most part, the dance itself was uneventful. Gideon kept catching glances of Samuel on stage when Donny looked that way, but his attention was clearly directed in a different direction the majority of the time.

Jessica was there, Jessica had noticed his interesting suit, and Jessica was interested in him. They talked and danced for hours. Gideon barely paid attention as he watched the dance pass by quickly as if he were using a remote to fast forward.

Gideon had spent years honing his mental abilities and, like everyone, had a specific way he viewed things in his mind. Some people saw things like filing cabinets; others saw them as pictures. For Gideon, it was an old-school DVD player. This also allowed for the functionality that came with DVD players, including play, pause, rewind, and fast forward. He was a product of his time, and this felt comfortable to him.

As the dance continued, Samuel would sometimes play music through the in-house system and come down into the crowd to mingle with the participants. Everyone seemed excited to converse with him. Gideon assumed Samuel had personal meetings with most, if not all, of those participating in tonight's festivities.

Gideon knew the final count but watched closely. Samuel would have a final list by now, but he wasn't against sending out a few more invites when the time came. Faces from the news stories that Gideon had read faded in and out of view. It was like seeing an in-memoriam video at an awards ceremony seeing these people at their happiest, enjoying the night with no knowledge that it would be their last. He, for the millionth time, thought of the families they'd left at home; some with babysitters, who'd waited all night for parents they would never see again.

Well, not alive anyway.

Donny wove his way through the crowd until he was face-to-face with Samuel. "Sammy."

Samuel hated that nickname, but he didn't let that show as he beamed at Donny. He reached forward as if to shake Donny's hand, then pulled him into an intimate hug.

"Are you enjoying yourself?" Samuel shouted over the music. Donny, not wanting to shout himself, nodded his head, causing Gideon to see the world slide up and down in front of him.

Samuel seemed to understand his mutism. "They always play music too loud at these events, don't you think?"

Gideon felt Donny pause. Even in his slightly inebriated state, he saw this as a trick question. If he agreed with Samuel, he would essentially be bashing Samuel's own choice of music and volume. If he didn't agree, then he was being disagreeable. He stood there for a little bit trying hard to think of a response when Samuel started laughing. It was a beautiful laugh that carried his musical talent within it, making it sound like a short song.

"I'm just messin' with ya," Samuel said. He took out his cell phone, messed with it a bit, and the music's volume faded enough to make talking a little easier.

"What a trick."

"The magic of modern technology. What can I say?" Samuel replied, smiling.

Gideon again noticed how great the smile looked as long as you didn't pay too close attention to his eyes. Those were smiling in a different way, a malevolent way.

Samuel placed his hand on Donny's shoulder and made piercing eye contact with his hypnotic blue eyes. Donny's breath caught. "Find your lady. Make tonight the greatest night of your life."

To Donny, this sounded like a Psalm or Proverb upon which he should base the rest of his life. Had Samuel's plan worked perfectly, that would have been the case. As it would turn out, the phrase would haunt him in his dreams at night, chasing him like a beast let loose by the dark memories. Those nightmares drawn by this memory tried to consume Gideon. However, the current memory, the one he was most interested in, was beginning to fade, so he forced them away.

This was the issue with remembering someone else's memory. It was like running on battery. Without a constant source, it would begin to run low. Had Gideon stayed in the bar, he could have continued to pull from Donny and grab whatever memories he needed.

He sighed, the first noise he'd made outside of his own head in what? Hours? It was hard to keep track of the time outside of his mind when he was in this state. The very means of finding this memory, his outfit, the drink, the questions, etc., was the very reason he had to leave and was unable to stay connected. Trial and error had led him to understand that this was the most convenient way to get the information he needed, but it was still a hassle.

He decided to skip to the end where everything went wrong.

Or, in Samuel's opinion, where everything went very, very right.

Samuel was on stage, singing a slow Elvis tune about the folly of being a fool in love. The room had paired up with the poor saps on the side looking longingly at the dance floor.

Gideon felt exceptionally bad for the ones in that group who'd been marked by Samuel; this would have been a last chance to truly enjoy life, to grab a partner and spend a few minutes in bliss. One last burst of living before the next song started. Gideon didn't know what waited on the other side, if anything. Maybe regret in death wasn't something these sad few would have to worry about. Gideon still felt a strong urge to yell at them, to wake them up to the wasted time they had left. Then again, people spend years sitting at home in front of a TV then die of cardiac arrest. Was that any more wasted time than these last few minutes? He didn't know. Regardless, the song was coming to an end and his revelry would have to be put on hold.

"Thank you, everyone, for coming out tonight," Samuel spoke into his microphone as the instruments began to fade away. "This next song will be the last one and it is exceptionally special to me. I think it will be one that you take with you, unto death."

Gideon noticed the body movement of the crowd. They were all smiling up at Samuel. But at that last comment, their smiles, while still there, dropped ever so slightly. On its face, it was a nice sentiment; a memory that would last a lifetime. However, any mention of death on a night that had been filled with so much life felt like a minor chord in a major song. Jarring.

Gideon felt Donny shudder and pull Jessica, whose hand he was holding, closer as if to pull in some of her heat after such a chilling comment. Gideon felt an almost parental pride for Donny. No sideline at the dance for this guy.

Then he remembered Donny in the bar, already drunk before two in the afternoon. Survival wasn't always a blessing.

Samuel began the song. This time, there was no music playing through the system nor any instruments at hand. There was only his voice. But there was no need for additional music. This was, without a doubt, the most beautiful song anyone in attendance had ever heard. It was tied into their very lives. Hadn't they all been humming it absentmindedly for weeks?

Gideon knew the song. He had heard it many times. The first time he heard it was years ago, when he was only a child in foster care. He mentally waved that thought away. He didn't have time to reminisce on his own memories when this one was still fading.

Donny's mind was lost in the song. Gideon's own mind was luckily separated, allowing him to continue to watch unswayed by the music. He watched as eyes glazed over as if a communal daydream had begun. When every eye had lost focus and people swayed lightly on their feet, Samuel left the mic and leapt down gracefully from the stage. The song did not diminish in volume or in beauty.

As soon as Samuel was on the dance floor with them, the crowd began to move. Samuel walked toward the big double doors, leading outside into the cool February night. Gideon watched in fascinated horror as the crowd split into two distinct groups. About three-quarters of them found chairs and sat, placidly placing their hands in their laps and smiling dreamily. One of them began to drool contentedly. The smaller group went to the table still laid out with hors d'oeuvres, desserts, plates, and most importantly, silverware. As Gideon watched, each participant reached down and selected a knife.

Steak as a meal option had been Samuel's idea.

One by one, with stupid grins on their faces, and a song on their breath, they picked up the sharp tools of their deaths.

Gideon, helpless to stop him, went with Donny as he, still holding Jessica's hand, picked up his own knife as did she. They looked at each other, singing softly, filled with love. Gideon's heart broke a little more, knowing it was the last time Jessica would ever look at anyone like that. He also knew that look would drive Donny to the bar every day from here on out.

Gideon was filled with selfish relief when she turned toward the door, toward Samuel, and toward her inevitable death.

Verse 18

Norton, Kansas

ELIZABETH was distracted. She kept thinking about her diary. She should probably call it a journal or something now that she was grown up. She decided that she was tired of changing the way she thought of things because she was a "grown-up." It was a DIARY, and she had a CRUSH. She sighed. There was no use fighting it. Hell, if she needed any proof, all she had to do was look at the last entry in the list of names in her DIARY. Was she embarrassed? She supposed she was, not that anyone else had any idea she had a crush.

Had he been flirting though? She'd felt like he had been, but she'd also not been flirted with in years. Having a young child attached on one hip and a wedding ring adorning that prominent finger were usually good deterrents. Well, they had been for her anyway.

They didn't seem to have slowed anything down in Jason's case. Not that he'd ever had the child-on-the-hip problem.

"Mom? It's your turn."

Her eyes came back to focus. Her dad and her son were sitting at the small table in the kitchen/dining room combo. There were dominoes before her, trains of them stretching out from the central hub in the middle. She looked at the disappointingly useless black dots in front of her.

"Trash bag," came her reply.

Wyatt giggled.

She was happy to hear it. His eyes had been a little too inquisitive. She once again had that feeling he was able to read her mind. Was he in on the secret between her and her diary? Did five-year-olds understand crushes and attraction? His understanding of a loving couple was her and his dad, which, by the time he was able to understand anything, was strenuous at best. If Samuel had been flirting, would he see that as anything more than friendly conversation between adults? Or possibly worse, had it only been friendly conversation between adults?

She drew a domino that she couldn't play and placed her marker, a pencil eraser in the shape of a unicorn, on her last domino to represent that her train was now officially open to be played on. Like vultures, they did just that, thanking her exuberantly. She stuck out her tongue at them as she closed her train with a new domino when her turn came back around.

Wyatt loved dominoes. They played with a set that only went up to nine, but she had a feeling he could have played with a set that went to sixteen. The first time they'd played in Omaha, she'd all but played both sides. The second game he took over and by the fifth game, he beat her fair and square. Now it was a staple in their house. A week did not go by without a dominoes game. Her dad had been delighted as it had always been one of his and her mom's favorite games. That thought made her pause as the reality of her mom's sudden death hit her all over again.

That was how unexpected deaths were, she supposed. Especially with people who lived far away.

It was easy to fall back into the normal flow of life; the flow of life that had a mother in Norton only a phone call away.

Then, while at the grocery store, a mango would prompt the thought, "I should call mom and ask how you know if a mango is ripe or not." *Bang!* Like a gunshot, that comfortable worldview would shatter, revealing what lay behind: a world without a mother.

When someone died from an illness, there was time to come to terms with their death before it happened. A pre-death acceptance. That was something they'd not been granted.

She watched as the game of dominoes continued. She saw her mom pull the double zero toward the end of a round, knowing it would give her 50 points if she didn't get rid of it, already knowing she couldn't. "Shit," she'd say under her breath. She was not a cursing woman by nature, but dominoes had a way of pulling a few minor curses out of her. That and Phase 10. Elizabeth saw all this with a clarity so vivid that she had to blink a few times to clear her vision.

Like the afterimage of a picture on a white page, her mother faded away and she realized she was on the verge of tears. Her remaining family were luckily looking at the dominoes and not her, so she was able to quickly wipe away her tears before they made it back to her.

"Out," she said as she placed her last domino on the open train her dad had been unable to close. "While you boys count up your points, I'm gonna hit the ladies room." She didn't need to use it for its intended purposes, but she needed to get away for a second and get her emotions under control. Again, to her luck, the two boys were so upset with their loss and busy counting their dots that they barely noticed as she made her escape.

Standing in her childhood bathroom as an adult made her age drastically. She stood in front of the mirror, oddly expecting to see a perky teenager with mild infuriating acne. Perhaps she was looking for a girl with pigtails that didn't quite match because she'd wanted to do them herself. Two little hands holding onto the counter in front of the sink, pulling her up onto the stool purchased just for her so she could brush her teeth and wash her hands without help. Those images were there, but lost behind the reflection of a tired, weary, older woman who looked like she'd been crying. This mirror stood as a stark reminder that she was no longer that little girl. That life had not stopped. Rather, it had crashed through time like a runaway freightliner and now she was looking back at the destruction left behind.

Like a sliver of light cutting through a thundercloud, she saw something at the top of the mirror. There, slid beneath the tiny metal frame, was a wallet-sized picture of Wyatt, beaming as if he'd been told that "Due to a scheduling error, Christmas would take place twice this year." She smiled. Then she realized that, due to a relational error, Christmas *would* be twice this year for him.

Could she not have one happy thought? Just one? Why did everything have to be tainted by the reality of her life?

She looked at the picture again. How could something so perfect come from something so flawed? She kissed her fingers as they hovered in front of her lips. She whispered onto the cool moisture left by her kiss, "Sorry." She then placed those fingers against her son's beautiful, joyful, unknowing face and let them linger. Her gaze returned to her mirror self. She rolled her eyes, let her hand drop, then flipped off the bitch in the mirror. "The next time we meet, you had better be a bit more forgiving or you can go straight to hell. I am not afraid of seven years of bad luck." She winked and her mirror self-winked back. Elizabeth left the bathroom ready to lose a domino game to a child, despite winning the last round. She was content with that.

Two fingerprints glimmered on the picture in the mirror before the lights winked off and the room was plunged into darkness.

Verse 19

Cherokee, Iowa

DONNY and Jessica, still holding hands, knives held tightly in the others, followed the joyously oblivious partygoers through the door and into the cold February night. The song was everywhere. Each person hummed, whistled, or wordlessly sang, acting as speakers to amplify Samuel's melody. It was intoxicating. Even though Gideon was separated from the event and the true power of the song, Donny's memory of it still worked on him like a strong drink.

They walked out the front door, down the steps, then turned. They stepped off the pavement and onto the grass. They followed Samuel as he led them around the stone building through the frosty lawn.

Gideon, safe and warm in his car, thought about the fact that it had been the middle of February when this took place. The sun was down as well, which meant it had to have been terribly cold. Yet, none of them had stopped to put on their coats or prepare in any way for the temperature. Not a single member of the group acted the slightest put out. They continued their progress toward the woods behind the gym.

It made a queer sight: this band of merry carolers. They all had giant smiles plastered on their faces and kept looking at each other expectantly. It all looked so fun, like a group of friends moving from one bar to the next. Then you noticed their hands. One of every pair held a steak knife, swinging around with the music, the partygoers oblivious to the little dealer of death in their possession. Gideon, powerless to intercede, could only watch, already knowing the outcome.

He again thought of the families at home. Children going to bed, missing out on a goodnight kiss, knowing they would get one when their parents came home. Spouses who'd been unable to attend the event finishing shifts, excited to hear about the dance when they got home. Parents already planning their kids' college careers and preparing for the heartbreaking day they would see them off. He'd seen the faces. He'd read the names.

Samuel had done the same yet, he'd read more than their names; he'd read their souls. At least, in his mind he had. He was the judge, the jury, and tonight, the executioner. A weight no shoulder should bear, yet Samuel took the responsibility willingly enough.

Ever since they were kids, justice weighed heavily on Samuel. Gideon had tried so hard to contain him in a partnership that would ultimately damn him. He again shook his head. He needed to focus. They were coming to the trees, a picture he'd also seen. The site of the massacre.

Jessica pulled on Donny's hand excitedly, ushering him along through the song. They reached the first trees, ducking to miss low branches. There wasn't much of a trail where they'd entered and everyone began to spread out, which had a haunting effect with the music. It appeared to be coming from everywhere. It echoed around them, the frozen trees doing nothing to absorb the sounds. They ducked and swirled around the branches like sprites, steadily making their way along, following a confident leader. Samuel walked in the middle of it all, never needing to duck, as someone would dart ahead and move the branches out of the way for him. He gingerly stepped around fallen branches littering the ground. The winter had done its work, weighing down weak branches until they'd finally given up, succumbing to gravity. Samuel turned toward his followers, letting the singing throng know that they were almost there.

Then everything spun, flipped, and Gideon, in his car, threw up his hands instinctively, hitting his left against the wheel hard enough to bruise.

The world came to a stop, and he was seeing the ground of the woods up close. Donny had fallen. He tripped over one of the frozen limbs. Gideon watched as Donny looked down at his ankle, which was completely bent in the wrong direction. Then he looked back at Jessica, still holding his hand, now with panic on her face. Through this all, neither stopped singing.

Verse 20

ELIZABETH lay in her bed. She'd excused herself early, claiming the drive had made her tired. This was by no means a lie, but it was definitely stretching the truth considerably. As was proven by her wide-awake status.

Wyatt had wanted to show her dad the most recent superhero movie that he'd brought, and while Elizabeth loved a good CGI-filled spandex fest, she assumed some movie time would be appropriate for them. This left her alone in her room with her thoughts, which were obnoxiously specific tonight.

Samuel kept popping up whenever she would try to think of something else. It was like the chorus to a pop song, playing on repeat in her mind, and there was no way to fix it.

Dress shopping meant she would be in Alma. Afterward, they would probably need other supplies, which meant she would have to go to the store, where she would run into Samuel, who would be buying something manly.

Manly? What the hell did that mean? Would he be buying aftershave or something?

Actually, that worked for her, because that sexy shadow would be a bit thicker. Not enough to look homeless, but enough to darken that chin line and make his blue eyes that much brighter.

"Oh, my God, stop," she said and realized she'd been reaching to put her hand down the front of her pajama bottoms.

What the hell was she thinking? She was literally about to do what she'd jokingly thought about doing earlier when her dad walked in. She'd only just met the guy—and with her son needing to pee, nonetheless. Not a recipe for romance.

She again turned her mind toward Rebecca and the wedding. Elizabeth started wondering what she would wear. Rebecca had impeccable fashion sense, so she assumed it would be great. Maybe a single strap over one shoulder, with one side of the dress ending at her knee, then cutting down to end on the opposite leg's heel. Samuel could run his hand up the exposed knee when he came to bring a drink. Then it would continue into the darkness, between . . .

"Oh, my God," she hissed, again yanking her hand away from her pants.

She felt that she could cut herself at least a little slack. It had been some time since anyone had touched her down there in the manner she'd intended. Jason had been terrified of anything below her belt ever since a tiny human had been yanked out of there. She thought of that stupid joke from childhood about the butt: "Exit only." Well, to Jason, that no longer only applied to the back door but to the front as well. She thought back to the last time they'd done anything intimate. Had it been years?

She thought about how awkward it had been. Everything had been fine during foreplay, but when it was time to place piece Y into opening X, Y had reduced to 0. It had taken far too much work to get him back to working order and by the time he'd entered her, she'd felt kind of gross. Her husband had been struggling to keep it hard inside her, probably having to think of some young girl who'd never had a child. Someone whose front door had only been used as an entrance. His eyes were shut so tightly, they'd turned white, and she knew that if he'd opened them and seen that it was in fact his wife under him, he would have gone flaccid immediately.

The sex ended as awkwardly as it had begun. He just kind of . . . finished? He'd been wearing a condom, even though she'd been on birth control, because what is better than one contraceptive? She honestly didn't know if he'd finished as condoms conveniently hide that fact. It wasn't like she followed him into the bathroom, saying, "Hey, let me see if there is anything in there." Afterward, he had all but ran to the shower, presumably needing to clean off the experience.

She'd stayed in bed, not quite crying. Not yet anyway. Wyatt had stayed at a gracious friend's house who'd agreed to take him overnight so that Elizabeth and Jason could have some much-needed alone time. Elizabeth remembered looking at the night ahead of them, without Wyatt as a distraction. She remembered feeling dread. That's right. The prospect of spending the night alone with her husband had filled her with dread.

Back in the present, she sighed and reached for her phone. If she couldn't get her mind off of this practical stranger, then maybe she could direct it productively.

She texted Rebecca: "Have you looked into music for your wedding yet?"

Innocent enough, right? She probably hadn't, other than the cursory conversations with her fiancé in regard to a band or a DJ.

The little dots popped up, notifying Elizabeth that the message had been received and an answer was incoming.

Despite growing up in a cellphoneless world, it was hard to believe there was a time before text messages or instant messaging. Here they were, miles apart, having a conversation as easily as if they were in the same room. Technology was nuts. All the information in the world was available at your fingertips.

She sat up, feeling exceptionally stupid. If Samuel Serenade was a singer, then he would have definitely left a digital footprint, right?

Her phone dinged, pulling her attention back to the conversation at hand. She made a silent promise to herself to check Google as soon as she was done with Rebecca.

"Not yet, but some friends of the family back home have given my dad some ideas to forward on to me."

The little dots popped up again, but only for a second.

"Why?"

There it was. Elizabeth had known this question would inevitably be asked and yet, surprisingly, she was unprepared to answer.

She loved Rebecca, but she also knew that she was the nosiest friend she'd ever had. She claimed it was only because she cared for Beth and wanted what was best for her. Elizabeth herself wasn't sure a new guy was what was best for her, and she didn't need other opinions clouding the matter. This would have to be done carefully and with the tact that comes from years of close friendship.

She mused on the tact of friendship and how every relationship you have involves tact. You learn how best to talk to your parents, which is drastically different from how you talk to a spouse or your child or your best friend. Even work relationships had their own tact. When you boil everything down, maybe that was what the human experience was: learning tact then living tactfully. It would explain how some people excelled at life and others failed. The inability to live tactfully. She sighed. That was definitely an oversimplification to life, but she felt that it wasn't so far off either.

"I had heard about a singer in the area looking for work and would look into him," she texted, a reminder to Google Mr. Serenade after this. "But if you had already picked someone, then it wasn't going to be worth my time."

She snickered. Like her time was so valuable at the moment. She was in bed by nine p.m. and could hear explosions on the television in the living room down the hall, and could pinpoint where they were in the movie. She'd tactfully shown interest in what her son found interesting and had, in turn, seen most of these movies more times than she would care to admit. It did, however, allow her to gauge how much time was left in the movie. Wyatt would be coming in afterward to say goodnight and would probably want her to read him a book, unless he was able to talk his grandfather into it.

She smiled, imagining her gruff farmer father sitting on the edge of the little twin bed, reading one of Wyatt's picture books. Would he do the different voices like he had with her? He was out of practice, but she assumed reading was like riding a bike.

Wyatt, who was only five, had become another statistic in the modern age of divorce. One out of every however many kids will grow up in a split family. He understood that his life was different and that his dad would no longer live in the same building as him, but she wondered if he fully understood the implications of a divorce.

Hell, she didn't fully understand the implications of a divorce. Take Samuel for example. Had it been long enough since leaving Jason to allow feelings for another man? She wondered how much of that decision was up to her, how much of it was up to Wyatt, and how much of it was held by the society around her. They would judge her sexless nights by the date of separation, not by the actual date that their relationship died.

Jason sure as hell lost no time moving on to a woman with an unused uterus. However, she understood that there was a fundamental difference to the perception of men and the perception of women in these circumstances. Society had decided long ago that it was okay for men to move on quickly, but that women should be more conservative in their romantic endeavors post-serious relationship termination. This hadn't been a serious concern for Elizabeth, because she hadn't felt any desire to move on romantically. She had Wyatt, her job, and the debris of the divorce to deal with. Why complicate matters with another man?

Then Samuel sauntered into her life. Well, he had done whatever the equivalent of sauntering was when one was straddling a motorcycle.

Ding went her phone.

"Samuel Serenade?"

Her heart skipped a beat reading his name from the other side of the phone. The little dots appeared, and Elizabeth realized she was holding her breath. What if Rebecca had already looked into him and decided she would rather have a DJ or bring in a band from out of town? Where would that leave her in regard to contact with him? She would have no reason aside from personal reasons, and that felt far too forward at this juncture of their relationship. Which, at this point in time, was no relationship at all.

"If that is who you are referring to, he is top of our list for possibles and comes highly recommended by the locals."

Elizabeth emptied her lungs in a long sigh. The dots returned, but the tension was gone. She'd been handed an excuse to get in contact with him and for now, that was enough.

"I hear he is cute."

One time in college, after Elizabeth had been dumped, she called Bex, bawling over the loss. "Fuck 'em," Bex had said. "Better yet, fuck someone else." That sentiment had gone through her mind the first night Jason spent away. Of course, she'd never acted on it or had any real desire to act on it, but now there was this man who sauntered up on a motorcycle.

"I guess we will have to see," Elizabeth texted back. "Just remember, you are engaged."

She turned her phone to silent and sat it on the table beside her. She would be seeing Samuel Serenade soon. She thought of those blue eyes. She began to breathe a little heavier.

She listened to the movie through the closed door down the hall. She could barely make out the speech that took place before the final confrontation.

Those blue eyes. She allowed her hand to drift this time, thinking what the hell, I have a little time before the movie ends. She saw those eyes above her in the dark and allowed herself, for the first time since before Wyatt had been born, to be carried away in the wave she was stirring up below the waistband of her pajama bottoms.

Intermingled with her soft moans and sighs was a melody. She softly sang herself into a sweet oblivion.

Verse 21

Cherokee, Iowa

JESSICA yanked hard on Donny's hand, but it was clear he would go no further. She looked at him sprawled amongst the fallen branches and tears began to fall down her cheeks. She didn't want to leave him, but she also needed to catch up to the group already leaving the two of them behind. Her beautiful voice, still singing the tune of the night, took on a tortured breathy note. She yanked his hand again. He understood that she was no longer trying to pull him with her but remove her hand from his.

Terror gripped him stronger than any emotion he'd ever known. He could not be left behind. The need to continue with them was so strong that to be left here by her would be a fate worse than death. He clamped his fingers down on hers, and without slowing the melody pouring from him, urged her with his eyes to please help him. She looked at him with pain. She wanted nothing more than to take him with her to the wonders that lay before them, but they were falling too far behind and if she stayed to help him, she would never catch up.

Donny and Gideon both saw her resolve as she looked at him, and they both understood that she'd made her decision and it was not him. Donny dug in deeper, planting his fingernails deep into the flesh of her hand, but her face only showed sorrow and the song never faltered. Then, with a quick and inexplicably strong motion, she yanked her hand toward her as hard as she could. Three of Donny's fingers dislocated. Everything within the joints that connected his fingers to his hand tore away beneath the skin and pulled free. They stared at each other, tears now freely running down both of their faces. They sang to each other for one final second—a moment within eternity—before she turned and fled into the woods, rushing to catch up with the rest of the Valentine's Day partiers.

Donny raised his hand and looked at the bumps rising above where the knuckles had been. A random flash of memory from school when he was a teenager popped into his head, pushing past the music: a balding, bespectacled man in a sweater vest, pointing at a diagram of the human hand. "These are your phalanges," he explained with a long stick. Donny's phalanges were now phalanfrees, as in freely floating under his skin. As he watched, his hand began to swell around the detached bones that had been pressing against the flesh in an attempt for more freedom. Everything about this moment was surreal, as if it were happening to someone else. He knew there was pain without feeling it. In fact, all feelings were drowned out by the terror of being left behind and the ecstasy of the song.

Donny tried to get up, placing his good hand to the ground, pushing himself up. He saw his hand, splayed out on the ground, all four phalanges still perfectly attached. Perfectly empty. Where the hell was the knife? He looked around frantically. He saw nothing. At one point, he thought he saw a glint of metal and attempted to crawl to it. He placed his other hand to the ground. It instantly buckled, dropping him hard to the cold, leaf-strewn ground. The song continued. His ears heard only his own raspy, breathless voice, but the melody in his head was just as strong as before. It spun around him, pulling him forward, beckoning him insistently to come join the party. He could feel that the song was coming to its conclusion. The terror at not being included became a drug, flowing through his veins, tearing away his sanity from him.

He understood that whether the glint he'd seen was the knife or not, he was out of time to reach it. The chorus was giving way to the bridge and the final notes would be right around the corner. He reached for what appeared to be the sharpest stick within arm's length, but again, he'd forgotten that where his hand had previously been was now a swollen mishmash of wrong angles. The frenzy of the song mixed with the unbearable desire to join in kept his mind from operating on a level necessary to understand that his right hand, at least in that moment, was no longer his dominant hand. He mashed it against the stick, crying freely around the music. Time and time again, he pressed the lumpy mass against what he saw as the only way to join the rest of them. One of his phalanges was bent entirely backward and the skin below, unable to take the continued strain any longer, had torn, exposing the torn muscle, tendons, and ligaments beneath. The bone pushed forward toward the opening, sliding out easier than Gideon would have anticipated. It was taking all of his power to not vomit in his car.

Gideon found himself sadly urging Donny to switch hands to end this self-inflicted torture. There was a grisly sound as more skin tore and another bone began to find its way to fresh air. Maybe it was the sound or maybe some clarity made its way through the haze of the music, but Donny finally reached out with his good hand, rolling his shoulder over to gain access to it. He of course grabbed it with the first try, wrapping those perfectly undamaged phalanges around the sharp, icy branch. As he grasped the branch, a jutting spike of wood slid painlessly into the soft flesh of his palm. Gideon saw the middle finger of the recently unblemished hand go slack and understood that the branch had severed a tendon.

Donny showed no signs that he'd felt the pain or even that his hands were damaged in any way. He could hear the others further in the woods still singing at the top of their lungs. He understood that he needed to be a part of the finale, even if he wasn't in the presence of everyone else. He lifted the branch and examined it, heedless of the blood now painting the cold wood and draining into the sleeve of his oh, so unique suit. The stick was not as sharp as he'd previously thought, but he was out of time and beggars can't be choosers. Noticeably, the voices up ahead began to lose volume. Gideon knew that it was not because they were singing quieter. Rather, fewer people were singing. Fewer people were able to sing. The night's festivities, propelled by Samuel's music, had finally begun, and consequently were coming to an end. Voices began to drop away. Gideon could sadly imagine the crowd of happy partygoers: one by one, slitting their wrists with the steak knives, falling to their knees, still trying to continue the song as their life flowed out of them.

Donny, however, sat alone in the cold with one hand pulverized and the other bleeding around a frozen stick. Still singing, he looked at the wrist under his right hand, not noticing that the fingers above were each pointing in a different direction, the skin pulling away from them. His suit, which had felt like such a great idea until now, posed the problem of covering up too much of his wrist, leaving only a sliver before the hard muscles of the hand began. The song would not wait for him. He began to slash at that exposed wrist while singing jubilantly, finally happy that he was part of the group again, if not in body, then at least in spirit.

The stick was not sharp enough to do what he requested of it. He did the best he could. Before long, his wrist began to look like a wild animal had gotten ahold of it. However, he never hit the life-sustaining vessel in the wrist that was the target of this melody. He sang and continued to furiously wreak havoc on his wrist, only stopping when the voice of Jessica, one he knew very well, fell away from the other singers. They were down to a handful now. Rather than slow him down, this sped his resolve; he would be with her soon, if only he could get deep enough. The splinter of wood in the hand holding the stick slid free as he adjusted his grasp and slid home in a new spot as he retightened it. Gideon could only guess at the damage being done.

Donny slowed then and looked at the blood freely flowing from the wounds around the stick. The song came to a soft end as the last voice faded away. Now it was only him. He realized dully that he was no longer singing. A black ring formed around his vision then quickly closed in, erasing the world in darkness. He felt, rather than saw, the stick fall from his failing grasp; he followed suit, hitting the ground hard enough to fracture a bone in his cheek.

Gideon was not sure if Donny heard the footsteps, but Gideon did. He also understood that the fractured cheek was a small price to pay for his life. Had the owner of those feet known Donny was alive, he would have stopped and held a small encore for one. Luckily, the bloody mess lying among the fallen branches could not have looked more dead as the cold of the night crept over him. The footsteps paused only for a moment then continued onward. Donny, in his delirium, heard the sound of a motorcycle starting up. Oddly, the last coherent thought to pass through his mind before slipping into the sweet release of unconsciousness was "Isn't it too cold for a motorcycle?"

Verse 22

Omaha, Nebraska

WHILE Elizabeth was enjoying some much needed "me" time, Jason was longing for just that. Ever since his discussion with the mirror, he'd been having these hard to explain thoughts. He'd grown comfortable with El and Wyatt living in the same town as him; it gave him access when he wanted it, but allowed for him to step back and be himself. It was the perfect Dad setup. Now that they were going to be gone for months, the idea that had at first felt like further freedom, now made him feel lonely.

Stacy pressed closer to him, focused on the TV. This was good because it kept her from noticing the way his face tightened in a grimace when she did. That asshole in the mirror had done a number on him. This amazingly sexy woman was pressing her mostly naked flesh against his, and he was wincing. He looked over her head, out the window of their apartment.

As a mostly-free-from-parentage-responsibility-adult-male, he'd sprung for the very best. Like the highest live-in apartment in Omaha. Arguably, it was not as high as the apartments in, say, New York, but it was high enough to make him feel like a winner.

That thought, passing through his mind in those exact words, made him grimace again. What the hell had he become? He thought about how he and El would watch movies and laugh at those people who talked like that. He also reluctantly realized that most of the people in the movies who talked like that were villains.

Was he a villain now? He looked at Stacy, wearing nothing but a pair of boxer shorts because at the top, baby, there is no reason to wear clothes or draw the curtains.

Who on Earth was saying these things in his head? It couldn't be him.

He thought about how El would send him downstairs to the main floor to make sure all the curtains and blinds were drawn so she could come down from their bedroom without revealing her pale flesh to the whole neighborhood. He smiled. She'd always made being naked seem scandalous, even in their own house. To her, the neighbors were always looking through the windows with binoculars, hoping to see a stray nipple.

He looked at Stacy's exposed nipple and had to struggle to hold back a sigh. Here he was, next to an actually scandalously-exposed nipple, thinking about his ex-wife.

The last he'd heard from her was when she'd made it safely to her dad's house via a picture of Wyatt covered in fudge. A joyous moment of which he was not a part.

"Are you okay?" Stacy's voice cut through the background noise of the TV and into his own guilty thoughts.

He looked at her and she rolled a little to make eye contact. He hummed a question and raised an eyebrow, hopefully conveying that he had no idea what she was talking about.

"You're so quiet." The concern in her voice was touching.

Jesus, was he ruining his new relationship by being concerned with the last one he ruined? Ruining relationships seemed to be his specialty.

"Would you rather I talk the whole time we watch TV?" He'd meant for it to come out as teasing. Instead, it came out sounding petulant. She recoiled a little. She'd heard the petulance more than the tease, it would appear. He sighed. Maybe honesty was the best policy, as long as that honesty was only a snidbit. "I guess I am just missing Wyatt more than I had thought I would." The truth, the partial truth, and nothing but some of it.

Her eyes softened, however, and the tension left the room like the tide. "You know, I miss him too."

It would appear telling the truth was for him and him alone tonight. Stacy did not like Wyatt. Not because he was a bad kid or because of any malice, but because she liked to live in a bubble of ignorance about Jason's past. It was easier to believe her boyfriend had not left his wife and child when the child wasn't standing there like a scarlet letter. Even his name, Wyatt, sounded like a question. *Why, why, why did you break up my parents?*

At one point, Stacy had floated the idea of their own children. To her, his failed marriage was Elizabeth's fault. She'd failed as a wife. He hadn't known how to respond, because telling her the reason he left his wife was because she had a child sounded shittier out loud than in his head. It sounded pretty shitty in his head, too, so he'd mumbled a noncommittal response and the moment passed.

"Maybe I will text El tomorrow and see about having him visit sometime this summer. I know I told her it was fine if he didn't, but I think it would be nice." That also meant he would get to see El. He left out that part, however, for obvious reasons.

Stacy seemed to muse it over, then gave him a rueful smile. "That would mean I would have to put on a shirt, right? That doesn't sound fun."

She moved and began pressing her foot into his crotch. Nothing happened, and he knew nothing would. He sighed, reached down, took her foot, and gently, but pointedly, moved it away from him. She sat up then. "Sorry. I was just joking. I would love for Wyatt to visit and obviously, I would wear a shirt." Again, that concern in her voice. This time, however, he felt that it was less about concern for him and more for their future. He wondered if she was picking up any of his other thoughts. He wanted to dissuade them, but he didn't have the words. Right now, he knew whatever words he used would be false, and he was afraid she might pick up on that as well. He leaned forward, kissing each nipple, then her lips.

"I think I can bear to see you in a shirt for a weekend. It'll be a struggle, but I think I can survive." He smiled and prayed it would look genuine.

She tentatively smiled back, which was probably the best he could ask for.

He stood, and the fact that he was also wearing only boxer shorts did nothing to hide the complete lack of action below the band. Her smile faltered a tiny bit. He leaned forward and kissed her lips again; this time, a little longer and with more tenderness. "I'll text her tomorrow. I think I'm going to go to bed. I'm so tired, I am finding it hard to stay up." He saw that she got the double meaning and hoped she bought it. He'd basically given his version of the "I have a headache" speech. She started to get up to join him. "No, don't feel obligated to go to bed now. It's still early. Feel free to stay up a bit longer, guilt-free. Make sure to give me a kiss when you do go to bed."

She relaxed back on the couch. She could take a hint, it would appear.

"Okay. Get some sleep. I will probably watch another episode or so before turning in." She favored him with a teasing smile. "I'm awake enough to stay up by myself for a little bit."

He also caught the double meaning. He assumed it was a joke but didn't care. She could do whatever she wanted. Hell, if it kept her from waking him up when she came to bed, hoping for some action, then he hoped she "stayed up" by herself for a while.

He made his way toward the bedroom and decided to use the restroom before laying down. Then he realized that, of all nights to not have a conversation with that interloping son of a bitch in the mirror, it was this night. Who knows what things he could convince him of when he was in a mood like this? His bladder wasn't that full anyway; it was more of a habit. If he woke up needing to go, he would do so, in the dark, where the man-in-the-mirror couldn't judge him.

Verse 23

Cherokee, Iowa

GIDEON came back to himself like pulling off a virtual reality headset. The real world came into dark focus.

Dark? How long had he been sitting there? Events went by faster in his head than in reality, but that didn't change the fact that he'd been inside Donny's mind for essentially the entire night. He'd been lucky that a cop hadn't come by to check whether or not he had died.

He looked around. The rest stop had basically been empty when he'd pulled up. Luckily, it had remained so during his long recalling of that night.

No wonder Donny was drunk in the middle of the day. Gideon would be surprised if Donny ever allowed himself to be sober again. The sick truth was that the survivors, of which Donny was only the second Gideon had found, retained all the memories of the events. It wasn't like blacking out while drinking. You remembered doing everything and even, sickly, remembered enjoying it and wanting to do it. Like Donny, the other survivor's memories had been easily pulled and displayed in technicolor, because that was how she saw them every day.

The other survivor, Emily, did not get midday drunk, but rather midday doped—and morning doped and, for good measure, nighttime doped. Also, it had been a long time since she'd worn a belt or shoes with laces.

Emily resided in a psych ward in Oklahoma. Based on what Gideon had read from her mind, she would reside there 'til the day she died, which, if she had her way, would be sooner rather than later. Not because of the song's suicidal pull, which she still heard in her nightmares, but because even the drugs had no effect on the memories hiding behind her eyelids. Ironically, a tree had saved her life as well.

The tree that had stopped her fall also gave her a superb view of the not-so-lucky ones who'd missed the tree. Gideon threw up after watching those memories. He thought back to when he and Samuel had been kids, talking about the Native Americans who'd forced herds of buffalo off cliffs to their doom. The books, with pictures Gideon considered graphic, had done nothing to prepare him for what he saw through Emily's eyes. It was like kids throwing watermelons off a building in science class.

And the sound. There was a wet, crunching sound, nothing like its counterpart on TV. The film industry can try as hard as they like. They, thankfully, would never be able to replicate the sound Gideon heard through the ears of her memory.

Unlike Donny, who was found within hours of the woods massacre, Emily had spent over a day in her tree, staring at the dead bodies of people she'd known most of her life. People she'd cared for. She'd had to watch and listen as birds and other animals came to look into what had taken place in their territory, leaving with prized mementos. By the time a ranger finally found the site, Emily had been so close to death that she'd not even had enough strength to shew away the birds who, unsatisfied with the measly portions left below, decided to find fresher portions.

Gideon thought about how Samuel never stuck around to see the repercussions of his musical massacres. It was easier for him to feel justified in his actions if he didn't have to see the broken families left behind; the devastation he caused with his fight for justice. Gideon, on the other hand, now following his back trail, witnessed it firsthand. In most towns, there were no survivors, which meant he had to track down family members. He saw the victims through their memories. Fathers, mothers, siblings, and friends, undeserving of the fates that befell them.

Samuel saw the world in black and white. He always had, since they were children. Had he stayed one day after, he would see the gray. The families and friends of the victims remembered them not as the sinners Samuel saw, but as their loved ones. People who may have been flawed, but were, nonetheless, loved deeply despite those flaws.

When they'd been partners, Gideon had been able to contain Samuel—at least, to a degree. His ability to read minds and see memories had given him a glimpse into the very souls of their considered targets. Gideon had been able to identify those truly deserving of Samuel's wrath. During those years, Gideon laid awake in bed many nights, questioning the morality of their crusade. He understood that Samuel had a need to cleanse the world of those he considered evil.

Gideon realized that he was lapsing into his own childhood memories of Samuel and himself growing up together. He decided it was probably time to find a less conspicuous spot to spend the night.

A different town down the road might be better. There had been a few people at the bar who had truly malicious thoughts in regard to his questions. He doubted anyone would do anything as foolish as pick a fight with him. But if on their way home from the bar they saw his car, they might feel inclined to let him know how much they disliked his line of questioning.

It had happened before. While Gideon did not hurt for money, it was inconvenient to get the words "Fuck Off" removed from his car door.

There was always a town within an hour of travel in the Midwest. He would pick a direction and hope that it was along the trail of his ex-partner, once best-friend, and forever brother.

Verse 24

Alma, Nebraska

GARY sat in the booth, sipping a regular beer, his once-a-week Thunderhead purchase having already taken place. He had a feeling, though, that his one a week rule would probably not last long. Once you had a better beer, it was hard to go back to something lesser. He sipped again and sighed. Sally was still away from her bartender duties and Jacob had other plans for the day. This left Gary with the new bartender—who was not new, just new to the shift—and his less than desirable beer.

The door opened and Gary's mood was lightened as Samuel Serenade strolled in, looking as chipper as always. Gary's heart panged as he thought back to when he was Samuel's age, deeply tanned from farming shirtless with barely an ounce of fat on his body from the nearly continuous manual labor, his dark hair lightened by the sun. He looked down at his belly pressing gingerly against the table in the booth. He didn't have much time for self-loathing as Samuel slid into the booth, calling to the bartender, "Two Thunderheads for my friend and I?" Gary smiled widely. His one a week rule was solely with regard to purchasing fancy beer, not drinking it.

"Mr. Serenade, as I live and breathe," Gary said, allowing his joy at no longer drinking alone to flow toward Samuel.

Samuel returned the smile, just as warmly.

As an out-of-towner, Samuel didn't have many friends in Alma and was probably just as grateful for Gary's company. Or so Gary told himself, warming to the idea of being this young man's friend. "What brings a striking young man like yourself to a dirty hole-in-the-wall establishment like this?"

"I resent that," the bartender said, smiling. "I just cleaned." He set the two tumblers, full of that delicious honey beer, onto the worn, wooden table. Gary tried to think of his name to say something witty, but he didn't know it. Sally had been gone a few days now. Gary should have learned the new guy's name.

"Thank you ever so kindly," Samuel cut into his thoughts. "I apologize, but I never got your name."

Gary marveled at how easily Samuel went right to it. Here was Gary, trying to figure out how he'd not yet learned the bartender's name, and Samuel took care of the problem without hesitation. The kid oozed confidence. There didn't appear to be a single ounce of shyness in the boy.

"Blake," the bartender said happily, obviously pleased that someone asked.

If he wanted people to call him by his name, maybe he should get a name tag, Gary thought. He quickly finished his less satisfying beer so that the bartender, Blake, could take the empty glass as he left.

Once Blake had gone, Samuel looked around, overexaggerating his movements. "He had things to do today," Gary answered. "Old fogies like us do sometimes have plans, you know?"

Samuel smiled.

"What brings ya back to my table in the middle of the day?" He sipped his fresh beer, enjoying the sweet flavor of honey and hops.

"I had a few questions for you in regard to the upcoming festivities." Samuel sipped his own beer, then pulled another business card from his wallet and set it on the table. "I actually never got an answer about whether or not you passed my card along, because our conversation turned to the unfortunate events of the night before."

The unfortunate events being a certain unpleasant individual blowing his unpleasant brains all over the walls.

"Speaking of which," Samuel continued, "I still haven't seen or reached out to Sally, per your request." Gary nodded affirmation. "I should tell you that I have a new lively bee in my bonnet with regard to the wedding gig. There is a . . ." He paused and considered. ". . . someone that I would like to see again who is involved."

"Hopefully, not the bride," Gary said, raising gray eyebrows in mock suspicion.

Samuel shook his head.

"No, I think she said she's the maid of honor. A friend of the bride, maybe."

Gary saw Samuel's anticipation as he waited for recognition from the old man's face. No luck, though, as Gary's face stayed blank. He was only able to give a look of interest in Samuel and his new lady.

"I don't think she lives in this town. She said she was driving through. Her name is Elizabeth?"

Still no recognition. "I will admit that I do not know all her friends as I didn't know her that well personally, just the family in general." Samuel's smile made Gary want to help him find this mystery woman. "I could text Jacob and see if he knows—"

He was cut off as Samuel's phone began to ring.

Verse 25

Norton, Kansas

ELIZABETH sat at her dad's kitchen table listening to Wyatt in the other room talk to himself as he did math problems. He'd promised both his parents he would keep up with preschool-type work over the summer. This had not surprised Elizabeth as she knew he enjoyed math. She assumed it shocked his father as he was not the type of person to do math for entertainment.

Again, she marveled at where Wyatt could have come from in the DNA that intermixed inside her one night during a thunderstorm. She didn't know why, but storms always put her in the mood. That only made them more depressing these days.

Attempting to push aside all negative thoughts, she looked at the text from Rebecca she'd received. It read "Samuel Serenade," followed by a number, followed by a winky face emoji.

Now that she had the number, it was real. What if she called and he didn't remember her? What if, worse, he remembered her only as that mother he'd met when she got out to use the bathroom?

In her defense, it was Wyatt who needed the bathroom. Regardless, the first time they met, bathrooms were part of the equation. That was never a great way to start a romantic relationship.

Having received the text relatively late the night before, she'd decided to wait until the next day and call him first thing.

However, when she'd woken up, she'd decided she should wait until after coffee, then Wyatt had woken up and they'd discussed plans for the day, then her dad had returned from wherever old farmer-type men go in the morning in Norton. Time had contented itself in moving along and she, still subconsciously scared of the phone call, contented herself in letting it. Until time seemingly stopped. Her dad had left again to run some errands and Wyatt decided to do his math work. Elizabeth found herself free of obligations and therefore free of any excuse to not make the call.

The blue phone number with the underline sat on the lit-up screen like an omen. Maybe it was because she'd never attempted anything like this that made it feel so heavy.

She'd met Jason in college and their friendship had melded into a relationship. One day they were friends and the next, they were more. There had been no complicated phone calls or worries about what the other thought. Heck, when they'd started dating, cell phones barely existed. Now, the blue underlined phone number on her phone felt like it contained all the weight of her past life. With this phone call, she would be admitting that she was ready to consider moving on with her life. That she was willing to let Jason go.

As if called from her overworked mind, Jason's name appeared on the screen and her phone began to vibrate softly. For a time, she stared at it, unable to comprehend what was happening. Was she imagining this? She'd been considering leaving this man in the past where he'd so efficiently left her and now, he was calling her. She seriously considered letting it go to voicemail, but reluctantly accepted the call.

"Hello, Jason." She'd heard somewhere that you could hear a smile through the phone. She wondered if you could hear a frown.

"Um, hi, El. Elizabeth. Sorry," he stammered and Elizabeth supposed maybe he'd heard the frown after all. "Are you all right?"

Great. He'd heard the frown so loudly, he was concerned with her wellbeing. She wanted to explain that he'd messed up her phone call to a man she was interested in, but suddenly had no energy for that discussion. So she hummed ascent to let him know she was all right, and either he accepted her allrightness or he understood that she didn't want to talk about it.

Either way, he pushed forward. "I know that I told you that I was agreeable with the two of you being away all summer, and that pictures and Facetimes would suffice, but I was wrong."

She sat up straighter. What was he saying? He missed them?

"I was wondering if you would be willing to drive Wyatt up at some point, and we could all go get dinner or something, then he could stay with me for the weekend or something."

Elizabeth was so flabbergasted that she couldn't respond. He'd never requested time with Wyatt. In fact, she'd all but forced the kid on him because she thought Wyatt needed to know his dad. Jason had always been reluctant about Wyatt being in his new apartment. He'd done everything he could to remove any evidence from his life that he was a dad and here he was, reaching out, wanting to be just that. For a weekend.

"I gave you that option and you said no," Elizabeth finally said. "Remember how busy the weekends are for wedding planning?"

Her emotions were all over the place. She felt like a cowgirl bandita with her limbs tied to different horses.

On the one hand, she was thrilled with Jason's new desire to see Wyatt. It had been everything she'd hoped for yet never saw. Even when they were still together, Jason's reluctance to spend alone time with Wyatt or watch him while Elizabeth finished some work or prepared supper had been evident. After they'd split, he'd become a specter, a ghost dad who would manifest only when summoned. On the other hand, he'd not been wrong in saying that weekends were busy. Bex would be in Alma tomorrow starting the process. Now Elizabeth would have to cater to his needs when maybe she could have prepared had he started off by saying he wanted to see Wyatt throughout the summer.

Wyatt was a consideration as well. He was the sole piece in this depressing game of chess they were playing. How would he feel knowing there had been no plans to visit his dad and now there were? Would it give him hope like it did her? When that hope turned out to be unfounded, would that be worse than when there had been no hope to begin with?

But what if this change of heart was genuine and Jason truly wanted to spend time with Wyatt? This could be the corner she'd hoped he would turn earlier. By saying no, would she be ending any chance of Wyatt having a real relationship with his dad? What if she told Jason no, then Wyatt found out later that his dad had requested time with him, and she'd kept them apart? Would there be resentment?

Wyatt was a poor soldier who had somehow been drafted for both teams and was now stranded in no-man's land as both generals took shots at each other.

Jason had called her, though. He'd reached out to her,

not the other way around. That had to mean something.

Throughout all of this, the other horse pulling the ropes taut was Samuel. How dare Jason call her and cloud the waters when she was finally considering diving in? Or, at the very least, wading in. She already felt exposed, like a woman putting on a bathing suit for the first time after losing her pregnancy weight.

She could almost see this analogy: Samuel already in the water, smiling at her, his gleaming blue eyes sparkling with the reflection of the water. She still has her towel around her. Why had she picked a bikini when she could have worn a one-piece? Because she wanted to feel sexy again and for Samuel to see her as such. Then, as she begins to unwrap, Jason cannonballs into the water, splashing her, messing up the hair she wasn't sure she'd get wet. As he surfaces, splashing more water around, he calls out to her . . .

"El? Elizabeth? Look, I know what I said earlier. I honestly believed that it would be better he didn't visit or vice versa. I know that it will be inconvenient for you to travel here, so I can come get him, if you are okay with that and he is willing."

It was a good thing this was a phone call and not a Facetime or in-person, because Jason would have seen her jaw drop. It unhinged like a snake preparing to eat an entire antelope. There was no way she'd heard what she thought she heard. He'd come pick Wyatt up?

There had to be more to this. People didn't change this drastically overnight.

Her untrusting mind, the one that had taken dominance after he'd packed his bags one night, walking out of their house and away from his responsibilities as a father, was working overtime to stamp down any feelings of hope. Her hopeful mind was not entirely gone, however, and it was playing one hell of an offense against the untrusting defense. She'd never taken Wyatt away from Jason for so long. Maybe, faced with that understanding, the reality of it all had finally woken him to the fact that not only did he have a son, but that he was his son's dad.

Elizabeth thought about what it would do to her if Jason said, "I'm taking Wyatt for the entire summer, and you won't see him." It would devastate her. She wanted to believe so badly that Jason had thought about the long summer ahead and had felt similarly devastated.

"How would your roommate feel about that?" She was shocked to hear no real malice in that comment. Honestly, the emotion behind it was curiosity mixed with concern. She knew that Jason's new girl-thing (Did adults, say "girlfriend"?) had no great love for Wyatt. She found it hard to believe that she was jumping at the chance to entertain a five-year-old, much less one who looked like Elizabeth. At the same time, maybe this new Jason hadn't cared. Elizabeth wasn't sure how that made her feel. Again, there was a battle between untrusting and hopeful, where the line of play kept getting pushed to either favor, then back again.

"She is excited." Elizabeth heard Jason pause before he continued. "Well, she has accepted it anyway."

His corrected reply was so unabashedly honest that Elizabeth's jaw fell open again. She could tell that he'd considered lying but chose the truth. For the first time she could remember, he'd all but admitted his new relationship wasn't perfect. Hopeful pushed against untrusting and moved the line of favor once again.

"It has been a while since I went to the zoo or the gardens," Jason offered. "I was thinking we could all go. Weather willing, that is, depending on the weekend you choose."

"I think that sounds great," Elizabeth heard herself say.

It was like an out-of-body experience. She heard the words but she did not know who'd said them. Horses continued to pull her limbs to the breaking point. It appeared that the desire for her son to have a stronger bond with his dad was too strong. Despite the mental battle still raging in her mind, the decision was made. With those words spoken, the smoke cleared, and the battle was done, come what may. It would be good. She could give her dad a weekend off from Grandpa duty.

"Do you want to tell Wyatt?" she asked.

Jason said he did so she walked into the adjoining room. Wyatt looked up expectantly and, for a brief second, Elizabeth almost screamed into the phone: "You can't have him! I won't allow you to break his heart." She held it back. Instead, she said, "Wyatt, it's your dad. He wants to talk to you."

She passed the phone off and listened with anticipation as Wyatt said the customary hello, yes, I am good, etc.

After Wyatt had explained how great Grandpa's house was and how excited he was to see the farm, the conversation lulled into silence. This was Jason's opportunity to back out, thought Elizabeth, if he realized this had been a momentary emotional mistake. He could tell Wyatt how cool that all sounded and that he would see him in the fall. Instead, Elizabeth watched as Wyatt listened intently, pressing the phone closer to his face. His entire face lit up and she knew she'd made the right choice.

She also knew that sometimes the right choice led to the wrong outcome. She prayed this wouldn't be one of those cases.

Wyatt began telling his dad how excited he was to go to the zoo and hang out with him for the weekend, and what he would like to eat, what toys he might bring—all the things important to a kid.

Elizabeth stood, feeling oddly jealous of Jason. Granted, doing things with Mom was par for the course; life as Wyatt knew it. Doing things with Dad was rare, unique, exciting, and new. She sighed, torn between jealousy and elation at seeing Wyatt so happy. She left the room, letting them have private father-son phone time.

She went into the kitchen to make herself some afternoon coffee. As it brewed, she remembered what she'd been planning on doing before Jason called. She felt a strange urge to go take the phone from Wyatt. All the nerves she'd been feeling about calling Samuel settled back on her. It felt like a literal weight being draped across her shoulders. Maybe it was good that Jason had called and distracted her; it gave her an excuse not to call.

Then Wyatt came in, still beaming, the phone no longer to his ear. There was no longer a valid excuse not to call.

"Daddy is gonna come pick me up and take me home."

A dagger slid into her chest, sliding easily between her ribs, entering the heart, and severing her lifeline. Her body seemed to forget what it needed for basic survival. Her lungs froze into useless balloons and the process of drawing air came to a stop.

Take me home, he'd said.

All her misgivings about letting Jason have this weekend

wrapped a cold hand around the hilt of the knife in her chest and gave it a cruel twist. *Take me home.* Foreboding seeped into her, taking the place of much-needed oxygen, solidifying the useless balloons in her chest.

"Mom?" The giant smile on Wyatt's face dissolved.

She imagined what she must look like to her son, suffocating in front of him, face turning to a dead gray as her bloodstream ran out of the oxygen it had been so accustomed to.

"Mom?" There was real concern now. The smile was gone. He stepped forward.

Take me home. She breathed in a deep breath and felt her lungs fill. With that act, the knife in her chest receded a little, though it remained. While no longer in her heart, pressure settled under her breast, a reminder that her decisions held weight.

"That's great, honey. He sounded very excited to have you over to his place and to take you to the zoo." She heard her emphasis on *his* and hated herself a little. She wondered if Wyatt was old enough to understand adult jealousy and, if so, whether he was able to read it in her language. His smile tentatively returned. "Did the two of you decide on a weekend?"

"Dad said it was up to you."

The man was literally bending over backward to make this work. What had happened to him? She looked at Wyatt and, shockingly, returned his grin with genuine joy. She was feeding off his joy. Also, much to her regret, she was feeding off her own hope.

"I'll look at the wedding plans and your grandpa's plans, and communicate with your dad, and we will come up with something. Those animals in the zoo aren't gonna look at themselves."

Wyatt laughed. "Maybe someone should give them a mirror so they can." Wyatt cracked up, set her phone on the table, and ran back into the living room with a new pep in his step.

Elizabeth looked at the phone. With the screen blackened, there was no underlined phone number staring at her. With all the excitement of the past few minutes coming to an end, the world seemed to stop along with it. It was as if everything in the world was holding its breath, waiting to see what she did. For some reason, that thought propelled her forward.

She dashed toward the table, nabbed her phone, and held it in front of her face. The facial recognition opened the screen to the last thing she'd been doing prior to the call. There was the message with the underlined number.

Afraid that her indecision would settle back into place, she pressed her thumb to the number. She didn't place it to her ear, though. She watched as the screen turned black, displaying the information of the call. She could hear it ringing softly, connecting to a phone she hoped would not be answered while she simultaneously prayed that it would. The ring stopped mid-jingle.

"Hello?"

Verse 26

Missouri Valley, Iowa

GIDEON had gone to sleep on a soft hotel bed. But when he'd opened his eyes, he was back in the forest behind the school.

He crawled along the forest floor, pulling himself forward with the better of two hands. He was now very aware of his pain and the fact that not all of his fingers moved. Jessica was up ahead, however, and if he'd survived, maybe she had too. Every part of him was cold. He was continuously on the edge of consciousness until he felt a branch jam itself above his right hip, tearing through his purposefully interesting shirt and burying deep into his skin.

The song was over, and the pain was more intense than anything he'd felt in his life. He rolled over and used the few remaining fingers that worked on the only hand that could grasp to pull out the branch. A red flower bloomed on the fabric. His mind screamed to give up and give in to the darkness pulling at his consciousness to relieve the pain. But Jessica might still be alive, so he rolled back onto his stomach, into the new puddle of blood, and continued to pull himself forward.

It felt like years passed as he continued to crawl. At one point, he attempted to stand despite his ankle, but in the process of pushing himself up from a kneeling position, his vision quickly tunneled. He knew that if he continued to stand, he would pass out.

After an unknown amount of time pulling himself forward, his arm feeling like there was molten lava flowing through the veins, his hand slipped into a puddle then against something soft. He got his elbows under him, forcing all the will he could muster to look up.

The little clearing was filled with bodies already turning blue in the cold February night. There was blood everywhere — splashed on the trees, staining their clothes, pooling on the ground where they lay. Gideon looked at the arm he'd touched and saw the overeager party goer had slit his hand in half from wrist to fingers, and it splayed out in two pieces like an alien prop in a sci-fi film.

Gideon yanked back his hand. Immediately, he began to see stars as a black hole formed in his vision. He took deep breaths and closed his eyes, waiting to see whether he would pass out or the feeling would pass.

With his eyes closed, his other senses were clearer. He could hear voices now, coming from the gym and the edge of the woods. Help was on its way.

He needed to find Jessica. With all this carnage, they might miss her. He opened his eyes. There was no movement in front of him. No twitching, no moaning, and most dishearteningly, no visible breathing. The voices behind were louder now, tearing through the trees. They would be here shortly.

He made his way toward the middle of the little circle the party goers formed with their bodies. Once there, he was able to get to a seated position. Finally, he got a good look at the chaos.

Steak- and bile-coated shreds of lettuce spewed forth into his lap to steam in the cold night air. He didn't notice the hot mixture soaking into his pants as his eyes jumped from body to body. When they landed on Jessica, everything inside him froze.

His heart threatened to finish what he'd been unable to do with the stick. While he, and many of those in the circle, had gone for their wrists, possibly pulling from some subconscious knowledge of attempted suicides, she'd taken a much more definitive route. The steak knife was hilt deep in her throat, her blue, lifeless hand gripping the handle in a literal death grip. The bones of that hand looked vibrantly white in the darkness. She'd slumped back against a tree. The already drying blood had flown like a waterfall down her chest into her dress. Her eyes were open, accusingly; not because Gideon hadn't been there to save her, but rather that he hadn't been there to join her. Though his consciousness had all but deserted him, he found the energy to begin screaming.

Gideon sat up in bed, a cold sweat broken out all over his body. The scream that had been in his throat stopped behind his lips, held together tightly by a strip of duct tape. Gideon had taken precautions as he did after a particularly horrific read. While the memories faded consciously, his subconscious had a way of leading him into the lingering memories when his guard was down. While awake, he was able to remind himself that he was watching someone else's memories, but when he was asleep, his mind had a way of forgetting that fact. It was like playing a virtual reality game while under the influence of a very potent hallucinogenic.

He worked to bring his heart rate down, taking deep breaths through his nose, filling his constricting lungs, allowing them to get acquainted with the feeling of being full before releasing slowly. His heart returned to a normal rhythm and a calm settled back over him.

He removed the duct tape and tasted the air. He was in a motel room in a small town south of Cherokee. The air wasn't necessarily fresh, but the feeling of air passing through his lips after being taped was relief enough. He thought back to when he was a kid, first learning to wear duct tape at night after reading someone. Samuel had always been by his side when he awoke, attuned to the signs of his nightmares before his mind realized they were dreams. Samuel, who'd helped him understand his little quirk. Samuel, who'd been his partner. Samuel, who'd broken his heart.

Samuel, who was now gone.

Verse 27

Alma, Nebraska

"HELLO?" Samuel answered the phone. He mouthed "sorry" to Gary who shrugged, not put out in the least. Gary picked up his beer and sipped, ready to listen in on the conversation Samuel planned to have in front of him.

"Um, hi. Yes, this is Elizabeth. I don't know if you remember me, but I am the maid of honor at Rebecca's upcoming wedding that will take place there in Alma."

Gary was pleased Samuel's phone was loud enough that he felt included. He did not believe in fate, but he had to admit it was putting up a good case for its existence right this minute. Samuel paused. Gary wondered if he was considering acting like he didn't remember her, despite the fact that he'd confided the importance of their meeting to Gary. Flirting was long in Gary's past, but he remembered the game, and how important looking cool and detached was at the beginning.

"Bombardier eyes?" asked Samuel.

That was a reference Gary did not understand. But he heard an intake of air and could picture the young lady's face turning red. He wondered if Samuel had gone too far. Gary again recalled flirting in his youth. Sometimes, a small jest could end a conversation before it started with the intended walking away upset and embarrassed.

"Yep." A loud sigh came from the phone. "You know, I was calling to set up an audition, but now I am so mortified from embarrassment that I am not sure I can be in the same room as you. My iPhone connected to the speakers, is less judgmental." There was a pause. Gary anticipated Samuel would break it but, before he could, the voice continued. "People still like the Spice Girls, right?"

Samuel burst out laughing and Gary smiled.

"If it makes you feel better," said Samuel, "I could wear sunglasses to the audition, so you don't have to see those bombardier eyes."

There was a sigh of exasperation from Elizabeth.

"I promise to be professional during the audition and, if I get the part, I will even take you out for a celebratory dinner."

Too far. Even Gary knew it. The silence drew on, long enough for Gary to believe she'd hung up. In fact, he was reaching out to comfort his new friend when she replied.

"I do like dinner," she said with a thoughtful inflection. "Completely professional, obviously. As a potential employer to a potential employee. So, a work dinner."

Gary, recognizing the potential drama was over, pointed at his drink, then cocked an eye in a request that was unabashed, but hopefully endearing. Samuel nodded and Gary waved over the bartender, Blake.

"I am obviously very busy with wedding planning and other maid of honor duties, so I am not sure how much time I can spare for something so. . ." Elizabeth paused to give her next word more emphasis. "Trivial."

"As trivialities go, it will be an enjoyable break from the stressful work that a maid of honor has to endure at such a critical stage in wedding planning." Yeah, Samuel could play as well.

Gary rolled his eyes at him as the new beers came to the table. Samuel had barely touched his first one and now had another. If Samuel left now, would Gary drink all three of the leftover beers? He rather thought that he would. The man liked his beer, and to waste good beer is next to blasphemous.

"How 'bout this weekend?" asked Samuel. "Do you have a venue yet? I could bring my equipment and do a little preview. Will the bride-to-be or lucky fella be attending?"

"They have full faith in my musical appreciation. While I am sure they will want to hear you eventually, I am the first stop. I could even be the last stop—if you are all huff and puff but can't blow me down."

Gary choked on his beer. Samuel had to suppress a laugh as the old man fought to catch his breath. Samuel had walked in declaring that someone he'd only met once had caught his eye, and here she was on the phone dropping innuendos. Impressed did not quite do justice to how Gary felt. Actually, it was kind of eerie how well the conversation was going, if what Samuel said was true and this was only the second time they'd talked.

A memory of the day Gary met Samuel pushed forward into his mind: Sally struggling to complete basic tasks or finish sentences while talking to this man. Before he could dwell on that memory, however, Samuel's reply pulled him back to the present.

"I appreciate a good nursery rhyme and will strive to be big and bad enough to suit your musical needs."

Jesus, that sounded like something an elementary kid would say to the girl he had a crush on, despite having no real understanding of what a crush entailed. Ironically, the terrible joke helped put Gary's mind at ease as the perfection of the conversation was tainted, removing some of the shine. It felt a little more real; some of that easy confidence was gone. Samuel was, after all, a normal man who was infatuated with a beautiful girl he had met. A tale as old as time, as they say.

Elizabeth's laughter came through the phone as a pure melody. Her laugh was infectious, and Samuel found himself laughing right along with her, their voices intertwining through the phone signals, creating something truly wonderful. Gary, who was only privy to one side of the laughter song, found himself chuckling at the pure joy of the moment.

However, as Samuel turned toward the bar, Gary's unease returned. Again, his mind returned to their first meeting and how easily Samuel had woven himself into their lives. As the laughing began to taper off, he had a fleeting thought as he looked at his beer: *I was okay with regular beer. I wish Samuel had never walked through those doors.*

The thought was so sudden and uninvited, it felt like a completely different person had thought those words. His smile was gone, torn from his face from the dark thought. Luckily, Samuel was still turned toward the bar and missed the look of confused fear passing across Gary's face. Gary decided that maybe he was done with fancy beer. He was planning to leave as Samuel finished the call by clarifying the details of the audition. When he turned back to Gary, his face shone like that of a child on Christmas morning.

All concerns left Gary, who grabbed his beer and tipped it toward him. "I feel that congratulations are in order."

Glasses clinked together and the fleeting doom dissipated like mist after the sunrise.

Verse 28

Norton, Kansas

HAROLD and Wyatt watched as Elizabeth systematically went through the clothing she'd brought for the hundredth time.

"None of these are good. I wasn't planning on going on a date, so I didn't pack anything like that. Not that this is a date. It's an audition, a wedding task that needs done." She held up a top she'd already decided against to reconsider. She threw it on the bed with the other discarded outfits.

"Honey, if it isn't a date and you don't want to give the impression that it is, why don't you just wear something casual like a t-shirt and jeans?"

She snapped her head toward her father so quickly, he felt like ducking behind Wyatt. Her eyes were manic, like a scared animal backed into a corner. It took him back to when she'd been in high school about to go on a date with a boy. He remembered how every word he spoke would draw that look. Only then, there had been two sets of eyes snapping toward him.

He could almost hear Judy scolding him: "What do you mean 'casual'? I swear, Harold, how you have had a daughter these many years and yet understand nothing about the teenage girl is beyond me."

That familiar pang of loss hit him again as he realized how much better she would be in this situation than him. He'd not understood his teenage daughter, and he was finding out he didn't understand his adult one either. Her eyes were still on him, burrowing holes into him, tearing through him to find his definition of "casual" to reveal his complete naivety of the situation.

Wyatt came to Harold's rescue. "I like that shirt, Mom. It makes you look prettier than Miss Montgomery."

Harold said a slight prayer of thanks to the seemingly less attractive Miss Montgomery, and to Wyatt for speaking up, because with that statement, every amount of anxiety in Elizabeth melted like the leftover snow in late March. She looked at the yellow blouse in a new light. A light that compared her to this Miss Montgomery, Harold presumed.

"You know, I believe you are right. That fresh-from-college bombshell has nothing on me when I wear this top." She beamed at her son.

Wyatt beamed back. But when Elizabeth turned, he made eye contact with his grandpa and kind of shrugged, and Harold saw a hint of blush color his grandson's cheeks. Harold may not have known much about teenage girls, but he knew something about young boys, having been one himself. Miss Montgomery was Wyatt's first crush, and unless Harold was wrong, Wyatt had been lying about his mom being prettier than her. The kid was smart. Harold saw a future of artful manipulation. Harold decided to keep up his guard a little bit more for the rest of the summer.

"While you have this casual meeting with a potential musician for your friend's wedding," Harold said, careful to not sound too sarcastic with his reply, "Wyatt and I will finally get to the farm."

Wyatt beamed up at his grandfather, expectation apparent in his glittering eyes. Harold knew he'd been waiting to go to the old farm ever since his mom had told him about it. Wyatt had regaled him with stories from the drive to Norton. Elizabeth had explained how there were giant machines no longer in use, where the grass and weeds had grown around them apocalyptically. The house had not been lived in for years and stood abandoned and decaying, the paint all but faded to nothing from years of sun and no recoats.

Elizabeth frowned a little, still holding the yellow top. "I thought we would all go out together." There was real disappointment in her voice.

Harold knew she enjoyed going to see her childhood home. Where Wyatt would see the end of the world, she would see the start of hers.

While the farm wasn't far from town, it was far enough that their family had been a solitary unit, entertaining each other more than guests. He knew she'd hoped to show Wyatt her first home and share the experience with him as he saw her old bedroom, even if it had lost some of its little girl luster from when she lived there. Harold's heart broke a little, but he still believed this was something Wyatt would enjoy more if his mom wasn't there, clouding his imagination with the reality of her past. Again, Harold pulled from his own memories of being a young boy.

"I think the first time he goes, it might be best if he sees it with his own eyes rather than through yours." He was shocked by how poetic his statement sounded and saw on his daughter's face that she was too. She looked stunned. Then, she slowly nodded, allowing a smile to touch her lips.

"It's a boy thing, isn't it? Something this ol' lady wouldn't understand. I would blather on about when I was a kid and take all the atmosphere out of it."

Wyatt looked a little confused by what the adults around him were talking about, but Harold nodded, and Elizabeth sighed.

"Fine," she said. "I see your point, but I will not miss my opportunity to ruin the farm for my son. I vow to go with the two of you at least once this summer to give him the boring tour of my childhood." She smiled and stomped down defiantly as if placing the dot at the bottom of her exclamation mark.

"I will dust the cobwebs from your room and make sure the posters of those boys with long hair are nice and shiny." Harold was rewarded with a touch of color on her cheeks, but he saw her gratitude just as plainly.

There was a moment of silence between the three of them. Two of them shared a moment of reminiscence; the third felt very confused but also very excited.

They all hoped this weekend would be one to remember.

Verse 29

Omaha, Nebraska

JASON was almost giddy as he went through the calendar on his laptop. He was looking for the perfect weekend where he would have no other distractions. Scenes of Wyatt and himself standing in front of the sea lions, laughing as they swam in circles. Wyatt with his face inches away from the gorillas, trying to communicate his delight by grunting their language. Most of these thoughts played out in a Hallmark movie-type montage as Jason had only been to the zoo once with Wyatt, and he'd been less than a year old and asleep in his stroller the whole time. That is, until he was awake and screaming in the car.

Jason shook his head as if an annoying fly buzzed around him. Those negative memories of Wyatt when he was younger were only going to serve to ruin the weekend he was planning. Wyatt was old enough to talk, reason, and enjoy the zoo.

Stacy sauntered into the room, fully dressed for once. She saw the screen of his computer. "Planning an elaborate get away?"

He wondered whether she deliberately forgot about their conversation about Wyatt or she disliked the idea so much that her mind blocked the memory.

"Sorta," he said, "the one with Wyatt that we talked about."

He knew she hated it when she said his name rather than "my son." His name made him a human; a person rather than a past hindrance.

If she heard the name, she didn't react. She was getting ready to go to work, in her own world more than his at the moment. That was okay with him. He wasn't sure if it would have led to a fight, but things had been a little tense ever since he announced his plans to have Wyatt up for a weekend. She came around the couch to kiss him before leaving, coffee thermos in hand. Again, Jason was struck by how young and attractive she was. He didn't know too many people who could make nurse scrubs look good.

Looking at her, he felt another pang of guilt. But it was an old pang with which he'd already come to terms. The fact that Stacy was a nurse at the office of the pediatrician Wyatt used to see had not eased tensions in the divorce talks. It had, in fact, convinced Elizabeth to look for a new pediatrician despite liking Dr. Johnson. Stacy wasn't going to quit her job because it made Elizabeth feel awkward.

Jason could still hear the venom in Elizabeth's words as she explained to him and a room of lawyers how she'd been forced to find a new pediatrician to satisfy his manly urges. The looks from her team were that of understanding; the looks of his team were barely hidden looks of understanding. While his team had fought in his favor, explaining that it was her personal choice to switch doctors, he could tell they thought he was on the wrong side of the argument.

Looking back, though, he still held to the fact that he hadn't had much choice. Feelings couldn't be controlled.

He remembered sitting in the pediatrician's office, wishing he were there for a reason other than his son's checkups. He would wear clothes he thought made him look cool and revel in Stacy's appreciation. This was something eventually noticed by the woman he thought less of as a wife and more of as an obstacle.

As Stacy walked toward the door, Jason's guilt settled into the chair next to him like an old friend. She turned, door open, and waved at him. He waved back, trying not to look at the empty spot next to him, the spot that was less empty to him.

After the door latched, the man-in-the-mirror, whom he saw on the couch in the laptop screen's reflection, said, "Now that is how you make scrubs look hot." The compliment to her was a slap to him. He purposefully set the laptop in the empty spot, hoping that would drive the disembodied voice away.

Coffee was what he needed. Coffee would help finish his plans with Wyatt and, hopefully, help banish this guilty spirit.

His shiny, spotless kitchen, however, did not lessen the guilt as he saw, overlaid over the black, glass table, a wooden one with crayon marks, spaghetti stains, and glass spots. His eyes fell to the tile floor where he saw the ghosts of toys, left abandoned, blocking easy access to the lower cabinets. Shaking his head to disperse the hateful apparitions, he went to the miniature espresso machine.

It had been one of the first purchases he'd made after moving out of his old house. No longer did he have the classic 10-cup Mr. Coffee pot, but a machine that ground the coffee beans, brewed the coffee hot and strong, and even frothed milk to top it all off. Espresso represented his newfound singleness more than anything else. A pot represented sharing, the understanding that the coffee was meant for everyone. Espresso, brewed into a tiny cup, was meant for only one. A personal drink, personally brewed, for one person. Don't take it personally. He sighed and brewed a single espresso for himself, forgoing the frothed milk.

He returned to the blessedly empty couch and sat. The coffee worked. Holding the little cup made him feel like he was at work and allowed him to look at his schedule with a more detached eye. He was penciling in a meeting, regardless of who the meeting was with. As far as his computer and online calendar were concerned, it was just another meeting amongst many. He sipped his bitter yet delicious coffee, feeling the warmth flow through him into his fingertips. He began to work, clinically looking up information on the zoo, upcoming weather, and upcoming movies that would be in theaters. Through it all, the guilty man who'd been haunting him stayed silent.

An hour later, he had everything planned out on his calendar. He had even pre-ordered tickets for the movies. The coffee was gone, allowing the reality of what he'd done to wash over him. His lips split apart in a smile of pure joy.

Images passed in front of him of zebras, giraffes, and spaceships, but, mostly, of Wyatt's face as he witnessed all of that with him. Wyatt's eyes glistened with tears of happiness as they walked hand in hand toward the lions. He saw himself lifting Wyatt with ease to place him on his shoulders. With a final little swirl of his finger, he invited Elizabeth to the event and breathed a long sigh of accomplishment. She didn't reply. Planning weddings was a lot of work, he reminded himself. He set the laptop on the hateful empty spot, stood, stretched, then went about getting ready for work.

Verse 30

Norton, Kansas

ELIZABETH saw the calendar invite pop up on her screen and felt a brief pang of hurt. Most of the hurt she felt was quick and unexpected. Each pang followed something that had once been common and no longer was.

Jason and Elizabeth had shared their calendars before they were married. Originally, while in college, they would pencil in their upcoming events and plans on each other's wall calendars. Over the years, their calendar sharing had evolved right along with the flow of technology. Dentist appointments, when keyed into one phone, were automatically shared to the other. There were bittersweet memories of adding after-work kisses, or more lewd acts, into the shared calendar, letting the other know their intentions for when they got home.

The hurt, as it so often did, turned quickly to anger. How dare he do something they used to do before as if nothing had changed? Elizabeth mused on the stages of grief. There should be a list of stages for divorce: hurt leads to anger, anger leads to confusion, confusion leads back to anger, anger leads to defiance, and defiance leads to resolution. She could almost watch those stages pass by in this recent act. She'd moved from anger quickly into confusion, wondering whether sharing his calendar was intentional or if Jason was being efficient without considering the larger implications. During her revelry, the phone had faded back to its heartless black screen.

She reached out and gingerly touched the screen. The notification of the shared calendar appointment swam back.

Jason had sounded different on the phone. He'd seemed interested in Wyatt in a way she could not remember. Then a memory popped into her head, leading her back to the next stage: anger. The memory of them putting the supposed due date in their shared calendar.

They'd been sitting in bed together, the night after their first appointment, no visible evidence yet of the life inside her. She swore that her stomach had begun to swell, and Jason dutifully had called her crazy. In perfect clarity, she saw them holding their phones, excitement buzzing between them.

"Who should be the sharer and who should be the sharee?" she'd asked, terms that had long ago become normal for their calendar sharing ways.

"Well, he or she is in you at the moment, so I think you should have the pleasure of typing it in," Jason had offered.

"So, like all the rest of this upcoming pregnancy, I have to do all the work," she said.

He rolled his eyes in the most exaggerated way he could, moving his head with the motion.

"If you wanna be the one who squeezes this human watermelon out of your genitalia, be my guest. However, since childbearing is chauvinistic, I will place the due date on our calendar."

They kissed tenderly. The event was added, and Jason blew into a cupped hand, mimicking a party horn. Love was so thick in the room, it was suffocating.

Elizabeth snapped back to the present and was surprised to find tears. Her pregnancy had been rough, and she'd been scared of being intimate for a large portion of it. Jason had seemed understanding, but, in retrospect, it had probably been the beginning of everything that followed. The memory that had flowed from seeing that calendar invite had been one of the last truly intimate moments they'd shared.

She was still angry; the memory had left her in a weird state of longing. Not for that moment or for the moments of intimacy before that, but rather for the future that moment seemed to promise. Jason's party horn echoed in her mind, reverberating down the halls of her memory. His excitement at that moment had been real. She knew it then and believed it now.

He had been excited like he'd been on the phone call the day before.

He'd honestly sounded excited about spending time with Wyatt. She heard the hand horn again. She realized there was another stage of divorce, possibly the worst of all: hope.

Hope. Not in reuniting. Not in falling madly in love again. Rather, hope that someday, things would finally smooth out. Hope that the children would be able to have a mostly normal life with two parents who didn't want to kill each other. Hope that the other stages of divorce would resolve, and life would move on.

The problem was that the divorce stage of hope had the potential to branch away from the other stages into new stages. Hope led to disappointment; disappointment led to hatred. She looked back at the calendar, hovered her finger over the accept button, then, without touching the screen, picked up her phone and slid it into her back pocket.

She wasn't ready quite yet to risk hope.

Verse 31

Council Bluffs, Iowa

GIDEON lay in his hotel room bed, wearing a towel around his waist and nothing else. It had been a hot day and after his shower, he'd been reluctant to dress again. Like many hotel rooms, the heater/air conditioner combo under the window either turned the room into a refrigerator or a sauna. There was no in-between. Gideon, at the moment, was content to let the room fall into a wintery cold as the remaining drops of water that had dodged his towel turned frigid. Summer weather was not suit-wearing weather unless you were a missionary going door to door. Gideon was not a missionary. However, he was going door to door. He was looking for anything that could be useful.

The trail had gone cold.

It was during these times of stasis that Gideon began to think about giving up. Maybe he would cruise down to Las Vegas, make a decent amount of money, and settle down somewhere. Was Samuel his responsibility? For that matter, hadn't he already tried and failed? Didn't that make up for his inability to solve the problem now? When a doctor tries his best to remove a cancer, but the patient still dies, no one blames the doctor. They nod solemnly with the understanding that there was nothing that could be done. Cancer does what cancer does.

For that matter, Gideon wasn't a professional private investigator or a cop. He wasn't even good at solving *Where's*

Waldo? The pictures gave him a headache if he looked at them for too long.

He was able to glimpse inside the minds of others. That was the only reason he hadn't given up yet. No one else knew what was going on. Even if they did, they didn't have the necessary tools to do anything about it. Not that his tool had done much for him that day. Lots of input was received; little was of consequence. Sifting through useless data was tiresome on a productive day, let alone when there were no leads to follow.

He would probably leave town soon. But without a direction to start out, it was difficult to make that next step.

If he went west and Samuel had gone east, that kind of mistake would mean more than wasted time. It would mean losing the trail entirely. Events tied to Samuel were hard enough to parse from the news. The further away Samuel drove, the harder still. Up to this point, despite being one step behind him, Gideon at least had been following the remnants of footsteps, chasing down a beach as the waves mockingly washed away the trail.

Despair began to settle over him like the cold air on his overly warm body. The combination of coming cold with the mental equivalent of taking a downer began to lead Gideon away from consciousness toward the release of sleep. Only, for Gideon, sleep was rarely a release.

Today, at the few locations he'd visited; he'd found no useful information, but plenty of terrible thoughts to haunt his dreams. He absentmindedly thought about his duct tape on the bedside table, but his exhaustion and depression made his extremities heavy enough that his will could not muster the strength to reach for it. Darkness swam toward him, dread filled him, and sleep took him.

Verse 32

Alma, Nebraska

ELIZABETH pulled into the parking lot of a church she hadn't been to since she was in high school. Yet, she remembered it very well.

Growing up, she'd been quite religious. It was hard not to be in a small Midwest town. In her grown years, she'd never left her religion, per se, but she also couldn't remember the last time she had been in a church.

Well, there had been her mom's funeral.

Again, the reality of her mom's death slammed into her, causing the air to whoosh out of her like a physical hit to the gut. In between gasps for air, as her lungs tried to figure out what had happened and course correct, she whispered a small thank you that she'd still been sitting in her car or else she most assuredly would have fallen over. Like a wave, the feeling hit hard, but subsided quickly, as it always did. She wondered, also as she always did, whether the waves were getting any smaller.

She shook her head, imagining the thoughts shaking loose and falling away. She looked back out her windshield at the church in front of her. It sat in the middle of a giant dirt parking lot, and the dirt that had been kicked up by her car was still hanging in the air like a light fog. The white building, with its tall spires, stood out in the dust like a gothic castle in an old horror movie. It was a beautiful church. If the people of a small

Midwest town knew what to spend money on, it was religious buildings.

The beauty, however, added to the horror film aspect. The church sat comfortably on a tall hill, overlooking the small houses and business of Alma, the last building before the bridge out of town. It was a sentinel watching over the flock, guarding them from intruders while judging them for their own sins. Elizabeth saw all this through the eyes of a younger Elizabeth, who'd come to many church services on her weekends with Rebecca; who'd stayed for a week with her friend to volunteer for vacation bible school, or as the townies called it, VBS. She saw the church through the eyes of someone who believed that the building held power. The power to protect. Also, the less talked about power to condemn. The dust settled back into the parking lot and the church lost some of its mythological look. Elizabeth now saw the venue for her friend's wedding.

She got out of her car, threw her arms above her head, and leaned backward, stretching out her muscles, easing the tensions away. Walking toward the church, she could all but see Rebecca and herself peeking around the bushes to the left and the right of the walkway to the front door. Rebecca ran past her, chasing a younger version of Elizabeth with a water balloon. Overlaid on that memory was her with a kid on her shoulders, around Wyatt's age, calling her a faithful steed. Tears traced down her cheeks, leaving traces in the light dust that had settled there.

Her friend would be married here soon, and the past, present, and future would meet in one glorious moment.

The door was unlocked and inviting. The cool air conditioning leaked out around her when she pushed it open. The darkness enveloped her as she let the door close behind her.

Despite the door's relatively large window, the darkness of an empty church is a darkness that can't be illuminated easily.

The minister had told her the doors would be unlocked, and that she would have the church to herself for as long as she needed as there were no activities scheduled for that afternoon or evening. In an attempt to help her eyes adjust, she turned back to the window, allowing her vision to simultaneously experience the darkness around the door and the bright light spilling in through the window. It was like waking up after someone rudely turned on the light, having to keep one eye closed until things adjusted. Was there science to back that up? Probably not.

Through the window, she saw a motorcycle pull into the parking lot, coming to an abrupt stop that kicked up more dust than her car's four wheels had. The vision, seen through the square of light surrounded by darkness, filled her with an unexplainable dread.

The man stepped off the bike and stood next to it, looking toward the church as she had. The dust, however, was thicker as he hadn't waited as she had. He, more than likely, was not dealing with the memories of a family member's death. This allowed for a nearly phantom look of a man, hidden behind a veil of dust, whose features were indistinguishable. Death himself was standing outside this hallowed building, barred entrance by ancient religious protections. The thought arose in her mind like an accidental crossing of phone lines, picked up from another conversation not meant for her ears, but concerning her. A gust of wind picked up the already stirred-up dirt. The vision became more haunting as he began to make his way toward the front door toward her. Her feeling of protection from this specter withered with each step he took. Where his face should be, there was only a mirror of black reflecting the gothic building. Faceless and foreboding, through the dust and the wind, he came for her

A hand fell on her shoulder. "FUCK." Her lungs emptied painfully. She took a long, deep breath. "ME." This time, she had the presence of mind to preserve some of the life-giving air, possibly keeping herself from passing out.

She took a few more experimental breaths as the specter outside ran toward the door, clearly alarmed by the scream. The hand on her shoulder had vanished immediately after the expletive flew. Elizabeth turned to see the owner of the hand at the same time the door burst open, turning the window of light into a doorway of light. It illuminated the young minister whose face was white with embarrassment from having scared Elizabeth and, presumably, from hearing the F-word screamed at the top of someone's lungs in the house of the Lord.

"Is everything okay?" the helmeted figure said, reaching up to unbuckle the clasp under his jaw.

The minister, still stricken, bobbed his head back and forth to the woman who'd sworn and the man whose face was hidden behind a helmet. His day was less than perfect, Elizabeth thought, as she continued to catch her breath with little breaths of air.

She nodded her head in affirmation as Samuel's face, as those beautiful eyes, came into view. The nod, complemented by the reveal of the stranger, seemed to reassure the minister, who smiled sheepishly.

"I'm so sorry," said the minister. "I assume you are Miss Elizabeth? I cleared my throat a few times, ironically attempting to get your attention without scaring you, but you were quite distracted by the window." His eyes darted to Samuel.

Elizabeth, now fully back in control of her senses, took her first good look at the minister. He was young, probably fresh out of college, as they often were in these smaller towns. He was short and thin with dark brown hair, wearing a t-shirt from a previous church camp and faded jeans. *Seen one, seem 'em all*, she thought.

Her ears were working again as well, and she caught the implication he'd made in regard to the window. She willed herself to not blush, wishing she could look again into the helmet's visor to see if her will was working. The helmet, however, was now hanging less forebodingly by Samuel's hip. Had she thought of the helmet as foreboding moments before?

They had a planned rendezvous, and one of the very few things she knew about this man was that he drove a motorcycle. So, then, why had that vision caused Elizabeth so much fear that she'd been oblivious to this poor young minister's approach? She must have been so totally grasped by the emotion to scream profanity at the top of her lungs in a church.

Oh no. She'd yelled the word "fuck" in a church in front of the minister. That realization settled upon her heavily, and she no longer needed the visor of the helmet to tell her she was blushing. "I am so sorry for yelling . . ." She paused, trying to find the right word or rather, a different word than the right word. "That word," she finished lamely. All the schooling that led to her becoming a teacher seemingly rolled its collective eyes at that response.

The young minister smiled, then laughed.

The spontaneity of his laugh took Elizabeth by surprise—and presumably Samuel, because they both jumped a little.

"Believe me when I say I have heard much worse at church board meetings." His smile was infectious.

Had Elizabeth been scared only moments before? Now, in the glow of this young man's innocent smile, she found that hard to believe.

Samuel caught her eye and winked.

"If you two want to follow me," the minister said, a hint of laughter still under his words, "I will lead you to the sanctuary, and show you how to set up the sound system."

"Sir," Samuel said, "I'm sorry, we haven't even introduced ourselves." He reached out with his right hand and firmly grasped that of the minister's. "My name is Samuel Serenade, and this striking young lady next to me is Elizabeth. She is the maid of honor, and I will be providing the music."

Elizabeth was struck by the fact that he'd introduced her, giving the impression that they not only they knew each other, but that they did so intimately. She was torn between annoyance at his audacity and warmth that he would treat her with such familiarity. Regardless of those mixed emotions, she was not going to let him have that last word.

"I have not made that decision, and frankly, an iPhone has much more versatility. So, you are not even my first choice at the moment."

The minister, who'd opened his mouth to introduce himself and was still holding Samuel's hand, shut his mouth and looked quizzically at the two of them, appearing to question how well they did know each other. He recovered quickly as all good ministers do after hearing something that makes them pause.

"My name is Gideon," the minister said.

Samuel's smile disappeared so quickly that Elizabeth's faltered a little. Shockingly, as quickly as it left, it returned. Had she blinked at the right time, she never would have seen it go.

But she had, and she now noticed his eyes no longer smiled with his mouth as they had seconds before.

Gideon, on the other hand, noticed nothing or, if he did, it did not show. "I usually go by my middle name, however. Bartholomew." He paused as if he'd told the punch line of a joke, but Elizabeth and Samuel just stood there with awkward smiles on their faces. He sighed. "Goes to show why I have to write and practice my material in front of a mirror before I preach it. Some things sound funnier up here," he said, tapping his temple, "than they do spoken aloud." He smiled that winning smile and everything was right again.

Elizabeth darted a look at Samuel. His eyes were smiling again. She was grateful for that, because while the smile had been gone, she'd felt a stirring of those feelings from the church window, feelings she didn't understand nor want.

"Because a bad joke is only good when explained," Gideon, or Bartholomew, continued, "my middle name is Bartholomew, and I actually do go by it. The joke is that a longer, more complicated name makes no sense to use when you have a perfectly good, short first name." He paused again. "Okay, so, still not funny. I am glad I tried this out on you two instead of on my congregation."

"Why would you go by a longer, more complicated name?" Elizabeth asked, more perplexed than ever.

Her middle name was Anne, which was probably the simplest, overly used middle name a girl could have. A big disappointment in life was that she'd not married someone with a last name that started with a T, because then her initials would have been EAT, and that was at least interesting. She was again struck by the fact that she had a second chance at that. Divorce was the opportunity she needed to be the EAT she'd always wanted to be. She had to stifle a laugh and play it off as a little cough. "Thank you, dusty day." Without warning, her diary floated into her mind's eye, theatrically, like a book bobbing to the top of the water after a boat sank. It was open to a page with names written. Her name, over and over, with the final one being Elizabeth Serenade. She could feel the blush infusing every part of her body, from her face, down her neck, entering her shirt, slipping under her bra, moving past the slightly damp straps on its way to her exposed shoulders, on a journey to her hands. Gideon—wait, no, he'd confirmed that he went by Bartholomew—was looking at her, confused. He'd been about to answer her question about his middle name when she began blushing with the intensity of someone who'd fallen asleep on the beach with her top off.

Samuel, who'd been lost for a bit in his own world, noticed the look on Bartholomew's face and turned toward Elizabeth.

Luckily, whether on purpose to save her embarrassment or because he wanted to explain, Bartholomew went ahead and answered. "To make a long story short, my parents disagreed on my name, so I got both. Gideon is my legal first name, but I go by Bartholomew. I honestly had no idea that my first name was Gideon until Preschool, during roll call. I looked around for the shy kid named Gideon, only to have the teacher, exasperated, tell me I was the shy kid named Gideon."

This did get a snicker from the two of them, and Gideon pretended to take a little book out of his back pocket and write in it.

"Joke has potential. Give the teacher a funny name to seal the deal," he muttered loudly. He mimed putting away the book. "Mrs. Muffinhead refused to call me by the only name I had ever heard or used, and it was a very confusing first year of school."

Samuel laughed with such genuine joy that everything else took a second to appreciate it. The wind itself stopped and allowed the creaking of the church to settle as Elizabeth watched with rapture. Bartholomew, beaming, took out his imaginary book, made another note, and put it away again.

"I don't know how you can relate that to God but definitely put that in a sermon. 'Muffinhead' is dynamite." Samuel was wiping tears from his eyes. "With that said, it is nice to meet you, Bartholomew. Lead us to your sanctuary. I do love to see where a man works."

Bartholomew, seemingly as caught up in Samuel's magnetism as Elizabeth, led the way with a huge smile on his face, explaining how Israel was originally named Jacob, or something along those lines, with regard to his story about Mrs. Muffinhead.

The short walk from the front door to the sanctuary was delightful. Elizabeth had that feeling of old friends reunited, falling back into an easy conversation. Samuel probably lived in a world like that, where everyone he met was an old friend. He seemed to bypass that awkward part of meeting someone new by acting as if that person wasn't someone new. This was extroversion on a level she'd never known existed. It was infectious.

With the two men walking ahead of her, focused in their discussion, she was able to revisit the floating diary without feeling embarrassment. Well, maybe a little embarrassment, but it wasn't being witnessed and that helped tremendously. She again saw the book float up, revealing the names, and she allowed herself to focus on the final listing. She wasn't so

foolish to want to marry this man she'd just met. She
understood the absurdity of that thought. Yet, the thought that
a man like this could be in her future at all warmed her. A man
like this wanted to be in her future. Well, as far as she could tell,
he did.

"Isn't that right, El?"

All of her attention snapped forward like a slingshot that
had been pulled back into her own thoughts. She suddenly
understood how Samuel could have a reaction like he did to a
simple name. With that one syllable, everything in her world
changed color. It tinged red.

"What?" The question came out harsher than it should
have. But hearing her ex-husband's pet name for her come out
of the mouth of a man with whom she'd, moments before, been
creating a future in her mind was like having an entire gallon of
reality poured into her cup of fantasy.

What the hell was she thinking about? Had she forgotten
she had a son? A life? Hell, an ex? What was she doing thinking
about this man in any way other than someone she met who
would potentially be at the same wedding she would be
attending, then go their separate ways? While thinking of
marriage was definitely absurd, it was equally groundless to
think that any future past this wedding was possible.

Samuel's dazzling blue eyes were on her, concerned and
possibly hurt.

She forced her face to calm and, with effort, managed a
smile. "Sorry. You took me by surprise. I don't much care for
that nickname, if it is all the same to you."

His eyes softened again in understanding.

"And why would you, when Elizabeth is a beautiful
name?" Had anyone else slathered on that kind of corniness

that thick, she would have physically gagged. Yet, when Samuel said it, her knees literally loosened.

She'd read about that happening in chick lits, but she had always rolled her eyes at the sensitivity of those women. She wondered, if anyone were reading her story, would they roll their eyes right now? Probably, and they would be justified. Nevertheless, she was weak-knee infatuated with this man and had to accept that, if she was planning on spending any amount of time with him leading up to this wedding. Let any future after that reveal itself to her then.

"I was saying that you have your doubts about my abilities," explained Samuel.

Elizabeth was back under control. The emotional rollercoaster she'd been riding since pulling up to that damn building was exhausting. She nodded, and added a sly "mmhmm" of affirmation.

He smiled back. "Just wait 'til you see me do K-pop. You will wonder why you have an iPhone when you could hang out with me."

They laughed together in fellowship as Bartholomew opened the doors to the sanctuary.

Verse 33

Norton, Kansas

HAROLD watched as his grandson slowly walked away from the truck toward the dilapidated, long-retired farm equipment. Harold felt a pang in his heart for the imagination of a child. He tried to imagine what Wyatt saw through the haze of wonder. Did he see an apocalyptic world that had moved on while they'd made the journey to the farm? Thick vegetation grown around the machinery left behind by a civilization long extinct? Giant vehicles of war, motionless, collecting rust on the blades attached to the front, no doubt placed there as a means of defense against the unending hordes of evil that had come from the deep, hundreds, if not thousands, of years before? Harold shook his head in an effort to pull himself together. Maybe he hadn't lost as much wonder as he'd imagined.

Wyatt slowly turned in a circle, taking it all in. Harold looked back at the old machinery. He tried to again let his imagination run free, but saw only expensive rust buckets, taking up space. He sighed, a little sad at the loss. Then he went to the back of the truck to retrieve his toolbox.

He planned on getting a little work done while Wyatt played nearby. He cursed. It had slid perfectly into the middle of the truck bed. As a younger man, he would have jumped up into the back, but old men did not jump into the back of trucks. However, young boys did. He turned to see if Wyatt would be willing to hop up and, at the very least, slide the box over to the edge.

Wyatt was standing stark still, staring at an old combine, its blades rising out of the tall grass like a shark's underbite.

Harold realized there was a flip-side to the beauty of imagination: The dark side of seeing your greatest fears come to life before your eyes. While adults rationalize everything into boring facts, like combines are metallic tools used by farmers, kids did not have the luxury of years of monotonous disillusionment. So, what looked like a giant, bladed death machine was in fact a giant, bladed death machine.

Harold hurried over and put his hand on Wyatt's shoulder, causing the poor boy to jump. "You alright?"

Wyatt looked at him, then back to the combine, then slowly back to him.

"There is nothing to worry about from that old thing. It doesn't even start anymore. I keep telling myself I should strip it down for parts, but then the tractor wouldn't have any company." He gestured toward an equally worn-out machine that was also being swallowed by the tall grass. For a second, he was afraid that Wyatt wasn't going to get past his fear of the combine and the day would be ruined. But Wyatt laughed a little and looked back at him, a tentative smile on his face.

"Can I touch them?"

"Touch 'em? Hell, I'll help you get in them. As I said, they won't move—" He stopped as his mind caught up to what he'd said. "Look, don't tell your mom I said the H-word."

"Help?"

Harold smiled down at him.

"Yeah, 'help,' 'cause if she knows I'm helpful, I'll never get anything done. I'll be too busy helping her pick her outfits, brushing her hair, and tying her shoes. She will never lift a finger to do anything herself again."

They both laughed. But as the wind blew the dust up, Harold saw images of his wife doing all of those things for their daughter and loving every minute of it. He could feel the dust sticking to a bit of moisture forming under his eye, and he wiped it away.

"Yeah. But I can help you."

They walked toward the towering machines hand in hand, and Harold knew he would love every minute of it.

Verse 34

Council Bluffs, Iowa

THE fist came forward, pistoning along an unseen track, growing from the size of a small fruit into that of a basketball and blotting out everything around it. The world in front of Gideon's swollen eyes was nothing but fist. He was moving to Fistland, where he would work a fist job, return to his fist home, and kiss his fist wife. There was nothing but the fist, not even peripheral shreds of blue to remind him that behind Fistland, there was another nicer land that had a sky.

There was a crunching, breaking sound, and, at first, Gideon worried he'd broken his glasses again, but then he remembered that before he was allowed entrance to Fistland today, the border control guard had removed them. Unable to see him, Gideon knew the boy was wearing them mockingly. Relief, oddly refreshing at a time like this, washed over him. Had he broken his glasses again, Mrs. Warren would have had to tape them with that electric tape that always started to unravel and leave a sticky residue on the bridge of his nose.

Speaking of noses, his was possibly broken. Blood was oozing out, rather than pouring out, so that could be a good sign. Noses healed; glasses did not. Count those blessings, count them one by one.

One thing could be said for Fistland: it wasn't a place you stayed long. The fist retracted on its track, a train with only two destinations and bullet speed.

Gideon returned to his second home, Blurrsville. The fist lost clarity as it moved away, blurring into a hideous tan oval that, like the moon, made a hellish face, an obscure skull with only four teeth. It looked quizzically at him, turning this way and that. There were words surrounding Gideon, but he chose to not pay attention to them. It was hard when he wasn't wearing his glasses and his face was smashed in to know which words were coming from lips and which were in his head. Phrases fell around him.

"Jeez, I think Andy went too far this time." Surely a thought. No one would admit that out loud, what with tickets to Fistland being freely given out.

"Hit him again." That was either the frantic command of someone caught up in the action or the thought of a kid getting off on the beating of another defenseless kid. Either way, not important.

"That is a ton of blood." Didn't matter.

"Mrs. Warren could come back any second." Either someone verbally warning the Mayor of Fistland or someone thinking about how this little event could be brought to a conclusion.

Then, cutting through all the confusing phrases, spoken or otherwise, came a song, whispered under the breath, yet clearly audible.

The train to Fistland stopped dead on the tracks, inches from Gideon's battered nose. It was close enough now that he was able to see its details: the wrinkles, scars, and reddened knuckles from hitting something that is hard underneath a soft outer shell. It hovered there, trembling slightly as if no longer an extension of the arm it was attached to, but its own entity, angry to have been leashed to a distracted owner. Gideon had been too distracted by the hovering fist to have realized that the voices around him ceased.

Well, that wasn't true. They'd all joined the song. This was something he'd never experienced. Everything he heard, both with his ears and his mind, melded into one. It was the most beautiful thing he'd ever experienced.

Then, from the source of the song, came a thought that Gideon alone could discern as it intertwined through the melody, riding the tones and pitches, becoming the very soul of the song. A thought that was broadcast to the receivers around Gideon, each one picking it up and internalizing it. Like sponges, those around Gideon drank the song greedily, taking in the thought along with it, allowing it to take over. "Beat him up" was the simple thought that would have sounded crass or foolish if spoken aloud, but was somehow the most melodious words any of them had ever heard. It was more than a command; it was a rewriting of their primary needs. Breathe, eat, beat him up, sleep, use the bathroom. Going without oxygen, even for a few minutes, could cause irreparable damage, and yet, that paled in comparison to not complying with the song.

Gideon, still without his glasses, watched as the blurry masses around him turned toward Andy. They were all now singing the same song. It was eerie to watch as they all followed a directive like mindless zombies smelling fresh meat.

Rarely do people act perfectly simultaneously, even when a loud noise causes everyone to look in the same direction. Some hesitate, others duck, some throw up their hands. Each turn to see what happened at their own volition.

This was different. Not a single person hesitated. It was perfectly simultaneous. They all turned to look at the kid whose hand still hovered inches from Gideon's nose. The song wove in and around them all as the blurry individuals began to advance on Andy, who did not run away, who did not scream. He stood like a statue with his invitation to Fistland left unanswered.

Then those who'd egged Andy on minutes before fell on him, each desperate to get to him. Those in the back were yanking at those in the front for the chance to kick at his face or rip out some of his hair.

Gideon lay on the ground, stunned, watching in shocked horror as the blurry masses became one solitary blurry mass, bumping up and down as they jostled around the now limp body of the kid who had been torturing him minutes before. The oddest thing of it all was there were no words, grunts, moans, or any of the other typical sounds coming from the mass. Music, punctuated by the thumping sounds of impact, accompanied by tearing and ripping sounds, all of which flowed perfectly with the song.

Then, as suddenly as it had started, the song was done, the final note ringing in their minds. Then the thoughts began to reappear like little blips on a radar screen. Confusion, revulsion, and fear.

Gideon heard it all as the kids standing around Andy realized what they'd done. They looked around at each other, not sure what to do, when Andy sucked in a rattling breath and began a choked sob. The sound, jarring after the beauty of the song, broke the spell of confusion and the crowd broke apart, realizing they wanted to be anywhere else but there.

With effort, Gideon got to one knee. He was preparing to use the other leg to push himself up the rest of the way when out of the haze, his glasses appeared before his eyes. He followed the hand up the arm to the face of the newcomer, standing close enough that he didn't need glasses to see him.

Blue eyes looked back at him. They were like glass reflecting the sea on a clear morning. Even at his young age, Gideon understood those eyes would open doors.

"Here." The boy wiggled the glasses in front of Gideon's nose. "We need to go."

Confusion clouded Gideon's thoughts, slowing his reaction speed. Finally, he reached up to grab the offered glasses. They slipped onto his nose and the world cleared. Blurry masses compressed into clean-cut lines and faceless blobs became concerned crowds, all of which kept a safe distance as they muttered to each other.

Glasses on, Gideon was able to see Andy clearly for the first time since the song. He felt something turn in his throat, then fall into his gut with a splash. Andy's nose had caved in on itself. His wailing mouth revealed a good number of his teeth were either missing or broken. His clothes were torn. Where Gideon could see skin, there were bleeding scratch marks and bruises already darkening. His eyes were swollen shut; his face a tie-dye of blues, purples, and reds. For some reason, however, his hair was what struck Gideon as the most terrifying aspect: there were patches missing, along with chunks of scalp. There were red, oozing, open wounds where brown locks had grown minutes before.

The daze following the beating and the song finally broke, and Gideon heard everyone all at once. Cutting through it all was Andy's thoughts. Broken pieces of glass, each with a different word for pain or suffering were trying to form into a coherent thought, leaving deep slashes in Gideon's mind as they tried unsuccessfully to make sense of the situation. Gideon turned to run, to get away from the terrible writhing thing on the ground, to get away from those thoughts, the pain. Vomit jetted from his mouth after only two steps, and he began to sway on his feet as consciousness threatened to leave him. Gideon could still hear the screams of anguish behind him as Andy writhed around in the dirt.

Gideon sat up with a start, groping for his glasses and not finding them. His room was dark. He was naked. He was confused. Voices from the hotel rooms around him filtered back into his mind as he struggled to gather his consciousness back from the dream and place it back in reality.

He rolled over. The towel he'd been wearing, still damp, felt cold on his leg, which helped to snap him back to the present. His glasses were in the bathroom, sitting on the counter where he'd placed them before his shower.

He stood shakily and felt his way toward where he remembered the bathroom to be. The lights were off as it had been sunny when he fell asleep. Once inside, his foot caught on the bath mat he'd left on the ground, and he had to catch himself on the counter before going face first into the toilet. Taking deep breaths, he stayed in that position for a short time to catch his equilibrium. Then he straightened and turned toward the counter to find his glasses.

A blurred figure stood in front of him. He gasped and fell backward, striking the glass door of the shower. It rattled in its groove but successfully kept him on his feet. Gideon could see its eyes: two blue dots, floating in darkness. Yanking the information from his short-term memory, he threw himself at the light switch on the wall. Light flooded the small room, and he was able to quickly find his glasses on the counter. With a quick gesture, he brought the man in the mirror into focus.

His green eyes looked back at him through the lenses of glasses. Green eyes filled with nostalgic fear.

Verse 35

Alma, Nebraska

BARTHOLOMEW led Elizabeth and Samuel to the sanctuary where the service would take place. Like most small Midwest towns, the sanctuary had an absurdly tall ceiling that came to a point in the middle, giving the feel of a Victorian castle. The last time Elizabeth had been there, the floor had been covered by an unimpressive green carpet and pews had been screwed in long rows all the way to the back where they were tucked under a hanging balcony. While the balcony remained, the carpet and pews had been replaced with hardwood floors and chairs. Chairs could be removed for children's activities, Bartholomew had explained.

"Or dancing?" Samuel had asked with a cocked eyebrow and crooked knowing smile.

"Some of the older members of the congregation frown upon such Godless activities," Bartholomew said, shaking his head. He then matched Samuel's smile. "So, to acquire funding for the new floors and chairs, the children stepped up. We had shirts and pamphlets with sad children questioning where God would want them to play: in the sanctuary or in the town dump."

Elizabeth stared at him with a shocked expression, but Samuel laughed.

"Seriously, though," Bartholomew continued, "we really did have to play church politics to get it done, and there has been some grumbling about the fact that we plan on having the after-wedding dance in this very room."

After walking halfway down the aisle leading to the stage, Elizabeth turned a slow circle in the middle of the room. It was like returning to elementary school and finding out that the kindergarten classroom has been remodeled.

Obviously, the church was never going to remain the same as it had almost twenty years before, but it still felt like another loss of childhood. Memories tied to treasured events no longer had an anchored setting. However, the tall, beautiful stained-glass windows helped. They had been there when she was young, and she assumed that long after they recarpeted the floor and changed the seats, maybe even remodeled the stage, those stained-glass windows would still refract the light in their multiple colors, serving as a portal to important moments from her childhood.

She turned to look at Samuel who was looking at the stage, talking to Bartholomew. Was this an important moment? Would the stained-glass windows bring her back to this very moment years from now?

A shudder ran down her spine as she thought about it. She kept her eyes on Samuel, scared that, if she looked to either side, she would see herself as a young girl or maybe an old lady. Perhaps she was living in the memory now, standing in the chapel years from now, at a funeral, as the colorful light played on her pale, wrinkled skin. She shuddered again.

Samuel's eyes left the stage and landed on hers, grasping immediately that she'd been staring at him. Her eyes quickly darted toward the next thing she could look at: the young, beaming face of Bartholomew.

"I remember VBS here," she stated lamely. Bartholomew smiled indulgently. "The pews, while in the way of some games, made for great beds if you were able to sneak away. Maybe let the older members know that by removing the chairs, their beloved grandchildren are forced to learn about Jesus instead of napping."

Bartholomew laughed and the weird mood Elizabeth had been in since walking into the sanctuary broke up and fell away.

Samuel smiled at her, and she felt witty, clever, and maybe even sexy. She wasn't sure why, but she always found witty men sexy, so she hoped men felt the same about their women.

Then a thought popped into her head: *Are you supposed to feel sexy at church?* She pictured some of the widows, divorcees, and single women looking for a godly husband and decided that yes, church was an acceptable place to feel sexy.

"Thank you for my opener at next week's board meeting," Bartholomew said. He turned toward Samuel. "So, based on our phone call earlier, you are hoping to borrow one of our guitars for this audition as you only had the motorcycle today and didn't want to deal with bringing your own? You will find a few different ones tucked into that room off the back of the stage. Be careful going in there. It is kind of cluttered, and I would hate to explain to our very energetic teenaged drummer why someone put their foot through his snare drum."

"Ah, the classic musical instrument closet," Samuel said, nodding. "Been in one, you've been in 'em all."

He began to make his way down the aisle, heading toward Elizabeth. Her breath caught a little with the understanding that he would have to pass her to get to the stage. Would he put his hand on her arm, her back? Would he touch her at all? Her mind swam. Without thinking about what she was doing, she stepped back into the nearest row of chairs to give him a clear path down the aisle. He walked by, turned, and, as those blue eyes caught hers, smiled a new, unique smile she'd not seen before. What had she been thinking, moving out of the way? She wanted to throw herself back into his way and force him to touch her. But, luckily, she had the state of mind to hold still until he'd passed.

Bartholomew followed after. When both had their backs to her, she closed her eyes to recenter herself yet again. This rollercoaster of fear, crush, joy, and nostalgia needed to slow down before she got sick.

Samuel was laughing on the stage about something Bartholomew had said. Elizabeth opened her eyes again, feeling confident that the floor was under her feet and staying still, at least for the moment.

"No, really I swear," Bartholomew said and laughed with Samuel about whatever had been said prior.

Elizabeth felt like the third wheel all of a sudden. It was a position she'd put herself in, what with the closing of her eyes and recentering moment that had just taken place, but it was still a feeling she didn't like. Not wanting to miss anything else, she sidled back down the row of chairs and hurried toward the stage.

"Honestly, he is like eighty-seven years old and plays better guitar than anyone I have ever seen, and I used to travel across the Midwest to go to Christian music festivals when I was in high school."

"He sounds great," Samuel said, eyes sparkling. "I would love to meet him,"

They turned toward Elizabeth. This time, thanks to the recentering, she was prepared and held her nerve when they landed on her.

"Doesn't he just sound so cool?" asked Samuel.

Well, the last sentence, which was all that she'd heard, sure sounded cool. She nodded, hoping he wouldn't press her on the details she'd missed.

Luckily, he turned again toward the door at the back of the stage. "And you're sure he won't mind me using his guitar?"

"Oh sure," Bartholomew mused. "His memory is so bad, I could tell him I smashed his guitar today, and come Sunday, he would head toward the closet, planning on tuning up for service."

They all laughed again, and Elizabeth was struck by how much she'd laughed in the past thirty minutes. She reflected on the fact that she'd probably laughed more since arriving at the church than she had since Jason first moved out. It was amazingly refreshing, like dumping cold water over your head after a long day's work in the hot sun. She looked at Samuel. His smile rarely left his face. He was such a breath of fresh air. There was so much shit in her life, it was sometimes hard to smell anything else. She breathed deep, as if the fresh air metaphor was real, reveling in the positivity surrounding her.

This moment was important. It felt like the beginning of a new chapter in her story, and it held a weight to it. It all revolved around this man; this character who'd shown up like an enigma and had changed her life. She obviously couldn't tell the future, but as an English teacher, she knew what a watershed moment was and she was fairly confident she was standing in one now.

"Are you ready?"

Her attention zoned in on Samuel. Had he read her mind? Had he seen her thoughts and understood the gravity as she had? Was she ready for it? Be it fate, destiny, or God himself, was she ready for the next chapter?

He saw her confusion and shared the look. "Are you ready to hear my musical talents? Because something as good as you are about to witness demands preparedness. An attentiveness from start to finish. As soon as I step up to the mic, this will be declared a no phone zone."

As if it had been waiting for that very moment, her phone began to buzz in her back pocket. She blushed. "After this phone call, you will have my undivided attention," she promised as she backed toward the door to the sanctuary. "Granted, it is yet to be seen if you truly deserve my undivided attention." Feeling she'd gained some ground, she spun toward the large double doors, and with a hand on each, pushed one open. The other was locked shut. She cursed under her breath. She heard Bartholomew move toward her, making an apologetic sound. She slipped through the one open door and let it shut behind her, trying to save a little dignity.

She pulled the phone from her back pocket, saw that it was her dad, and her thoughts filled with concern. With all that had happened since she'd shown up in Alma, Wyatt had been far from her mind for the first time since his birth. She'd felt like someone other than a mother. Seeing her dad's name on her phone's screen brought that reality back to her hard. Was Wyatt okay? She tapped the answer bubble and brought the phone to her ear, hand trembling a little.

"Hello?"

Verse 36

Omaha, Nebraska

JASON sat at his desk, his mind a million miles away from the stock market to which he was supposed to be paying attention. Well, not a million miles. Two hundred and sixty-five miles. That was the exact distance from him to his family. His real family.

He couldn't help but play through scenarios. First, he would have an amazing weekend with Wyatt, who in turn would tell his mother about it. She would be impressed and a little confused. That confusion would lead to hope; hope that maybe things could be different. Then he would plan another amazing weekend. This time, he'd drop a hint about how much Wyatt might enjoy it if she tagged along. No big deal. It would be just the three of them going bowling or something like that. She would agree to appease Wyatt, but also maybe because she wanted to herself. Then while Wyatt was picking out a bowling ball, he would put his arm around her shoulders companionably and make a comment along the lines of "That is one good boy we got there." In his imagination, he could feel her tense, then soften, allowing his arm to remain. Because it wasn't about them; it was about Wyatt. Throughout the weekend, he would make a point to get closer to her. He would grab her hand when they needed to move forward in line at the movies, they would share a popcorn, maybe he'd "accidentally" bump into her while reaching for something, allowing his arm to brush against her breast. He felt a stirring below his belt.

He got up from his desk and made his way to the office restroom. He bent over the sink and splashed some cold water in his face. That would have to serve as his cold shower for now. When he straightened up, he was face to face with the man-in-the-mirror.

It would appear he had followed him from his apartment. He was a persistent little asshole, that was for sure. "Did you get an erection thinking about your ex-wife?" A very forward asshole to boot.

Jason considered drying his hands and leaving the bathroom, but this confrontation had been coming for a while now, and he felt like having it out. "What if I was?" Great start. He was really putting the screws to him. "She is an attractive woman with whom I used to have sex. Does that not entitle me to get aroused when I think about the prospect of having sex with an attractive woman? Especially one that I know is good in bed?" Again, somewhere in his mind, maybe a room over, someone was telling him to leave the bathroom or at the very least, have this conversation in his head. It didn't have to be spoken out loud. But Jason felt like it did.

There was something about spoken words that gave them force. They were more real than the fleeting thoughts that came and went like vapor. This conversation was important. He could feel it.

"Sure, sure, you can imagine having sex with an attractive woman. Or you could go to your new apartment and have sex with an attractive woman."

Damn. That was a compelling argument. Stacy was extremely attractive, all things considered. She put El to shame in the looks department. She was young, fresh, tight, and boring. Shit. Had he just thought of the woman with whom he was living as boring?

"Did you just think of Stacy as boring?"

Oh great. Now the man-in-the-mirror was commenting on his thoughts as well. That didn't seem fair.

"Shut up. Thoughts like that don't count, and you know it." Did they, though? He looked back on the past few months. Stacy had been amazing. He focused specifically on the sex: athletic, fun, sweaty romps that always left him panting. Then, like turning a dial on a microscope, he looked a little closer. There was something missing. Sticking with the microscope analogy, he thought of his relationship as DNA. The sex was almost a perfect strand, a building block toward the perfect relationship. But there was a link missing; a link that had not been missing with Elizabeth. He turned the dial still more. The missing link came into focus and Jason's mouth went dry.

"Familiarity, you pitiful prick."

The past few months had felt like a dream to Jason. He'd considered them some of the best in his life. In fact, he was fairly confident he would have continued living blissfully in that fantasy had it not been for El taking Wyatt and going to Norton. Without him. That had been the first domino that led to his introduction to the man-in-the-mirror who'd pointed out certain truths he'd not wanted to face. Now, however, he was seeing the past few months in a new light.

He slid a comparison slide next to the one in the microscope. Now he was able to see two different nights of sex simultaneously. He saw himself bent over Stacy's back, reaching around her, cupping her perfect breast, ramming into her like a teenager discovering sex for the first time, grunting while she screamed out. He saw this and understood why he'd felt like everything was perfect. It was like living in the porn he'd always watched. Who wouldn't want that kind of sex?

Then his eyes drifted over to the other slide. Elizabeth was lying down in front of him, naked, grabbing at her breasts. "What are you doing?" he asked, getting into position between her legs, smiling at the absurdity of it all.

"When I am on my back, my breasts have a way of melting into my armpits like a couple of cracked eggs. I thought that since it is your birthday, I would make sure they are extra perky. So, I have decided to help and bounce them as we go." She demonstrated by manually bouncing them up and down.

He'd been ready to enter her, but everything about what she'd said and did was too much for him. He started laughing.

She looked at him with a smile of pure joy. "If you think that is good, another benefit of hand bouncing is that they can go in different directions." Again, she demonstrated, the right going up as the left went down. It was too much. He bent over her, kissing her earnestly as she continued to help her breasts defy gravity, only letting go long enough to guide him in with one hand.

It was pure magic. Not pornographic. Not hot and sexy but full of love.

Jason looked at the mirror in shock, the color draining from his face. "Love," he said, feeling slightly sick. "Love is the missing link."

Familiarly was an aspect of that, he realized. Love was the difference in the two slides.

Another thought popped in his head; another stop on this trail of discovery. Had he passed gas in front of Stacy even once? No, because he was too scared. He was scared that something like that would break their perfect pornographic life. No one farted in a porno.

He thought back to another time with Elizabeth. She'd been kissing his left thigh, a clear destination in mind, when he'd gently pulled her up to kiss her. She'd looked at him questioningly, then reached down to squeeze him questioningly. His answer to her questions came in the form of a little squeaky toot.

Her eyes became round in shock. Then, smiling, she exclaimed, "My hero!" and kissed him deeply.

Again, it was nothing like the sex he'd been having with Stacy, and yet . . .

His mind trailed off. The man-in-the-mirror snapped his fingers at him to get his attention.

Only it wasn't the man-in-the-mirror. It was someone else's man in the mirror, standing next to his.

"Oh, uh. Hi Josh," Jason stammered. How long had he been there? For that matter, how long had Jason been there?

Josh rolled his eyes and washed his hands. Washing his hands meant that he'd used the restroom, right? Had he been in one of the stalls?

"Uh, so, um, nice weather out there, right?"

Josh looked at him and smiled. "Yeah, I think that the sun was the missing link, don't you?"

For the first time since he could remember, Jason had a reaction with which Elizabeth would have sympathized. He blushed. Josh dried his hands, turned back to Jason, winked, then left him alone in the bathroom. Well, almost alone. There was still the man-in-the-mirror.

His phone buzzed. He reached for it and felt a second buzz as he pulled it from his back pocket. He looked at the screen. A picture with a text flashed open from his ex-father-in-law.

"Elizabeth wanted me to share some pictures from the day. Here's a good one."

Good was questionable as the picture had clearly been taken with an older phone, but it still caught his breath. Wyatt was making hay angels in a pile of hay in what Jason could only assume was a barn. Despite the poor picture quality, Jason found his eyes filled with tears. He wiped at his eyes and looked toward the mirror. The man there, thankfully silent, looked expectantly at Jason. It made him feel uneasy, like the man-in-the-mirror knew something Jason did not. He turned back to his phone and realized there was another message. That must have been the second buzz. It was from Stacy.

There were two words: "Call me."

Verse 37

Alma, Nebraska

GARY and Jacob sat together, quietly drinking their beers during a lapse in the conversation about their new friend. Neither beer was a fancy wheat beer as Gary was taking a break from them. Not because of the feeling of unease he'd felt the other day, he told himself. Rather, because, as the Good Book says, "All things in moderation."

"She was the maid of honor, I think he said," Gary explained.

Jacob nodded understandably.

Who else would be looking into the music for an upcoming wedding? The main aspect of the story, that Gary had tried to convey to his friend, was Samuel's joy at being on the phone with the mystery maid of honor.

When the door opened, they both looked up, expecting—or maybe hoping—to see Samuel leading a young woman over to meet his new, old friends.

Instead, their eyes fell on Sally, looking a little worse for wear, leading a young boy.

Verse 38

Council Bluffs, Iowa

GIDEON swung on the old wooden swing, letting his toes drag along under him where the grass had worn away. The other kids had not messed with him today. In fact, they appeared to be making a point to avoid contact with him at all costs.

While getting breakfast, he'd felt as if he were under a dome; all the other kids breathing the fresh air on the outside as he felt oddly suffocated by the distance between them. An introvert by nature, he'd always desired his own personal space, but to be shunned to such a degree felt different. It made him feel dirty, or stinky, or most of all, guilty.

Andy's beating had been severe enough to land him in the hospital where he was still recovering. The kids who'd taken part in the beating had such conflicting thoughts and memories of the event that they were continuously screaming in their own minds: *Why? Why would I do that to him? I didn't want to do that. Was that a dream?* Those thoughts, and more, swirled around Gideon. The one thing they all seemed to agree on was that Gideon was involved. *That little freak did it. He was the one who was being hit. He made us hurt Andy.*

His own mind was a mass of confusion as the feelings of guilt fought with the understanding that he'd done nothing wrong. He was, in fact, the victim.

"Bad day?" The voice came from his left, close enough to be under the dome with him. He looked up and saw the kid who'd handed him his glasses the day before. "My name is Samuel, by the way." The kid reached his hand around the swing's chain.

"Gideon." He grasped Samuel's hand, unknowingly bonding their future together. "Was that you yesterday? Singing?"

Samuel smiled with a shocked expression on his face, but Gideon heard the affirmation in his mind.

"Thank you." He tentatively felt his nose. While still sore, the bleeding had stopped quickly, and the swelling was already going down. That was a good sign it wasn't broken. It could have and probably would have been a lot worse. "Andy likes hitting me for some reason. I don't have to say or do anything to provoke him." Yesterday, Gideon had been sitting under a tree, reading a book, when Andy and his cronies jumped him. "I mean, I know why he does it, even if he doesn't say it out loud. He is afraid all the time. Afraid that the other kids will see him as weak or that he might lose some of the influence he has over them." Gideon thought for a second. "I guess, thanks to you, those fears have come true. As much as the others are avoiding me, there is no way they will want to have anything to do with him after yesterday."

"What makes you say that?"

"Because I can hear their thoughts." Gideon had never blatantly stated this out loud, but he'd also never met a kindred spirit.

Samuel's eyes widened in awe. Gideon could read Samuel's joy at no longer being alone.

"Neat trick, by the way," said Gideon. "I wish my thing was as useful as yours. I know when I'm going to get punched, but I can't do anything to stop it, like you." Then, almost as an afterthought, he added, "You have a good voice, by the way."

"Thank you. I plan on being a singer when I grow up."

That made sense to Gideon. The ability to make people act without their consent would lead to an extremely lucrative singing career. Samuel could be one of those guys who stood at a corner with a guitar, and he'd end up making more money than most of the people passing by to their "real" jobs. Gideon, however, could see into Samuel's plans and saw that his only desire was to make money singing. Gideon was shocked to know that this kid, who had the power to bend people's actions to his will, would not exploit that at every turn. Innocence was a blessing.

Innocence? Was that the correct word? This kid had forced a mob of children to beat another kid senseless. Could the term "innocence" be attributed to someone who would do that?

"I think being a singer would be the perfect job for you," Gideon said lamely.

Samuel, on the other hand, beamed as if Gideon had given him permission to follow his dreams.

Samuel was roughly three years younger than Gideon and had arrived at the home a week or so prior to the incident. Gideon found himself wondering where Samuel could have come from. That led back to the question he asked himself every day: Where did he come from? Two people with extraordinary gifts showing up in the same town could not be a coincidence, could it? Gideon was pondering this when a thought from inside the building cut through his own thoughts like a hot knife through butter:

Oh, my God. He died?

The thought struck Gideon like an arrow to the heart. His memory flashed back to the bloody mess that had been

Andy lying on the ground. He'd been bleeding from multiple cuts, and spots on his face and arms were already turning blue, well on their way to bruises. But dead? He closed his eyes, cutting off Samuel's concerned expression.

Voices floated around him. He shifted through them, trying desperately to pinpoint that thought and home in on it. He found it and used all his will to shut out everything else. Had it been an idle thought, hearing it would have been impossible at this distance with so much surround sound, but it was a panicky, stressed thought that shone brighter than any around it. Even still, he could only pick up bits and pieces.

Collapsed . . . shard . . . internal . . . emergency surgery . . . everything they could. . .

The thoughts then became too hard to follow as the person transmitting them completely broke down. He knew, without seeing or hearing her, that Mrs. Warren was weeping.

He opened his eyes and turned to Samuel whose face still held the concerned look. Gideon tried to smile, wondering how he could tell Samuel that at such a young age, he'd committed murder.

Had he? His hands hadn't touched Andy; the other kids had done the deed. Gideon remembered the command: "Beat him up." Samuel hadn't told them to murder Andy; they'd been the ones who took it too far. "Shard," like a piece of a bone? Visions of dark purple bruising flashed into Gideon's mind. Had Andy's eye been draining out between the lids?

Samuel couldn't be blamed. He was a kid who'd seen another kid being punched, and he turned the tables the only way he knew how. Gideon stood from the swing.

"I gotta use the restroom. I will be right back." He speed-walked toward the building and the restrooms inside.

This meant getting closer to the distraught thoughts, but if he wasn't in a stall in a minute or so, he would vomit on the floor.

The thought of bodily fluids on the floor did him in. He'd barely entered the bathroom before turning to the sink and jettisoning his breakfast. It splashed up onto the counter. Was he an accomplice if the act was done in his defense? He threw up again.

"You okay?" came Samuel's voice from the other side of the door.

That poor kid had no idea what had happened. It would devastate him. He would have to live with the knowledge that he'd taken someone's life forever. Gideon felt his stomach roll over again with a new thought: What if he had known what he did? What if Samuel had meant to kill him? Did Gideon want to look behind that curtain?

Gideon woke up in the bed in Council Bluffs. There was no scream this time. His stomach was a little upset, but that could have been from dinner as much as from the memory.

He'd revisited that swing set over and over in his mind, both asleep and awake. Was Andy's death an accident or a beginning?

Verse 39

Norton, Kansas

"HELLO, honey. I just wanted to call real quick, give you an update on our farm day, and ask about sending pictures to Jason." Harold swore he heard Elizabeth breathe an enormous sigh of relief. Deciding he must have heard it wrong, he forged on. "I have a really good one of him making hay angels like you used to. I would show you later tonight, but I wondered if I should send it to Jason or if that would be inappropriate?"

Wyatt had told him all about the phone call with his dad. Things seemed to be trending up between Elizabeth and Jason. Harold was glad. Wyatt needed both of his parents, even if they weren't together.

Harold's thoughts on divorce had always been a little old fashioned, he knew. When Elizabeth had first told him, he'd been both angry and dismissive. Looking back on it, he felt a pang of regret. Her mother would have been more understanding. She definitely would not have said something along the lines of "Maybe you two just need a weekend alone to, you know, work it out." He felt shame thinking about the memory. Elizabeth had not talked to him for days after that. During a time in her life when she'd needed her parents, her remaining parent had let her down. Of course, the fact that the shithead had shacked up with some floozy almost immediately after leaving his daughter had shifted Harold's views on divorce significantly.

Then along came this phone call that seemed to be worming its way into everyone's thoughts toward Jason. And Harold, sad to say, was feeling the all too dangerous feeling that Elizabeth had been feeling: Hope. Like Elizabeth, the feeling had nothing to do with the two of them getting back together. Rather, it was about Wyatt having more contact with both of his parents. A child needed that. Harold still held to that belief, regardless of where his feelings toward divorce fell. So, after hearing about the phone call, he wondered if maybe some cute pictures of Wyatt might tip the scales toward a mutual parenting relationship where everyone won. *Well, maybe not that nurse*, he thought and smiled.

"Update first. Then send him the picture. Make sure it's a really cute one." He heard the hope in her voice as much as he felt it in his thoughts. *Oh Judy, maybe Wyatt would be okay*. He watched as Wyatt pretended to drive an old tractor, wondering what amazing scenes were coming to life in his imagination. Probably not farming scenes, if Harold was being honest with himself. He snickered a little, then recounted their activities at the farm so far. Telling her about the rope swing in the barn; the snake they'd seen (having to explain it had been just a bull snake, no rattle to be heard); how Wyatt had been playing on the old machinery for the past hour or so.

"There was a weird moment at the beginning," he added, then wished he hadn't started. There was no reason to worry Elizabeth while she was out having fun. Oh well. It wasn't that big of a deal. "He'd been staring at the combine, and when I touched his shoulder, he jumped, acting kind of scared. It's probably nothing, but I figured I'd give you the heads-up in case he brings it up tonight."

There was a pause as Elizabeth thought about it. "He's always been a cautious boy and, if I remember right, the front attachments look like giant torture devices. I'm sure he was—" She broke off and Harold heard distant voices on the phone. Elizabeth returned. "Look, I gotta go, but thank you so much for the update. Give Wyatt my love. I love you, Dad. Thank you so much for watching him. Oh, and don't forget to send that picture to Jason. Melt that heart for me."

Then she was gone, off to her adult life. She was no longer the little girl who played on the old farm machinery.

Wyatt, his face full of joy, looked out of the tractor windshield. Harold snapped another picture with his flip phone. Oh yes, he planned on melting that heart, and he hoped it hurt a little more than a little.

Verse 40

Alma, Nebraska

SALLY sighed. She wasn't sure what she'd wanted to see as she entered the bar. Over at the table were her two regulars, like they always were. It was just the two of them; there was no third man buying Thunderhead with dazzling blue eyes. Her feelings on his absence were complicated. She was glad that she didn't have to confront him in her current state, but, at the same time, the thought of seeing him had made her heart beat a little faster. Samuel's absence at the table hurt, more than she would have liked to admit. She absentmindedly slid her hand into her back pocket, cupping a folded napkin with the words "you are so much more than your past" scrawled within a ring of long dried condensation.

Gary looked up at her and smiled warmly, compassionately, and she felt better.

"How are you doin', Sally?" His voice was filled with a grandfatherly tone that helped dissipate some of the fog of depression that had hung over her since the day Jack confronted her in the bar then went home to end his life. His smile was like the sun breaking through the gloom. She decided right then that this was better than dealing with Samuel. Not complicated, purely good.

Jacob had turned in his seat. Now the three of them looked at each other with Boomer a passenger along for the ride.

"I am coping," she finally responded. "Still trying to figure out what is next in my life and where everything lands in that." The "everything" she was referring to looked up at her from where he stood, holding her hand. She had a feeling that he intuited that himself and she felt ashamed. "Came to get my last check," she explained. "You guys may be without me for a little while. Think you can handle it?" The familiarity of their relationship was doing more for her than any of the recent well wishes from family and ex-in-laws had come close to doing.

"Do we get free beer to soften the blow?" Jacob asked, clearly trying to bring some levity to the situation.

A situation that, as far as Sally could tell, had no concrete ending. Jack had a life insurance policy. A good one. The assumption of an early death must come with the guns. However, it did not pay out—or, at least, hadn't yet, barring a court case—because the fucker had killed himself. The only good news was that the guns no longer needed a home, and she was in the process of selling them off, which, up to this point, had kept her on her feet while she wasn't working. She knew that was a temporary fix, however.

A future was ahead of her where she would either have to pay for daycare, which was almost as much as she made working, or find a job she could do from home until Boomer started school again in the fall. All of this was like a wave, coming toward the shore, building up in pressure and size and all she could do was watch the news coverage.

Then there was Boomer himself. She'd never thought of herself as a good mom. Hell, she'd barely thought of herself as a mom at all. She'd never wanted to get pregnant and would have "taken care of it" discreetly, but Jack had found the test. The serendipity of him dropping his phone into the trash on the wrong day had completely changed their lives. Despite the fact that he'd agreed to never have kids, upon finding out she was pregnant, his whole belief system on parenting had completely reversed. He'd refused to let her end the pregnancy, going so far as to threaten taking her to court. She wasn't sure what the laws were surrounding that, but in a small town in Nebraska, she knew what it would have done to her reputation.

So, she'd dealt with her pregnancy, full of heartburn, restless leg syndrome, hypertension, and pain. Then Boomer was born, and Jack had become Super Dad, devoting his life to their new child, while Sally tried to become the mom she knew she should be. She often wondered if she would have felt more love for her son had the events surrounding her pregnancy been different. Had she not felt pressured to have a child, but rather chosen to become a mom on her own accord. She would never know. Suffice it to say her relationship with Jack deteriorated quickly after Boomer's birth.

Sally loved Boomer. Hell, she even liked him. Since Jack had died and she'd been thrown back into full-time motherhood, she'd realized just how much she loved him. However, that did not change the fact that he complicated her life. She no longer knew what her future held.

On top of all that confusion, she had to deal with the emotional confusion of having a kid whose dad had recently taken his own life while dealing with the emotional confusions of having someone she'd loved at one point in her life kill themselves. Yet, every night since the event, after she crawled into bed with Boomer and they cried together as they cuddled close for comfort, she realized that she would do anything for this boy. She would even face the confusing emotions, something she'd always tried to avoid. She loved Boomer more now than ever. Late at night, after his breathing had slowed into a sleepy rhythm, she would send a prayer up to Jack. A complicated prayer of thanks.

"Look," she said to the two men she'd come to see as her stand-in fathers, "I may have given you two the wrong idea. I don't own the place. I acted like I did to make you like me." She smiled, a touch of her old spirit flaming to life. They beamed back at her, happy to see the light hadn't been snuffed.

Again, she thought about how grateful she was that Samuel hadn't been here. This uncomplicated exchange had been the perfect distraction from her otherwise complicated life.

Then, as if called by her thought, the sound of a distant motorcycle came echoing down the quiet streets, getting louder with every quickened breath. Boomer made a grunt of pain and pulled his hand from hers, looking up at her confused. She hadn't realized she'd been squeezing his hand so hard. There were plenty of motorcycles in Alma, so there was no reason for her to believe it was him. But she did believe. More than that, she knew, without a shadow of a doubt. Her day was about to get a little more complicated.

Verse 41

Council Bluffs, Iowa

GIDEON sat in the little chair off to the side of his bed, willing himself to stay awake. He was exhausted. Not from the continuous search for Samuel, that was winding to a close in this city, but by the continuous dreams of the past.

He found himself longing for another read like the one he'd had in Cherokee. At this point, that nightmarish bloody scene would be a welcome distraction from the childhood he'd lived through. From the regret that was always waiting around the corner. His chin started to dip toward his chest, and he yanked his head up. He wasn't done sifting through everything he'd seen today, already knowing none of it was useful.

Samuel had driven through this town on his way to another bloodbath, leaving behind no trail to follow. Gideon had already decided that, at the end of the week, whether he had a lead or not, he would move on, hoping it was in the right direction.

His head dipped again toward his chest. What was his plan anyway? Stay awake forever? He considered walking down the hallway, trying to look into the minds of his fellow hotel guests, looking for something to haunt his dreams tonight, but he had always tried to avoid going into the minds of those that had nothing to do with Samuel or his search. His chin bumped his chest this time, and he pulled his head up to look into the blue eyes of the young boy who'd saved his life by taking another.

"Wake up," Samuel said. This brought Gideon out of the daze he'd been in since returning to the swings. "I asked if you were okay. You seem distracted."

Distracted was an understatement. Andy was dead and he was partially responsible. Samuel was also responsible, yet, for the moment, unaware of what he'd done. Gideon wished for the millionth time that he was unable to read minds. Then this terrible knowledge would be unknown by him. Had he not had this ability, he would be a kid, swinging next to another kid who could potentially be a friend. He thought about telling Samuel, breaking the news himself before it became common knowledge. He wondered how that news would be shared or if it would at all. They could say that he was transferred to another home after such a savage beating from his peers. That would not be far from the realm of possibility. A believable story. No one would have to know that he was dead. No one aside from the boy who could read minds. Gideon decided to not tell Samuel. Spare him the truth for a little longer at least.

"I'm fine. Just thinking about you and me." What were the chances of two people with abilities only found in comic books meeting under the same roof? Samuel was thinking similarly. Gideon knew, though neither had questioned it out loud. The next question, forming in both of their minds, was "Now what?" He came to a decision for them. "We need more information. We should find out where we came from."

"Yeah" was all Samuel said, but his blue eyes burned with the conquest. Gideon wondered what look would be in those blue eyes if he knew that he'd caused another kid's death.

His mind flicked to Mrs. Warren. She was still weeping,

the word "investigation" repeating over and over like an alarm in her mind. Gideon suddenly had a vision of police questioning the kids who'd beat Andy to death. What would they say? Gideon, as the one who was being beat up, would certainly have some explaining to do. What would he say?

"Look, I think the sooner we start, the better," Gideon said, hoping his voice sounded full of purpose and less of anxiety. Samuel nodded enthusiastically. "Between the two of us, I think we could find out where we came from, don't you? With our . . ." He paused, pondering the best word. He landed on "abilities. I believe we could find out just about anything."

"Where would we start?" A good question. Gideon thought the foster parents would probably be the best bet. He could look inside their minds and find out what they needed to know. For any information they couldn't find there, Samuel could persuade them to find it for them. "We should have superhero names," Samuel added. Gideon had almost forgotten that he was talking to a kid and that he himself was a kid. To Samuel, this was a game. Gideon again thought about what would happen if Samuel knew about Andy. "I want to be called Super Samuel."

Gideon couldn't help it. He laughed. "Sorry, buddy, but that is one of the lamest superhero names I have ever heard. It should be something specific to your ability and, if possible, an alliteration."

"What's an alliteration?"

Again, Gideon reflected on how young this boy was. "It's when two words start with the same letter."

"So, like Super Samuel."

Well, Gideon should have seen that coming. Foot, meet mouth. He thought for a little bit. How could he make Samuel understand? Maybe if he came up with his own name first? What started with a "G" that also had to do with looking into people's minds? "Gideon Glimpse." It was perfect. He wanted to never be called anything else. "Do you see how it sounds cool, but also explains my ability? I glimpse inside people's minds."

Samuel thought for a long time. Gideon could feel time passing like a physical thing. Like water flowing past him. Then Samuel looked at him, his name decided.

"Singing Samuel." Goddammit, he was bad at this. That sounded worse than Super Samuel, but it was moving in the right direction. The singing aspect seemed important to him, which raised another question.

"Samuel, can you use your ability without singing? Like, can you just tell someone what to do?"

Samuel thought about it, pushing himself a little to make the swing drift back and forth. "I don't know. I haven't done it much. The few times I have, it has always involved singing."

Fair enough, Gideon thought. He once again reminded himself that he was talking to a kid and not a veteran of magic with years under his belt. Regardless, singing worked, and why fix a clock that isn't broken? So, the name could or should have singing be a part of it. But the word "singing" was so lame. No one would take that seriously. "Glimpse" was badass; he needed his partner to have an equally badass name. He ran through all the words he could think of that started with "S" and had to do with singing. Soprano. Only for a few more years, probably. Staccato. Ha. Only if he wanted to explain that to each person to whom he introduced himself. Serenade.

Gideon's breath caught. It was perfect. "Nice to meet you, Samuel Serenade."

Samuel's eyes widened and his mouth formed an O of astonishment. They both felt the moment. They felt its weight on them. Something had happened. They'd gone from being two kids alone in the world with superhuman abilities to a team. It was like the creation of the X-Men or the Fantastic 4. Samuel was beaming at Gideon as if he was his dad, and this was his birth. In a way, Gideon mused, it was like a second birth. They were both born anew into their new roles.

Like birds pushed out of the nest, it was already time to test their wings. He threw his mind toward the hysterical woman who'd hung up the phone to head toward the bathroom to be alone. Gideon knew this in the same way he knew he was 12. It was knowledge that was in his mind.

Knowledge that pushed him again to get moving. He did not want to be questioned by the cops, and if he had his way, Samuel would never find out about Andy. "The first thing we need to do is figure out where we came from."

Verse 42

Omaha, Nebraska

THE man-in-the-mirror was, for once, blessedly quiet, listening to Jason try in vain to come up with a satisfactory explanation.

"Look, El—" He caught himself: "—izabeth." *Great start, douchebag.* "I know this sounds like the most cliched excuse in the book of excuses, but I swear to God and all the saints in Heaven, Stacy's grandma is sick. Like, dying sick."

He looked at the man-in-the-mirror, willing him to say something snarky to explain how lame that sounded. God, should he tell her that his dog ate his schedule for the weekend too? He was so angry at the look in the mirror that he balled up his hand, prepared to slam it right into that piece of shit's face. His face. His piece-of-shit face. He was in the ultimate lose-lose situation. Elizabeth would kill him, but he could not say no to going with Stacy to visit her grandma. It was possibly the least ethical thing he could think of.

"Oh. Sorry, honey. I know that we are in a relationship, and I live with you, but my ex was counting on me. So, have fun dealing with this emotionally crushing burden on your own. I'm off to hopefully rekindle a flame that I put out."

The man-in-the-mirror had spoken this so clearly, Jason's neck popped as he swung his head, first toward the mirror in surprise, then toward the bathroom door to make sure Stacy wasn't standing there, even though he knew she was finishing her twelve-hour shift and wouldn't be home for another hour.

Still, the man-in-the-mirror had laid it out clearly. It was hard to find a fitting argument for him. He could not spend this much time in a relationship only to bail on it when there was a real emotional need. However, he dreaded having to call El to explain despite finally acting like he gave a shit about their son, which he did, he would spend the weekend with his new girlfriend on a trip out of state. The reason for the trip would be irrelevant. The moment she heard he was canceling, she would be upset. When she found out the reason had anything to do with Stacy, she would be furious.

"You could lie," the man-in-the-mirror offered.

The idea had first occurred to him at work after getting off the phone with Stacy. The idea had followed his first thought of telling Stacy, "Sorry. I have plans that weekend." While that idea sounded far more pleasant, for the reasons previously discussed with his doppelganger, it was quickly quashed. Then came the impulse to lie. To tell her work was forcing him to go on a business trip or maybe his own family member was sick instead of hers. Maybe he could shove his finger down his throat while he was on the phone with her and wretch loudly, letting her know he was in no condition to see Wyatt or anyone else for that matter anytime soon. All that sounded fine. Until a picture of him with Stacy and her family or any other incriminating status or tag brought out the truth. If canceling plans hurt their relationship, lying would kill it. It would be near impossible to recover after that.

No, it was better to be honest. Take the hit and hopefully get back in the ring after Elizabeth had some time to cool down.

He looked at his watch. He still had about an hour 'til Stacy got home. He would text her to pick up some food on the way home. That would add fifteen to thirty minutes. He hoped that would be enough time to talk to Elizabeth before Stacy got home and made everything more complicated. He looked back at the man-in-the-mirror.

"Any words of advice? A script for me to follow? A book for how to cancel important plans for dummies hidden in your version of our cabinets? No? Didn't think so."

He turned to leave, then turned back and looked at himself in the mirror. Could he loath someone more? Tears began to form in his eyes, and he felt a lump in his throat. Coughing, he worked to regain his composure before making the phone call. He took deep breaths and wiped at his eyes. Then, before he or the man-in-the-mirror could talk him out of it, he pulled his phone from his back pocket, found her number, still under favorites, and with one press of his finger, sealed his fate.

Verse 43

Alma, Nebraska

ELIZABETH bumped into Samuel who'd stopped almost immediately after stepping through the door of the bar. She herself had been distracted, trying to fix her hair after taking off the helmet.

It had been ages since she'd ridden on a motorcycle. Elementary school, in fact. Her uncle had driven one down to see them for the Fourth of July and had taken her for a spin around the block. It had been exhilarating, despite her mother's apprehension. That specific uncle had gone on to flip his bike a month or so later. He was only hurt a little, but he never found the courage to get back on his bike or any bike thereafter. He sold it and that ended Elizabeth's foray into two-wheeled motor vehicles. That is, until today.

After the not-so-scary phone call with her dad, she'd returned to the sanctuary, explaining what happened to the four worried eyes that fell on her as she reentered. A few mesmerizing songs later, Samuel announced that the space would be perfect for him to use at the wedding.

"Oh?" Elizabeth said, raising her eyebrow as tall as she could to emphasize the OH. "Did Rebeca call you while I was on the phone to give you the job? Sorry. The 'gig'?"

Samuel started to flash that winning smile, below those winning eyes. However, Elizabeth threw up her hand, blocking both.

"I dare say, mister Serenade, you are being presumptuous. Your singing is good. I will give you that. But I will need more assurances."

He started to lean toward a confused look, still smiling.

"Good musical talent at these events needs to be able to carry a conversation, keeping the guests entertained with not only the music, but their words."

His smile began to return. She was glad he was catching on, because this was all a bluff to get him to take her to an early dinner. She wanted to make that clear in a fancy "I have got control of this situation" kind of way, and she was afraid that she would have had to settle with a lame explanation after her monologue. She finished strong, however.

"You will take me to an establishment near here and convince me that you can carry a conversation, even when there is food or drinking involved."

She nailed the landing. She could tell because Bartholomew and Samuel were both looking at her as if she'd delivered the speech in a movie before they all marched to certain death. Admiration mixed with surprise. It was delicious.

"You drive a hard bargain, Elizabeth."

Her name came out of Samuel's mouth like another song, and her strong command of the situation was almost lost, but she remained calm and kept her face steady, giving him no satisfaction. Not yet anyway.

"I feel up to the challenge, however," he continued, "and know of a delightful establishment where I can introduce you to the only two references you will need to talk to."

Her heart sped up. This was working out perfectly. Then she eyed Bartholomew, standing sheepishly off to the side as the conversation took place before him. Her heart dropped.

She'd totally forgotten about him and now realized how rude it would be to exclude him.

Bartholomew caught her eyes and smiled warmly. "That all sounds exciting, but I have a sermon to write tonight, and so I won't be able to join you, much to all of our disappointment, I am sure."

What was this? A convention for witty people? Elizabeth wanted to reply with something just as witty to keep the upper hand, but her little speech had wiped her out. She nodded thanks toward him. Still smiling with compassion, he nodded back.

Samuel bowed toward the young minister. "Your presence will be missed mightily." The guitar dangled below him as he bowed. Reaching down, he strummed a note in a minor key to exaggerate their collective sadness. The guitar was no longer hooked up to the sound system, so the sound was quiet in the large room and did, in fact, give Elizabeth a shiver. All the warmth and witticism of the conversation seemed to get a little colder as the note hung in the air. Samuel let it die on its own instead of snuffing it out with his free hand.

Elizabeth turned toward Bartholomew and got the impression that he felt the same way. The smile that had been radiating mirth and warmth now looked a little forced. She looked back at Samuel who was straightening up, beaming with the joke of it all. Then he seemed to read the room. He reached down and placed his palm on the still vibrating strings. The note died instantly, and the sanctuary was flooded with silence. It felt like a fourth person in the room with them, a presence that kept the rest of them from talking.

Bartholomew, after what had to be a shorter time than it felt, broke the silence, banishing that unwanted guest. "Thank you for those kind words and for emphasizing them so poignantly. I honestly considered changing my plans, if only to keep your hearts from breaking further, but that sermon won't write itself, and I am trying to not get any notes from Karen this Sunday explaining how it could have been better. The thousandth time's the charm, I tell myself. One of these days, that lovely old lady will have no criticisms, and on that day, she will be ready to go to our Lord in peace. Or so I believe." He pondered what he'd said for a moment. "Now that I think about it, I might add a double negative, just to make sure she sticks around a little longer. You two have a wonderful evening. I am sure I will be seeing both of you again soon. You know, if Mr. Serenade gets the job, that is." He winked at Elizabeth, turned, and made his way toward a door off to the left. When he reached it, he turned back toward them. "You two don't have to worry about locking the door or anything. I will lock up after I work on Karen's lifeline."

They looked up at him, startled to realize he was still in the room. Samuel straightened, one hand holding the guitar case, the other flashing a thumbs-up. Elizabeth copied him, but with both hands.

Bartholomew gave a little wave and disappeared through the door, leaving them alone for real this time.

Samuel stood there for a moment, holding the guitar. Then he turned toward Elizabeth. "Do you like motorcycles?"

The question was completely out of left field for her. So much so, she was unprepared to answer. Did she like motorcycles? "Like" was a strong word. She didn't hate them. One of her neighbors drove one around the block, and it was excessively loud and that was not cool. Of course, there was that ride with her uncle that had been fun.

Grasping onto that memory as all those thoughts flew through her mind, she responded, "Of course, I love motorcycles. Do I not look like a biker girl?" Way to grab onto one random memory and overcompensate big time on the response.

He held his free hand up in an apologetic gesture and turned toward the instrument closet to return the guitar. "I meant no offense. I just wanted to make sure before I offered you a ride on mine. It would appear my concerns were horribly unfounded, however, and I should probably offer to let you drive."

She blushed for the millionth time. Luckily, he'd already ducked into the small room with the guitar.

He appeared a second later, eyes wide. "You will never believe this, but I just spent years in another land where lions rule and there are men who are half-goat."

"Oh, come off it, you son of Adam." God bless her English teacher cred, or she would have had no idea what he was talking about. It had been many years since she'd read The Chronicles of Narnia and she was impressed she remembered the son of Adam part. She could tell by his delighted expression that he was as well. "While you were away, I did some thinking, and I don't think it would be right for me to upstage you by driving your bike better than you. My consideration should be noted, and I will ride behind you."

His smile widened as he made his way down the steps from the church's modest stage. "I am humbled by your generosity." He bowed again, this time with no guitar nor lingering note.

Without the note, the gesture was silly as it was intended to be, and she giggled. There was something about him and the ease of their interaction that made her feel young again. Something she hadn't felt since before getting pregnant.

"We can leave your car here, and you can wear my helmet. It covers the whole face. I have a spare half-helmet in case I need to help someone on the side of the road."

Or drive a cute bridesmaid home from the wedding at which he was performing, Elizabeth mused. She was surprised by the sting of jealousy she had at that thought. They'd only just met. He didn't owe her anything. Regardless, the thought that she might be one in a long line of wedding hook-ups gave her a slight moment of pause. Then, she thought, *Fuck it. If that is all it is, it has been a long time and I could definitely do worse.*

She followed him to the front door, turning back as they left the sanctuary, looking toward Bartholomew's office door. She felt guilty for not inviting him, but her eagerness to spend some alone time with Samuel eclipsed her guilt. Still, the guy seemed lonely. She made a mental note to have lunch with him at some point before the wedding. With that note taken, her spirits were lifted, and she left the large, empty sanctuary.

Samuel stopped at the glass door leading outside to the parking lot. "Looks like the wind has died down," he said. "That will make riding the bike more enjoyable, because you will be able to see your surroundings."

Now that they were looking at their vehicles, she was nervous. Motorcycles were dangerous, and she was a mother now. Was it worth the risk?

"When we get on, you will have to hold onto me tight. Is that all right?"

Yep, totally worth the risk. She nodded at him, and he opened the door. The warm summer air pushed at them as the air conditioning behind them fell away. The wind had died down. That was true. Now the heat sat, unmoving. The best word Elizabeth could think of to describe it was "thick." Samuel absentmindedly took her hand and led her into the sun toward his bike. She was unsure if she lost her breath from the temperature change or from his hand around hers. Either way, it was amazing.

Verse 44

Alma, Nebraska

THEIR eyes met: Samuel's electric blue and Sally's dusty brown. Everything seemed to stop. Then there came a miniature "oof" from behind Samuel. Sally released the breath she'd been holding, and time continued its relentless march forward.

A pretty woman with light brown, shoulder-length hair and matching eyes looked around Samuel at the collection of people in the bar. Sally's chest tightened with an emotion she didn't want to define. It wasn't like she and Samuel had been in any kind of relationship other than casual flirting at the bar and that had only taken place one time. Yet, she'd felt a connection with him, something she'd assumed he'd felt as well. Maybe he had. It's not like she'd been easily accessible recently. Still, she was hurt, at least a little.

Samuel blinked, his dazzling eyes hiding behind their lids for a split second. When they reemerged, they brought with them a similarly dazzling smile.

"Sally, how are you doing? I have been so worried but didn't know the proper way to go about checking on you," he said, looking at Boomer then back to her, "given the situation."

The situation being the fact that her ex-husband blew his brains out the day they met. What was the best way to reach out, given that situation? Boomer tugged on her hand, questioningly.

"I am doing all right, given the situation." That seemed like an adequate response to the question. "This is Boomer, my son. Boomer, this is . . ." She paused. What was Samuel? Had they known each other long enough to even be considered friends? Would "acquaintance" be the proper title? That felt wrong as well. She decided to just go with the safest route and not stress on it right now. "My friend, Samuel," she finished.

The pause in between, probably only a second or so, had felt longer. She noticed the woman behind him, watching the exchange with keen interest. She was probably focusing on the pause, trying to parse out if there was any hidden meaning to it. Samuel, for his part, seemed oblivious to all this, smiling at her and Boomer as if they were old friends who haven't seen each other for years. His eyebrows went up a little as he seemed to realize it was his turn to introduce his guest.

"Nice to meet you, Boomer. Your mom is the coolest person that lives here, I dare say. This is Elizabeth, hopefully, my future employer and also a friend. She lives in a different town, so your mom doesn't have to worry about her status as the coolest person in Alma being in jeopardy."

Boomer looked at him with mixed confusion and unease.

Samuel continued, not noticing Boomer's expression. "Elizabeth, this is Sally, the best bartender in the Midwest, and these two miscreants are Jacob and Gary, and recently, the only reason I come to the bar."

They nodded their greeting as she nodded back, and hellos were tossed hither and thither.

"Sally, it's good to see you. I had planned to share a meal with Elizabeth while discussing future arrangements, but if you want to talk, I am sure that Elizabeth would be more than accommodating."

Elizabeth's eyebrows creased. Clearly, she had no idea what was going on, but was hurt that Samuel was willing to bump her for another woman.

Sally could relate. Had she not felt a similar pang of jealous resentment toward Elizabeth when they'd walked in? How dare Samuel bump her from his mind to find this new, attractive woman. She considered taking him up on his offer, if for no other reason than to make Elizabeth be accommodating. Then she felt Boomer tug on her hand and her reality rushed back in on her.

"Thank you, but that won't be necessary. I am only here to pick up my last check. Boomer and I have to rush to get to the bank before they close, then do some light shopping. I want to eat something other than casserole and fruit salad. No one ever brings over burgers for consolation. So, we have been eating green beans in a gravy with a breadcrumb crust for breakfast, lunch, and dinner."

Elizabeth's look softened. Sally was unsure if she was happy about not having to give up Samuel for the evening or relieved to find out the reason she'd almost been shunted aside was because of a death in Sally's family. Either way, Sally resented it. Briefly, she considered inviting Samuel along to help her shop and cook, since she was "so upset." Then she realized she was being petty and unfair to everyone involved, including Boomer who appeared to be more eager to leave with every passing second.

"Good luck with your future employment, Samuel. Elizabeth, it was nice to meet you. And you two geezers best be here when I get back."

Jacob and Gary nodded and raised their glasses to her. Had she been bartending, she would have already refilled Jacob's. It was getting low.

With Boomer leading the way, she began to follow him out, then realized she hadn't grabbed the check, the only reason she'd come in. Well, not the only reason, but the other reason seemed foolish at the moment.

She let go of Boomer's hand. "Stay right here for a second, buddy."

She hurried behind the bar into the kitchen where the manager's office was tucked in a corner and the employee lockers next to it. She opened hers and found her check waiting. She turned to leave and saw Samuel standing in the kitchen. Her breath caught.

"You aren't supposed to be back here." Her voice sounded weak, even in her own ears. Without speaking, he crossed the kitchen and wrapped her in his arms. She leaned into him, smelling a musky smell of dust, sweat, and Old Spice. It was perfection. She started to cry, but, luckily, had become very good at keeping her emotions under control over the last few days, so only a couple of tears squeezed past her closed lids. After what felt like an eternity, she looked up into his perfect blue eyes.

"I am so incredibly sorry for your loss," he said. "I would do anything for you. I hope you know that."

Her mind went to the attractive woman presumably back in the bar. *Would you leave her?* she wondered. Again, she realized how unfair that was. There was no future here. Not for the two of them. Why should he give up something potentially good to get swept up in all her bad? She took a deep, calming breath.

"Thank you," she said softly. The way they were standing, she had a strong urge to throw caution and common sense to the wind and kiss him. To escape out the back and sneak around to his motorcycle and drive away. The image was so vivid that his words felt like part of her daydream. She realized that wasn't the case. "What?" she asked, hoping her voice sounded more in control to him than it did to her.

"I said, I think maybe you and Boomer should leave town. There is nothing for you here any longer. You should pack up and put Alma in your rearview mirror until it isn't. Then keep driving 'til you find a new life in a new town."

It sounded like a line from a movie or something. Like when a bank is about to be robbed and the bandit tells the pretty woman waiting to cash her check that maybe she should be somewhere else at the moment. The melodrama of it gave her chills and a sense of foreboding.

Seeing the look on her face, he smiled as if to reassure her everything was fine. She saw that his eyes, those beautiful blue eyes, did not share the joy of that smile. No. They were the eyes of a bandit about to rob a bank.

"I'm being overly dramatic, aren't I?" He paused, let her go, then ran a hand through his hair. "I am just concerned. You understand, right?"

She did not, in fact. Her life had gone from complicated to next to impossible since stepping into his arms. She was at a complete loss.

Samuel also, surprisingly seemed to be at a loss for words. He took her hand, lifted it to his lips, and softly kissed between the knuckles of her middle finger and ring finger. "I hope everything works out for you, no matter where you come to rest." With that, he turned and walked out of the kitchen, leaving her alone with her whirlwind of thoughts.

"What?" she asked herself, not sure if it was in regard to what he'd said, what had just happened, her own feelings and thoughts, or some combination of it all.

She followed Samuel out of the kitchen and saw that Elizabeth was sitting in a booth, discussing options with Blake, as Samuel talked to Jacob and Gary. Boomer was waiting at the door, and she could tell he was stressed about still being here, now alone. She hurried over to him.

"Goodbye, you scallywags," she called toward the bar at large, not making any reference to whom it was directed, afraid that if she attempted to look at them, she might make eye contact with Samuel. At the moment, that felt like the worst thing that could happen. Boomer in tow, they exited the bar into the late afternoon daylight.

Samuel's motorcycle was parked in front of the door. Boomer stopped so abruptly that Sally nearly ripped his arm out of its socket as she kept walking. She turned and followed his gaze to the bike.

Guessing at his expression, she said, "Don't even think about it, mister. Not until you have enough money to pay for your own funeral can you consider owning one of those things."

Had she looked closer at his face, she would have seen fear, not greed.

Verse 45

Council Bluffs, Iowa

"BEFORE we start, I guess I should ask: Do you remember anything about your parents?" Gideon asked Samuel as they got off the swings. Gideon saw, even before Samuel shook his head, that he did not. "Neither do I. I have been in the system for as long as I can remember."

He didn't even have memories of the first few homes he'd been in as he'd been moved around quite a bit, even as a baby. His current case worker, Travis, had not come right out and said why, but Gideon hadn't needed him to. Turns out most of his previous families had found it eerie how perceptive he was, to the point that they'd requested different placement for him.

The sad part was he'd always only been trying to help.

Like when his foster dad had been watching TV and think to himself, *I'm thirsty*. So, Gideon would get up, go to the fridge, and bring him back a soda. Then he would have to hear his foster parents thinking about how strange and unsettling he was. It hurt, so he would try to not preemptively help as much.

Sometimes, however, if he wasn't paying attention, he had trouble parsing out what was said and what was thought.

He'd been removed from his last house because he'd heard his foster mother thinking about suicide and he'd felt obligated to intercede. He'd walked up to her, sitting at the kitchen table, a forgotten coffee cooling in its mug.

"Delores?" he'd said. "I know things seem
overwhelming right now, but I think you can beat it. You are
stronger than you know." Most of those statements he'd pulled
from her memories of conversations with her minister. The
minister had been trying hard to work through her depression,
but based on what Gideon was hearing, he was failing.

Gideon was a kid, though. He hadn't been trained in
counseling. He'd guessed that hearing these reassurances again
would help, especially if it came from someone who cared
about her. The reason those memories had been so easy to pull,
however, was because she was focusing on them as she
considered what ending her life would be like. To hear her
thoughts, voiced out loud by the young boy she'd taken into her
house, was enough to make her stifle a scream as she abruptly
stood, striking the table and causing her lukewarm coffee to
slosh over the side of the mug.

His foster mother had backed away from him, and he
was struck by each thought like a slap to his face. *Demon. Witch.
Warlock. Devil. Evil.* They struck him like gunshots, coming fast,
heavy, and hot. He jerked with each one, which gave him a
possessed look. She took off at a near run and he heard the door
to her bedroom slam shut. While her frantic breathing and near
hysterical crying were muffled by the door, her thoughts were
not. He heard every twisted accusation and terrible new belief
as they bloomed in her mind. He was no longer welcome in the
house. He considered calling his case worker himself, but he
was unsure as to whether that would improve the situation or
hurt it further. After listening to her jumbled, terrified thoughts
for another minute or so, he had turned and walked to the back
door behind the kitchen table, slid it open, and walked out into
the cool fall air. By the time he returned to the house later that

night, Travis had been there waiting to take him somewhere new.

Now, as fate would have it, he was here. Prior to the day before, he'd not believed in fate, but he was beginning to consider it now. How else could he explain being at this house at the same time as Samuel? Samuel, who was also gifted. Samuel, who was also a kid looking for his place in a world that would never understand him.

"So, where do we start?" Samuel asked.

Gideon thought about it. He was no expert on the adult side of foster care, but he assumed that there was paperwork that new foster parents received with each new kid. If they could find their papers, he assumed they would have general helpful information, such as age, general description, medications, and, most helpful, for them now, birth parents. He didn't know that with full certainty, but it felt like a good place to start.

"We should talk to our foster parents. They will know something I can read off their minds, and, if they don't, they are bound to have papers with helpful information you can sing to get."

Samuel looked exuberant. He nodded his head up and down repeatedly until Gideon reached out, stopping it mid-nod.

"Calm down. We gotta play it cool or their guards will be up."

God knew their guards were up after that last phone call. He let go of Samuel's head, and Samuel took on a more serious look, a disquietingly adult look. It made Gideon shiver. He felt as if he'd looked through a window and saw the man Samuel would become. A man who had at least one death on his hands. He shivered again.

They made their way toward the house. The few kids in front of them quickly got out of their way. That was fine with Gideon. He was antsy to start so that they could get on their way, hopefully, before news broke about Andy.

They went in through the back door. Gideon heard crying in a room to their left and decided that with emotion like that, getting any real information would be difficult. Mrs. Warren's husband was not crying. He was standing stoically in his at-home office, considering what to do after that phone call. Gideon realized now, for the first time, that these two would probably lose all the kids here and not be allowed to continue fostering. He also realized that he did not care too much. This placement had been less than perfect, and these two had barely lifted a finger to stop what they had to know was going on in their backyard.

"Sir?" Gideon had never felt comfortable with these two so had never moved past "sir" and "ma'am" when talking to them. They'd not openly minded that, but he'd heard them thinking about how weird it was. Their thoughts had not swayed him, however, because he'd learned to not change his behavior based on the thoughts of others. "We were hoping to talk to you about our parents."

Mr. Warren turned to look at them, silently taking them in. Silent on the outside anyway. On the inside, he had something to say:

Trust me, your guys' mom doesn't want anything to do with you, and you should be grateful.

Verse 46

Norton, Kansas

HAROLD sat in his chair, his bitter microwaved coffee resting on a stack of magazines about Midwest life and farming. He'd been raised by parents who lived through the dirty thirties and had taught him to never waste anything. The chair he was sitting in had in fact been repaired multiple times and was still his favorite chair. He sipped his coffee, involuntarily grimacing, like taking a shot of straight vodka. Coffee was a tool, dammit. It wasn't about the flavor; it was about the caffeine.

He got up, joints popping like fireworks as he rose to his feet. He walked down the hall toward Wyatt's room and peeked in at his grandson, sprawled out shirtless on his bed. Harold had heard of kids crashing after a busy day, but, until this afternoon, had not fully grasped how adequately that word described it. Wyatt had fallen into his bed, seemingly asleep before his head had hit the pillow. Harold, who could no longer take naps without messing with his sleep cycle, which was tenuous at best, had himself required coffee to get through the rest of the day, à la the microwaved, stomach-curling brew sitting beside his chair.

Prior to this visit, Harold had known he loved Wyatt. As a grandfather and the father of Wyatt's mother, it all made sense. He'd known it in a purely hereditary way, however. Wyatt was his grandson and, therefore, he loved him.

Harold had seen him on weekends when he was younger, and he would take a seat on a nearby chair while Judy sat directly on the floor with him, actively interacting with him as he showed her his toys and brought books to her to read. When Wyatt brought him something, he would acknowledge the item, then Wyatt would be off again, Judy on her hands and knees crawling after him as he went. Judy had loved Wyatt, in a pure way; in a way Harold had not understood until today.

There was something about sharing his world with Wyatt, and watching Wyatt open up to it and enjoy it that had touched Harold in a way he hadn't anticipated or been prepared for. He'd never taken drugs—a strong conservative man was he—but he thought he understood addiction better now. He was addicted to this sleeping, beautiful child. He was addicted to being a grandpa.

"It's about time, you old fool," Judy said from behind him. "You only needed me to get out of the way so that you could take center stage. Sorry for not seeing it sooner."

Tears began to form in the corners of his eyes. "God, I hope you don't believe that," he whispered, unsure if he was talking to Judy or to himself. Wyatt stirred, moving into a slightly different, presumably more comfortable position. Harold eased the door closed to mute the one-sided conversation he knew was about to take place and made his way back to his chair. Sitting across from him, in her own favorite chair, was Judy, a knowing look on her face.

"Did you enjoy your day?" she asked, smiling a half-smile. "What all did you do at the farm?"

Obviously, as a construct of his own imagination, she had access to his memories, but she was clever. Aye, so she was. It felt so familiar. Coming home from work, she would be

sitting in her rocker like she was now, sipping iced tea. The
Judy in front of him was holding a tall glass of iced tea now,
condensation dripping down the side to puddle on her hand
before continuing its path to her lap. She would first ask how
his day was, then follow up with what had taken place in hers.
The ol' two-punch knockout. She genuinely wanted to know
about his life. More than anything, she'd just liked talking with
him. Now, as she sat in front of him, all his memories at her
disposal, she again just wanted to talk to him.

"I did enjoy myself, honey. It was a perfect day. You
should have been there."

He was struck by the fact that she wasn't. She may be
able to see the memories, but she wasn't part of them. She
hadn't been standing in the barn's shadows or sitting in the
overgrown grass by the tractor. It had been Harold and Wyatt, a
team of two. Judy had taken the day off. He looked at her and
she looked right back, nodding without taking her eyes from
his. She sipped her iced tea.

Had there been a day that Judy had not tagged along
since her passing? She judged his food choices at the grocery
stores, told him from over his shoulder what vegetables were
ready in the garden, and reminded him of proper folding
techniques during laundry. She was a comforting presence to
which he'd become accustomed. One that had been noticeably
missing today.

"You didn't need me to be there. You don't need me to
be here."

A new two-punch knockout. It hurt. Of course, he
needed her. How on Earth could he live without her? He could
not remember a time without her.

"Today at the farm?" she interrupted as his thoughts
were coming to terms with her first statements.

His eyes cut back to her, full of tears, hurt, and a little bit of anger. The rocking chair was empty. There was no movement to signify a recent occupant's departure. There was no iced tea. There was emptiness. She was gone.

He closed his eyes, rubbing at the tears threatening to get out of control.

"So, what's next?"

Harold's eyes sprang open. Wyatt was sitting in the rocking chair, working to get it going, having to sit at the front of the chair to get enough foot on the ground for a good kick. He sat where his grandma, who he wouldn't remember, had been sitting moments before. Wyatt filled the space that Judy had been occupying. Harold could hear sweet musical laughter coming from the kitchen. It seemed to signify an "I told you so" sentiment. Wyatt, feeling he had the chair moving enough, pulled up his feet, crossed them under him, placed his hands in his lap, and looked at Harold expectantly.

"Well, buddy, it's just the two of us. We can do whatever we want. I think a pizza buffet sounds like the perfect plan."

Wyatt's smile threatened to engulf his face as he shot out of the rocking chair, putting it in more motion than his kicking efforts had achieved, and threw himself into Harold's arms.

Harold held him tightly, unable to rub away the tears. Through them, he thought he saw a figure standing in the kitchen doorway. Maybe it was shadows moving as the curtains blew in the vent under them. Whatever it was, it was gone as quickly as it had been there, blinked away with the tears.

Harold and Wyatt were alone in the house and that was okay.

Verse 47

Council Bluffs, Iowa

GIDEON had slumped in his chair. His body would let him know tomorrow what regrettable choice he'd made by not moving to the bed and accepting his fate. His body would remind him that he paid for the decisions he made. The pain he felt as he stood and straightened his muscles and bones into a more human shape, each joint popping in protest, each ligament straining to return to how it had been. They would be a painful reminder that there are consequences for inaction as much as for action. Those reminders would hurt, but not as much as the reminder he was actively viewing in 3D surround sound with motion seats.

"Our mother?" Gideon mumbled, slumping further into the chair. He watched, helpless to change anything as the two boys followed the trail that would inevitably lead to the creation of Samuel Serenade in earnest.

"Our mother?" Gideon breathed out, not even a full whisper.

Samuel turned to him, a little kid looking at his older brother. That was what Gideon was: Samuel's older brother. They had the same mother. The thought had hit him like a wave, and each new revelation that came with it hit him again. He could almost visualize himself on a beach, trying to sit up only to be knocked flat again and again against the sand. Unable to get above the water. He was drowning in revelation.

His mother was alive. He had a brother. They both had abilities. They were together. And this man in front of them had information about all of it.

He felt a small hand, his brother's hand, sneak into his.

Round and blue, like the waves, Samuel's eyes questioned him, looking up into Gideon's green ones. Gideon thought, *You certainly got the better eyes in this family,* and a maniacal, frantic laugh tore its way up his throat. Thankfully, he was able to cut it off before it made it to his mouth.

He had to calm down. Each new thought threatened to crack open his head like an egg. He closed his eyes and took one long, calming breath. Then, eyes still closed, he turned back toward the man with the answers.

"Tell me about my mother."

He'd made a split-second decision as he was forming the words to go with "my" instead of "our." The decision followed his earlier thought process about what he'd heard about Andy. This was not the time nor the place to put that kind of pressure on Samuel. The last thing Gideon needed was for Samuel to experience the same inner turmoil Gideon was. After they were away, with a clear-cut goal and destination, he would tell Samuel.

"I don't know anything about your mother," Mr. Warren lied.

Gideon was too unfocused to do a good read, so he was unsure if he lied out of fear or obligation. Did the foster program tell foster parents to not share information about the kids' parents or was he afraid that they would act on the information and that would make a bad situation worse? The last thing he needed after Andy was for two of the foster kids to go missing. Thin ice could only take so much pressure after all.

Gideon didn't care about any of that, however. Hell, he'd all but forgotten about Andy after hearing he had a brother who was now holding his hand. Information he'd wanted had become information he needed. He tried focusing and saw headlines flash inside the man's mind.

All the headlines were about fire.

The man looked at Gideon and, for the first time, Gideon wondered if people could feel him working in their minds. He'd never dug past the surface level, and no one had ever reacted to his little glimpses into their thoughts. Now, however, he was digging, and he was planning to go deep. The fact that he'd asked after their mother had already lifted this information, but the man's mind was occupied on other matters. Matters that involved a dead kid whose eyeball had drained out of his skull.

Mr. Warren looked at Gideon more closely, maybe with a sense that something wasn't right about this exchange, and he no longer wanted to be a part of it. "I think the two of you should go back outside for a little bit."

Gideon could hear the unease in his voice. Or maybe he heard it seeping from his mind. Regardless, he was not letting this opportunity slip away. He intended to dig deeper, to find out what the fire meant, but the man was now walking toward them, preparing to usher them out and away.

Gideon turned to Samuel, his little brother. "He knows more than he is saying. I need more time. Stop him."

Samuel's eyes widened with understanding and purpose. His mouth began to move, and the song began, flowing from Samuel's mouth and mind in perfect unison.

It was beauty made audible.

The man stopped. His eyes lost focus and his lips moved to unheard lyrics as he picked up the song, and his older, deeper voice added a new layer.

He has a respectable voice, Gideon mused, then, shaking his head, got back to business. He mentally reached into this man's thoughts and began to excavate. The headlines cleared like a microbe under a microscope. Gideon began to read. The music faded away as he was lost in the stories.

Verse 48

Alma, Nebraska

ELIZABETH and Samuel sat in a booth two away from the two old men he'd introduced to her. The other woman had left with her son. Despite the beginning of this post-audition interview not going according to her plans, it was now falling back in line.

When Samuel joined her after a quick chat with his friends, he'd explained the circumstances surrounding Sally and her son's late father. Elizabeth had complicated emotions as she listened to the tale. She was obviously horrified and saddened to hear about the loss of life and Sally's own life being completely turned upside down. Yet, she also felt a sense of relief; relief that a potential opponent for Samuel's attention had been taken off the board. She felt sick to her stomach that she should feel relief at all in regard to a suicide, but she also wanted to be honest with herself and acknowledge the fact that she was relieved.

When they'd first walked into the bar and Samuel had reacted the way he had to this other woman, Elizabeth had felt like another in a long line of women with whom Samuel flirted. Flirted. Dear lord. Where was she? In junior high? Regardless, that was how she'd felt, and it had made her question many things. Her diary with his last name guiltily drawn after they first met, for example.

After everything with Jason, the feeling of jealousy that a man she liked could be interested in another woman had cut into her in what felt like a physical way. All of this because Samuel had spoken kindly to an attractive woman when they walked into the bar. No context. Samuel being kind. She'd hated herself for those feelings. She had no right at all to those feelings, other than the fact that they were hers. She had ownership of those feelings, and, by that right, she was allowed to feel them. Right or not, she'd been jealous.

While Samuel explained meeting Sally, the confrontation with the man who had been her husband and the father of her kid, then his horrible death, Elizabeth felt the physicality of her jealousy lessen from a stabbing pain to a residual ache in her chest.

God, Samuel had such a strong effect on her. Only a week ago, she'd been the woman who'd sworn off men in general, and now she was on the verge of death by jealousy over a man she'd just met.

It was the eyes, she thought. *Or his voice, the musical quality of it as he spoke.* It was encapsulating.

She'd read in romance novels about defenses being destroyed by men and had always scoffed at that. Now, here she was, crumbling and melting despite herself. She made a mental note, as she sipped her long island iced tea, that she would keep full control of herself around this man.

Then he turned toward her and smiled gently. The walls weakened, and she could feel the crumbling and melting begin again. She looked away, looking for something less attractive. Her eyes fell on the back of one of the older gentlemen's heads.

"That's tragic," she said absently. The head in question still had a surprising amount of hair, all white, of course, and in need of a haircut within the next week or so.

"It was tragic in that any loss of life is tragic," said Samuel. "Less tragic in that the man was human trash and the world is better off without him."

The man's hair length quit being interesting. Elizabeth turned to look at Samuel, meeting his blue eyes. They were shimmering with an emotion she wasn't sure she liked. She processed that last statement, trying to fit it into the puzzle that was Samuel.

She herself had voted against the reinstatement of the death penalty in Nebraska when it had been on the ballot. She'd felt real disappointment when it passed anyway. Now, she'd heard a man she'd all but fallen in love with (*slow down,*) speak like the pro-death commentators during debates. The puzzle piece did not fit into the puzzle she'd begun, and she wasn't sure she wanted it to. It would ease her mind to learn that the piece was from a different puzzle that had somehow got placed in the wrong box by accident.

He must have read some of her thoughts from her expression because his face softened. "Sorry. That probably sounded a little . . ." He searched for the word.

"Extreme?" she offered helpfully, mentally beginning to remove the piece from the box altogether.

"Yeah, that's right. You have to realize that when I care about someone and someone hurts them, I take that very personally." There was that jealous pain again. "That day when he came in and said those terrible things to Sally, I felt the urge to fight for her. I don't know." He ran his hand through his hair in exasperation. "To defend her honor or something. But I know my own limitations. I am not a strong man. He would have taken me to Fistland with an express ticket." She smiled a little at the term he'd used, softening a conversation that threatened to be a little too serious. "So, when I heard of his passing, I was sad for her, her son, and his family. But I won't lie and say I didn't also feel a sense of relief for her as well. He was a roadblock in the way of her happiness, and that roadblock is now gone. Yes, it's terrible, especially right now, but in time, her life will be better for it. I can guarantee it."

She wanted to see it as he did, but death was death, and she was unable to completely remove that puzzle piece from the set. Instead, it was set next to the box, a potential puzzle piece that was troublesome and would have to be reevaluated after the puzzle was a little further along.

"I understand," she said and watched as relief flooded over his face. It helped, but the piece remained.

There was an awkward silence after that. Again, her eyes drifted as she looked for something to change the subject. Her eyes again landed on the fine white hair a couple of booths away. "So, aside from Sally, it seems you have been making multiple friends since you arrived. Those two seem like interesting company."

He did a slight turn to follow her gaze, then turned back. The smile met the eyes and her disquiet dissipated immediately, the puzzle piece forgotten for the moment.

"Aren't they the best?" His excitement was infectious, and she was smiling back at him, fully engaged yet again. "They were the ones who first turned me on to the wedding taking place. They graciously shared my information with those who needed it, and that has led to us now. If anything, you have them to thank for the audition today. Well, that and your son's fortuitous need to use the restroom when he did."

Another reminder that she was a mother, always just below the surface. Yet, the way Samuel talked so breezily about it was refreshing. He didn't treat Wyatt like baggage attached to Elizabeth, but rather another aspect of her life. Jason, Wyatt's own father, rarely spoke about him with such ease. To Jason, Wyatt had been baggage.

After he was born and they would get ready to go out, either to a restaurant or to a friend's house, she could feel his agitation with how much more effort it all took because they had a baby. She'd told herself that, as time went on, it would become so routine, he would stop noticing. He never stopped noticing. Even after Wyatt was potty trained, Jason still saw the toys, and books, and car seat, and everything else as work. It was spelled out clearly when they would hire a babysitter and go out on their own. The relief she'd seen in his eyes on their nights out had hurt more than their time alone had helped.

"We have some time before the wedding," Samuel continued. "We all should go to a pool or a lake or something. I would love to get to know master Wyatt a little better."

"You just want to see me in my two-piece." The words came out before she had time to consider the consequences, and she had to fight perilously with her pigment to keep it to a relative pink rather than a deep red.

He winked, shrugged, held his hands up to signify she'd caught him, and took a sip of his beer. "I think that sounds wonderful."

Her phone buzzed and she looked down.

"Home." The text was from Rebecca, preceded by a couple of innocent emojis. This was followed immediately by emojis that could mean fresh produce or that she was being inappropriate. Elizabeth smiled and turned over her phone. That kind of distraction was unneeded. She was embarrassing herself fine on her own.

"Should we get down to brass tacks? The audition was..."
She paused for dramatic effect. "Pretty good."

His eyebrows raised in question.

She held up one hand, palm forward, to calm him. "I just
think it wasn't enough to convince me. I'm going to need
another one, maybe in an open-air setting? To gauge if it was
your own talent or the acoustics of the church that made you
sound so good."

"Will your parents be willing to watch Wyatt again? I
mean, he is invited, obviously. I do like a crowd. But it sounds
like I need to convince you specifically, and I might be better at
that if it were. . ." He also paused for dramatic effect. "Just the
two of us."

His expression changed. He must have noticed how the
joy that had been radiating off her had dulled.

"I'm sorry. You are right. I was being silly. He is more
than welcome to come."

She shook her head, eyes glistening with a layer of tears.

"It's not that. I'm sorry, it's . . ." She paused. This time, it
was not for dramatic effect but in search of the proper way to
continue. "It's just my dad. You see, my mom died in a car
accident. A drunk driver ran a stop sign and . . ." She stopped
then. She looked at her empty glass, wishing there was
something to sip as a distraction. Why had she turned down
another drink when the bartender had come around last time?
"It's like I forget because it's so unreal, it doesn't fit into my real
life. Then something will remind me, and it hits again and
again, and each time is like the first time." What was she doing?
This had to be the worst topic for a date that she could have
come up with. Hell, she wasn't even sure if this was a date. But
if it were, she was doing a fine job of driving it into the ground.

Like a grave. Two tears, one for each eye, had swelled enough to start their trek down her cheeks.

Samuel took her hand. "I am so incredibly sorry to hear that." The sincerity in that statement was the last straw. She stood, needing to be away for a little bit. She planned on using the restroom as a safe space to get her emotions under control. But before she could make her way in any direction, he was up, and his arms were around her, and she was crying. For her mom, for her divorce, for her life as it was systematically torn down around her. She cried into his shoulder, and he held her to him. They stood together for what felt like an eternity, a release of everything she'd held on to. She had not realized that they were outside the bar. When had that happened? He'd slowly eased her toward the entrance and outside to give her as much privacy as was possible on the side of the road in the late afternoon.

He looked down into her eyes. His blue eyes had their own film of tears over them, though his never quite broke the seal. "I will take you back to your car."

Half of her told her to grab on to him, to grab his shirt and twist her fist into the fabric so that he couldn't let her go. The other half was so incredibly grateful for his willingness to let her handle her emotions on her own that a minor battle took place inside her. She realized she was exhausted. The emotional rollercoaster she'd experienced throughout the day was slowing down now, and she was ready to see her son and her dad, and have a nice bath with a glass of wine.

"Thank you" was all she could manage.

He helped her onto his bike. She was about to put the helmet on when she realized she'd left her phone on the table. She started to get up when he reached out, phone in hand.

"I grabbed this on the way out. Don't worry. I didn't look. I swear."

She looked and saw a couple more texts from Rebecca and a missed call and voicemail from Jason. Her heart sank a little more. It would appear that the rollercoaster had a couple more loops after all.

"By the way," he said sheepishly, "there is a cute little grocery store in town that I believe sells both eggplants and peaches, if your friend needs them."

She was unable to hide the blush. Even her hands were red.

Loop the loop. Fucking rollercoaster. Loop the loop.

Verse 49

Council Bluffs, Iowa

GIDEON woke up. His right arm had lost all feeling and his body ached. His muscles felt like they'd solidified under his skin. His joints were like bubble wrap.

As he stood, every part of his body made noise. He felt old, partly because of his aching body and partly because he'd been living in his memory of childhood. Regardless of why, he felt a moment of dissociation as his reality and his dream overlapped. He was both twelve and thirty-five. He took off his glasses and rubbed away the lines that had formed where they'd pressed into his skin.

There had been fires. The headlines he'd read had been about the fires. There had been two. One per child.

He walked into the bathroom and looked in the mirror. He was shirtless, so he was able to see the burn on his side clearly. He'd grown older and his skin had stretched over the years, causing the scar to lose some of its shape. He knew, though. He could still clearly see the handprint that had been welded into his skin. Prior to that day with his brother, he'd always thought it to be an interesting birthmark. Something he'd had since birth.

Come to find out, it had come later at the hand of his mother. Of his and Samuel's mother.

There had been two fires. The day he read those articles, there was a third.

Verse 50

Alma, Nebraska

SAMUEL'S bike rolled to a stop in the dirt parking lot. The wind had died down so the dust from his tires settled quickly. There was no creepy moment this time. Just the two of them, sitting close, her arms still around him. He turned. As he did, she reluctantly let him go. He looked back at her, and she realized he couldn't see her face because of the visor. She undid the clasp under her jaw and took off the helmet, allowing their eyes to meet again.

"I had a wonderful evening," he said as she stepped off the bike. He reached for the helmet. She handed it to him, and he took her hand to help her as she dismounted the bike.

"I did too. Aside from getting my makeup on your shirt, it was delightful." She offered a weak smile. The afternoon had not gone the way she'd planned or hoped. But she enjoyed it, for the most part.

She'd missed giving into her emotions, even a little bit. As a single working mother, she always had an audience. Either her students or her son. Twenty-four seven.

The sun was already going down over the Midwest. This had been a day of emotions. As it came to an end, she was glad for it. She found that sometimes giving into her emotions felt good.

Without thinking about it, she gave into her emotions yet again, needing to know that she could, needing to know that what she'd been feeling all day was real. She threw her arms around Samuel's neck, pulled him in, and placed her lips against his, probably more forcefully than the chick lits would have suggested. To hell with those.

She felt him stiffen in surprise. Then his arms were on her back, responding to her kiss. Their lips parted, and their tongues met. God, this felt so good. Her night of lustful imagination had not prepared her for this moment, and her knees were weakening. Thankfully, his hands were ready to support her and keep her close to him. She could give into this like a drug. Everything else be damned.

Then she was pulling away, breathing heavily, looking into his flushed face. Sadly, everything else could not be damned. She had responsibilities and it was getting late. He smiled at her; his eyes electric. He would be ready to go if she stepped forward.

He ran his hand through his hair and looked toward the sunset. "Beautiful, isn't it?"

"It is. People joke about the Midwest, but if you don't flyover, you get to see some truly breathtaking sights." Her breathing was returning to normal. The rollercoaster was coming into the station.

He smiled, put his hand on her back, this time in a far less sensual way, and they walked to her car together.

"Thank you again for a wonderful night," she said. "I will call you tomorrow to go over your next audition, if that's all right."

"It sounds wonderful. Thank you, as well. You have been a wonderful surprise." He looked back toward the horizon where the sun was no longer visible. A pink hue remained against the darkening sky. Elizabeth saw a look in his eyes she was unable to place. A harder look than she'd seen yet. "I may be up late tonight practicing, so if I don't answer your call, please know that I am probably sleeping in, resting my vocal cords in preparation for that final audition."

"Then, to be safe," she stated as formally as she could, "expect a follow-up call in the afternoon."

He laughed and nodded appreciatively. He softly shut the door and she started the car. Her phone connected to the car with a little *ding*. She remembered she had a voicemail from Jason. She waved a final goodbye and pulled out of the parking spot, aiming her car toward the road. She watched in her rearview mirror as Samuel mounted his bike and put on his helmet. Before she pulled onto the road, she opened her phone, opened her voicemails, and hit play. Jason's voice came flowing out of the car's speakers.

Before she'd made it over the bridge, her fury hit a new high. The rollercoaster had left the station yet again.

Verse 51

Council Bluffs, Iowa

GIDEON continued to read as Samuel continued to sing. Mr. Warren sang along, his eyes staring into nothing, all expression gone. Gideon saw that there had been two fires, separated by about three years. He turned to Samuel who was still singing, sweat beginning to slide down his forehead and cheeks. It would appear that it took some energy to use his ability. Gideon realized, now that he'd pulled back from the memories, that he himself was exhausted and sweating. He'd never gone that deep. He supposed that these abilities were like muscles, and they were both flexing them pretty hard.

"How old are you?" Gideon asked.

Samuel, continuing to pour out the melody, cut a quick confused glance at him, then held up four fingers on his right hand and five on his left, signifying nine.

Okay, so if Gideon did the math right, then both of the fires came shortly after they were born. Dear God, had their mom tried to burn them to death? Is that what he was reading? He wanted to read further, but either the man was somehow blocking it, or, more likely, he had no memory of the events past the headlines. A start and a dead end all in one. He pulled back and returned again to himself.

He turned toward Samuel. "I got some information, but not enough, we need our paperwork."

Without stopping, the song Samuel was singing changed, ever so slightly, and the man turned into his study. The two boys followed. He sang along as merrily as could be as he opened a drawer in his desk, removed a key, turned to a filing cabinet that he then unlocked, and slid out one of the drawers. Still singing, he rifled through the folders and pulled out one, set it on the desk behind him, returned to the cabinet, closed that drawer, opened a second, searched through it until he brought out a second folder, and set it on the first.

"Make him leave," Gideon instructed as Mr. Warren walked toward the desk.

Samuel, clearly getting tired, changed his tune yet again and the man casually walked out of the room, now humming the song.

For a time, Gideon could only hear Samuel singing, then he heard a car start. He went to the window and watched as the man backed his car out of the driveway and drove off down the street. Samuel finally stopped singing and crumpled into a chair in the corner.

"Where is he going?" Gideon asked.

"I convinced him the house was out of food. So, he is off to the grocery store. He may get all the way there. He may not. I don't know. I haven't done anything quite like this." He looked so tired.

Gideon felt for him, but he also realized that meant they were back on the clock, and they needed to hurry. "You did great, Samuel Serenade."

At the mention of his superhero name, Samuel sat straighter, looking exuberant again.

"Let's grab the documents and get out of here before he returns. What do you think?"

Samuel launched out of the chair, fully recovered as only little kids can do. His energy was back and twofold. Gideon smiled, grabbed the documents, and they ran out the office door into the hallway. Samuel made to head downstairs to their rooms, but Gideon put a hand on his shoulder.

"Um, this information might be sensitive. I don't want the others to see it." He was quickly trying to think of the spy movies and books he'd read and how they spoke. This seemed to fit the moment. "We don't want any wandering eyes to see it." Samuel still looked confused, so Gideon gave up and said, "Let's head to the park down the street so that we can look at them without anyone around."

Samuel nodded his agreement, and they went running down the hallway, out the front door, and away from the house.

Verse 52

Omaha, Nebraska

JASON paced back and forth. He shouldn't have left the voicemail. It would have been easier to explain had he been able to talk to her. What had he been thinking? He paced past his phone again. Still no response. What did that mean? Was she mad? Was she coming up with a response or freezing him out? Stacy was out with some friends after work, thank God. This was stressful enough without having to explain to her and having to deal with her being upset that he was upset. He rubbed his temples, trying to expel the headache forming from the tension. He caught his reflection in the microwave. "Shit."

"Shit is right, you motherfucker." The man-in-the-mirror was back and in grand style now.

Jason took back his previous thoughts about Stacy. He would have preferred her over this.

"If you go with her, you will be sealing the deal on El. You know that, right?"

Jason avoided looking at the microwave, hoping it would block out the accusations.

"You can't ignore me. Stacy is hot, though, so at least you can console yourself by fucking her on the trip to visit her sick grandma."

If looking away didn't help, maybe he could block him out by covering his ears.

"Ha ha ha ha ha." The laugh rang through his mind.

Fine, confrontation it was. He turned violently toward the microwave. "Shut the fuck up. I don't need you to tell me how complicated my life is. I'm the one complicating it."

He was angry at everyone. He was angry at Elizabeth for letting the situation get as far out of hand as it did. He was angry at Wyatt for being innocent. He was angry at Stacy for showing him attention he didn't deserve. Mostly, he was angry at himself for being a wife-leaving, child-abandoning piece of shit.

He crumpled into the couch in the living room. The leather made a delightfully new noise that further angered him. He didn't need any of this new stuff.

He thought back to when he and El had moved in together. They'd bought a used couch off the internet. It had been very used, but it had been the first furniture they'd bought together. They'd loved that couch. They'd made love on that couch. He sighed deeply.

He'd fucked on this couch. He stood, disgusted.

There was no going back, no turning around. Yet, for a split second, there had been a better path forward. He'd seen a way out of the trap in which he'd caught himself. It had been so clear.

"You are an idiot," the man-in-the-mirror interjected helpfully. "That plan was never going to work. You were never going to get back with El—izabeth."

Jason turned toward him, on the verge of tears, and saw . . . compassion?

"Look, you fucked up. There is no denying that. But if you had to fuck up, you did it in the right direction. Most men who leave their wives at your age end up living in a basement apartment with only their hand and porn to keep them company. You landed an amazing apartment and a smoking hot girlfriend who is way out of your league. Why are you so upset about landing on top?"

Jason walked around the island to stand face-to-face with the slightly distorted version of himself. He worked on a response that would express his feelings, to adequately explain why none of that mattered. To bring this bastardized version of himself over to his side. To show him that the family he'd left behind was more important than the gains he'd made after.

Instead, he plunged his hand through the protective glass front, which shattered into a million pieces, cutting him in a million places. He pulled back his hand. Blood had already begun bubbling up around some of the deeper cuts.

"How am I going to explain these cuts to Stacy's grandma?" he asked the missing man-in-the-mirror and began to laugh hysterically. He walked toward the bathroom, drops of blood dripping onto the brand-new white carpet.

He didn't notice.

Verse 53

Norton, Kansas

ELIZABETH listened to the voicemail again. She wasn't sure how many times she'd listened to it, but with each listen, her anger grew. Not because of what he said, or what it implied, or anything specifically in this voicemail. She was mad at herself for allowing herself to hope that things would be different.

Despite her better judgment, despite every fiber of her motherhood telling her to protect her son, she'd allowed hope to blind her to the possibility that change was around the corner. She listened to the voicemail again. Hope wasn't a double-edged sword. It was just the blade. It cut you regardless of how you held it.

"Hi El—izabeth. Sorry, um, but I won't be able to pick up Wyatt this upcoming weekend. Stacy's grandma is sick and it's not looking good. Um. Dammit. Look, I swear to God this is not what I wanted. I have been looking forward to this weekend since before I brought it up to you. I swear I will pick another weekend and I will, I don't know, take the two of you to Disneyland or LEGOland or wherever a kid Wyatt's age would want to go. I just feel like I have committed enough to this current relationship that I can't bail on Stacy and her dying grandma. I don't know if she's dying, I guess. Hopefully, she isn't. I don't know. She is sick, like most elderly people probably are, but it must be something different or we wouldn't need to go. Sorry. Please, please call me back. We can

reschedule right away, and I will take care of everything. I lo . . .
Bye." *Click.*

She screamed, not for the first time. She was not sure if
the roller coaster would make it back to the station tonight. Her
fury was becoming a living, breathing thing, taking sustenance
from each listen of the voicemail.

That selfish, sadistic, son of a bitch. Literally any other
excuse would have been fine. But Stacy's grandma? It was the
most cliched get-out-of-work card there was in the deck. Who
would it be next time? Stacy's aunt? Hell, she'd even heard
students use that excuse on multiple occasions. One of her kid's
grandmas must be suffering from chronic dying syndrome for
how often he used it.

She was driving fast, trying to drive away from this
mess in which she'd allowed herself to be placed. She would
have to tell Wyatt. Goddammit, she would have to deal with the
loss of his father all over again.

She'd allowed herself to think everything in her life
could be okay. Jason would be a participating father. Samuel
would be a participating something. Her dad would be a
participating grandpa. There would be participation from all
attendees.

She crested a steep hill and felt her tires lift off the
ground a little. She had decided to slow down when the lights
illuminated a deer in the road.

She yanked the wheel to the side, knowing in the back of
her mind that was the incorrect thing to do, knowing that her
instincts didn't give a fuck. The deer, for its part, decided to
leap out the way, but too little too late. She felt the side of the
car make heavy contact. She heard glass break, and a thick,
meaty, snapping sound. She veered to the side as she slammed
on the brakes. Finally, her car came to a stop.

Her heart was pumping a million miles per hour as her body dumped adrenaline into her bloodstream. Her eyes took on a new focus as every detail and color stood out in high definition. She heard sounds on a new level: the creaking of metal bent into a new shape, some mechanical sound that had not been there before, and the sound of a living creature in severe agony.

She got out of her car, taking a moment to steady her feet. Her body felt like ants were crawling under her skin and, at the same time, as if it were shutting down. The adrenaline was starting to run down, and her body was unsure of what to do with that information.

She crossed in front of her car and saw that her passenger headlight had been shattered. "Shit." There was a splash of blood near the jagged hole, and she saw that a bit of her bumper had crumpled in. That would cost a pretty penny, she mused, as she continued her progress around the car. There was a smear of blood that went up on to the hood and down the side.

Then her eyes fell on the body of the deer lying on the side of the road. It swelled with each panicked breath. She saw its rear leg, bent grotesquely to the side with a jagged piece of bone tearing through its hide. The useless leg lay in a puddle of its own blood.

Without warning, anger swelled into Elizabeth. "Good!" she shrieked. She watched as the deer tried to pull itself away from what it perceived to be a new threat. Some deep inner voice was compelling her to march over to this thing that had further complicated her life and stomp on its skull. To end this pitiful life. It would be a mercy, wouldn't it? Isn't that what you were supposed to do when there is no hope? To kill swiftly?

The deer made a low, squeaking sound, like one of those stuffed animals that you squeeze, and her perspective changed yet again. The rollercoaster had slowed down, at least a little. She had a vague understanding that yes, this poor creature's only fault had been trying to live in a world that had been slowly taken away from it. Each new road was less world to walk in.

She looked at the poor thing, trying and failing to get away from her. She reflected on her previous thoughts: Isn't that what you were supposed to do when there is no hope? To kill swiftly? The deer had laid its head on the ground, too exhausted to struggle any more. It had accepted that whatever Elizabeth had planned for it would happen.

For a moment, she saw the deer as a metaphor. When there was no hope, what was to be done? She turned and walked around the front of the car again, taking cautions to not look at the blood steaming on the hot hood. She pulled herself into the front seat and dialed 911. Isn't that what you were supposed to do when there is no hope? To kill swiftly?

"911. What is your emergency?"

Verse 54

Alma, Nebraska

A computer sat open in a hotel room in Alma, Nebraska. The door to that hotel room clicked shut. A motorcycle started outside the room, and the engine faded as it moved away. On the screen of the computer were two browser windows left open.

The first was an article from *The Norton Telegram*. It was in regard to a drunk driving accident that had taken the life of a woman as she'd crossed an intersection on her way back from the grocery store.

The second was a Facebook page. The latest post stating "Join us tonight at the First Methodist Church of Norton in the basement for Alcoholics Anonymous. 7–8 p.m. If you are ready to change, we are ready to assist in that change. It is possible, with help."

Verse 55

Council Bluffs, Iowa

GIDEON and Samuel walked down the street toward a park the kids often went to when the weather allowed it. Today was one of those days. However, with everything going on with Andy, Gideon felt safe in assuming no one would be allowed to leave the foster home. Well, aside from the two of them. He held the two folders tightly, working out how he would break the news to Samuel that they were brothers.

When they'd first left the house, Samuel had peppered Gideon with questions about what he'd seen in the man's mind, eager for any information regarding his past. Gideon had carefully sidestepped the questions, explaining that he wanted to look at the files before he said anything, and that they shouldn't do that until they were safely away from the house. Samuel had persisted a little after that, but upon seeing Gideon's resolve, had given up.

Samuel hummed a little song as they walked, and Gideon could feel little tendrils of energy radiating from Samuel, despite the fact he didn't appear to be actively using his ability. For that matter, he realized that if Samuel had wanted to make Gideon tell him what he'd seen or to hand over the documents at any point, Gideon would have been powerless to stop him. Would he see it coming? Samuel would at least have to think about doing it before he started, wouldn't he? That gave Gideon a small advantage. He tucked that information away in the back of his mind, labeling it Kryptonite.

"So, after we find out where we come from, what do we do then?" Samuel asked the question Gideon had been struggling with since they'd left the house.

What were they supposed to do with that information? Go see their mom? He'd not glimpsed anything about their dad. Maybe they didn't share the same dad and they were half-brothers. There were too many questions and no real answers yet to formulate a plan.

He shrugged at Samuel. "Let's see what is in our documents first, and we can go from there, all right?"

They walked in silence for a little while. Well, relative silence. Gideon got to listen to Samuel's humming, and his thoughts. He was again surprised to find that, although they'd walked away from their foster house with the use of superhuman powers, his were still the thoughts of a child. It was like a slideshow of cartoons, commercials, and comic books with flashes of concern over their future mixed in.

In short, Samuel's thoughts were exhausting.

Gideon focused on closing his mind to the inflow of thoughts and managed to dull the constantly running video montage. He needed to think.

Should he feign ignorance and act surprised when he opened the folders, or should he tell Samuel beforehand to prepare him? He looked at his little brother and all those thoughts disappeared. This boy was his own blood. He had a feeling they were going to be in each other's lives for the foreseeable future. Starting off with a lie felt wrong.

When they reached the park, Gideon led Samuel to one of the benches and set the folders between them as they sat.

Samuel reached for them, but Gideon put his hand on top, holding them shut. Those blue eyes rolled to question him.

Gideon swallowed hard before saying, "Samuel, there is something you should know before we open these. Something I am pretty sure I read from that guy's mind."

The confused look remained, but Samuel waited patiently.

"Look, I'm not sure how to tell you this, but, um." He stopped, looking out toward the playground where a boy and a girl who were clearly siblings chased each other around the plastic castle rising from the sandy moat. Gideon smiled, finding strength in their joy at being together. "You and I are brothers."

Once it was out, Gideon felt a plethora of emotions: relief that the secret was out; fear that Samuel would be mad at him for waiting to tell him; most of all, and most unexpectedly, a tremendous wave of love for the boy. This kid in front of him was his brother, and the implications of that fell on him like an anvil. He loved this boy and would fight to the death for him, if it came to it.

Samuel, for his part, had nothing to say. His mouth hung open; his eyes wide. He was unable to articulate his own whirling thoughts, but Gideon didn't need him to. He was watching them tangle together and try to untangle right in front of him. He hopped down from where he'd perched on the bench, walked around to Samuel, and hugged him hard like a brother would. Samuel immediately melted into him and began to cry.

Gideon held his brother. And now that they were together, he was never going to let him go.

Verse 56

Norton, Kansas

AFTER telling the local sheriff's department about the deer, Elizabeth called her dad, then continued her trek home.

Her anger had been swallowed up in the exhaustion that followed her body's response to high levels of stress. The adrenaline that had flowed through her body now dissipated, leaving her drained.

She didn't want to talk to Jason. She didn't want to think about Jason. She wanted to get to her dad's house, see her son, hear about his day at the farm, pour a glass of wine, and slip into a bath that was too small to be perfectly comfortable, but would get the job done if she made a point to move every few minutes to submerge a different limb.

She kept seeing the deer's face as it looked at her, terrified. She kept remembering how she'd wanted to kill it quickly because there was no hope and therefore no reason to let it live in misery. The police officer she'd spoken to all but confirmed they were going to send an officer out to do just that.

She pondered the idea that something that has no hope of survival should be put down quickly. That it was merciful to do that rather than to allow something to live in constant pain. The thought kept replaying in her mind. Hadn't she been thinking of how all hope for a new fatherly Jason was lost? That she was never going to allow herself to be fooled into hoping things would change again? In light of what had happened to her, she wondered whether maybe it was time to do that. To give up on hope and end things a little more permanently. To kill this relationship quickly to make sure they didn't continue to suffer.

Jason clearly was not willing to commit to anything. Any thought he had of reigniting some father-son relationship was unattainable as long as that bitch was around. She could almost see the events playing out in her mind: Jason telling Stacy that he wanted to see his son; Stacy not loving the idea; Jason, for once, pushing back; Stacy half-heartedly agreeing, only to come up with some story about her poor, sick grandma, conveniently dying the weekend that Jason had been planning to see Wyatt. Stacy batting those long, fake lashes, begging him to not leave her in her time of need. Oh, how was she to survive this traumatic experience without his big strong arms around her?

Elizabeth realized again that she was speeding, falling back into the mindset that had led to her little wreck. She took a deep breath and slowed down.

Another set of events played out in her mind: The deer continuing its lamenting cries as it tried unsuccessfully to pull itself away from that hellish concrete. Its dark mass splashed first with red light, then blue, then red again; a shadow in the ever-changing light, first huge, falling on the doomed animal, shrinking with each click of boot on road. The officer coming to a stop, towering over the deer like some god prepared to dole out heavenly justice, as he pulls iron from leather, sliding his sidearm from its clutch, cocking it with one motion. The deer looking up into the black hole that has become its whole world before the sun rises from that hole, bringing with it an eternal night.

In that flash, in that eternity, Elizabeth recognizes the deer's eyes. They are Jason's eyes, and they are filled with fear and understanding.

Elizabeth screamed again the same sentiment she'd originally felt toward the deer: "Good!" She took a deep breath, ears ringing from her unexpected exhalation. Then, softer, her throat sore, she said, "That is what you are supposed to do when there is no hope. Kill quickly to end its suffering."

Elizabeth drove on, still engrossed in her thoughts. Had her mind been a little less occupied, she may have noticed the lone headlight behind her: a motorcycle's headlight, following her path to Norton.

Verse 57

Omaha, Nebraska

THINGS were not good in Stacy's apartment that night.

For starters, their microwave was destroyed. Jason had explained that he'd slipped and ran his hand through the glass while trying to catch himself. Then there were the blood stains on the new carpet, installed before they moved in. He argued that the medical supplies, the few they had, were all stored in their closet in their bedroom and maybe, moving forward, they should at least have a few in the kitchen for such an emergency. However, all of this paled to his apparent anxiety over Elizabeth's impending call.

Stacy's fists were white, the blood flow cut off by the increased pressure she was asserting to keep them down at her side. "My grandmother is dying. This might be the last chance I get to see her, so your ex-wife's opinion, as far as I am concerned, means less than the random hobo's outside our building. At least he might have some empathy."

Jason had tried to explain the shaky ground he was on, infuriatingly painting Elizabeth as an innocent bystander rather than the evil witch that was trying to keep Stacy from visiting her dying grandmother. Like pressure in a shaken soda, her anger continued to grow with every statement Jason made that was not a simple agreement.

She was baffled that there was pushback. Her fucking *grandmother* was dying. Hell, he would have the rest of his life to reconnect with his son. Her grandmother was *dying*. The rest of her life could be a week. "I bet you secretly hope my Nanna dies before this weekend so you can reinstate your plans with your son and his mother." It was a verbal slap, which she considered fair play as she was trying hard to not physically slap him as well. It had a similar effect, though, as he recoiled as if struck.

"You know that isn't true," he said under his breath.

What the hell had she been thinking getting involved with a married man, with a kid, nonetheless? Had she not anticipated this? But the attention he'd shown her at work, when most men only had eyes for their kids and their wives, meant something. She was important enough to cause his eyes to wander from what should have been the most important things in his life. That meant she was more important to him than the most important things in his life. That feeling had propelled their relationship until now. What had happened? Distance makes the heart grow fonder, they say, but doesn't there need to be fondness there to begin with?

She looked at the microwave, the fist-sized hole with spiderwebbed cracks racing away from it. It looked like an accusing eye staring at her, compelling her to question his story, and possibly their entire relationship. She took a deep breath. She needed to focus on something else for a moment to clear her mind.

She fell into nurse mode easily enough as she took his hand, still wrapped in a towel. A white towel. Deep breath. She peeled it away and saw that there were only a few cuts on his hand. Of those, only one looked remotely deep. She took him into their bedroom, into the bathroom, and began to tend to the wounds. They were silent, neither willing to break this momentary reprieve to the current fight. Using hydrogen peroxide, she cleaned out all the cuts, relishing as he sucked in air between his clenched teeth. Then she bandaged a couple of the cuts on his fingers and put a small gauze strip, taped down with medical tape, across the top of his hand. She noticed how the knuckle around his middle finger was already turning dark and wondered if any of the myriad of little bones in his hand had broken.

"Tomorrow, you may want to go into a clinic or something and look into getting an X-ray to be sure nothing is broken." The words came out with a clinical, emotionless tone. Like a robot, designed to sound human, that didn't quite meet the function perfectly.

He looked at her, eyes moist with barely held back tears, and she had a moment of softening where her resolve broke a little. He'd been a married man and was still a father. He was doing his best to still be a father. Should she be so mad at him for that? He'd chosen her, after all.

Yet, she couldn't get over that sense of jealousy; that sense that this weekend had been about more than reconnecting with his son. That, in fact, it had involved, at least to a small degree, some reconnection with his ex-wife.

Her resolve hardened yet again. "I think tonight I will stay at Nancy's house. I think you need some time to think and be alone." She watched as his eyes darted toward the mirror. When they returned, she thought she saw fear there. She shook it off. She needed to keep that resolve hardened if she were going to make it out the door. "Also, if your ex calls, I don't think I want to be anywhere near it or things might change." She took a deep breath. "For good."

She stood, stepped around him, and left him alone in the bathroom.

As Stacy gathered her things on their bed, Jason's phone began to ring in the kitchen. The sound echoed throughout the apartment, tearing through the silence that had fallen. Possibly, tearing through their relationship as well.

Verse 58

Council Bluffs, Iowa

GIDEON sat in a bar. He was tired. He'd not been sleeping well and had decided that a drink might do the trick. Maybe a few drinks.

He was on his fifth Rum and Coke, enjoying the buzzing blend of alcohol and caffeine. He knew he would dream of his past again that night as he always did when he was separated from Samuel for too long. Whenever the trail was cold, and his mind had no other pertinent memories gleaned from those around him to distract him, his dreams turned toward his and Samuel's origin story. Their origin story, like real-life super people. He mused on the fact that he could no longer think of the two of them as superheroes. He wasn't sure what to call them.

He finished his drink. The lack of sleep feeding into the alcohol made him feel drunker than he was. He stumbled on his way to the bar, ordered two more to take back to his seat, and closed the tab before it was closed for him. The bartender, a cute, young thing, obliged. She made eye contact with him. His glasses magnified the dark circles that had taken root around his eyes, giving his pale face a skeletal appearance. She smiled and he smiled back, showing all of his teeth to clench the skull look. He returned to his seat as she returned to the customers closer to her who were presumably less terrifying.

God, he was only thirty-seven. Why did he feel like he was sixty? He needed one good night's sleep. One night of actual rest would lighten those circles and he would look like a living, breathing human once again. However, there was little chance of a dreamless night for him, and he knew it. He had a better chance of wooing the bartender while looking like a Halloween decoration than avoiding his childhood. He considered reading the room to find something good enough to distract him from tonight's foray into memory, but, as always, he was scared he would see something. Something worth judgment.

Before, he'd always had Samuel to take that burden. But Gideon didn't have the resolve that Samuel did. If he were to read this room and dig deeper than the trivial thoughts floating around him, he may stumble into something dark, something deserving of death.

The man at the bar chatting up the cute, young bartender might be a serial rapist. If Gideon found that out, what was he supposed to do with that information? He couldn't call the cops, claiming he'd read the man's mind nor could he confront the man as he was shit in a fight and couldn't finish the job even if he were able. That would leave him to live in the memories while knowing that he'd let the man go, possibly to rape the cute, young bartender he was chatting up this very minute.

No, it was safer in his own memories, as terrifying as they were.

He quickly downed his two drinks, one following the other, and stood to leave.

As he made his way toward the door, he had one last look at the cute, young thing behind the bar, now fully engaged in conversation with the man. Gideon clearly heard her think, *He's cute.* He paused for only a moment, then walked into the warm night, hoping that the man at the bar wasn't a serial rapist.

He threw up a block away from his hotel room. Then, to really clear out his system, he threw up two more times once he was safely behind his locked door. Great. Not only would he have to worry about his dreams tonight, but he would also have a hangover to deal with tomorrow.

He dry-heaved, phlegm clinging to his lips and nose like a wet spiderweb from his face to the water below. He wiped it away, stood, and washed his arms and face in the faucet.

Shit. Should he tape his mouth tonight? He had a vision of himself waking up in the middle of the night needing to vomit, unable to get the tape off in time. Would he drown? He decided that his hotel neighbors might have to deal with whatever new horrors this night brought. They were already surely front-row participants to the sound effect arena of the vomitorium he was setting up with his handy little trash can.

He stripped off his shirt and threw it in the growing pile, making a mental note to do laundry tomorrow. The alcohol continued to tip his brain as he laid his head onto the pillow. The room felt like it was on the sea, rising and falling with each cresting wave. He felt seasick, but managed to keep whatever was left in his stomach from making a return visit. He closed his eyes. He could all but hear the waves lapping at his bed and smell the foamy, salty air, taking him further and further away from land, and further and further into his past.

Verse 59

Alma, Nebraska

SALLY lay awake in her bed staring at the ceiling. She kept going over the events of the night like a record with a scratch.

She'd gone to the bar to get her check, but she knew all along that was not the main reason she went. She'd hoped she would run into Samuel.

Her life was confusing, to say the least. Life-altering events had hit her left, then right. This marked the first death of someone close. Along with that, it was the first time she was without work since high school. She was an unemployed, widowed, single mother. How cliché. One would think that these thoughts would be all-encompassing, yet, cutting through everything were two blue eyes, holding her attention.

Until this evening, they'd been an irritating daydream that she couldn't shake, but seeing him with another woman had shaken her. Then, their meeting in the kitchen had downright haunted her. That scene was the one that played on repeat, his blue eyes penetrating her soul as he said, "I think maybe you and Boomer should leave town."

It felt like an ominous warning rather than advice. Maybe even a threat. How many movies had she seen where that line precluded the final shootout, or the missile strike, or a giant monster spewing fire from its throat? Never did those words preclude something good.

Then her mind would slip onto a different track, based on his next line: "There is nothing for you here any longer."

Was Samuel telling her that he'd moved on and didn't want her to see him with that other woman? Maybe he was afraid she would complicate the new relationship he found himself in after his attempts at the bartender failed. Dammit. His attempts wouldn't have failed if it weren't for her piece-of-shit ex-husband painting his oh, so special mancave with his brains. Now, not only did she have a son in her life again; she had a son who'd walked in on his father missing most of his head.

The psychiatrist at the hospital had gotten Boomer to talk about it, thinking it would help him get past it. But when Boomer started talking about the recently exposed muscles of Jack's throat still flexing in an attempt to sing, the psychiatrist had mercifully ended that part of the interview.

The singing part perplexed Sally as she'd so rarely heard Jack sing. Only when he was really drunk. Even then, it had to be at a party, or at a bar, or somewhere the music was turned up so loud, it was as if he wasn't singing at all, only mouthing the words.

She rolled over and looked at the clock on the nightstand. Boomer squirmed next to her. He'd spent every night in her bed. Like vampires, they fed off each other's grief at night, but rarely communicated during the day. A shy boy by nature, he'd always found it hard to talk to her, hesitantly asking for things as if he were afraid. Before, that had been something she overlooked. Now, however, it was heartbreaking. He'd lost his dad who, despite his failings, had loved Boomer and had been loved by Boomer. Then, he'd been placed with someone who was little more than a stranger to him. Yes, they'd spent time together—going to movies, parks, or any other distracting activity she could think up—but rarely had they spent time together in an intimate way. She'd been more like his fun aunt than his mom, and she had liked it that way. Hell, as far as she could tell, he'd liked it that way. Now they were both relearning their roles in each other's lives under the worst circumstances.

She thought about Jack's house; the house they had at one point shared, before she moved out. Boomer's room was there along with his belongings, waiting for their owner to return. Right now, she wasn't even sure about the owner of the house. Jack had not left a will. He had not even left a suicide note. So, did the house and everything else he owned go to her? Did Boomer, at his very young age, get everything as next of kin? A lawyer was parsing that all out for her, wanting to make sure that his other family didn't lay claim to any of it because of the ambiguity of the situation. She could care less about the house or anything in it, aside from the monetary value she could get from selling it all. The few guns she'd already sold fell through a legal crack as she'd been the one who purchased them. There were guns he had purchased himself—mostly after their split when he was forced to use his own money—that were still off limits to her. But that could wait.

Money would be an issue soon enough. For now, there were far more pressing issues. Like Samuel.

She rolled back onto her back to stare at her ceiling fan, rotating lazily in the dark. What if she did leave town? Where would she go? She had a sister who lived in a town in Iowa with some Spanish-sounding name. Amanda had, in fact, called her yesterday asking what she could do to help. Assumedly, she'd not meant taking the recently outcast family into her house.

"There is nothing for you here any longer."

She felt a surge of anger, burning through her as if she'd downed a fifth of whiskey. She relished in the feeling, letting it burn in her chest. How dare he presume to know anything about her life outside of that bar? He who'd breezed into town, flirtatious from the start, only to dump her for someone with less drama? How dare he tell her what she did or did not have here?

She sat up, suddenly needing to move, adrenaline pouring into her veins. She wasn't sure what she would do. Run a mile? Break something? Stand on her roof to scream at the sky? All of those felt like legitimate options at the moment.

She stood, moving to put on a shirt before realizing she was already wearing one. Another change that came with living with her son.

Her son.

The thought stopped her, and she felt all the adrenaline slide through her veins, into her lungs. She exhaled it out, suddenly feeling exhausted to her very bones. She would do none of those things because Boomer was sleeping, and she was responsible for him. She sat back on the bed, put her face into her hands, and began to cry.

Fuck Samuel and his tidings of doom. But, mostly, fuck him for being right.

Verse 60

Norton, Kansas

RANDALL sat at the back of the small room in the church basement and sipped his cooling coffee. Sobriety had been hard for him, but he was trying. He'd be damned, if he weren't. He'd successfully stayed away from any semblance of alcohol since the accident.

Pictures flashed in his mind. Not memories of the night, because he had no memories from that night, only empty time. No, these pictures had been placed in front of him on a metal table by a police officer. They were pictures of a crime scene. His crime scene. Tears, always so close these days, welled around the corners of his eyes, and he hastily wiped them away.

He looked at the woman at the front of the room, clearing his mind to listen to her story of woe. Every story here was one of woe. Even the good stories, about steps forward and family forgiveness, were set against a backdrop of woe. A woeful life was what he deserved, though. Hell, he didn't deserve any life, let alone a woeful one. He sipped his coffee to keep from sighing deeply.

The meeting was coming to an end with only a couple of people left to speak. He'd already given his updates for the evening, proud of his continued sobriety and still haunted by past mistakes. Mark those two off the AA bingo card. He stared into his coffee and stifled a little laugh. He should write up an

AA bingo card. That would make the meetings a little more interesting at least.

The truth of it all was that he didn't need the meetings because those pictures on the metal table were enough to keep him from the bars. He would never drink another drop in his life, knowing that each time he considered alcohol, he saw red, like spilled paint, dripping down the hood of a car. He shuddered.

He noticed that the woman had been replaced by a balding, middle-aged man, whose name was probably not John. Randall settled back into his chair, already writing up squares for his bingo game.

A teenager in the row in front of him turned to look at him, annoyance showing on his pimple-speckled face. The woman a couple of seats down from the boy turned and gave him an angry look. What the hell?

Then he heard it: a little song, a little more than a hum, tickling his ears. Reflexively, he turned to his right, then to his left, unsure from where it was coming. The woman rolled her eyes at this display and returned her focus to Not John, but the teenager continued to stare daggers at him, clearly hoping his look would have an effect. Randall gave him a bewildered look, hoping to convey his own confusion.

Then he realized the song was coming from his own lips. He, himself, was softly singing a wordless tune.

Upon realizing this, he allowed it to take hold of him. It was beautiful. Something this beautiful should not be coming from him. He did not make anything beautiful; he was far better at destroying beautiful things.

He stood and nodded slightly to the teenager who finally turned to face the front again. Randall, on the other hand, made his way toward the back, the song wrapping around every strand of his DNA, leading him out the door.

He was in ecstasy. The song was better than any alcoholic high he'd ever experienced. He danced up the stairs to the foyer, the song growing in pitch and intensity as he went. The church had amazing acoustics and he relished in the sound, no longer caring about the meeting he was surely disrupting.

He kicked open the front door, stepped into the summer night, threw open his arms, and began to sing at the top of his lungs, spinning like a princess in an animated kids' movie. He skipped to his truck, slid behind the wheel, threw an elbow out the already open window, turned the key, and drove away from the church, leaving the meeting and the bewildered members behind.

Entwined with the song flowing from the truck was the sound of a motorcycle, keeping pace with both the speed of the truck and the flow of the music. Together, they made their way out of the town, warming the hearts of those they passed with the interlude on their way to the finale.

Verse 61

Council Bluffs, Iowa

GIDEON and Samuel decided to open one folder at a time and look at the files together to make sure nothing was missed. They started with Gideon's folder as he was the oldest.

Gideon undid the clasp on the envelope and pulled out the files, holding them out so they could view them together. He held tightly, scared to lay them on the table in case a gust of wind came and carried off an important document.

There were many documents, including notes on previous housing, medical records, and, most importantly, a copy of his birth certificate that included his mother's name. He noted that all the spots where his father's information would be filled in were left blank. His mother's name, however, was plain as day: Roberta Charles.

As he shuffled the papers around, a clipped-out newspaper article slid from between the papers onto his lap. He returned the other papers to the envelope for safekeeping and handed both envelopes to Samuel to hold, then turned his attention to the newspaper clipping that had two pieces stapled together. It would appear the story had begun on one page of the newspaper and continued to another page. He cleared his throat and read aloud for Samuel's sake.

"House fire nearly claims the lives of Roberta Charles and her one-year-old son, Gideon Charles."

He stopped. Hearing his name paired with his mother's hit him deeper than he'd expected. Samuel perked up, hearing his own last name, and Gideon realized they'd not discussed last names and he hadn't considered reading a last name from his new friend. How had that not come up when they were coming up with new last names?

Maybe it had something to do with connection to family. When that connection didn't exist, the ties to it didn't matter as much. Gideon had never thought of himself as Gideon Charles, but, rather, just Gideon, and, from now on, Gideon Glimpse. He felt a momentary pain, realizing that he and Samuel were brothers who shared the same last name but had decided on having two separate last names. That was something to ponder after all of this was worked out. Right now, he needed to focus on what was right in front of him.

Gideon continued to read:

"At 3 a.m., emergency services were called to the house on 1590 West Birch St. by a neighbor who'd been awakened by their dog's barking. Upon looking out the window and seeing the smoke, Gretchen Hendrickson dialed 911 immediately.

"'At the time in the morning, I was afraid that Miss Charles and her child might very well be sleeping through the fire,' Mrs. Hendrickson said.

"Emergency personnel were on the scene within fifteen minutes and took control of the situation. They were able to find both Roberta Charles and her son, Gideon, who'd taken refuge in the nursery.

"Roberta Charles suffered no injuries, while the one-year-old boy had significant burns. They were both taken to the hospital but are otherwise stable."

Gideon handed the paper to Samuel absentmindedly. He lifted his shirt to look at a scar that had stretched through the years and softened in color but was still quite visible. Many nights, as he fell asleep, he would place his hand on it, placing his finger on each of the five lines that spread out away from the larger middle scar. The scar stood out clearly in the morning light, and Samuel's eyes grew large as he saw the unmistakable shape of a handprint.

"I think we need to read your report now," Gideon said as he lowered his shirt over the scar. Samuel said nothing, but nodded seriously as Gideon replaced the newspaper article in the open folder and closed the metal clasps. He shifted the folders so that Samuel's was on top, undid the metal clasp, and reached inside, both nervous and excited about what they would discover next.

Verse 62

Norton, Kansas

RANDALL'S truck cruised along the highway west of Norton. The radio was off, but music flowed from the cab. Randall felt better than he had since he was eighteen at the first party beer had been available.

He remembered thinking beer was revolting, wondering why anyone would drink something that tasted so terrible. Later that night, four bottles in, he decided he'd been too hasty. Eight bottles in, he wondered how anyone could not enjoy beer. Twelve bottles in, he didn't wonder much of anything.

His life had taken a radical shift at that party. No, he had not become a raging alcoholic, never to be sober again, but he'd opened the door to it. Instead of politely declining party invites that might involve drinking like he had previously, he started to seek out the parties. If a party wasn't scheduled for a certain weekend, he made a point to schedule one. All that had been while he was in high school. After walking the stage, what little restraint he'd held over graduating was gone, and he was free to do whatever he wanted. He found that what he wanted was to keep drinking.

What had originally been a social event, something done to loosen up around friends, became a private event. It was shockingly easy to get booze in a town like Norton. The only thing holding him back from being a fully-fledged alcoholic at the ripe young age of eighteen was money. The two were always at odds with each other as he tried hard to hold down a job while trying harder to chase the buzz. He continued walking that fine line of finding and losing work while earning enough to keep a healthy supply at home. His parents, unwilling to curse their child to homelessness but also unwilling to watch his complete degradation, had allowed him to live in their basement for free, but they tried hard to have nothing to do with him aside from that. That was perfectly fine with Randall as he didn't need their constant nagging and disapproval in his life.

As the years dragged ever onward, Randall moved from job to job, always finding one reason or another to move on. His reason for moving on to another job was usually because the current job told him to go. Being a functioning alcoholic was tricky as you had to maintain a certain level of sobriety to get through your days, despite the heavy drinking at night. Often, he was unable to maintain a level of sobriety, either showing up to work still drunk or battling a hangover. Most employers frowned upon either and would show him the door. He'd graduated to straight vodka with the understanding that you got more of a buzz for your money. This was his life, and he'd come to terms with it relatively easily. He saw no escape and, therefore, chose to not look for one.

That was until the accident. Everything had changed after the accident.

That was sort of ironic as he barely remembered the accident aside from flashes of images like those strobing fireworks. It was the most important night of his life, and he couldn't remember more than five minutes of it.

Randall turned off the highway, past the sign for Prairie Dog State Park, headed to the lake, smiling and singing despite the content of his memories.

While he may not have remembered the night of the accident clearly, the following days were burned into his memory like a brand. Memories of being in jail. Of cops treating him as if he weren't human. Memories of pictures being shoved under his nose. Shaking with the effects of withdrawal as horrific pictures were spread out like playing cards: pictures of two mangled vehicles. One of a car, bright red splashed all down the hood in front of a shattered windshield. The other of a truck, despite its front being irreparably damaged, the rest of it, including the windshield, looking relatively okay. He'd instantly recognized the truck as his own.

His shakes had kicked up a notch and his stomach had clenched. Without warning, he'd turned toward the man calling himself his defense, and ejected everything that had found a way to stay in his stomach from the night before. It had not been a lot, but it doesn't take much vomit in a small room like that to make it uninhabitable. His appointed defense attorney had just stared at him, yellow streams of bile dripping from his face onto what Randall assumed was an expensive suit. He mumbled an apology as he turned, shakes gone for the moment, to lay his head down on the metal table, on the pictures, and cry. They left him in the stench of his own vomit as he wept.

He remembered those memories vividly.

Randall had spent about a week in jail before being released. He had to appear in court, to sit next to the man he'd spewed regret all over, who, despite a rocky beginning, somehow kept him from going to prison. Randall spent much of that time coming to terms with true sobriety. He'd been cut off cold turkey and had dealt hard with the consequences. He'd spent that first month—yes, an entire month—in pure misery as withdrawal raked through him. When that ebbed away, there came a pure, almost unbearable need to drink alcohol; not to keep the high, but to return to what had become normal life. Randall didn't know how to be a sober person anymore, and that scared him more than anything else.

By court demand, he had to attend AA meetings basically every day. At first, he hated them and hated the people attending them. They could, if they wanted, go grab a beer on their way home. What the fuck did they have to complain about when they were free to drink whatever and whenever they wanted? His hatred of their freedom kept his ears closed to them as he sat in the back, absorbed in his own self-pity and anger. While the court forced him to go, it did not stipulate that he had to share. So, meeting after meeting, he sat in the back, brooding over just how unfair his life had become. Could he honestly be blamed for how things went down? Sure, he'd driven into her lane and, sure, he'd been drunk, but she'd been the one who neglected her seatbelt, after all.

With each meeting, however, and the continued sobriety, a shift began to take place in his understanding of blame. He began to take ownership of the mistakes he'd made in his life. His alcoholism wasn't his high school friends' fault nor was his nearly continuous unemployment the fault of his employers.

He began sharing. His story was not much different from those around him. The others showed him compassion and understanding that he did not feel he deserved, but that he accepted gratefully.

A rebuilding was taking place within him, and, like many construction projects, the initial phase was a teardown of what had come before. His old life was dismantled with each meeting until it was stripped clean. Then, with each meeting from that point on, a new structure started to take shape. He landed a job at a local restaurant that he was able to hold onto by showing up to work on time and for every shift. He worked hard and found that he liked the work and the people with whom he worked.

At the meetings, he'd become well known, taking more of a leadership role and even sponsoring a few people.

There were dark times. When he was alone at night, he would think to himself how fortunate he was that the accident had happened at all. Without that event as a catalyst, his life would have continued as it was until a different accident claimed his life. He often wondered, if the tables had been turned, how many people would have attended his funeral? Then he would see that splash of red on the car in the picture, realize what a terrible thought that was, and say a prayer requesting forgiveness to the higher power of his choice.

He turned off the main road that led to the camping grounds and to a dirt road well known to the fishermen of Norton. It led to a free area of the lake where you could fish without needing a park pass. During the day, especially this time of year, it was packed with men on their days off, killing time away from the family, drinking beer while watching their lines, content to catch nothing, happy to be out fishing. At this time of night, there would be no one around; only Randall and whomever was following him on the motorcycle. Oh, and there would definitely not be any beer.

He sang louder, throwing his head back, drowning out the sound of the motorcycle behind his truck as it handled the bumpy dirt road with ease. They continued to the lake.

Verse 63

Norton, Kansas

HAROLD and Wyatt sat at the dining room table; their playing cards forgotten as they listened to one side of a very heated discussion taking place in the living room.

Multiple times, Harold had the feeling that the best thing he could do for Wyatt would be to take him out of this house. Maybe for a walk or for ice cream. Anywhere other than sitting here as his parents severed their last remaining ties to each other. Harold thought back over the years of fatherhood. He could only think of two times prior to this that Elizabeth had been extremely angry, and neither of them compared to this.

The first time was when her first boyfriend broke up with her for one of her friends she'd considered second only to Rebecca. He tried to remember the friend's name, but, seeing as she never came to the house again after that, she'd faded from his memory.

The second, and most recent, was when they'd found out that the man who'd taken Judy from them had been released. That last one was probably the most comparable to this moment. But even it didn't have the venom this attack did.

He looked at Wyatt whose eyes were glued to the archway that led into the living room. Every once in a while, Elizabeth would flit into sight, usually slashing with her free hand with deadly force. Then she would turn on her heel,

precise as a soldier, and pace back out of sight, keeping up a
continuous string of threats, curses, accusations, and promises.

Harold looked again at Wyatt and saw a statue of a little
boy. His skin, despite the summer sun it had been absorbing in
great quantity, looked pale as carved stone. His expression was
blank, not letting a single emotion leak out.

Harold weighed his options for a little bit, then stood.
"Come on. Let's go get some more ice cream."

Wyatt didn't turn to look at him. Instead, he kept his
eyes glued to the little bit of the living room he could see. "No
thanks" was all Wyatt said as Elizabeth strode back into view,
eyes blazing, seeing nothing around her, completely oblivious
of the potential damage she was doing to the little statue in the
kitchen who was absorbing all the negativity aimed at his
father. His eyes were glossy, probably as unaware of his mother
ripping at the air in front of him as she was of him.

Harold walked around the table and placed his hand on
Wyatt's shoulder. Wyatt jumped in surprise as he was yanked
from the flood of negativity in which he'd been drowning.

"I desperately need ice cream. Think you could help me
with that?"

Wyatt turned from him to look back toward the living
room. His mother was now back behind the wall, but still just as
audible. He turned back to his grandpa and Harold could see
the tears that had been held back by sheer force of will.

"Come on," Harold said again, compassionately.

Wyatt stood and allowed his grandpa to lead him out
the back door, choosing to go around the house outside rather
than to use the front door, which stood on the other side of the
living room.

When they were safely in Harold's truck, Wyatt's force of will broke and he began to weep. Harold said nothing, pulled out of the driveway, turned the wheel, and left Elizabeth to stew in her hatred alone. He decided he would bring her ice cream too. She would probably need it as much as Wyatt by the time she was off the phone.

Verse 64

Omaha, Nebraska

JASON sat on his bed and absorbed everything. There were two women in his life and, at this moment, both hated him.

His phone call with Elizabeth had been like talking to the radio when the musician took breaths: pointless.

Matters were made worse as Stacy had been in and out of the room as he tried desperately to get one cent into the conversation, let alone two. She was only able to hear his side of the conversation, which came off sounding extremely apologetic and regretful with regard to her dying grandmother. Clearly, she did not take that well. By the time he was off the phone, reeling from shock after receiving a healthy dose of hatred injected into his ear, Stacy's bags were packed. She'd not just packed an overnight bag either, signifying that her stay at Nancy's might be a little longer than a night.

Then, mere minutes from ending his phone call with Elizabeth, another dose of hatred and accusation were fed directly into his bloodstream from Stacy. How dare he value time with his ex-wife over supporting her in a time of emotional need? She was now questioning how invested he was in this relationship and whether there was a future past the end of the week. There had been more words, more accusations, some names, and a promise or two thrown in for good measure before she, her bags, and possibly their future walked out the door, slamming shut behind her.

He'd stood looking at the door for a long time. His mind seemingly shut down, not knowing if he should go after her, make a drink, or call Elizabeth.

Was the weekend trip to see the grandma off? What did that mean in his life?

He thought back to his daydream about Elizabeth and their reconnection, realizing now that he had to let that go. Even if things between them could be mended, they would never be fixed. They could not be fixed after a phone call like that, and Elizabeth had known it. She'd intentionally and effectively killed their relationship as he stuttered and protested feebly.

He sighed deeply, tore his eyes from the door, and made a drink. Jack and Coke, minus the Coke and the glass. Terrified of reflective surfaces, he wandered around his apartment, only looking up briefly from his feet to check what surfaces looked back at him, finally finding a corner of bed where he could sit without the man-in-the-mirror pestering him. Only then did he allow everything that had happened to wash over him, trying desperately to see where it went wrong, to find some way out of the flow that didn't end with his life shattered on the floor. He went back further than the fights tonight, further than his planning the weekend, further even than the picture of Wyatt that El had sent before their trip. He went back and back, like a movie reel played in reverse.

What he saw tore him apart. He watched a shitty man treat his family shitty, all because of his shitty understanding of what it meant to be happy. He saw himself at his son's pediatric appointment, staring down the front of the young nurse's scrubs. He saw the way he laughed when she made a joke about parenthood. He now saw the look of confusion on Elizabeth's face. "It wasn't that funny," she'd said after Stacy had left the room. He'd shrugged, knowing she was right, but knowing also that his laughter had made the young nurse smile more and that had made him happy. He saw himself alone in the bathroom at his old house, Elizabeth down with Wyatt doing God knows what, his eyes closed, imagining slowly taking off the nurse's scrubs as she worked on his belt. His muscles tensed and he breathed a long sigh as the tension released.

He saw the fights he'd had with Elizabeth, trying desperately to weasel out of taking Wyatt to the park while she cleaned the house, or made lunch, or, God forbid, took a well-deserved nap. He'd never wanted to be alone with Wyatt, afraid that the lack of feelings he felt toward his son would grow exponentially if they were alone and he had to interact with him.

He opened his eyes and was not surprised to find that he was openly crying and the bottle was much lighter than it had been when he'd entered the room.

Without thinking about it, he lifted the bottle to see how much was left and found himself looking into the dark obscured face of the man-in-the-mirror. He was the only one enjoying the night.

Verse 65

Norton, Kansas

RANDALL brought his truck to a stop, turned the key, and sat for a minute, relishing the beauty of the night. He realized that his life had not been perfect; it had, by definition, been total shit. However, by one chance encounter, his life had been split in two. Now there was the life before and the life after.

The life before had been the type of life parents warn their disobedient children of as they start experimenting with social circles. The life after was the life preached about at revivals. He'd died the night he wrecked his car, as effectively as the other lady. They'd died together, only to be resurrected on different sides of the veil.

Based on what he'd read about her and the funeral, she'd been a good woman. That meant she'd closed her eyes in this world and opened them to paradise. Randall, by comparison, had not been so lucky. But he understood that by opening his eyes on the world again, he'd been given a second chance; an opportunity to make sure that the next time he died, he would not open his eyes to the infernos of Hell. He owed everything to that night and, in turn, to the death of another. He meant to make sure that her sacrifice was not in vain.

As he sang, alone in his truck, he could see the beautiful future stretched out before him as the softly rippling lake did now.

He opened the door and stepped onto the hard dirt, packed down by fishing boots, folding chairs, and tackle boxes. His song echoed across the lake, bouncing back at him from the trees sporadically sticking out of the waves, dead monoliths from when the water level was lower. His voice joined him over and over with each echo, turning his little song into a choral concert for the fish and the stars. He bent to remove his shoes, not wanting them to get wet. With shoes and socks carefully placed on his seat, he began to walk forward into the water.

Despite the hot days, the water was still cold enough to make him catch his breath. It washed around his ankles as he took his first steps. However, the song continued unchanged as the surrounding voices filled the minor gap. His legs disappeared into the inky blue depths as he continued his forward progress. Once the water had reached his crotch, causing his balls to suck up against his body in a feeble attempt to avoid the cold, he stepped onto a long-forgotten fishhook that buried itself deep into his foot. His song did not waver as he continued to step deeper into the lake, even as the fishing line stayed fastened on the stick that had originally caused the loss. The hook tore through skin and muscle as it opened his sole from forefoot to heel. The song never wavered. Soon, the water was to his chest, and a dark cloud trailed behind him as his foot poured red into the dark water behind.

Finally, he stopped, the water now lapping at his chin, and turned toward the bank where his truck sat, waiting for a driver that would never return. There, beside it, was a parked motorcycle and the dark silhouette of a man.

Randall, still singing despite little waves splashing into his open mouth, looked at the man curiously. He understood that this man was the only way he could find the future for which he was fighting so desperately. This man was the key to his happiness.

Overwhelming joy filled him as he took a couple steps back. Water flowed into his singing mouth. He inhaled the water into his lungs, trying desperately to get enough air into them to keep singing. The song was all he knew, and it was all he cared about. The song, as they say, must go on.

But it was getting harder and harder to get a full breath as with each inhalation, more water flowed down his windpipe, causing him to wretch, which hurt the song. This was something he could not bear. The song represented his life, and he was ruining it by drinking again. The only answer he could see was to take deeper breaths with the understanding that deeper breaths meant more oxygen.

The man on the bank watched and listened as Randall tried desperately to continue singing the song that the man himself hummed softly from the safety of the land.

Randall was crying tears of frustration and defeat, understanding that he could not save the song, that his drinking had once again ruined everything. The world was growing darker with each breath as he continued to exhale what little air had made it in only to inhale more water. His contribution to the song had stopped many notes before as his lungs began to give up on a job they'd been doing since birth. They no longer pumped lifesaving oxygen into his bloodstream. His vision gave out as consciousness left him.

The last thing he ever saw was the man mounting his motorcycle, and the last thing he ever heard was the song wrapping around the engine as it started. His last dying act was to smile as he slipped beneath the waves, grateful that the song would continue, even if he could no longer sing.

The silence of the water gave way to the silence of death. He sank ever deeper.

Verse 66

Council Bluffs, Iowa

"OPEN mine now," Samuel said. He pawed at his folder, trying to grab it himself, his excitement tangible.

Gideon had just read about the fire that had surely caused his removal from their mother's house, and Samuel was acting like that had been a cliffhanger ending to the first episode. Based on the thoughts that Gideon heard, the next folder would have a similar story involving yet another fire. Their mother was either an exceptionally careless candle owner or there was more to the story. Gideon wondered if he wanted to know the answer. Would it be better that their mother was a bad mom or that she'd tried to forsake her motherhood through fire?

Samuel was persistent and, honestly, a little whiny. Again, Gideon had to remind himself that Samuel was only nine. Hell, it was probably a good time to remind himself that he was only twelve, and all of this was heavy for two children to handle. He started to open the second envelope, then paused.

Where did this knowledge lead? Two fires was what the man had been thinking, which meant the careless candle ownership theory was hard to swallow. Which, then, left what? The only plausible answer Gideon came up with was their mother had tried to burn them alive. If that was true, did that knowledge lead them toward their mother or away from her? Yes, he understood that knowledge was power, but he also knew that sometimes ignorance was bliss. Had he not just taken Samuel away from the knowledge that he'd caused another kid's death?

Throughout Gideon's revelry, Samuel was getting more and more upset that they hadn't moved on to his information. Reluctantly, Gideon opened the folder, resigning himself to whatever happened with the knowledge attained.

More files with basic information like birthdate, social security number, and everything else were on top. Again, he saw their mother's name and, again, the reality of his family hit him as his brother excitedly looked over his shoulder, soaking up the information the best he could.

Did they have any other siblings? The thought struck Gideon like a blow. He had not known about Samuel until today. Maybe in another home, possibly due to another fire, another file with their mother's name existed. If that were the case, did that other sibling also have special abilities? Were they lonely as he'd been? Did they feel like no one else could understand them?

With that thought, Gideon understood their next move. They needed to find out if they had other siblings, siblings who might be as confused and afraid as they were.

That meant they would have to meet their mother after all. The idea filled Gideon with excitement but also a good amount of fear. If what he believed was true, it meant they were actively going to seek out someone who'd tried and failed to kill them.

The newspaper article in Samuel's folder, eerily like the one in his own folder, felt like a solid confirmation of that thought. He read the headline, then looked over the article, letting key words jump out at him: Survivors. Fire. Roberta

Charles. Hospital. He handed everything over to Samuel who took it greedily and began pouring over everything.

Gideon was already thinking about their next move. He knew that you could use a computer to search for information. He also knew there was a computer at the library as he'd seen it on their weekly trips. He'd always been attentive during car rides in case he got left behind; a fear that was strong despite the fact he'd never experienced it before. This meant that he had a good idea where the library was and, if he was slightly off, he could get them close enough to ask someone on the street who should be able to direct him.

He turned around on the bench and stood. Samuel, whose eyes had been glued to his files, looked up.

"Let's go to the library," Gideon said.

Samuel, who'd not been privy to Gideon's thoughts, gave him a very confused look that was mirrored in his questioning mind, but he stood obediently and they walked out of the park.

Gideon opened his eyes to the hotel room that was beginning to feel a little too familiar. He'd spent the day in the neighboring city of Omaha, directly over the Missouri River. He'd discovered no real leads. Again, he was beginning to feel like the trail was gone and he should move on. He had a very clear vision of himself living comfortably after using his specific skillset to prepare for a comfortable future.

He imagined himself sitting at a small table while his significant other prepared breakfast. A normal job would be waiting for him as he finished his coffee and prepared to go. His attention would be drawn to the radio that, up to that point, had been playing some soft, relaxing, prework music. Then there was an urgent alert about a mass suicide or some accident that had taken place at a town event somewhere near him. He could visualize the color draining from his face as he understood that he was partially responsible. That had he continued his search and found Samuel, maybe he could have done something to stop him.

What did he intend to do if and when he did catch up with Samuel? Talk to him? Try to make him see reason? That little endeavor was what brought about their unfortunate split. So, what? Kill him? Barring the fact that Samuel's abilities would surely make that a difficult task in general, did Gideon have it in him to kill his little brother? He absentmindedly ran his hand up under his shirt to place it over the burn scar.

It helped to center him, to bring him back to where it all began. The two of them sitting at that picnic table; one life already taken by Samuel, Gideon unknowingly guiding them to the next.

Verse 67

Norton, Kansas

ELIZABETH sat in one of the chairs her dad kept rain or shine on his back deck. Luckily for her butt, it had not rained for days, and she had no fear of wet drawers. This was especially good tonight as she was on a hair trigger, and merely sitting on a wet cushion could have been the deciding factor in how she spent the rest of her night. Driving to Omaha to kill her ex-husband was an option, and had this seat been wet, the dry seat in her recently damaged car would look a lot more appealing.

Thankfully, the cushion had been dry, so Norton, for the moment, continued to be where she sat, waiting for a text back from Rebecca after desperately sending, "You up? I need to vent about something!"

She felt a little guilty for texting Rebecca so late. But now that the door to their friendship had reopened, she felt that she was the best source for venting. However, with each passing minute, she wondered if Rebecca would call or if she was one of those do not disturb-type people who have their phones set on timers to keep unwanted calls from interrupting their beauty sleep. If only kids came with do not disturb options.

She sighed. Bad joke.

Wyatt actually did fine these days. It was her piece-of-shit ex-husband who kept her awake at night and woke her early in the morning. Hating him was like a full-time job, and she couldn't be late to clock in and out.

She reflected on the word "hate." Until tonight, she didn't think she'd hated him. Did she resent his attitude toward Wyatt and his own fatherhood? Sure. Was she upset with how he'd treated her and his marriage? Absolutely. Had she hated him, though? That was a very strong sentiment that her childhood days in VBS and Sunday School had told her to avoid at all costs.

In fact, had he said nothing during this little summer vacation, she would have only resented him more for his flippant dismissal of their absence. Resentment she could handle. But by giving her hope, by making her think that things could change, he'd taken that resentment, squeezed it like a clam, and ground it into a pure, black pearl of hatred.

Worst of all, Wyatt wouldn't understand any of this. Not why his dad bailed on him, not why she was so angry, not the well of emotions that sat below his parents' recent interactions. All he would know was that he was less loved than he'd thought, and that his mother was angrier than he'd seen.

Great. Fucking fantastic. Two amazing things for him to take away from tonight.

Hopefully, he got a good job when he grew up because therapy was not cheap.

She sighed heavily, feeling the sigh like a weight pressing the air out of her chest in a whoosh. She looked one last time at her phone, decided maybe she would try to get some sleep, and stood. Then she felt the familiar buzz in her palm. Without looking, she hit accept.

"Oh, thank God, you called. I was getting nervous that you wouldn't, and I would have no one to vent to, and my head would shoot off my neck from all the pressure."

There was a pause. Then a voice that was clearly not Rebecca's said, "Um, so I honestly thought I would get your voicemail, but it would appear you were waiting for my call? Are you psychic?"

All the feeling in Elizabeth's body fell away. Starting from the top of her head, it emptied out as if there were a hole on her foot and she were a human-shaped pitcher. She sat with the phone up to her ear, mouth moving silently, brain struggling to come up with an explanation for her explosive greeting that would not end with Samuel hanging up, packing up his guitar, and fleeing to places unknown.

Silent sentences formed and unformed, but a sighing, whispering sound was all she could produce.

"Elizabeth, are you okay?"

She felt her phone buzz and a slight pause broke in on Samuel's voice. With a numb hand, she revolved the phone away from her ear to look at the screen that clearly showed her current connection to Samuel and a call waiting icon with Rebecca's smiling face. It buzzed and flashed mockingly, laughing at her mistake. Her mouth kept moving as she willed words to come out.

"Elizabeth? Are you having a stroke?" It sounded like a joke, but she could also hear real concern in his voice.

That, more than anything, finally got her motor skills working. She flicked the message option to Rebecca and sent her a preprogrammed response letting her know she was busy on another call, then canceled the new incoming call.

"Sorry. No, I was expecting someone else is all." Okay, good. That ought to buy her a second to explain her manic outbreak when she'd answered. "Just so you know, the head exploding bit was in regard to something completely unrelated to our evening, and my desire to vent had nothing to do with you."

"I am not sure if I should be glad that I didn't cause you undue anxiety, or disappointed that it had nothing to do with me and you weren't waiting anxiously by your phone for my call. I will admit, at first, I was incredibly flattered with your opening line about how nervous you were that I wasn't going to call, only to realize you were waiting for some other late-night caller."

Elizabeth found herself at a disadvantage once again with Samuel. Had she looked at who was calling, she could have had control of this conversation from the beginning, granted to her by the late hour. She could have started with cute admonishments and cutting remarks about propriety, maybe even quoted some *Sense and Sensibility*. However, she'd practically had a mental breakdown in front of him and was therefore on clean-up duty, struggling to get back to level ground. While he got to be cute and funny about the situation. If there was a God, he'd recently decided that Elizabeth looked good in red.

"If it makes you feel better, said late-night caller has called since we started talking and I sent them straight to voicemail." She purposefully left out the gender of the other caller to make him sweat a bit. A little give and take. He would get to have the ignored phone call, but not who was making it. She felt that she'd made some progress in her uphill trek to even ground. Now that the original shock of who was on the phone had subsided, she felt a little better and was ready to pivot back to where she should have been at the beginning of the call. "Why, pray tell, would you be calling a single lady at such an improper hour? Perhaps you need a lesson in propriety?"

Boom. She loved the word "propriety." It made her feel like she was in a Jane Austen story. Level ground had been reached and she was reveling in it.

"I apologize. That kiss has left my sense of propriety a little mixed up tonight."

Kiss? Elizabeth's position shifted again, and she felt a backslide. What kiss? Then she remembered. Images and feelings spun around her as if she were in a child's kaleidoscope. The kiss before getting into her car.

The fight with Jason had all but wiped that moment from her mind. It had, in fact, wiped almost everything out of her mind. She'd been in such a blind rage that she could not recount much else that happened that evening. Thank God for her dad who had all but singlehandedly put Wyatt down as she fumed, plotted, and cursed herself into a miserable state. She'd kissed Samuel, then promptly forgot about it after listening to her voicemail. Goddamn Jason for taking that away from her as well.

". . . concerned about you."

Wait. Was Samuel still talking? Dammit, she'd slipped ever further back. Level ground was again out of her reach. "I'm sorry, what?" Great, great. Now she was psychotic and scatterbrained. She was looking like a real winner with this phone call.

"I was saying that the reason I called, and, again, I assumed I would be talking to your mailbox, was because I was concerned about you. You seemed kind of down after talking about your parents and I wanted to check in. That, and I was hoping to schedule another get-together. One a little less about music and more about getting breakfast and or coffee."

A date? Obviously, with a kiss like that, there was clearly chemistry, but a breakfast date felt big, especially for her. She thought about how she hadn't had a real date in years and almost said no.

Then, two memories struck her at once: the kiss and her recent fight. She decided that a breakfast date could kill two birds with one stone. It would allow her to get closer to Samuel while simultaneously punishing Jason. She didn't know with certainty that Jason would care that she was going on a date, but she had a feeling he might. Once a man claimed ownership, it was hard for him to renounce it, even if he'd moved on. Like a child playing with toys, even if he wasn't currently playing with one, that didn't mean anyone else could play with it. Elizabeth was not owned by anyone. It was time to prove that.

"That sounds delightful. Can we make it a little later in the morning? It would appear neither of us went to bed at a decent time." She smiled. Level ground felt pretty good under her feet.

Verse 68

Council Bluffs, Iowa

ON average, two kids would find it difficult to move around town unsupervised. But when those two kids can read the minds of those around them and make people do as they wish, they become unfettered and essentially free to roam.

Gideon and Samuel made their way to the library, using the thoughts of those around them to guide them when Gideon's memory failed him. At one point, a middle-aged man watering his lawn got a little nosey but was left absentmindedly singing a song as he held his hose.

Thinking back on that trek later in life, Gideon would realize that walk was the template they used from that point on, until their split. Gideon would use his ability to glean information while keeping an eye out for anyone that might be paying too much attention, and Samuel would manipulate anyone that stood in their way. Money? Not an issue, sing a little song. Lodging? Sing a little song.

Samuel and Gideon walked into the library. The tall, domed ceiling made them both feel small without the rest of the kids around them. These two children, now alone in the world, felt that solitude heavily as they made their way to the row of computers in the little room at the back of the library. There was someone sitting at every computer in the room. Some checked email, some did homework, a few played pixelated video games.

Nowhere to sit? Sing a little song.

Every eye turned to look at them, glossed over. Samuel looked at each of them, his song never missing a beat as he walked further into the room. Gideon watched as Samuel decided to force one of the kids playing a videogame to give up his seat, rather than any of those using the free computers for something productive.

Once the kid had left, singing softly to himself on the way to check out Samuel's favorite book, Gideon took a seat in front of the computer.

He realized very quickly that he had absolutely no idea how to use the internet as he'd never used it before. He closed his eyes and allowed his mind to drift into those around him.

As they were actively logged on—as the act was called—to the internet, their minds were hyper-focused on exactly the information Gideon needed to get started. Each click took a couple of minutes to load. He was soon on a webpage which listed names, numbers, and addresses. It was essentially a digital phonebook. From there, he was able to search and find Roberta Charles. She was still in town, living in a new, less burnt-down house.

"Do you have any money?" he asked Samuel who gave him a sarcastic look. "Right. Sorry. The singing thing. Duh."

He hit print and somewhere behind the librarian's desk, the information they needed began the slow process of transcribing itself from digital to physical. There were only two pages. At a penny a page, it would have cost basically nothing, but who had time to deal with money when there were songs to sing and people to meet? They exited the library, papers in hand, leaving the librarian humming softly.

The two boys waved down a taxi, got in, sang a song, and headed toward the address they'd found online. To the home of their mother and, inevitably, the damnation of their souls.

Verse 69

Norton, Kansas

ELIZABETH set the phone down on the little table next to her, took in a long breath of warm summer night air, then sighed it out. She picked her phone back up and looked at the time.

Holy hell. She'd been on the phone for over two hours. It was coming up on five in the morning now. The sun would be up shortly.

She set the phone back down and let the past couple of hours flow slowly into her mind like the tide coming back in. She started with the last statement Samuel had made: "So when can I see you again? Preferably in person and at a reasonable hour."

She smiled and wrapped her arms around herself as if he were there. She'd essentially become a dump truck full of baggage, unloading it all on this man she barely knew. A man who she wanted to get to know better who she assumed would almost surely run for the hills after a conversation like that.

However, he'd listened, commented seldomly, encouraged compassionately, and miraculously requested further interaction.

She hugged herself a little tighter, then released. She needed to get to bed. She had a full day of wedding prep with Rebecca, and that would be after dealing with the fallout of Jason's phone call with Wyatt.

She had realized fairly quickly that calling within listening distance of their son had been wrong. When she first pulled up Jason's number, though, all she'd wanted was for Wyatt to hear what a piece of shit his dad was. After Wyatt and her dad had gone to bed, however, regret settled in with the reality of her bad decision.

The rest of the conversation with Samuel pieced itself together as she sat alone on the back deck. She'd essentially given a near stranger an autobiographical description of her divorce, followed by a list of grievances, starting with the phone call with Jason that night. He now knew more about her than her best friends did.

Sure, there was that kiss—that wonderfully sensual kiss. But that spur-of-the-moment indulgence could hardly be considered a concrete foundation to a relationship worthy of the information exchange that had just taken place. She thought about how it was like needing to pee: when she stepped into the restroom and her body knew it was about to feel the sweet release of urination, the need intensified. However, if the toilet was out of order, with the process already initiated, there would be no stopping it and there had better be a sink or a trash can nearby or she would have wet pants.

That was not a great metaphor. But it wasn't about the actual act. It was more about the urgency. When the phone rang, the need to empty had become so intense with the knowledge of coming relief that if it had been the pope calling the wrong number, he would have heard a long, unexpected confession.

She smiled at the image of the pope hearing all about her hatred of her ex-husband, then saying something like "I had meant to order some takeout Italian, but okay. Um, do five Hail

Marys and you'll be good. Now, do you know the number of
Fazoli's?" She laughed out loud at that. Italians probably don't
call their food Italian food. She laughed a little harder.

God, she was tired. Staying up this late was always
tricky. The sun would be up in the next hour or so, which meant
she would be getting little to no sleep. Was it worth it to try?
Should she get the coffee brewing instead and maybe try to take
a nap at Bex's parents' house in between her maid-of-honor
duties? She snickered at the thought of the word "duties," then
decided that even an hour or so of sleep would probably help
her not seem like a lunatic.

She was out within a minute of lying her head down.

Verse 70

Council Bluffs, Iowa

GIDEON stepped out of the shower and reached for the towel.

"How was your shower?"

He looked toward the door to the bathroom. Without his glasses, he saw only the blurred color of skin. He chose instead to reach for his glasses, resting on the counter, and put them on, bringing the body of the woman he'd brought back from the bar into focus. She was standing in the doorway, completely naked, as she'd been when he'd left her snoozing on the bed. Her thoughts did not match her nudity as they kept jumping back to her husband and kids.

He'd read her need for some kind of release while at a new bar. He'd needed a distraction. They were a perfect match. She felt regret for the potential loss of her family; he felt regret for helping mold a serial killer. Tomayto, tomahto.

This was a mistake, her mind said through her smile.

He smiled back at her as if he hadn't heard. He began to towel off, leaving her to take her own shower.

He was in bed, looking through news items, when she came out of the bathroom, surrounded by a cloud of steam. He wondered if she'd made it extra hot to help clean away that dirty, adulterous feeling. She smiled sheepishly, pulling the towel up further over the breasts his mouth had tasted only minutes before. He smiled back and politely looked away as she gathered her things and got dressed.

Having sex with a stranger was kind of like stealing something. Leading up to that moment, and the moment itself, was full of the excitement of breaking societal rules and the possibility of being caught. Once the deed was done came the worries and concerns. What at first seemed exciting turned scary. All the variables that were easy to overlook before became starkly clear after the fact.

He was pulled from these thoughts as she cleared her throat, buttoning the last two buttons of her blouse. She looked around as if seeing where she was for the first time. She again smiled, and again, Gideon heard her thoughts.

Oh, my God. What was I thinking?

What came out of her mouth, though, was "I should probably be going, but thanks for the nice evening."

"Thank you, as well," he replied. He was ready for her to leave, taking her storm of confusion and heartache with her, so that he could hopefully sleep without seeing his younger brother's childhood face.

She awkwardly bowed, with her hand in front of her holding her clutch, then turned and walked briskly out the door.

He smiled, feeling both bad for her and happy for her. She was clearly not happy with her current life. Maybe this event would act as a catalyst and give her the determination she needed to either fix what was wrong in her relationship or abandon it. Either way, a change was needed, and he may have facilitated that.

He mused on the fact that Samuel would have seen tonight as unforgivable. Gideon understood it for what it was: the start of a healing process long needed. It was one of the things he always tried and failed to convey to Samuel. Samuel lived in a world of black and white that Gideon's constant eavesdropping didn't allow. Gideon's ability to read minds meant he had a deeper understanding of people's motives and their hearts.

He waited a few more minutes in case she'd forgotten an article of clothing or something else. When she hadn't returned after half an hour, he turned off his phone, pulled the duct tape from the drawer beside his bed, slapped a strip over his mouth, and turned off the lights. He was hopeful for a quiet night, but had always lived by the mantra "hope for the best, plan for the worst."

He rolled over, closed his eyes, and found himself in the back of a cab with his little brother on their way to meet their mother.

Verse 71

Omaha, Nebraska

JASON woke up unsure of where he was. He stared at the ceiling for a little while. It was familiar, but the sleep haze clouded his mind and made it difficult to pinpoint. He struggled to sit up. Upon doing so, he found himself in his room. He looked up at the ceiling, then back to his surroundings, realizing why the room looked off. He'd fallen asleep at the foot of his bed, probably while still figuring out if there were any way to salvage any relationship in his life. It was unnerving that things could look so different from this angle. There was probably a metaphor there. But he was too tired and too emotionally exhausted to chase it down.

He needed coffee. More than anything, he needed coffee.

Stretching, he willed himself to his feet. His body ached. It was never meant to sleep in the slumped over position it had found itself in for hours. His joints were stiff as he worked the sleep out of them on his way to the kitchen. He was greeted by the spiderweb of cracks on the front of the microwave. Thank God he'd seen that reflection last night rather than one in the coffee maker or this morning would have been a complete bust.

Soon, the smell of espresso filled the apartment. With it came clarity. Today he would start the process of fixing his life, building back bridges where they'd been burned. A list began to form in his mind as he sorted who he would call first. Tricky, he knew. Each phone call had the potential to domino effect the next and bring the entire day crashing down around him, leading to another night like the night before.

He should probably call Stacy first as it was the plan to visit her grandmother that kickstarted this fiasco. He honestly didn't know if he was invited on that little trip. That information could be useful.

Then again, maybe calling Elizabeth first was the right thing to do. That way, he could explain the situation better and use the fact that Stacy was so upset about the situation that she'd left. Would that information help or hurt? Would she realize how important his relationship with Wyatt was to him or see it as him bailing on both Stacy and Wyatt?

Maybe he should cut out the middleman and go straight to Wyatt. Remind him that he loved him, and, no matter what he heard last night or what he might be thinking, his dad did want to spend time with him.

Then again, El might see that as an attempt to undermine her authority. Goddammit, this was all so fucking complicated.

A thought struck him like a bolt of lightning. The first call he needed to make was to work. He was in no state of mind to sell stocks to rich fucks who had absolutely no worries in the world while his life fell apart around him.

He walked back into the bedroom to find his cell phone, his cup of espresso steaming lazily on the counter.

Verse 72

Council Bluffs, Iowa

GIDEON and Samuel rode in silence in the back of the cab. Both could feel the weight of everything happening. First, they had met. Two boys with powers no longer alone. Then, they found out they were siblings. Now they were on the road to meet their mother.

Gideon's beating and rescue had already taken on the air of a memory from long ago. He had to keep reminding himself it happened only yesterday. It was hard to believe so much happened in such a short time. He'd been resigned to live a lonely life, overly informed about those around him. Now, with Samuel by his side, their future was limitless.

Before they could think about the future, they had to face their past.

Gideon Glimpse and Samuel Serenade. He smiled as he pictured the cover of a comic book. This trip to see their mother felt like the issue where you learn how the superheroes got their superpowers and why they'd been separated. He shook his head, reminding himself this was real life.

He looked at Samuel and glimpsed into his mind. His thoughts were entirely on their mother. He was a young boy, meeting someone he'd been dreaming about meeting his whole life. Gideon watched as different faces of women, famous and mundane, flipped through Samuel's mind as he tried to picture their mother. Gideon couldn't help but smile when Cher popped into Samuel's mind. She was holding his hand at a zoo, pointing at a giraffe as Gideon stood at the fence on tiptoes with his arm up, pretending to be one himself.

As their trip continued, Gideon began to realize that the neighborhoods got worse the longer they rode. They were progressing into a part of town that, under normal circumstances, they would have avoided. Yards where the grass was hidden by forests of weeds left unattended. The paint on most of the houses was falling off like dried flaky skin after a good itch.

The cab slowed to a stop in front of a house that was no worse, but no better than the ones that surrounded it. The yard had been mowed recently, so that helped, but he still felt out of place and, in all honesty, scared as he ushered Samuel out the door.

"Hey. You gonna pay or what?"

Gideon had been wound so tightly as he exited the cab that the voice behind him caused him to jump and grip Samuel's arms. Samuel let out a little yelp of pain. They both turned toward the bearded man who was looking at them in a perplexed way that clearly showed his confusion at driving two young boys to a part of town where he never came. However, he'd been driving a cab for over ten years and some things are ingrained in a person. So, despite his confusion, he understood that he got paid for the work that had been done. That is, he understood it until he heard the little boy begin to sing to him. Then he understood that it was time to go. He put the car in drive and soon was happily singing along to a radio that had never turned on, returning to a part of town he knew better.

The two boys turned toward the dilapidated house, both filled with trepidation. Samuel's stress and excitement were leaking from his mind, infusing with Gideon's own, as they took their first steps up the cracked sidewalk toward the front door.

Gideon thought about what it must be like to be a normal kid, walking toward the front door to their mother who would greet them with a hug or a kiss and ask them about their day. Maybe she would have freshly baked cookies waiting.

Normal kids did not walk toward the door with their mother behind it in fear.

This thought seemed to cement the day in unreality, giving it that hazy feeling of dream all over again.

They took the slanted steps onto the worn porch and stopped. Gideon could hear Samuel wondering who should knock, but he was too afraid to voice his thoughts as whoever was inside might hear him and come out. Again, that sense of unreality and oddness at the situation flowed around Gideon. He put a reassuring hand on Samuel's shoulder and knocked two times, as hard as his nerves would allow.

Time appeared to slow as they waited for a response. After what felt like an eternity, Gideon decided to knock again. But as he raised his fist to do so, they heard a chain slide above them. The knob turned a little as they heard another lock revolve. Finally, the knob turned entirely and the door opened a fraction, showing a figure in the slit.

The only feature Gideon saw clearly was a blue eye, glaring out at them from the dark silhouette.

In a hotel, in Iowa, a much older Gideon groaned in his sleep, unable to escape the nightmare. He rolled, his body trying to wake him up and save him from his own mind, His mother's blue eye continued to glare at him. Nightmares born from memory do not let go so easily.

Verse 73

Alma, Nebraska

GARY and Jacob sat in a coffee shop, looking out of place as they sipped from cute, little white mugs. Both would be busy the rest of the afternoon, but they wanted to meet up regardless. They decided to meet at the only other spot the two of them frequented.

Alma had a local coffee shop owned and operated by a hardworking young woman and her partner. When it first opened, there had been some controversy. There often is when two members of the same gender do anything together in love: date, get married, have kids, or, in this case, open a small coffee shop.

The owner, Susannah, had grown up in Alma and always felt on the outside. She decided to make it her mission to turn that perception around once she was older. She'd done this by returning and opening a business that people loved despite their political or religious whims. She'd landed on coffee as everyone loved coffee, and it was hard to be hateful in the morning over the delicious smell of a fresh brewed cup. She'd dragged her girlfriend, Johanna, all the way from Iowa to be a part of her mission to bring love to a small Nebraska town.

Gary and Jacob had been two of the first customers through the door and made a point to be seen in the little shop as often as their schedules allowed. Neither of them had any ill will toward those who believed differently than they did.

Susannah and Johanna had loved them from the start. They even dedicated a table to them.

Gary and Jacob were quietly sipping their coffee when the little bell dinged to signify the door opened. They instinctively turned to see who'd stepped in. There was a strange moment of déjà vu as the man flashed his blue eyes around the room, seeing someone neither knew in an establishment that rarely had new patrons. Both of their minds instantly went to Samuel, but this was someone else; another stranger in their otherwise set lives.

Gary was struck with the feeling he had the last time he and Samuel sat together. He remembered clearly wishing he'd never met him. He wanted to reach over, grab Jacob's arm, and beg him to remain quiet; to let this stranger grab his coffee and go with no interference, no life-altering meeting. That would come off as crazy, he knew, because he understood those feelings he had with Samuel had been just that: feelings. Yet, those feelings were hard for him to shake, and as Jacob's arm rose in a friendly greeting, Gary's heart dropped heavily into his stomach. He was done with his coffee. He didn't think it would stay down, even if he attempted to drink it for show.

The man saw the raised hand, smiled warmly, and raised his own. He then turned back to the counter to study the little menu behind it written with white chalk on a black board. Gary's heart began to trek back toward his chest, and he began to think maybe he'd be able to finish that coffee after all. It appeared the man was on a mission and would breeze past their lives with a simple friendly wave and nothing else.

He was wrong.

After the man placed his order, and Susannah began grinding the beans, he made his way over to the two old farmers to further his greeting. "Good morning, gentlemen. How's the coffee here?" He paused for a second. Before either could reply, he continued, "I guess I should have asked before placing my order. Hopefully, I won't regret my decision."

Gary could not find words. The man looked nothing like Samuel, yet, the whole situation felt so familiar that he was having trouble placing himself in time and location.

"My name is Patrick," the man said, reaching out.

Was he at the bar? No, this was the coffee shop, and this man hadn't ordered fancy beer, but fancy coffee. He shook his head a little and was relieved to hear Jacob return the greeting.

"My name is Jacob. This here statue across from me was made in honor of an old friend of mine named Gary."

Patrick laughed as he shook Jacob's hand. The sound was so easy and weightless, it finally broke through the tension that had seized Gary upon seeing him walk in.

He extended a hand for his own shake. "Better a statue than a leathery bag of bones," Gary harrumphed, reaching for the coffee he was willing to drink again. "What brings you to our favorite little coffee shop in the Midwest?"

Susannah, overhearing, flapped her hand toward him, waving off the flattery as she squirted some flavoring into one of the to-go cups she was fixing for Patrick.

"My fiancé had a late-night phone call that woke her up for a bit, so I figured I would surprise her with coffee. I found this place via Google. It is pretty much the only standalone coffee shop in town, so I decided to give it a try."

They smiled and nodded, looking like a Norman Rockwell painting from the *Saturday Evening Post*.

"I take it the coffee must be pretty good, if you two get up so early to enjoy it."

"When you are our age, getting up early is the norm, not the exception," Jacob said. Gary nodded an elaborate agreement. "However, that shouldn't take away from how good the coffee is. Granted, we old fogies are more into the black kettle type, rather than whatever comes out of that there fancy hissing machine."

Susannah walked over to Patrick, a cup in each hand. "One of these days, I'm going to force you two closed-minded old fools to try a cup of that fancy hissing machine's coffee, and it will change the way you see coffee. I swear you will never want the original again."

Gary, again, felt a momentary jolt as the fancy wheat beer appeared in his mind's eye. He felt weight settle onto his shoulders as the déjà vu returned. He struggled to catch a breath. Luckily, everyone else was engaged and laughing together too merrily to see his struggle, and he was able to take deep breaths in through his nose and out through his mouth. His heartbeat began to slow, and the clear glass full of a light yellowish beverage faded from in front of him. He smiled, both with relief and to pretend to be engaged in the conversation still.

"But then who would drink the normal coffee, if not for us?" Gary said, finding his voice more or less steady. It showed no sign of the fear he'd felt; the fear that still made no sense to him as he'd never had anything but pleasant interactions with Samuel.

He had no idea why he felt that meeting Samuel was such a big deal. It felt like a precipitating event; a precursor for things to come. Those things to come felt very large indeed. Upon looking at those things, the sheer size of it all was what was causing him distress. He was a simple man, with a simple life, and he only wanted to continue living in his simple world. Yet, he felt he'd been pulled into something far less simple.

To make matters worse, he felt that no one else felt it, adding to his sense that he was being paranoid and creating something out of nothing. Which, upon reflection of his relationship with Samuel, felt highly likely.

He realized Susannah had directed her last comment toward him, and he'd missed it. "I'm sorry. My train of thought must have derailed back there. What did ya say?"

"I said that since you two are the only ones drinking that normal coffee, if you stopped, I could free up some counterspace by getting rid of that coffee pot." She threw a thumb over her shoulder in the general direction of the coffee preparation area.

"Speak not blasphemy, my child. The Lord is always listening."

They all laughed, even Patrick, who, after catching his breath, started excusing himself to return to his fiancé with her morning surprise. The joviality of the moment was enough to help Gary clear his mind of his strange misgivings, but he still didn't like the idea of drinking the new coffee. He had enough new things in his life. No need to go adding something else.

Verse 74

Council Bluffs, Iowa

"I don't want any cookies, popcorn, or whatever it is that you boys are selling, so have a nice day." The door began to close as the blue eye turned back into the darkness behind it.

"Mom?"

Gideon jumped a little as Samuel spoke. Gideon himself had been locked in place. He had even stopped hearing the thoughts around him. Everything had stopped as he had seen his mom. Samuel, on the other hand, had the courage of youth and was not shy. Gideon, not for the first nor last time, found himself wishing he was more like his little brother.

The door stopped mid-close and the eye under the disheveled black hair returned. "What did you say?"

Gideon decided, as the older brother, it was high time he stepped in. But as he opened his mouth to introduce the two of them, his other hearing kicked back in, and he clearly heard their mother thinking, *No, God, no. Please, oh God. Please no.* Again, he could do nothing. His jaw locked in place.

So, yet again, Samuel, blessedly free of the curse of mindreading, went on for him. "My name is Samuel Serenade, he's Gideon Glimpse, and you are our mom."

Gideon was caught off guard when Samuel used their new names and at his frank description of the situation at large. Their mother's dismay continued to grow as she recognized the first names, and the reality of the situation grew in her.

Gideon felt her recognition moments before she shut the door in their faces without another word. They heard multiple locks slide into place and a chain lock dragged into its notch.

"Mom!" Samuel shouted. Gideon found himself wishing Samuel would stop using that word. It was like a trigger on a faulty gun that was dangerously close to blowing up in their hands. Gideon went to stop him, but Samuel was on a roll and was too fast. "We have superpowers!" He yelled through the closed door.

Then everything went silent. The wind stopped. No one was on the street. There was no traffic. Not even a dog's bark broke the tense lack of sounds as what Samuel said echoed in their minds.

Then their mom's thoughts came through. *Oh, God, no. Why? Why is this happening?* Gideon threw his hands up over his ears as if that act could stop her mental screams.

Then, in a shaky tone through the door, she spoke: "Please, please leave. I don't want to see you. I don't want to talk to you. I don't want you anywhere near me."

Samuel stepped back as if struck. Gideon, who'd felt the words before they were spoken, merely frowned. The scar on his side seemed to prickle. What he was sensing from her was not hatred, but fear; thick and revolting fear. At that moment, he was ready to comply. He was ready to take Samuel and run far from this door, this house, maybe even this city. He wanted to put as much distance between himself and this woman as he could. He was reaching for his brother's shoulder when Samuel began to sing.

There were no words in the song that could be heard with ears, but Gideon heard them loud and clear in his mind. It was a song of welcome, of beckoning, through the door to offer guests a nice, cold beverage on this hot day.

Gideon heard first the chain lock, then the others sliding out of place, concluding in the knob's lock turning with a click. The door opened, and they saw their mother fully for the first time.

She had a pleasant smile on her face as she hummed along with the song. But Gideon saw the sweat beading on her forehead and dripping down her face as if she were straining to lift something heavy—something like a mind-controlling song, perhaps. She was wearing a black t-shirt with a logo he didn't recognize and men's athletic shorts. If he was being honest with himself, her appearance was equal parts shocking and disappointing.

Every foster kid who is taken from their parents before they can form a memory of them makes up their own memories of them. In all of his, she was a business woman who'd given up her children to focus on her career. The news stories had messed with that image, then the neighborhood and house cracked it quite a bit. But it was seeing her dressed like this, with her pale skin standing out against the dark circles under her eyes, that had broken his imaginary mother for good.

He again had the urge to grab Samuel and run before they stepped in. Any answers from this woman would hurt more than help.

"Please, come in," she sang the words, mixing them perfectly into her humming without missing a beat. As she did, tears began to spill from her eyes, intermixing with the sweat that was actively running down her face. She was fighting hard to break the spell of the song, but Samuel, now on the doorstep, would not be denied.

They stepped into the house. They were both shocked by how empty it was. They'd walked into what would be considered a living room, but there was only one chair, a rocking chair, set in front of a small table with a small TV on it. There were no pictures on the walls nor any other decoration to be seen.

Samuel turned, shut the door, then, as an afterthought, while still singing, locked every lock before turning back to face their mother. He stopped singing and the tune echoed around them until everything returned to silence. The silence held just long enough for their mother to fall to her knees and begin openly weeping in front of them.

"Mom, we just want to talk," Samuel started. But Gideon saw something in his mom's head that made him grab his little brother and pull him into the nearest door he could find. They stumbled and fell onto the tiled floor of a kitchen. Their mom screamed and the living room was suddenly engulfed in flames.

The boys gasped at the unexpected turn of events and the sudden rise in heat. They could feel it on their skin. They crab-walked backwards, further away from the raging inferno that had been their mom's living room. Then, in the door frame, they saw her, a dark silhouette with glowing red eyes.

"I never wanted you. I knew that a freak like me would only make more freaks." The fire began to pour into the kitchen.

Gideon was terrified they were all going to bake in there. But Samuel's thoughts stuck to those words, no longer afraid of the fire, no longer caring if they made it out of the house.

"I have made many mistakes in my life," she continued as Samuel got to his knees, "but you were the two biggest."

Samuel made it to his feet. The walls in the kitchen were catching. It would be a matter of minutes before this room was as bad as the one they'd left.

"People say the reason they won't have children is that they don't want to bring them into such an evil world, but my concerns were the complete opposite. I had to worry about bringing more evil into this world." She took a harsh breath. The air around her shimmered with the heat, making her expressions impossible to fully read. "Yet, both times I couldn't go through with it, couldn't bring myself to . . ." She paused, searching for the right words. ". . . erase the mistakes I had made. Both times I failed to follow through. But not this time."

She was still crying, but the tears were evaporating as fast as they came. Gideon only knew she wept because he could feel the tears in her mind. He began to cry as well. Samuel, on the other hand, was now standing, still and emotionless. Gideon shivered despite the spreading fire as cold hatred poured out of his little brother.

Samuel began to sing.

Gideon turned his attention back to their mom who'd stopped talking. She had, in fact, stopped doing anything. A shred of flaming wallpaper fell on Samuel's shirt and started to smolder. Without saying a word, he stripped it off to stand shirtless before his mother. Gideon was shocked as he saw the man Samuel would grow up to be before their mother, eyes full of murder.

"We could have been heroes." The words fell around them musically as Samuel stepped closer to their mom, who was standing right inside the door.

Gideon heard the song's meaning change again and understood what Samuel was doing. In horror, he finally stood, planning to grab his brother to make him stop, to try to reason with him. But the fire was too intense. Reasoning was out of the question. There wasn't any time. He grabbed his brother and yanked him toward the back door, dragging them out into fresh air. Samuel never stopped singing.

Mom, stop using your powers and stand completely still.
Those were the unsung words in Samuel's song.

Samuel and Gideon made their way back around to the front of the house to stand safely across the street. Their mom, unable to use her powers to protect herself from the flames, screamed loudly enough for them to hear over the fire tearing through the house. Her screams had a minor key musicality to them and sounded surprisingly beautiful. Eventually, the song ended, as two voices became one, satisfying Samuel enough to stop singing.

Gideon fell to his knees. He looked up at his younger brother, who stood shirtless and emotionless, watching the house burn. "We need to go. There will be questions."

Samuel turned to Gideon who pulled away from him, falling to a sitting position before him. *Do I need to sing for you?* The voice in Gideon's head cut into him, and he quickly shook his head no. Images of their mom singing flashed into his mind. Samuel nodded and walked past Gideon, away from the inferno.

The sounds of sirens were coming closer. Gideon scrambled to get up and hurried to catch up to Samuel. He spared one look back at the house where their mother had lived. Another fire, another news story. This time, however, they would list no survivors.

Gideon looked away and began rewriting the narrative in his mind to make Samuel a hero who just saved their lives from a woman who meant to kill them with fire.

Verse 75

ELIZABETH woke to her phone buzzing next to her. Having learned her lesson last night, she looked at the incoming call notification before doing anything else. It was Rebecca.

Her eyes moved up to see the time. 8:00 a.m. She had only three hours of sleep. But, at the same time, she had plenty to do, and had already lost plenty of the morning. Anyway, Rebecca deserved an explanation for last night, so she hit the accept button with her thumb and rolled on to her back. "Hello?"

"I'm sorry it took me so long to call back after your text last night, but as it was at two in the morning, I'm not that sorry."

Elizabeth was struck by two thoughts at the exact same time: that she'd missed her friendship with Rebecca more than she'd known and that she was in desperate need of coffee. She decided that, with wedding planning on the books for today anyway, she could kill two birds with one stone.

"Apologies. Can I make it up to you? Let me take you out to coffee. I have to get dressed and it's a thirty-minute drive to your place, but I promise I can make it worth your while." She said the last bit in her most seductive, porn star voice before continuing in her normal voice once again, "By paying for your coffee."

They both laughed and Elizabeth felt good. Everything was great. She'd been kissed, she and Rebecca were back on joking terms, and Samuel had talked to her all night. Then, the reason for last night's call and everything with Jason started to float into her mind like a storm cloud, threatening to rain on her so far pleasant morning. She filled her lungs with air and blew at the ceiling, imagining the dark cloud there, and further imagining it burst apart in the gust of breath. Those concerns would come. But at least she could enjoy coffee with an old friend while dishing about a hot boy she had a crush on. Maybe she should take her diary. Rebecca would get a kick out of that.

"Sure," Rebecca said, "my parents have a fancy, self-grinding coffeemaker, but going out sounds better. I hear there is a cool new coffee shop in town here, and Patrick is nowhere to be found. May as well make him jealous for missing my morning by spending it with some hottie I know."

It both shocked and amazed Elizabeth how they fell right back into their old dialogue. She ran her tongue over her top teeth, expecting to find her old retainer. It also dawned on her that, despite seeing multiple pictures of Patrick online, and a few risqué ones from Rebecca recently, she'd never met Patrick in person. Well, today was the day. Maybe they could surprise him by bringing him some coffee.

"I am getting up now." She sniffed her armpits, deeming them passable as long as she put on a thin layer of deodorant, and said, "I will be there in, let's say, forty-five minutes."

Rebecca squealed excitement and the line was broken.

She left her phone on the bed as she dug through her bag, looking for the right outfit to meet a man she'd seen almost naked, aside from a well-placed top hat. A very classy and tasteful pic, if she and Rebecca did say so themselves. She giggled as she found some clothes that were both cute and comfortable; a must for a day of hard wedding work that involved cute boys. The cute boy she was most excited about was not the groom to be, but the musical talent who had agreed to meet her after they got their needed sleep after such a long talk. Holding her pants to her chest, she fake-swooned back onto her bed.

Then she turned her head and saw a notification from Jason. The swoon and happy feelings fell away as fast as an avalanche, threatening to take the rest of the day with it.

"Can we talk?" the text said.

What a fucking safe thing to do: text a request to talk. Nope, no. Not today, mister. She took her phone, went to her messages, and erased the most recent one from Jason, pretending she'd never read it. Eventually, she would have to talk to the father of her son, but she was not going to let him ruin this day, Goddammit.

She slid on her pants, happy that it was less difficult to get them over her rear. That was something she'd been working hard for that brought her joy in seeing results. *YouTube Pilates and better eating*, she thought to herself as she left her room. She grabbed a doughnut from a box in the kitchen, placing it between her teeth. *Life is about balance, after all*. She took a leaflet from the pad and began to write a note, giving the basics.

"Surprised you are up so early" came a well-known voice from the same old rocking chair.

That only enhanced her teenaged mood, causing her to bite down in a smile. *Plop!* The doughnut fell in a powdered cloud onto her hastily half-finished note. She turned, smiling devilishly at him.

"What is an old man like yourself doing awake at odd hours of the morning?" she exclaimed, swiping up her doughnut, causing it to disappear in a few bites. Doughnuts were her kryptonite. She walked into the living room, put her lightly powdered fists to her hips, cocked her head to one side, and gave him her best mother accusation look. Her own mother had been a pro.

"Hard to sleep with all that talking. Gosh, it was like having a high schooler in the house all over again."

They smiled at each other. Again, Elizabeth felt time slide backward. It did, in fact, feel like she was back in high school, when she'd first got her license and went off to see her friend in Alma.

"Are you okay?" The question took her by surprise, hitting her like the text had. Again, she hardened her resolve to enjoy the day.

"I'm fine. Just some stuff I need to work out with Jason. Nothing new." She sighed heavily. "Can you do me a huge favor and watch Wyatt again today? Bex called, hence the reason I am up, and wanted me to come over so we can start diving into the wedding planning." She made her way back toward her note and, not inconsequentially, the doughnuts beside it. She finished the little note with *I love you*, left it on the table, and grabbed another doughnut. "I appreciate it, Dad." She bent over and left a powdered kiss on his stubbly cheek.

"Can I make a suggestion?"

She cocked an eyebrow and lowered the doughnut that had about made it to her mouth. She nodded.

"Take tomorrow off from wedding planning and . . ." He cleared his throat. ". . . auditioning musicians and spend the day with Wyatt, then at the end of the day, call Jason."

Her anger at Jason began to fight through her defenses, desperate to get to the fresh air on the other side. She wanted to lash out at her dad and tell him to mind his own business, but she also understood that he was trying to help. Another deep sigh. If there was one good thing to come from thinking about Jason, it was that her oxygen saturation levels would be amazing.

"Fine. I will do my best. Not in regard to spending time with Wyatt, because that sounds wonderful. I will do my best to call Jason in a cordial manner at the end of the day. For Wyatt, and because you asked so nicely." She patted his head with her powdered doughnut. She wasn't above being a little mean to him for his unwanted suggestion.

He brushed at his hair while harumphing under his breath.

"I love you, Dad. And don't worry. The powder blends in perfectly with all that white." She slipped out the door, cutting off his retort.

She slapped a smile on her face, already planning to listen to Avril Lavigne on the drive to see Rebecca. If she were going to be back in high-school spirits, she would go all in, baby.

Verse 76

Council Bluffs, Iowa

GIDEON sat in the lone chair in the room on his laptop. He'd set up alerts for anything that might stand out as a potential Samuel sighting. In doing so, he had a plethora of alerts to go through. He was looking at weddings, suicides, bar mitzvahs, accidental deaths, birthday parties, and unexplainable deaths. He'd gotten good at weeding out the standard deaths and was again disappointed that all the ones he'd read so far this morning had been just that: standard, unspectacular deaths. The list of events wasn't going much better. Most of them had the musical talent listed. He supposed listing the performer enticed those on the fence about attending.

He kept broadening his net each day, but he decided that enough was enough. The day after tomorrow, he would flip a coin three times. Once for east and west, once for north and south, then a final round: sudden death between the winners of the first two. Then he would strike out and hope he struck lucky. If he didn't have anything by the end of the month, he would go to Vegas again and pad the bank account a little before starting over with absolutely no leads.

Restarting would be hard, but Samuel had never strayed far from the Midwest. He always claimed the flyover states got far less attention than the coasts. He probably had a point. When a bunch of people died in Iowa, it was chalked up to cult activity and compared to Children of the Corn. Because of course it was.

"Samuel, you piece of shit."

He decided to put the laptop down as the emotional rollercoaster of seeing cute baby pics on birthday invites paired with crime scene photos of blood seeping out from under a tarp were beginning to make him a little queasy.

He decided to spend the day exploring Council Bluffs and Omaha. He'd look for unique things to do there as he was planning on leaving and wanted to experience the towns. He decided to start at the Henry Doorly Zoo after he got breakfast at a local cafe or diner.

He looked at his clothes and decided to go comfortable over fancy. He didn't plan on doing much important reading today. After all, there would be no reason to line up the shoppers at the zoo.

Verse 77

Omaha, Nebraska

SO far, the only phone call that had happened— Jason's phone call to his job to take the day off—had been successful. He'd decided to play it safe with Elizabeth and text her for permission to talk. That seemed like the correct thing to do there. He'd then attempted to call Stacy but had been sent immediately to her voicemail. Maybe she was at work. He couldn't recall which shift, if any, she had today.

"Or maybe," the man-in-the-mirror said from the unlit TV screen, "she is sending your pathetic attempts to reconcile directly to her voicemail. Face it, buckaroo, the best person at ruining your life is you."

Jason was starting to regret not going into work. The apartment was deafeningly silent, which was the perfect setting for discussions with someone who both did and did not exist. Deep down, he understood that the person in the mirror was his subconscious mind feeding off his regrets. "Feeding" was a good term. And it was hungry, so it continued to farm for more regrets, digging deeper and rooting out the depressing thoughts that every divorcé had, he supposed.

"I'm going to go out and get a coffee," he told the empty room. More specifically, he told the man-in-the-mirror who watched him pass in every metallic face of every high-dollar appliance he'd picked out to show off his new life. Each one polished so finely, he often wondered if the man-in-the-mirror was the reality as he seemed far more realistic than Jason himself did.

He grabbed his keys, flung open the door, and walked into the hallway. He was blissfully alone. He breathed deeply, his lungs feeling full for the first time that morning as if a band around them had loosened. He had the whole day to come up with something useful. He had time.

Right now, he needed coffee. He walked toward the elevator, big plans swirling in his mind.

Verse 78

Alma, Nebraska

ELIZABETH and Rebecca walked into the coffee shop and were greeted by a most unusual sight: Patrick, seated in a chair, two cups of coffee sitting on a table in front of him, laughing away with a couple of old men.

Elizabeth recognized them immediately as the men Samuel had introduced her to the night before. She had the oddest feeling that she was in a play and the budget only allowed for a certain number of characters to participate.

Scene 29: Elizabeth and Rebecca enter stage left. The coffee shop is well lit and inviting with cute decorations on the walls. The two women see the two old men, now with Patrick in company. The room goes quiet. Rebecca says, "Patrick?" Big laugh.

Well, at least Elizabeth started laughing, without any warning. The entire coffee shop escapade was due, in part, to Patrick not being around. The whole thing had the surreal feeling of being written. Everyone began laughing, the two older men joining merrily, even though they had no idea why.

"Rebecca, dear, I, uh, got you this coffee. Granted, that was . . ." Patrick looked toward one of the adorable clocks on the wall. "Close to an hour ago. However, if we drop some ice in it, we can call it an iced coffee." He smiled a winning smile, but Rebecca was having none of it.

She threw up her chin in an exaggerated manner. "I am on a date. I have come to realize that men are unreliable and decided to move on. This young hottie behind me is my new forever love, and she knows how to treat a lady. She is going to get me a coffee and it'll be hot when I drink it."

Elizabeth had looked behind her to see to whom she was referring before realizing it was her.

"Nice to meet a fellow convert," Susannah said.

Elizabeth whipped her head back toward her. Everything was happening so fast, she didn't know what was going on. She decided to say the only thing she could think of: "Wait? Did I say I was paying?"

The room died as if she were doing standup at open mic night. Patrick, gasping for breath, finally made it to his feet, walking over for a proper introduction. After that, he kissed his bride-to-be and bought the two of them fresh, steaming hot coffees. He again got a decaffeinated one for Rebecca, which, at first, confused Elizabeth. Her mind had been so filled with information the past few days, the fact that her friend was pregnant had spilled out the top. A little gasp escaped her lips as that reality sank back in and she hugged Rebecca unexpectedly, nearly spilling her hard-won coffee.

They, as a group, sat at the table nearest to the men with whom Patrick had been conversing and introductions were made. Elizabeth was grateful as the men's names had gone the way of the pregnancy, flowing right over the brim of her mind.

It was one of the more pleasant mornings Elizabeth could remember having. Everyone was in high spirits. Even the barista spent time chatting with the little group. At one point, Johanna, Susannah's partner, was brought up and Rebecca apologized profusely, only to have Susannah wave it off cheerily.

"You think it's a joke, but there's still time before you tie the knot, and you weren't lying about your friend here. She's pretty cute."

Again, there was laughter all around as Elizabeth blushed. She did not remember the last time her looks had been brought up so many times in one day, let alone one hour.

She found herself wishing Samuel was there, though. She kept feeling like the fifth wheel as Gary and Jacob were basically one couple, Patrick and Rebecca were another, and Susannah, despite being engaging, also had a job to do and was often not at the table. She popped up sporadically when there were no other customers to attend to.

Elizabeth knew she was seeing Samuel later that day, but it felt like this would be the perfect time to introduce him to Rebecca. Every time the door jingled, she expected it to be him. The feeling that this interaction was a play had never quite left her. She kept thinking, *Samuel, you missed your cue. Enter stage left, please.* Alas, as they gathered their things, waving to Susannah and thanking her for a wonderful morning, she consented that maybe it wasn't the right act.

"End scene. Fade to black," she said under her breath as the door to the coffee shop closed behind her.

Verse 79

Omaha, Nebraska

GIDEON was having an amazing day.

First, he had a great breakfast at a local diner in Council Bluffs, then he went across the river to the zoo. It had been years since he'd been at a zoo. That was back when he and Samuel were children, playing Tom Sawyer.

He remembered how they stood in front of a large gorilla, each attempting to use their abilities on it. First, Gideon tried to read its mind, interested to know what a gorilla would think. But he heard nothing aside from the general thought stream of those around him that he always heard. Next, Samuel had stepped up to the bars and began singing to it. At first, they thought it was working as the animal turned to look at Samuel, but upon realizing it was nothing more than a boy singing, it turned its back to the boys again and paid them no more attention. They'd left the gorilla to try their abilities on other animals around the zoo, but quickly decided that their powers were for people alone.

Today, Gideon enjoyed the animals, not trying to use his power. Instead, he let the thoughts around him blur into white noise.

Next on his to-do list was to visit the Old Market, specifically a candy shop that he'd heard good things about.

After arriving and purchasing a decent amount of taffy and fudge, he'd meandered around, looking at all the shops with no real destination in mind.

The final thing he'd planned was a baseball game. The Storm Chasers were playing.

She'd said she'd been out interviewing the wedding singer, but something in her voice . . .

Gideon's thoughts went blank. He spun around in place, looking at all the faces around him. Holy shit. Was he actually going to catch a break? He took deep breaths, reminding himself that there were hundreds of weddings that needed hundreds of wedding singers. But he also realized that stray thought was the closest he'd gotten to a lead in days. To think that Samuel might have been in Omaha all along was both mind blowing and aggravating. He threw his mind out like a net, opening to everyone around him, shifting from one thought to the next quickly, trying desperately to not become overwhelmed and lose it. He'd not realized how busy this street was until now. Thoughts poured into him like a dam breaking.

Maybe if I drove to Harold's and surprised her, showed up apologizing on my knees.

The voice. He turned all of his focus to that voice and let everything else fade away. The man was walking away from him, but now that Gideon had locked on, that would not matter too much. It was like playing Marco Polo if Polo never stopped talking.

He followed and listened. The wedding singer was no longer important, but the information leaking out of this man was possibly the most interesting thing he'd heard in a long time. The man turned around and, for a second, their eyes met as he scanned the crowd behind him.

Someone's following me. Fuck, did the man-in-the-mirror make it out of the apartment? Is nowhere safe?

Gideon found himself wishing he had popcorn. This was

amazing. There were some people that reacted to his presence in their minds, portraying the awareness as paranoia. Often, the belief was that someone was watching them. He was never too concerned with it as they never understood what it meant, aside from feeling off in their minds. Like in this scenario, where this man—Jason, by name—thought his presence was someone that lived in his mirror. As entertaining as all this was, Gideon was not getting what he came for yet, so he decided to dig a little deeper.

"Hello, you worthless piece of shit."

Gideon found himself in a bathroom, looking at a man in a mirror who was looking back at him, maliciously gleeful. Gideon was stunned. This was something new. The concept of the man-in-the-mirror was so strongly ingrained in Jason's mind, it had become its own entity and it knew he was here. He opened his mouth to say something, but before he could even think about what to say, the man-in-the-mirror held up his hand.

"Don't speak. Your voice is like nails on a chalkboard to me."

Gideon was so perplexed by everything happening that he did not notice the firm hand against his chest until it pushed him back a little, breaking his concentration.

He found himself looking at a sharply dressed doorman to the tallest building in this part of Omaha. Confused, he looked around for Jason. He realized that as he was being confronted by the man-in-the-mirror, Jason had entered this building and Gideon had been stopped. The doorman looked at him suspiciously. Instead of trying to explain an unexplainable situation, Gideon turned and walked a short way down the walk. He then focused with all of his might until he made contact with Jason's mind again, only to find himself standing in front of the mirror. He pulled his mind back.

"All right," he said aloud, "the old-fashioned way it is."

He made a note of the address and began to walk back toward his car. He would have to confront this Jason guy head-on in person and verbally extract the information he needed. There was an inexplicable block in his mind unlike anything Gideon had run into before.

Gideon smiled. Despite this little setback, this was potentially the first lead he'd had for days, and he was excited at the prospect. He'd been planning to leave, letting the wind in his sails guide him, and now the wind had seemingly picked up in the right direction. Or, at least, he hoped. It was not a lot of information he was basing this hunch on, but his desperation made any lead significant. If all else failed, maybe tonight he would dream about something other than his brother and their mother's dying screams.

That alone was a reason to be happy about how the day had played out.

He sat behind the wheel, then remembered he had plans to see a baseball game that night. He could not have asked for a better day. Tomorrow, he would confront Jason while dressed to impress. Hopefully, by tomorrow night, he would be in a new hotel, hot on the trail yet again. Maybe this time, he wouldn't be late to the main event.

He was humming as he backed out of the parking space. By the time he was pulling out of Old Market, he was singing loudly, "Buy me some peanuts and Cracker Jacks, I don't care if I never come back."

Verse 80

Alma, Nebraska

ELIZABETH and Rebecca had a splendid morning. The years seemed to fall away as they made out-of-date jokes about boy bands and crushes they had when they were younger. The years apart felt more like days as they fell back into an easy rhythm.

Elizabeth was upset with herself for not making more of an effort to stay connected with her old friend. In the digital age, where everyone had phones in their pockets at all times, the best she could do was like a random post here and there. She'd not even commented on any recent ones that she could remember.

As they looked at wedding magazines and dress options, and talked about food and beverages, she made a deal with herself to never let this friendship lapse again.

Inevitably, as she knew it would, conversation turned to Samuel. When Elizabeth admitted to kissing him the night before, Rebecca let out a squeak of excitement. Elizabeth rolled her eyes and tried to keep her own excitement at bay, which was difficult with Rebecca grabbing her arm and shaking it.

"You little so-and-so."

That was what they'd said as kids when they wanted to use more adult words like "slut" or "bitch." It was a substitution Elizabeth started reusing since becoming a teacher, then a mother. It helped avoid situations like the one from the other day, when Wyatt had heard, then replicated her foul language.

"Look, don't get too excited. He's a traveling singer and there is probably nothing to it." This thought had been with her since she got off the phone with him the night before. It helped to keep her grounded; to hold her back from running full throttle into the arms of this man she barely knew. For both her and Wyatt's sake, starting any kind of meaningful relationship with a person she knowingly could not be with was not an option.

Rebecca let go of her arm, but the sparkle in her eyes did not diminish as they got back to work on wedding planning. "What about just a casual fuck?"

Elizabeth gasped and her face went scarlet at the surprising exclamation.

"No one is saying you have to follow in Jason's footsteps and move in with the first person you have a crush on, but, babe, sometimes you gotta let out some steam."

The casual nature with which Rebecca made such statements helped normalize them, and Elizabeth felt her calm return quickly. "I've never done anything like that. Also, in case you have forgotten, we hate Jason, and his post-separation choices are top of the list as to why we hate him. Not to mention, Wyatt complicates things. He seemed to like Samuel when we met him, and if I get much closer to him, it could end up hurting Wyatt, and that's the last thing I want, especially right now." She sighed. All the debates and conversations she'd had with herself in the early hours of the morning were now being verbalized, and she was dismayed to find she was on the side that she'd spent so much time internally fighting against.

Rebecca sighed, raised her palms skyward, and they moved on to a new topic.

The girls broke for lunch. Rebecca's mother brought them ham and cheese sandwiches, grapes, and soda. It was delicious. Elizabeth, lounging on the couch in the living room, felt the dozy warmth and peace of the afternoon working on her. "I think if we are going to continue this hard work, I, at least, will need some of that fancy coffee your parents have."

Rebecca frowned with jealousy.

"I know you already hit your caffeine limit, but how 'bout you watch me drink it and imagine that you are me? I will describe the delicious flavor, the warmth, the aroma—all of it to make it more real."

"You are more than a so-and-so. You are a real bitch, you know that?" Rebecca said and they both fell into a bout of laughter.

Rebecca's father came in and gave them each an agreeable nod. Then his eyes lost their humor. "Elizabeth, there is something I think you should know. It appears that they found a body in the Norton lake."

All humor left the room. Elizabeth no longer felt dozy. The warmth that had moments ago been leading her toward a nap turned to ice. Her mind raced as to why he felt it pertinent to tell her specifically. The faces of Wyatt and her dad appeared in her mind, each underwater, pale and bloated. Her mind raced as she tried to remember what their plans had been for the day. Had it involved the lake? She'd been so tired and excited from the night before that she'd barely paid attention to her dad as he laid out their plans.

"It was Randall Earlman."

She was so distracted by the images of her dead family members that, at first, the name meant nothing to her, and she was filled with relief. Then the name fit into place and all the air left her. The man that had caused her family so much pain, the man who'd taken her mother, Wyatt's grandmother, and her dad's wife, was dead.

What emotion was the appropriate one to have? Should she be happy that he was dead after all the hurt he'd caused? Should she feel remorse at yet another death involving this man?

"Are you okay?"

The warmth in Rebecca's dad's voice helped to clarify her thoughts. She realized that the hurt she was feeling wasn't for a man that she'd, in all honesty, hated, but was in the thought that with his passing, her mother's chapter in her life was done. While Randall lived, she'd kept her mother alive in pure anger at the injustice of it all, thinking almost daily about how it was unfair that a piece of garbage like Randall was allowed to continue drawing breath while her mother was six feet underground. She saw now that while it hurt to let that go—because it meant letting go of her mother that much more—it was good. It would be better now as she would be able to think of her mom's life rather than the life of the man who'd taken hers.

She smiled up at the man who'd always felt like a second father to her. "I'll be all right. Thank you for letting me know."

He smiled and looked relieved that he'd not ruined the previously good day with the news.

"Is there anything I can do for you?"

She felt like a kid again, hanging out in Rebecca's bedroom, making photo collages out of *Seventeen Magazine*. He would walk in, say hi, and ask if he could get them anything or be of service in any way. Then he would hurry off to get them the requested soda, or cookie, or whatever it was they'd asked for.

"Actually, I have heard a lot about a special self-grinding coffeemaker that sounds far too advanced for me to figure out."

"It would be my pleasure." He turned to his daughter who, after tensing up at the mention of Randall's death, had lounged back in her chair. "What about you, fruit of my loins?"

Rebecca made a retching sound. "Nothing for me. I lost any appetite I had at the mention of your loins. Gross."

Laughter traveled with him as he left the room to get Elizabeth her coffee.

As it died down, she found herself back in her own mind. Thoughts of Randall battled against thoughts of Samuel for dominance of her mind. By the time the coffee had been delivered, Samuel had won out. She was back in the right mindset to continue wedding planning, thoughts of her upcoming meeting with Samuel giving it all a rosy hue.

Verse 81

Norton, Kansas

FOR Harold, the news about Randall would have to wait, for he and Wyatt were at the local swimming pool. Harold was on a bench, shaded from the warm summer sun, talking to a young man from his church as Wyatt speedwalked his way back to the waterslide, intent to make it all the way to the rope by skidding on top of the water. He got to the top of the slide. While waiting his turn, he waved down at his grandpa who waved back then gave him a double thumbs-up. Harold mused on his previous reluctance to house his little family for the summer. He was starting to wonder how he would handle life after they went back to Omaha. He'd become used to their presence and already felt the loss just thinking about it.

For the first time, he began to wonder if moving a little closer wasn't such a bad idea. Was there anything holding him to Norton? He thought of Judith poking fun at him while preparing the beds for company. Ghosts were tied to locations, but memories were free. Maybe when he got home, when Wyatt inevitably took a well-earned nap after swimming, he would get on his laptop and peruse listings in and around Omaha. He didn't need much space. One thing memories and ghosts had in common was that neither took up much room.

He watched Wyatt duck his head and moments later, arms crossed around his narrow chest, he came shooting out the bottom, skipping across the water, and Harold was pretty sure his toe touched the rope. He clapped his hands and gave a little shout. People looked at him, but the only person looking who mattered was Wyatt, and he was beaming.

Verse 82

Alma, Nebraska

SALLY looked at the packed suitcase on her bed, telling herself for the hundredth time that she was only packing one. She wasn't leaving Alma like Samuel had bid her to do. Rather, she was taking some time away with her son.

Samuel had nothing to do with it. Her family had suffered a loss and getting away was the most appropriate form of recovery. Being with family made the most sense to her, so she'd called up her sister, Amanda, who lived in Des Moines, Iowa, and immediately agreed to host them. Boomer had not spent much time with Sally's family, and this felt important after everything that had happened. Samuel's foreboding message about nothing being here for her was shallow at best. It didn't take into account that Boomer had grown up in Alma and had friends there, and friends were also important after losing a family member. So, she wasn't moving away. She was taking a break from Alma.

And she was taking a break from Samuel.

Well, from the constant hope that she would run into him.

The trip to the bar had not been her first attempt, only the most successful. Prior to that, when at the grocery store, she would find her heart speeding up with each aisle she walked down, hoping that as she turned into the next one, there he would be, deciding on a brand of chips. When at a restaurant with Boomer, her head would snap up as the bell rang over the door. It was exhausting. Seeing him with another woman had changed the situation. Now she knew she would fear the next aisle as it might not be just him looking at chips, but the two of them as they planned a midnight snack back at his hotel.

Yes, getting away from this town for a little while would help clear her head.

Verse 83

Alma, Nebraska

BOOMER was thrilled. Ever since the incident, he'd wanted to leave Alma.

He'd never been close to his mom and was not sure how best to approach these types of conversations. It was like talking to a stranger, something at which he'd never been good. He preferred to let his dad do the talking, something at which he'd excelled. Now, Boomer, who struggled to tell his mom he didn't want broccoli with dinner, had to find a way to tell her he wanted to move. Even with the maturity he felt he had gained by going through the recent traumatic events, the idea of having an adult conversation with his mother terrified him. So, when she'd announced the visit to his aunt's, his relief felt like a physical weight had been removed from his shoulders. His mom had smiled and told him to start packing. He could not get out of town quick enough.

His dad would never in a million years have left him like that. Something—or someone—had made his dad do that. Boomer was scared that it might come for him or his mom next.

While the reality of death was something new in his life, the concept of death had been with him since his first memory. His dad would talk about hunts he'd been on, bragging while pointing at the antlers, the pictures, and the one prize buck head that hung in their old living room. Yes, death had been a common topic in their house.

Yet, it was his dad's singing that haunted him most. The song that had preceded his dad's death played on repeat in Boomer's head, but never came out his lips. He had the sinking feeling that if he ever allowed it to get past his clenched teeth, he would start singing, and as the song took his life, he would hear a motorcycle drive away.

He did not know what got his dad, but he knew it was still out there. He was the man of the house now. It was up to him to keep his family safe.

Verse 84

Alma, Nebraska

BARTHOLOMEW and Samuel sat together in the cool office in the back of the church, each holding a tall, cold glass of lemonade. The lemonade was compliments of Dorothy Jenkins, a delightful lady in the church who'd taken it upon herself to keep Bartholomew well fed.

"I know the good Lord used the dry bones to get his message across," Dorothy had said, "but that doesn't mean we need a skeleton preachin' to us every Sunday."

So, along with the lemonade, they also had a heaping plate of chocolate chip cookies.

"God forbid she bring me a salad," Bartholomew commented as he took his third cookie.

Samuel shrugged and took another cookie himself.

"I used to never work out before moving here. Now I have to wake up an hour earlier than I want to so that I have a fighting chance of fitting into my Sunday best."

Samuel choked on the bite of cookie he'd attempted to swallow and laughed it out.

Bartholomew, reveling in this new friendship, joined Samuel in laughter. "So," Bartholomew finally got out, wiping tears from his eyes, "how are things with the young lady? The two of you looked pretty friendly the other day."

"That is still in development and, if I am being serious, a bit complicated. All I can say, with any certainty, is that she is different from anyone I have ever met. You see I have a . . ." He paused as if looking for the right word. ". . . a certain charm about me, I guess you could say, that makes people generally want to interact with me. I have never once put on that charm for her and yet, we seem to click without it. That is something I have never experienced before." He stopped and looked out the office window contemplatively.

Bartholomew was confused. He didn't know what Samuel called it, but everything he'd seen in regard to their relationship was the definition of charming. He considered asking for clarification, but Samuel continued, and Bartholomew forgot his confusion.

"The complication, therefore, does not come from my feelings for her, which are genuine, but rather our very different lives. Neither of us are sticking around here after the wedding. So, it's hard to consider any future being feasible between the two of us." He sighed, signifying to Bartholomew that it was something with which he'd been struggling.

"You know," Bartholomew said cautiously, knowing that he was already on shaky ground, "Omaha is a pretty cool city. Not too big, not too small, but just right."

"Am I Goldilocks in this scenario?" Samuel asked with a smile.

But Bartholomew heard the sincerity behind the question. Bartholomew wondered if Samuel had already considered this. He'd never believed in love at first sight, but, as someone who'd never found love, it was easy to discount such fanciful things as that. To think that Samuel had not only considered a future with Elizabeth but had considered changing his to make it work showed how much he already cared for this woman he'd essentially just met. "I am not saying you would have to stop driving your little motorcycle around."

There was a scoff from Samuel, but he smiled regardless.

"But wouldn't it be nice, as you are traveling the country and sleeping in hotel rooms, to know there is a concrete place to return to? Something fixed, not so static?" Again, Bartholomew who'd lived at home, then lived at college, and now lived in the parsonage across the street from the church wondered how he could be giving any advice in these matters, having never experienced anything like Samuel's life.

"I don't know. Wouldn't it make it harder to sleep in a hotel bed when I knew I had my own bed waiting for me somewhere else?"

Bartholomew understood that what he said could influence the future of this man. He'd been a minister for a few years now and had never felt his words held so much power as he did now. It gave him pause. Up 'til this point, he'd been pushing the narrative because he thought they were a cute couple, but did that give him the permission to influence their relationship in such a dramatic way? For that matter, if he told Samuel he didn't think it would work, would Samuel end it immediately at his recommendation? That would possibly do more harm than good.

Suddenly, the room felt very small. As he sipped his lemonade, Samuel's electric blue eyes locked on to him.

He swallowed loudly, then took a deep breath. "It sounds to me like you have never had a reason to try. The very fact that you are considering it makes me think you should. Understand that I have never experienced either the open road or the type of love that would make me consider giving it up.

However, when I see the two of you together, I see potential. I see something that, if I had, I would at least fight for before giving up." He sighed heavily to illustrate the end of his lofty monologue and took another cookie to add a period.

Samuel fell back into his chair and ran his hand through his hair. "It's like you pulled the words from my own mind, like. . ." Samuel's face grew troubled. "Like, um, you could read them." He finished, trailing off toward the end.

There was silence then, as everything that had been said settled around them, filling the small office, taking up the space not filled by theological books and desk decor.

Finally, Samuel said, "Thank you for talking to me about this. I haven't had anyone to talk to about these things for a while. I will admit, as much as I love my job, and my life, it has been pretty lonely lately." He smiled, but Bartholomew could see there was real pain behind it. "No matter what happens, I want you to know that this friendship, as short as it has been so far, has been tremendously meaningful to me. No matter what happens, I will be forever grateful for these times we have spent together."

Bartholomew was stunned by all that Samuel had said. In the era of cell phones and email, it was rare for someone to talk with such finality in their words. He was acting like they would never be able to talk again after the wedding. Bartholomew could not remember a conversation feeling as heavy as this one was, and he'd talked couples away from divorce. He cleared his throat and asked, "When do you see Elizabeth again?"

"Tonight," Samuel said, his face lighting up. "She is in town right now with the bride, going over wedding plans. We will meet up after."

Bartholomew would have traded all the cookies left for a mirror to hold up, showing Samuel how happy he looked at the thought of seeing Elizabeth later. He had no mirror, so he took yet another cookie. He held it for a bit, considering eating it for an excuse to not add any pressure to Samuel's visit tonight, but decided against it. "Have you considered telling her how you feel? Specifically, that your relationship with her could last longer than the wedding? She might be thinking the same thing, afraid to mention it because she doesn't want to get her hopes up if there is no chance." He bit the cookie and watched as Samuel considered what he'd said.

Samuel took another cookie and took a bite. They were becoming quite the handy distraction when a little more thought was needed, Bartholomew mused.

"I guess I'm scared that she doesn't feel that way," said Samuel. "She is on vacation, at a wedding, away from her hometown. What if she sees me as a fun fling before returning to her real life and I start telling her I want more, something I am not even sure of myself yet? She might run for the hills or, worse, laugh in my face."

Bartholomew felt time fall away. He was back in high school with one of his friends dealing with a crush. Teenage insecurity never goes away; it just gains greater stakes.

Bartholomew set down the half of the cookie he held, catching Samuel's full attention.

"When I was in high school, I had a crush on a girl named Jennifer Platte." Samuel's eyebrows shot up, showing confusion and interest in equal measure. "We were in the same friend group, and I was pretty sure she liked me too. As prom neared, I knew that I wanted to go with her, but I couldn't find the courage necessary to ask her. In the end, one of our other friends went with her. We danced, we had a good time, but I did not take her." He paused to sip his lemonade, and to add dramatic effect. He was a minister, after all. He knew how to play up a story. "Jennifer and I are friends on Facebook. She is married now. Not to the friend who took her to prom, if you were wondering. Honestly, had I taken her to the prom, I doubt we would have ended up together or that our lives would be any different than they are now. However, I can tell you that there is not a day that goes by that I don't regret not taking her."

Samuel leaned back in his chair and ran his hand through his hair again.

"If I daily regret something as trivial as asking a girl to the prom, how much more are you going to regret not telling Elizabeth how you feel and at least giving it a shot? Who knows? It might lead nowhere. But I can guarantee that if you don't try, you will always wonder if it could have gone somewhere."

Samuel was quiet for a long time. Bartholomew's story clearly had an impact on him.

At last he stood, brushing stray cookie crumbs from his pants. "Thank you. I think I should get going."

Bartholomew stood too, afraid he'd hurt Samuel in some way.

But Samuel smiled and shook his head. "Don't worry. I'm fine. I just think that tonight's meeting might be more important than I had originally planned. I'm gonna go back to the hotel and do a little prep. Maybe run some lines in front of the mirror for a little while. Make sure I don't mess it up."

Bartholomew smiled, relieved, and walked Samuel out of his office, leading him to the front door with words of affirmation.

As the sounds of Samuel's motorcycle faded away, he walked back to his office and sat in front of the much-diminished plate of cookies. He maneuvered the half cookie left from before into a smile with giant cookie eyes above it. "So, Jenny, you wanna go to the prom with me?" Had anyone heard the laughter coming from his office, they may have wondered why it sounded so sad. But he was alone.

Verse 85

Norton, Kansas

HAROLD and Wyatt were on the back porch drinking iced tea, sitting in silence. After the pool, they'd returned home. Waiting for Harold, were numerous texts and voicemails informing him of Randal's death. All the color had faded from his face and he'd needed to grab the back of a chair to steady himself. Wyatt had started forward reaching out to help. Harold, upon seeing Wyatt's concern, had explained in very vague PG details what had happened to his grandmother and, more recently, at the lake. Now they sat, neither speaking.

Finally, Harold turned to his grandson. "Your grandmother loved you. I know you know that, but since she isn't here to tell you, I figured I would. The day you were born, she cried for close to an hour, tears of joy, because her body couldn't contain it all. She no longer wanted to be referred to as 'Harold's wife' or 'Elizabeth's mother.' Instead, she wanted to be known as 'Wyatt's grandma.'" Tears began to fall down his cheeks. "She was so excited about seeing you grow up. She actually had a birthday card for each of your birthdays all the way up to forty, along with graduation cards for elementary school, junior high, high school, and college. She even got two extra ones in case you decide to go on to get your master's and doctorate. And I will make sure you get every single one." He had to wipe his face as it was getting hard to see now. "She loved every second of time she got with you, and she spent every second away either remembering the last time or planning the next."

He stopped then and looked out over their backyard at the big tree Elizabeth had climbed innumerable times. Wyatt had shown interest in climbing in it, as there were still random boards nailed into the bark, but there were too many branches that no longer produced leaves. It was too much risk. "Your grandma was taken from us, taking the future she'd dreamed of from both of you. The future always seems inevitable; time keeps moving so the future is always going to be in front of you. The future is something I think we all take for granted." He stopped again.

"I'm glad that man died," Wyatt said with no emotion.

Harold turned toward him, the tears no longer flowing. Wyatt sat before him, confident in the statement he'd made.

"We should never be glad at anyone's death, Wyatt. Randall's future is now gone as well. Perhaps in his future, he'd gotten things together, had made something of himself. Two wrongs never make a right." These were the words that came out of his mouth. But in his mind, he was glad as well. The only disappointment he felt in the matter was that Randall had taken his own life and Harold had not had the pleasure. There were many sleepless nights where he could clearly imagine his hands wrapped around that miserable throat, squeezing as the flesh protruded between his fingers, feeling things break and tear beneath the pressure. "No, we should never be glad at anyone's death," he repeated, willing himself to believe his own words.

Verse 86

Alma, Nebraska

ELIZABETH, Rebecca, and Patrick walked through the doors to the bar as the afternoon was rounding third base toward evening. Samuel was sitting alone at the booth he often occupied with his older friends. Upon seeing the three enter, he stood, straightened his shirt, and walked over to greet them.

"Hello, my name is Samuel, and it's a pleasure to finally meet you." He raised his hand which was gripped by Patrick's own. Then, without warning, Rebecca threw herself into his arms, almost knocking him over. He laughed. "You must be Rebecca." He spun her in a circle, setting her gingerly back on her feet. "Elizabeth, and basically everyone I have talked to in this town, have spoken very highly of you."

Elizabeth watched all of this. Her initial nervous anticipation turned into relief as she saw how effortlessly familiarity bloomed amongst them. Whenever introducing someone she liked to those she already knew, there was the trepidation that they would not be liked by others. Could you plan a future with someone who would limit your future with those already in your life? Every introduction was a potential sacrifice and, as such, could never be taken lightly.

"You, sir, are striking," Rebecca cooed. Samuel smiled dutifully. "Your eyes . . ." She trailed off, then finished with a question: "Do you wear contacts?"

"Nope. These, along with my voice, are the only things my mother ever gave me."

Elizabeth felt like she was struck by lightning. Until this point, he'd not mentioned a single thing about his life growing up. For him to drop that information so willingly shook her. That, and the mention of any mother today would probably hit her like that. Suddenly, she was filled with curiosity. What had happened to his mother—or his father, for that matter? Did he have siblings? Where did he grow up? She'd been feeling like she knew the book that was Samuel pretty well, but she realized that she'd skipped to the middle, forgetting to read through the first chapters.

She realized that those eyes, given to him by his mother, were on her and that Samuel had asked a question. "Sorry, I was wool gathering." What on Earth? Was that even a phrase normal people said? It certainly wasn't one she said.

He smiled at the phrase, however, and she felt better. "I said it was nice to see you and asked if you would like a drink before we sit down to discuss my employment."

The other two had made their way to the bar. She presumed there would be the purchase of one beer and one non-alcoholic, fruity beverage. It was thrilling to see a secret in play and be a part of it.

Samuel turned toward the couple at the bar. "She sure is something."

Elizabeth nodded, feeling a slight burst of jealousy; a feeling leftover from when the two of them were younger, and Rebecca was always considered the pretty one and Elizabeth her smart friend. She knew the jealousy was unfounded. She allowed it to pass by her like a scent tied to a memory that pulls emotions quickly before blowing away in the breeze.

"She sure is. Good thing, for me, she is getting married and is no longer available." He turned to protest, but she cut him off, meaning to maintain the high ground this time. "I will take that drink. A Manhattan sounds nice."

She walked away, toward the booth they would share, and slid in, joined shortly by her friend. Patrick was still waiting at the bar for the drinks and Samuel walked over to him.

"We did good for ourselves," Rebecca said, nodding toward the bar.

"You did good for yourself. I am considering what is good for myself." Again, Elizabeth had to wonder why she was fighting so hard against her own desires. She supposed that after getting burned while taking something out of the oven, it doesn't make sense to reach back in without precautions. Her constant reality checks were the equivalent of oven mitts.

"No one is saying you have to get married, you know." Rebecca made a gesture with her hand.

"What was that?" Patrick asked as he slid in next to her.

"Oh, nothing. We were talking about Molotov cocktails."

Luckily for Elizabeth, Patrick's confused expression was funny enough that she forgot to blush. Samuel joined them shortly after, and Elizabeth started to wonder if maybe it was time to take off the oven mitts.

Verse 87

Council Bluffs, Iowa

GIDEON stood behind the provided ironing board, making sure his one and only suit was impeccably crisp. It had been a long time since he'd had to get information he was looking for without reading someone's mind. The suit had to be perfect because that initial look might be enough to break through, saving him a lot of effort. But, if not, it would give him an excuse to ask the questions he needed to ask.

He looked over at the bed, toward his open wallet with the badge and ID showing. The photo on the ID was of a younger man, but Gideon reminded himself that most people don't have the most up-to-date pictures on their IDs. Samuel had acquired their fake FBI credentials with a song directed at a target found by Gideon. He sighed, thinking back on the years they'd worked together before Samuel started deviating.

After they left their mothers, they'd found another park with another bench and had held a meeting. This, of course, was after Gideon had vomited up everything in his system at the thought of their mother, left behind in a fire, unable to move. He kept seeing her in the doorway, imagining as her clothes caught fire, her skin melting, and her hair turning black and curling toward her scalp. He wondered how long Samuel's song had held her in place before she fell to the ground. As her muscles disintegrated, had her mind continued fighting to stay

standing because of the command her son had left her as they
walked into fresh air? Cue the vomit.

At the bench, Samuel started crying. He was a kid again;
one who'd met his mother for the first time, been scorned by his
mother for the first time, and killed his mother for the first time.

As hard as it was for Gideon to comprehend everything
that had just happened—in fact, everything that had happened
since he met Samuel—he understood that he was an older
brother. With that, came certain duties. So, he held Samuel and
comforted him until he stopped crying. He'd cried as well, but
he made sure to make no sound as he did not want to
exacerbate Samuel's own grief or make him feel responsible.

But wasn't he? He'd saved their lives, as it definitely
appeared that their mother wanted them dead, but couldn't he
have commanded her to put the fire out?

Gideon could hear Samuel's thoughts, but there were
too many to get a good sense of them and his emotions were
complicatedly mixed. At one instant, he was mortified at what
had happened; in the next, he was happy to be alive then proud
of himself for saving them. This emotion would be followed by
a hatred at their mother for her actions and, more importantly,
her words.

With effort, Gideon tuned out Samuel's thoughts, held
him, and cried.

Time passed. Gideon had no sense of it. It could have
been a few minutes; it could have been a few hours. He held
Samuel until he was ready to talk.

When he'd finished crying, and they'd cleaned up their
faces, leaving snotty messes on their shirts, Gideon said, "I love
you, Samuel. Thank you for saving my life." It came out
without any plan or forethought, but he instantly knew it was

the right thing to say. Samuel's tumultuous thoughts evened out. That was good as Gideon was still trying to sort out his own.

"You aren't mad?" Samuel asked, looking up. His blue eyes cut into Gideon, solidifying his resolve that, while everything had gone to shit, Samuel was a kid at heart who'd been in an unprecedented situation and acted accordingly.

"Why would I be mad? Did you think that maybe I wanted to be torched to death? You saved our lives. Samuel Serenade, you are a hero!"

Samuel's eyes, still damp with tears, gleamed at this declaration. Gideon felt that they would be okay. At least, in regard to their past. However, now they had the future to think about. "Samuel, we need to talk about where we go from here."

"What? Like, back to the house?"

Gideon had a vision of cops waiting at the house they'd left earlier, wanting to question them in the death of Andy. No, the house was done. It was part of the past like everything else that had happened today. But where did that leave them? They were two children on their own in the wide world. Ah, two children with the power to know and manipulate the thoughts of those around them. Had they not already been using their powers to get to where they were now? In fact, he realized now that they could essentially do whatever they wanted. Between the two of them, nothing was off limits. "How 'bout instead of going to the house, we do our own thing?"

Samuel's eyes widened and his eyebrows raised. "Like what? Save the world?"

Gideon laughed, threw an arm around his little brother, and they walked out of the park toward a world that belonged to them. "Let's start with lunch. We can save the world after that."

Gideon saw a picture of Samuel in spandex with a flowing cape. Why not? Superheroes save people from burning buildings all the time. It's one of their more iconic cliches.

Gideon hung his ironed pants on the inner part of the hanger, followed by the shirt, then the jacket, not a wrinkle in sight. Samuel was close, closer than he'd been for years. He could feel it.

Tomorrow, Gideon would talk to this Jason guy and be back on the trail. After what felt like forever, he felt hope again, something he'd been a day away from letting go. He thought about that day in the park and how he'd convinced himself they were superheroes. Sometimes even the ability to read minds cannot help if you are blinded by love.

He watched himself in the mirror as he brushed his teeth, thinking about the read he'd gotten today from his new target about Jason's man-in-the-mirror. Tomorrow was sure to be interesting. He looked forward to the challenge.

Verse 88

Omaha, Nebraska

JASON held the phone away for a moment and breathed a sigh of relief. One fire might be out. If not, it was smaller than it was. Hopefully, just coals.

Stacy had finally answered her phone. The first five to ten minutes had been about what he'd expected, a lot of accusations, name calling, questions about the relationship and their future, etc., etc. She'd then begun to wind down a little, at which point he was able to get a few words in. Soon enough, they were having a real dialogue. He was adequately apologetic while not openly admitting he was wrong. He'd felt that, had he done that, it would have set a bad precedent going forward in regard to his ex-wife and son.

To be honest, he was not sure what his future relationship with either of them looked like after the previous night, but he knew he wanted to continue to try for one. As they talked, his mind kept drifting in that direction. Sure, he was attempting to soothe his current girlfriend. But it was his relationship with El about which he was most concerned, and she was the one who was refusing his calls and not answering his text messages.

As he talked, he walked. He'd never been able to stand in place while on the phone. He had to be in constant motion, which was odd as he was able to sit for hours watching TV, working, or playing video games. However, when he was on the phone, if he was not pacing, his anxiety would rise little by little until he was ready to scream into the handset if the person took too deep a breath. So, he paced, walked from room to room, stopping occasionally when he needed to think about a response.

This evening, as he talked to Stacy, he kept noticing spots on the walls where mirrors had been. When he moseyed into the master bedroom, he saw the giant lump of sheet that had been thrown over the vanity, knowing who lurked beneath. Every reflective surface had been covered or removed, and he was, at last, in peace. This was a blessing as he did not need that know-it-all interrupting the sensitive phone call he was on.

He knew that he'd heard the man-in-the-mirror speak without reflective surfaces, but that was a rarity. Then there had been that moment when he was out for coffee. He'd felt the man-in-the-mirror in his mind, almost in a physical way, but that had passed as well. He shuddered thinking about it. It had been something altogether new, and he'd not liked it. His unwanted guest had no right to bother him outside in the clear daylight.

"Will that be all right?"

Shit. Right as the fire had been going out, he lost his train of thought and now risked setting it ablaze again. If he admitted to not hearing her, it would come off as a lack of sincerity, but if he agreed without knowing to what, that could lead to a worse outcome. He went back and forth for a second and landed on agreeing with whatever she'd said. Being agreeable seemed the correct option. He decided to grunt his agreement in case it was something to which he shouldn't have agreed. That way, he might have an out by declaring the grunt had not meant what she thought it did.

"Great. I will be there around ten tomorrow morning to grab my stuff and help you pack your own, then we can grab lunch."

It would appear he'd agreed to go with her after all. Which, all things considered, was probably the best option. Yet, his mind began to drift again to El and their last explosive discussion. Here, he was trying to make up with the woman who currently shared his bed while constantly thinking of the woman who'd shared his bed.

There was one thought in particular: the wedding singer.

During their little tiff, she'd mentioned a wedding singer not once, not twice, but three times in different contexts. Once in regard to what she'd been doing when he initially called; the next in regard to her upcoming wedding-planning duties. Both were innocent enough. Then she'd said something about how good the night had been. She had started to say something else about the singer when she'd stopped herself, taken a deep breath, and began to tear into him again. He could not stop wondering what she'd been about to say. Had there been more than an audition that evening? Had there been some flirtation— maybe more? Jealousy rose in him, filling his chest with uncomfortable pressure, tickling his throat like bile.

With the man-in-the-mirror behind cloth or in closets, he took up the slack and berated himself for being jealous. Did he want to be with Stacy while knowing that Elizabeth had not moved on? He realized clearly how hypocritical that was and how unfair it was to think like that. Yet, here he was. He kept seeing his ex-wife through the eyes of another man. Maybe at a nice dinner or, God forbid, in a hotel room with the sheets pooled around her waist. That man wouldn't look at her exposed breasts and think about how they'd been used to feed a baby; he would look at them for the first time and see what he had not been able to see after Wyatt. They were great breasts.

He stopped his pacing, put thumb and forefinger to the bridge of his nose, and took a deep breath. These thoughts were unhelpful, both in general and, more importantly, during this phone call.

"That sounds great," he told Stacy. "I'll pack the essentials, like deodorant and face wash, and wait for you to help me pick out the clothes. Meeting the grandmother is a big step. I want to make the right impression." He had a moment of anxiety where he wondered if his lack of attention would be found out if he'd misunderstood the packing aspect of her statement.

"Oh, for sure. I would hate for you to meet her in the shirt you were wearing when we first met. Let's leave the rock band t-shirts at home, shall we?"

Ironically, he'd left that shirt at his old home with his old wife in his old life. He didn't even remember which band it had been. He got it at a music festival while in high school. He felt a hard pull toward his past: for the simpler times before he'd grown into such a shitty person.

"Yeah, I don't think that would win me any points. Unless Nana is secretly a metal head at which point she might end up liking me more."

God, he felt like a mediocre actor. All the words falling out of his mouth felt like they'd been written for him and rehearsed backstage. Luckily, she didn't seem to notice. She continued to talk about tomorrow and the upcoming trip. He practiced smiling.

Verse 89

Alma, Nebraska

ELIZABETH sat across from Samuel. Rebecca and Patrick had left. It had been one of the most enjoyable evenings Elizabeth had had in a long time. Just adults in conversation took her back to before Wyatt was born when Jason and she would call up another couple to see if they wanted a spur-of-the-moment outing to the bar. After you have kids, there is no such thing as spur of the moment. Either you brought your kid, which meant no late-night bar scene, or you found a sitter, which was usually more work than it was worth and had you starting the night already in debt. She had to remind herself, even now, that her dad's presence was temporary, and she would return to full parenthood after the wedding.

Still, the freedom she'd been allowed invigorated her and made her feel young again. Young and free to look at the man across the table from her with her guard down. Free to be herself and not a divorcee or a mother or a teacher, but a woman on a date. A real date. At least, that was what she was allowing herself to consider this little hang out now that the other two had left them alone and she had no curfew. The idea that she was living in her old room at her old house with her dad with no curfew made her smile. Samuel noticed and smiled back.

The meeting of Samuel and the two getting married had been delightful. Everything clicked, easing away the last of the tension she'd felt about Samuel. She'd been allowing herself to see him as a presumptive something, but his meeting her friend had held more weight than even she'd known until they arrived at the bar.

A few minutes into conversation, she realized that she'd been metaphorically holding her breath, and, again metaphorically, she'd been able to let it out as she saw how easily the talk came for everyone at the table.

Had she needed Rebecca's stamp of approval to pursue this? No. But it certainly helped and made her feel that much more comfortable.

Her son had liked Samuel and her best friend liked him. Again, she smiled as she realized that the last person whose approval would be important was her dad's. And again, she had that feeling of being back in high school as she considered bringing home a new boyfriend to meet her parent.

"What is so funny?" Samuel asked, pulling her from her musings.

"Oh, you know, thinking about how time is thin and how easy it is to fall back into the past."

He raised his eyebrows in question, so she explained all her musings on being back in her childhood house and how it made her feel like a high schooler.

He chuckled dutifully. "I would love to meet your father at some point and, even more, to get to know your son better. That little bit at the gas station was hardly enough time for me to demonstrate how awesome I am."

She choked on her drink as a laugh tried to make an appearance as she swallowed. He began to stand with concern, but she waved him back down, catching her breath.

He continued. "Sorry. I will make sure to only show my hubris when you are not drinking a beverage. The last thing I need is for you to drown because of my pride."

She felt struck as if she'd been slapped. Her face must have shown because the wry half-smile she was coming to know so well dropped away instantly.

"Are you all right?"

She hesitated, knowing that her mother's death had ended their previous time together, but also desperately wanting to vent some feelings about what had happened out at the lake. She thought about their long phone call, and how receptive he'd been to her soul-emptying speech. She decided to tell him about it. But she would keep it short to make sure the night could survive.

So, she told him about Randall's death and about her mixed feelings. She began to touch on memories of her mom before she realized that might do her in.

"Anyway," she said, cutting off the start of a story about her mother, "that is neither here nor there, but now you understand why I reacted to you saying 'drown.' It was funny, so you can put that silly half-smile back on your face."

Surprisingly, despite all of what she'd said, he did, and she knew she was falling in love.

With his help, they led the conversation away from serious matters, back to safer ground. Everything was going great. She'd begun to play with more adult thoughts about where she would like to spend the night. She had a fleeting image of trying to sneak Samuel through her bedroom window, shushing him as he bonked his head on the sill; both pausing when they heard a creak in the hallway, giggling under their breaths. She was wondering how she could tell Samuel about this funny new thought without sounding too forward when her phone chirped. A text message had come in. Without thought, doing something she'd done a million times, she flipped up her phone to look at her most recent text. It was like breathing, like blinking, like any other action the body does without conscious thought. When a phone chirps, you look; it's as simple as that. There, on the screen, was Jason's name, followed by Jason's text:

> Look, I want to talk to you in person, try again to explain everything, but I realize I will have to wait for the opportunity. I am sorry that I made you think that my priorities are out of whack. I am trying my best and would love to explain that to you if you would give me a chance. However, since you refuse to answer the phone, I do have to say via text that I am going to go with Stacy to see her family, as it seems more pressing at this moment. And I think if you honestly looked at the situation with unbiased eyes, you would agree. Please call me.

That simple act, that simple turning of the phone, something she could have resisted as easily as resisting to breath, had done what the talk of her mom could not. Her night was about to come to an end.

Samuel could sense it, too. The half-smile was gone as he looked from her face to the phone and back to her face. "Jason?"

Her ex-husband's name on the lips of the man with whom she'd been fantasizing about spending the night added another layer of confused emotion to the already complicated mess of feelings stirred up by that text. She looked up at him, not sure what to say. So, without thinking about it, she said everything.

He listened, taking it in, as she told the story of Jason and herself from start to finish, the good and the bad, leading to everything that had happened recently. Her story came to a shaky stop as her breathing became ragged and tough. Her throat was dry, and she regretted that they only had alcoholic beverages at the table instead of a simple glass of water. Samuel, as if reading her mind, got the bartender's attention and requested water. He hurried over with two ice cold glasses. Elizabeth drained hers, both to soothe her throat and as a distraction from Samuel's gaze. Those blue eyes had never left her. It was as if he'd been watching her story like a movie.

"How do you feel?" he asked.

Despite her feelings for Samuel and her recognition that he, too, had feelings for her, she'd honestly expected him to stand up, throw some bills on the table, and walk out, shaking his head in exasperated shock at ever considering being with a woman with a past like that. So, she was not prepared for his question and stated the truth: "I don't know." Sometimes the truth sounded pretty pathetic.

Samuel stood and threw some bills on the table. The similarities of his actions to her imagination made her head swim with déjà vu, and she thought she would be sick. But instead of walking away shaking his head, he reached down to her. "Come with me."

She had a new flash in her mind of Jasmine being offered a ride on a magic carpet. She took his hand. Together, they left the bar, and Samuel took her to his magic carpet. She reached for the helmet as she had before, but he stopped her hand with his.

"Not tonight." He tucked a strand of her hair behind her ear. "Trust me."

The image of the magic carpet came again as he helped her onto the motorcycle, then got on in front. She reached around him and held on as he started the motorcycle. He pulled out of the parking lot and soon they were flying down the road, her hair untethered by a helmet, streaming out behind her. It was one of the most freeing feelings she'd ever experienced. She could physically feel her anxiety being pulled away from her as they drove down the highway with no destination, riding the pavement. Time lost all meaning as she entered a state of euphoria. She thought, *Maybe Samuel should stop singing at weddings and become a therapist.*

Eventually, they came slowly to a stop, back in front of the bar. For a moment, they stayed on his bike, her arms still around him. She set her chin on his shoulder, her mouth next to his ear, and she whispered, "Thank you."

He turned and, instead of responding, he kissed her. It was not the passionate, sexual kiss it had been the previous night, but one that confirmed that her feelings toward him, becoming more serious every minute, were not one-directional. The thought filled her with excitement and trepidation in equal measures. She leaned into it.

They drew away, his blue electric eyes so close to her own. She took a deep breath, understanding that tonight was not the night to sneak him home or follow him to his own temporary home. She understood that it would break something that had just become solid. She kissed him again. "Thank you," she whispered again.

"Anytime," he replied, then helped her off the bike or magic carpet or whatever it was. He walked her to her car.

"Can I see you tomorrow?" she asked, not loving that her need sounded so apparent.

"Sadly, I have errands to run that will keep me tied up most of the day."

She'd opened her car door. It was beeping to let her know that she had. Each beep reminded her that the night had come to an end.

"The next day, however, I should be free. Depending on your wedding planning plans, maybe I could meet you in Norton?"

She saw herself in a prom dress, holding a clear container with a flower attached to a safety pin, waiting for Samuel to show up in a rented tux; her dad, arms crossed, ready to do his fatherly duty and disapprove jovially. She smiled at both the comical thought, and the idea of introducing Samuel to her dad and reintroducing him to her son.

"That would be wonderful. I am sure Rebecca can handle planning her wedding alone for a day."

They kissed again and, for a moment, she considered throwing herself at him, no longer caring if they broke whatever it was she'd been afraid of breaking. Instead, she withdrew, took a deep breath, bade him goodnight, slipped into her car, and turned the key.

Instantly, her car connected to her phone's Bluetooth and started playing the last song she'd been listening to: "He was a boy. She was a girl. Can I make it any more obvious?" She drove away, face scarlet, watching Samuel bent over laughing in the rearview mirror. She had to admit Avril had a point: It was feeling pretty obvious.

Verse 90

Council Bluffs, Iowa

GIDEON opened his eyes to yet another hotel room, one he remembered all too well.

He pushed the now cold steak around his plate. The few bites he'd managed to swallow sat heavily in his stomach, sharing space with his anxiety. Next to the plate was an ad for a karaoke night sponsored by his little brother. A karaoke night that Gideon had not known about. He was well past concerned and completely scared now. What had begun as a carefully executed agenda was spiraling quickly out of control. If he'd not accidentally read the FBI agent a few months prior, while they were waiting for coffee, who knows where they would be? Luckily, the agent had only a couple of very loose leads into the strange deaths taking place, and Samuel hadn't even broken a sweat steering the agent in a completely different direction. Still, as hard as it was for the general public to believe a singer was magically killing people, if enough bodies drop, the government does notice.

Looking at the steak, Gideon allowed his mind to run back over the years since leaving their mother's house. How the world had opened up to them. At first, they lived like little kings. Every child dreams, at least a little, of complete autonomy with unlimited resources, and that was exactly what they were given. Or, possibly more adequately, that was what they had taken. Gideon could pinpoint the exact moment things had changed and exactly who was to blame.

Two years after walking away from their still screaming mother, they'd found themselves eating pizza at a Chuck E. Cheese for no reasons other than they could and that's what they wanted. When singing on a street corner could bring in thousands of dollars, nothing was off limits. Gideon had been raising a steaming, melty piece of pizza to his mouth when he overheard a thought from a table near them: *God, I swear I am going to put her in a cast this time. Fucking bitch forgot the cake.*

Loud rambunctious children milled around the table from which the thought had originated. Gideon turned to see a man and a woman having a quiet, but heated discussion off to the side. Samuel, who could only hear the kids and found them less than interesting, continued to stuff pizza into his mouth with gusto, but Gideon set his piece down and focused on the thought, following it like a shining wire, deeper into the man's twisted mind.

Bruises in easily hidden areas; hospital visits for the ones that couldn't be hidden. Gideon's face paled as he saw not just the man's wife, but his two children also feeling the wrath of the man's fists. "Welcome to Fistland," he'd muttered under his breath, causing Samuel to look up from the quickly disappearing lunch. Even now, Gideon remembered the violent episodes parading through the man's mind. Fresh tears welled at the memory of the man slapping his newborn son in the crib for crying.

"Gideon, what's wrong?" Samuel had asked. Without thinking, Gideon explained what he'd seen. Samuel's look of interest dissolved into something else, something dark. Unable to take it back, Gideon remembered those blue eyes slowly turning away from Gideon and, like laser sights, landing on the man. Gideon knew, even then, that he'd made a mistake.

When the singing started, Gideon had raised his hand to stop his little brother, but the swollen face of the infant swam into his vision and his hand fell back to the table.

"Happy birthday to you, happy birthday . . ." Samuel's voice had joined those of the children as they sang hyperactively to their friend, excitedly waiting to see him blow out the candles jutting from Chuck's face on the very recently purchased cake. Their eyes glossed over as the song's melody changed. The man standing next to the birthday boy brought the serving knife to his neck.

Gideon was torn from the memory as the door slammed open and Samuel came rushing in, eyes blazing. "We gotta go!" he shouted as he unceremoniously shoved the few articles of clothing that had not stayed in his duffle with the rest.

"What have you done?" Gideon stood, caught up in Samuel's frenzied packing.

Samuel stopped, turned to his brother, and gave him a confused look. "What we came here to do." He did not elaborate, but, of course, Gideon didn't need him to. The images, still fresh, flowed freely from Samuel's mind. Color drained from Gideon's face, and he sat back down heavily. He saw the faces, saw the mayhem that Samuel had inflicted upon them.

"We weren't ready. I was still finishing the list and you—"

"I had my own list," Samuel spat. "I'm sick and tired of waiting as you whittle away at your so-called list, until eventually you decide that maybe two or three people are truly deserving. I don't need you to read minds when I can clearly tell you who was unfaithful, who beat their wives, and who generally deserves to die for being terrible."

Gideon had spent the years since that day in Chuck E. Cheese regretting his inaction and had, in turn, been doing everything in his power to rein in his brother's murderous compulsions. Now, it appeared the reins were no longer in his hands. He opened his mouth to protest, to try to get a grasp on the situation again, when a face he'd been recently getting to know flashed in Samuel's mind. All other thoughts vanished.

"Veronica?" Gideon's vision doubled as he saw her beautiful, smiling face interposed over the face from tonight's karaoke, blood sliding between pale lips. "Why? How did she make *your* list?" He injected so much venom into his question that he felt Samuel's resolve falter the tiniest bit.

"She slept with her student," Samuel said defensively. "Everyone knows that."

Gideon remembered when he'd first met Veronica. He remembered how weary she was of the completely baseless rumor going around town that she'd slept with a member of the football team at the local high school where she worked.

"Honestly, Gideon, you have no one to blame but yourself. You can literally read minds, yet have trouble doing anything about the evil you see there. Some of us aren't so passive." Blue eyes met green. "Some of us want to make the world a better place."

Had Gideon been in his right mind, he possibly would have devised a plan, would have thought through his next actions. But all he saw was the double exposure of Veronica's face. His hand closed around the serrated knife next to his plate. He rose to his feet.

"Stop messing around," Samuel said, not a trace of concern in his voice and zero belief in his mind.

It was that unbelief that allowed Gideon to get as close as he did. The knife flew forward, followed by all of Gideon's regrets and convictions. He screamed in rage and sorrow as the knife took its deadly course. His scream dropped into a deep bass note, then moved beautifully into a rich baritone as the knife pressed softly against Samuel's shirt. For a moment, the only movements in the room were the muscles of their throats as they sang a wordless song together and the tears that fell down their faces.

Moving slowly, the knife began to arch back toward its wielder, the sharp point coming to rest against the soft flesh under his jaw. With each note, Gideon felt the blade press a little harder, the skin flexing against it. His skin soon lost the battle and split, allowing the tip to slide in. Blood began to dribble down the blade onto his hand. They both heard the finality in the melancholy chords they sang as Samuel backed away from his older brother. Neither stopped singing as Samuel gathered his remaining possessions, including the keys to their car, and left the room.

Gideon knew he was truly gone when his hand began to sag, and the song dried up in his throat. He dropped the knife then fell to his knees beside it. Placing his bloody hand over his face, he continued to weep.

Verse 91

Norton, Kansas

WYATT had gone to bed hours before Elizabeth's car pulled into the driveway, but Harold was still awake, sipping a decaf coffee and reading the news. He wondered about tomorrow's newspaper and the article he knew would be in it. What would the headline be?

"Body Found in Lake."

Sounded right. Maybe it should say:

"Man Who Killed Local Woman that Everyone Loved Dies from Karma."

Maybe he should skip tomorrow's newspaper altogether.

The door opened and Elizabeth walked in. Their eyes met and he knew she knew. He stood, every joint in his body sounding off like a 21-gun salute. She walked over to him, took him in her arms, and, together, they cried.

No words were needed. Words would have gotten in the way as they so often did.

Verse 92

Alma, Nebraska

SOMETIMES, however, words were important.

Elizabeth had said many words as she told Samuel her story. Words like "Top floor of the tallest residential building in Omaha" and words like "even has a doorman." At one point, she'd said the words, "They walk across the street sometimes to eat at La Hacienda, which had been one of our favorite date night restaurants."

When fed into Google, these words, with a few others pulled here and there from her story, brought up an address and more words:

"Three hours and twenty-four minutes away."

Verse 93

Council Bluffs, Iowa

GIDEON awoke with a new determination. The now physical need for any other dream, and that of a new lead right as he'd been ready to give up, filled him with energy and purpose.

With renewed vigor, he whistled as he went about his morning routine, taking extra precautions to make sure he looked especially spiffy, smelled fresh and clean, and had the overall air of someone official. He had to admit there was an undercurrent of nerves running alongside his excitement.

It had been an exceptionally long time since he'd had to get information the old-fashioned way. The few times it happened before, due to similar mental blocks, Samuel had stepped in and wrenched the information from their lips, carried on a melody. Since Samuel's departure, there had only been one time he attempted to pull information from someone without his powers. In that case, about halfway through, the defenses in her mind crumbled after he asked her an unrelated question about pie. Sometimes that was all it took: something so unexpected, the brain doesn't know how to process it correctly and a crack appears. More often than not, a crack was all Gideon needed.

He tied his solid red tie under his collar, pulled on the black coat, and adjusted the sleeves. He looked in the mirror. He pushed his glasses up onto the bridge of his nose and admired how intellectual and official the whole outfit looked.

FBI, IRS, detective . . . it didn't matter. If he showed up on a doorstep looking like this, it took very little effort to go from stranger to "Please come in, officer." People respected a uniform, and this was a uniform they'd seen a million times on TV, preconditioning them to trust the black suit.

His reflection in the mirror reminded him of why he was in this predicament, and he wondered if the man-in-the-mirror would interfere with his "investigation" in any way. But he also knew he didn't have much choice.

He packed the rest of his things, planning on following the trail while it was hot and never seeing the room again.

Verse 94

Omaha, Nebraska

JASON was up early, his coffee made and a smile on his face. Today would be a good day. He could feel it. Stacy would come over at ten, which gave him plenty of time to call in with his continued illness, start packing, and reach out to Elizabeth. Stacy's forgiveness—or, at least, acceptance—had bolstered his belief that things would be okay.

Elizabeth was the mother of the son he'd realized he loved; that had to count for something. She couldn't shut the door on their relationship when they were literally connected by blood. Wyatt was a bond that could not be severed, and she had to appreciate that. For that matter, he was the one who'd reached out to spend time with Wyatt. That had to count for something, too, right?

He shook his head, not allowing himself to spiral down the rabbit hole; positive thoughts were the key to this morning. He sipped his coffee. Damn, it tasted good. He always felt better with his fancy coffee in hand.

"Elizabeth needs one of these coffeemakers," he thought aloud to the room. "Then perhaps she would be in the right headspace to listen to me."

He mentally placed the coffeemaker on a Christmas list, then decided to move it up to her birthday. It was sooner, and he didn't know if he could wait 'til December to have a civil conversation with her. He looked at his watch.

Shit, it was already nine? Where had the time gone? Had he spent all morning fantasizing about making things right with El, never actually attempting to do it?

Visualize, then realize; that was his old motto, but he'd run out of time to realize. If he called her now and Stacy showed up early, he would be in a worse spot than he was as he would have to remain on the phone with El—bad—or hang up—worse. But they would be leaving once Stacy finished helping him pack, which meant, for the foreseeable future, they would be by each other's sides. That would be a hostile environment for a call to his ex-wife, pleading to make up.

Fucking rabbit hole. He had to keep his head above water or he would drown, and he wasn't even done packing yet.

He felt it then: the joy he'd felt that morning; the belief that everything would be all right. It welled up inside him, filling his chest. He began to sing.

Verse 95

Omaha, Nebraska

GIDEON dropped the coffee he was holding, and the ceramic mug clattered onto the saucer. For the past hour or so, he'd been faintly connected to Jason, despite being across the street. He'd arrived at Jason's building around eight, allowing his mind to open up, probing gently for Jason's mind. He didn't want to poke too hard, aware that the man-in-the-mirror might notice him again and lock Jason down before he showed up on his front doorstep. He brushed the now familiar mind at the top floor.

He smiled. Rich people were extremely susceptible to men in uniforms as they were already in constant fear of them. The men in the black suits who could take away their hard-earned money, because they listened to a friend tell them about a stock that may or may not belong to a business that may or may not be going under, information that may or may not be public knowledge. He scoffed a scornful laugh, not yet daring to dig deeper to see if that were the case here.

Instead, he had looked across the street at a cute, little coffee shop. He decided that he would get one and see if any useful information leaked out without his prodding. He would make his move after his cup was empty.

Two things had held him up. First, the coffee was out-of-this-world delicious, so he'd decided to have a second cup instead of the planned one. Second, he was getting a lot of information without much effort and decided to milk that for as long as he could.

He'd learned about Stacy, the girl he was seeing, and El, an old flame with whom he had a kid. While both were mad at him, one had forgiven him. He'd also learned that Jason and the forgiving one, Stacy, were going on a trip. The purpose of said trip had yet to be gleaned, but based on what he'd heard the day before, he was willing to bet it was a wedding and, furthermore, that Stacy had a crush on the wedding singer. This had been the only time he'd pushed a little deeper. When he found himself standing in front of a mirror, he'd quickly backed out before being noticed, but it had been close enough to keep him from pushing too hard again.

Since that point, he hadn't gotten much. He had decided to finish the coffee he was on and go visit the man at the top of the elevator, the man who would set him back on the path. His coffee had just reached his lips for a sip when Jason's thoughts began to flow into a melody.

Samuel dropped his mug. It hit the saucer, recoiling enough to send a minor tsunami of hot, brown liquid on to the front of his perfectly kept white shirt. He stood slowly, trying to see everything at once, listening to the receiver on the top floor while also listening for the transmitter below. His heart raced. He could hear it, heavy in his ears, each beat momentarily muting the song. He walked toward the door to the shop in a daze, one thought louder than the song:

Samuel is here.

Verse 96

Omaha, Nebraska

JASON felt all of the tension, stress, and uncertainty drain away from him. He danced around his apartment as he sang, seeing a clear future, knowing exactly how he could fix all of his problems. It was as if, for the past few weeks, a fog had settled around him, blurring his path. Now the sun had come up, dissolving the early morning mist, revealing the path he'd known was there all along. Stacy was on her way, which was good, as she was a stop along the path.

But first things first, he needed his phone. Before he went any further, he needed to call El and tell her about his newfound peace. He needed to tell her how he would make everything better.

His phone was sitting on the kitchen counter. On the face was an unread text from Stacy: "I will be there sooner than expected. See you in a few."

Jason's smile was beginning to hurt, but he couldn't help it. He'd thought he would have to wait for Stacy, but the universe had intervened and now he could get right to work on making things right.

He sent a thumbs-up emoji, then opened his phone to his favorites.

El was number two. The heart emoji that once followed the name had been removed before their divorce was finalized. Hell, before he'd left the house. He had opened up his phone in front of Stacy at the clinic and been so embarrassed by that childish sign of affection, he'd removed the emoji while Wyatt was getting his shot and Elizabeth was holding his hand.

He was a real class act.

Without thinking about it, still singing a song that seemed to fit perfectly with his current reality, he went into the contact info and added the heart back. Then, with a flick of his thumb, the phone was ringing.

Verse 97

Norton, Kansas

A familiar, and currently unappreciated, face lit up Elizabeth's phone as it began to buzz quietly on the side table next to her bed. It moved slightly around the tabletop as it tried desperately to get someone's attention.

However, it tried in vain. The owner of the phone was currently in her son's room, hearing about the nightmare combine that had been chasing him through the tall grass, consoling him with platitudes and warmth.

The phone stopped its relentless jitterbugging and fell silent.

A few minutes later, it buzzed again, lit up with a new icon showing a voicemail.

Verse 98

Omaha, Nebraska

GIDEON stood in the doorway of the little diner, his alarm turning frantic with every second the song continued. His plan was quickly changing from gaining information to saving a life.

He gave up on searching for Samuel and began to move. Time became very tangible to him as he could all but see it draining away. He could visualize an hourglass, each grain of sand a note in the song he was hearing in his mind, catching deadly phrases interwoven throughout the melody.

Traffic was heavy in the Old Market. It moved slowly as people meandered from side to side, looking at the shops. Gideon was able to weave around stopped cars, shouldering his way past slower shoppers and tourists.

The song continued and he began to sense a line from the top floor to a location down the street. He froze in indecision. Samuel was at the other side of that line. Did he have time to get to him? If he chose to go after Samuel, would he be leaving Jason to die?

He had an idea. He reached deep into Jason's mind, past the song, past the hidden words, and found what he was looking for. He was standing in front of a mirror and the man-in-the-mirror was looking back at him. "You know I'm here, don't you?"

"Yep." The man crossed his arms in front of his chest and looked down at Gideon who was unsettled by the smug look on the man's face.

"Look, I don't have much time, but you should know…"

"Oh, I know exactly what's going on. I can hear the hidden words."

Gideon was struck silent at that.

"Catchy song, if I do say so myself." The man-in-the-mirror began to whistle the tune, snapping his finger as he did. "Really kickin'."

"If you know what the song is, then do something. Reach out to Jason, snap him out of it."

Someone bumped into Gideon. He was standing on the sidewalk, looking up toward the top of the tall building. He was so focused on the conversation, he didn't see the people milling around him, giving concerned looks. One person who passed him continued on her way, smiling and waving at the doorman as she went. Had Gideon seen and recognized her, maybe everything would have been different.

But maybe the man-in-the-mirror had known that too. Maybe he knew he needed to hold Gideon's attention that much longer.

"'Cause I agree with the song. I think this is exactly what should happen. Been sayin' it for a while now."

Pain slashed through their arms like a blade making deep cuts. There was another slash across the side. Gideon almost broke the connection after that but was so shocked by the man-in-the-mirror's statement, he held on.

"You and he are the same, mirror images of each other," Gideon pleaded with the man-in-the-mirror. "One cannot live without the other. You must see that this will bring about your own death."

Tears were beginning to fall down Gideon's cheeks. They were not of sorrow, but of frustration. He'd woken that morning so hopeful and now, with Samuel in his grasp, everything was falling apart around him. Samuel was here, on this very block, possibly within sight if he looked the other way. But he'd looked the other way for far too long. He had an opportunity to save someone. For once, he was on time and on the right side—only to be stopped by the very person he was trying to save.

"To be honest, I am grateful to the singer. I have been trying for so long to do what he is doing in a few minutes. If I was a proud man, I would be jealous, but humility has always been an attribute of mine."

Gideon, caught up in the dialogue even at this crucial moment, wanted to comment on the irony of bragging about humility, but had enough sense of urgency to let it go.

"You see, Jason wants this. Has for a while now. That's why I'm here. Only, he has a strong sense of survival that has always gotten in the way until your friend came along."

"Please," Gideon begged, "you can stop this. Give him a chance. Everyone deserves a second chance."

"I disagree." The man-in-the-mirror paused and, for the first time since they'd started talking, he looked away. "Looks like she's here. Look, you've been fun, but, honestly, I was stalling to make sure you didn't interfere with anything, and we are to a point, I believe, where it no longer matters."

The mirror cracked down the middle, then spiderwebbed out. Gideon watched in horror as the man-in-the-mirror broke into a million smiling faces, all of which began to laugh in a malevolent chorus.

Verse 99

Omaha, Nebraska

JASON sang and danced around the living room, droplets of blood splattering the walls and carpet as he swung his arms joyfully. The dark, long-sleeved shirt he'd put on hid the gashes well, only revealing the bloody lines when the sleeves pulled enough to open the slashes in the fabric.

Remotely, beneath the song, the joy, and the peace he felt, he could hear voices in conversation. He vaguely wondered if the people who lived on the floor below him had raised their voices to compete with his singing. Rather than diminishing his desire, it bolstered it. He began to sing louder, pounding his feet in his bloody dance around the apartment.

The doorbell rang. Jason's eyes glittered with glee.

Ever since El had taken Wyatt to Norton, his life had been a steep rollercoaster climb and this morning it finally crested the top. Now he could feel the wind in his hair, and he wanted to throw up his hands, laughing. That he did, a few drops of blood reaching the ceiling. Hands above his head, he did a clumsy pirouette on his way to the door.

He flung it open and found Stacy, who was already smiling, having heard the singing from the other side of the door.

Verse 100

Omaha, Nebraska

"JASON, wha—?"

But Stacy couldn't finish her question as Jason took her hands and pulled her into the apartment with him, spinning her around in gay circles, singing exuberantly with her.

Taken by surprise and filled with a happy confusion, she did not notice that all the reflective surfaces were covered nor did she notice the blood, splattered on the floor and walls, and still draining freely from his arms. She was blinded by the joy of dancing with the man she knew she loved and the belief that the past few days of darkness were finally over.

She tried to sing along with him, enjoying the melody, wondering where he'd heard it as she'd never heard him sing it before. They twirled and laughed and sang, her white blouse becoming pink in patches, unnoticed.

Soon they were dancing on the balcony, the warm air matching the warmth she felt radiating through her. In a fluid motion, he grasped her around her hips and lifted her in the air. It was exhilarating, like being in a romantic movie, swept from her feet in the final dance scene. She was so swept up in the moment that she threw her arms out like wings.

At first, she did not realize that Jason's hands were no longer on her waist, and the momentum of the lift was not stopping. She opened her eyes to a world blurring past her. She barely had time to scream before it all came to a stop.

Verse 101

Omaha, Nebraska

GIDEON blinked repeatedly in disorientation as the fluorescent lighting of the mental bathroom he'd been in gave way to the brilliance of the morning sun. His eyes had adjusted, and his mind had found its footing back within his head, when an ear-piercing scream yanked him around.

He turned just in time to see Stacy hit the road, imploding from the head down as the front of her body stopped without letting the rest know its plans. He watched in slow motion as her face split open from the pressure of her skull breaking apart with nowhere to go. Her body accordioned down, the discs of her spine trying desperately to move aside as the others came to take their places. Blood exploded away from her like a dropped water balloon, coating an uneven halo around her.

Blessedly for him, a car, despite slamming on its brakes, slid over the whole scene, removing the horror from his sight. Blood, the only visible indication of what just happened, continued to flow from beneath the front bumper.

Gideon didn't watch for long, however, as he again heard the singing clearly; this time, not from within his mind, but through his ears, coming from above him, getting louder.

In a desperate hopelessness, he looked up.

Verse 102

Omaha, Nebraska

AS Jason fell, he continued to smile, singing to an audience of one. The man-in-the-mirror was there, reflected in every window, smiling with his success. Each window was another picture drawn at the bottom of a kid's notepad, flipping as Jason moved through the open air. Jason sang to the man-in-the-mirror, letting him know in a blissful melody that he understood now that the man-in-the-mirror had been right all along, and Jason's hesitance had been the folly. The two of them celebrated together for the few seconds it took for Jason to make his trip from top floor to ground level.

They sang. They smiled. They became one, finally joining their ideologies into a single harmonic note.

Verse 103

Omaha, Nebraska

THE driver of the car that had come to rest over Stacy's crumpled form, one Christopher Duggan, stepped out of his car to see if what he thought he'd run over was, in fact, what he'd just run over. This act possibly kept him from joining the woman under his car in death. No sooner had he stepped out, car door handle still in hand, did Jason hit the roof of his car like a missile shot from a drone.

The metal crumpled toward where Chris had been sitting moments before in the part of his life he would always remember as separate from everything that followed. Glass from the windshield exploded into a million dagger-like fragments, one burying itself deep into Chris's forearm, something he would not discover until his shock subsided and an EMT, using comically large tweezers, pulled it free, placing four stitches there on the scene.

While Jason's body had come to a sudden stop on the roof of Chris's Ford Fusion, his left arm had, unfortunately, been held away from his body. Later, it would be described to police officers as if he'd been attempting to flap his arms. In reality, Jason had been joyously clapping. In doing so, his left arm had fallen over the edge of the car and made an attempt to finish the trip to the street, snapping violently. A large, jagged edge of bone unzipped the muscle and flesh of his upper arm, allowing the rest to dangle loosely in the sleeve of his shirt that darkened around the sliver of white that had torn through the fabric. A pendulum, waving both hello and goodbye to Chris, then and in his nightmares for years to come.

The rest of Jason's body looked oddly unharmed at first glance, having shattered on the inside, turning everything within into a soup of bone fragments, floating in fluids that had recently been held in organs, perforated a million times by shards of bone and impact pressure.

Verse 104

Omaha, Nebraska

GIDEON was still able to hear Jason's thoughts, even as they grew fainter, and heard the man-in-the-mirror consoling him in his final moments, assuring him that this was the best for everyone. Gideon was finally able to move his feet.

A crowd had begun to form a circle around the stalled vehicle and Chris, who still stood holding the driver's side door, his face and torso splattered red with Jason's blood. Gideon forced his way past the crowd and, finally, past the man-in-the-mirror who'd grown weaker as Jason lost his own strength. He reached into Jason's mind for any happy thought and found a day at the beach with a boy of two years old and a young, beautiful woman. He quickly pulled the names Elizabeth and Wyatt from the memory as his shoes crunched on shards of windshield. Gently, he pushed Chris aside and laid his hand on Jason's shoulder, trying not to notice the fact that it was not in its socket.

"Jason, I want you to listen to me and think about Wyatt and Elizabeth that day on the beach."

Jason tried to smile. Gideon hoped briefly that he'd made it in time to give this poor man a final comforting thought. But Jason opened his mouth and, with his final breath, he breathed out the final line to the song that had taken his life. His eyes glazed over, and Gideon felt the connection break completely. Despite the crowd pushing forward, the tell-tale clicking sound of phones taking pictures, Gideon felt utterly alone.

Until he heard the familiar song in his mind. He looked up in time to see a man weaving his motorcycle around the scene of the accident. The sun glinted off the visor as the man turned his way. As the glare moved aside, Gideon's green eyes met the cold, blue eyes of his younger brother.

Time slowed as Gideon reached out toward Samuel's mind. Samuel knew this game. He sang Gideon his own song, holding his mind and body in place as Samuel found a break in the crowd. Without another look back, he left his older brother standing next to the lifeless body of his most recent victim and Gideon's most recent failure.

Verse 105

Norton, Kansas

AFTER Wyatt had been consoled, he'd quickly fallen back to sleep, leaving Elizabeth to marvel at this ability with a hint of jealousy. Now that she was awake, she decided to make herself some coffee. As she entered the kitchen, however, she smelled the familiar, delicious aroma and saw her dad sitting at the kitchen table, sipping out of his favorite KU mug.

"Bad dream?" he inquired as she filled a mug that humorously reminded her that Mondays were, generally speaking, the worst.

"Guess so. It was all pretty confusing. Something to do with the combine at the farm trying to scissor him."

Her dad's eyebrows rose. "I told you he was scared of that thing. He nearly jumped out of his skin while looking at it. Wonder if he saw something on TV, like that movie about the car that came to life and started killing people."

"Wyatt has never seen *Christine*, Dad. What kind of mother do you think I am? I mean, when he started asking if we could have a dog, I did let him watch *Cujo*, but hey, I am not leaving work every day at lunch to walk a dog I didn't even want." She sat next to him and placed her coffee down to cool.

"Ah yes, you learn from the best. Remember that time you wanted the parrot from that pet shop in Philipsburg?"

She raised a single eyebrow, beckoning him to continue.

"Do you also remember the first time we let you watch Alfred Hitchcock's The Birds?"

Her mouth fell open.

"I was kidding about the *Cujo* thing, Dad. Dear Lord, I still can't drive by a telephone wire with more than three birds on it without breaking into a cold sweat."

He smiled mischievously.

"How many other childhood traumas did you inflict on me to keep me from getting what I wanted?"

He thought for a moment. "Well, you watched the killer doll movie at a friend's house, but it was conveniently when you were also getting into those expensive collector's dolls. So that was a happy coincidence."

She laughed openly then, throwing a hand up over her mouth as she remembered Wyatt asleep down the hall.

"Yep, you can read all the parenting books you want, but nothing works quite like a good scary movie."

This brought on another bout of laughter, muted poorly behind their hands. They fell into a happy silence as they sipped their coffees contentedly.

"Thanks again for helping out," Elizabeth said. "It's been a blessing."

Her dad nodded, conveying all of his emotions on the matter in that nod, something all older men master in time.

"Sorry if it feels like I've dumped Wyatt on you. I plan on taking some time away from wedding planning and whatnot to spend time with the two of you."

"Speaking of Mr. Whatnot, is he 'meet the father' material?"

"Oh my God, Dad. I just met the guy. We have barely

had two dates, and I started crying during both of them, I think. It's no wonder he hasn't called me today. I . . ."

It was then that she realized her phone was not in its traditional spot on the table next to her coffee. Had he called her or texted her? They'd joked about maybe waiting 'til later in the day, but one man's "later in the day" is another lady's "early morning." She stood. "I'll be right back."

This was a flippant saying that gets thrown around with little thought. But she would, in fact, spend the rest of the morning, and a good part of the afternoon, in her room in a state of shock and disbelief. Her coffee would be cold by the time she returned to the kitchen; forgotten along with the contentment she'd felt while drinking it.

Verse 106

Council Bluffs, Iowa

GIDEON stumbled into his new hotel room. He could barely breathe. The drive from the Old Market had done little to calm him; his mind kept pace with his rapid heartrate.

Samuel had been in Omaha this whole time, and Gideon had barely crossed the river. He looked down and almost broke into frantic laughter as he realized that, figuratively and literally, he had Jason's blood on his hands. He began to tear at his clothes, realizing there was blood on the suit he'd so carefully prepared to meet Jason. He felt his stomach turn and fought to keep down his breakfast. His tie caught and his mind almost broke as the knot pulled tighter; that little act of resistance was almost enough to send him over the edge. Then something loosened and the fabric slid through the collar. Soon he was standing naked in the shower, his body glowing red as the scalding water fell. The steam was instant, and he imagined everything that had happened burning away.

He forced his mind to slow and evaluated what he'd learned.

Samuel was in Omaha—or had been earlier that day. Jason had somehow ended up on his radar in a way that made Samuel act before whatever big event was next in his schedule. Jason had been with a woman named Stacy, but his fondest memory was of a woman named Elizabeth and a boy named Wyatt.

After an hour, once the water had cooled on its own, he started to compile a mental list of searchable items he'd gleaned from the scene. He smiled as the water drained down his face in miniature rivers, realizing that, despite everything, he finally had a solid lead. Purpose swelled in him once again, and he turned off the water. He stood naked in the shower, his body broken out in gooseflesh. He placed his hand on the burned handprint before reaching for the towel.

Verse 107

Norton, Kansas

ELIZABETH'S room had been spinning since she'd picked up
the phone and heard "Good morning, this is Detective Dawson,
am I speaking . . . ?"

At one point, she reached out with a shaking hand
toward the lamp next to her bed to see if the lamp would bump
into her hand as it continued its revolution around her. She'd
heard mention of surrealism, had even believed she'd
experienced it from time to time, but she'd never experienced
anything like the phone call that morning.

The spinning room was making it hard to pay attention,
which made everything worse as she had to keep asking for
information to be repeated. She kept forgetting if they'd
explained how her ex-husband and first real love had died. Was
he in a car accident? Did the father of her child get hit by a car
outside his apartment? Did the second man she'd ever slept
with get in a fight with someone?

She also had to deal with a strange doubling as Jason's
smiling face kept popping up in her mind, overlaying a much
angrier face. Her two views of this man, who'd been such a
presence in her life even after the divorce, were dueling for
control of her memories.

". . . last time he talked to you?"

"Sorry, what was that? I am sorry. I am trying, but I'm
sorry." It took a physical effort to stop herself from

continuously apologizing, her teeth clamping together painfully.

"I asked, when exactly was the last time he talked to you? It might help us get a better timeline for what happened."

Had she fallen into a police procedural? She pulled the phone away from her ear and looked at the screen, the need to vomit coming on as the spinning room now used her phone screen as an axle. With multiple loud swallows, she was able to relieve the urge. She was shocked to see that Jason had tried to call her and had left a voicemail, possibly minutes before his death.

His death.

The room became dark, blessedly dimming the spinning, and, for a moment, she almost gave in to a faint to escape the nightmare. She fought against it, pulling herself back to the surface. A noise escaped her lips as she willed her consciousness to stay intact.

"I'm sorry, what was that?"

"I have a voicemail from this morning. I haven't had my phone, so I must have missed his call. I only caught yours as I walked in the room." She took a deep breath. "I don't know how to listen to it while on the phone or how to share it or if I should listen to it first or . . ." She stopped, again having to reign in her words as they tried to gallop away from her. She heard a noise and turned to see Wyatt in the doorway. What color had remained on her face faded, leaving her a mannequin, sitting on the bed, showcasing the newest model of dread. "Um, officer, I need to let you go for a moment. Is this a good number to call you back on?"

"Yes, but I don't think—"

She ended the phone call with learned precision, never taking her eyes from her son. From Jason's son. She began to cry, and he joined her.

Verse 108

Omaha, Nebraska

EVENTUALLY, Officer Ian Dantez reconnected with Elizabeth. He heard her shaking voice and commended her for keeping as controlled as she was. With effort, he was able to explain that on an iPhone, you can send a voicemail via a voice memo. Soon, he was looking at a sound bite, possibly the last heard words of the deceased. With the reassurance that he would call her back as soon as he listened, he hung up and hit play.

"El, I have made a decision. I am picking Wyatt. I get that for you and me, it's too late, but your absence has made me understand how important Wyatt is to me and how much I want to be a part of his life. I called Stacy and told her, so please let me know when I can come." There was a pause then. "Hold on. Sounds like maybe Stacy just came in. I hear her in the kitchen. Stacy!" He called out on the voicemail and Ian heard the tell-tale sounds of movement. "Stacy, hi. Wait! What are you doing? Stacy, put the knife down please. Look, we can talk, please don't do anything rash. Stacy! Stop." At this, the phone must have fallen as there was a thump followed by scuffling sounds, and, finally, a cracking sound that led to silence.

This voicemail connected every dot for Ian. He finally could see what had happened with crystal clarity.

There had been multiple slashes on the man's arms and one on his side that had not been from the fall. After the police entered the apartment, they'd seen what looked like a struggle:

blood splatters on the walls, floor, and a little on the ceiling. They'd found the phone that had been stepped on as well. All of this left a winding, spinning trail that had clearly been a person struggling to keep the other from killing them. The trail led out to the balcony where the struggle had come to a deadly end. They'd fought. She'd fallen first, pulling him along with her. He'd been able to grab the ledge, but, after sustaining the injuries he had to his arms, there had been no hope. He'd joined her shortly after.

The voicemail provided the motive and gave context.

Ian frowned. The only aspect he couldn't quite place was the singing. Multiple eyewitnesses mentioned they thought the man had been singing as he fell. Had the voicemail had a bit of musicality to it?

He shook his head. As someone whose line of work often involved screaming and panicking, he knew that sometimes screams could sound almost musical; panicked words almost following a melody.

No. As far as he was concerned, this was an open-and-shut case. Devastating, but simple.

Verse 109

Omaha, Nebraska

OVER the following week, Elizabeth kept coming back to the word "surreal."

Everything that happened felt like a nightmare. She found herself checking to make sure she wasn't wearing pajamas and began to wonder when she would wake up. When talking to one of the lawyers explaining Jason's life insurance policy, she swore the young lady's tongue turned into a snake. It turned out to be a tongue ring that compiled the surrealism of her life. She was shockingly relieved that, at least that time, it was just a figment of her imagination.

As if that was not hard enough, the amount of information heaved onto her by the police, lawyers, and morticians, mixed with the well wishes of friends and family, kept her so distracted that none of it seemed to stick properly. She was hardly aware she'd left Rebecca to carry on wedding planning without her for the foreseeable future. She was vaguely aware that her ex-husband had an exceptionally good life insurance policy that had never been changed after their separation, bumping Wyatt and herself into a new tax bracket. She was slightly more aware that her husband had been murdered, like, actually murdered, something she knew was real, yet had subconsciously always thought only existed in books and TV shows. She was mostly aware that her son had lost his dad and that he'd loved his dad very much. This last fact was what she anchored her mental ship to in the midst of the constant storm.

Surrealism finally gave way to realism when they attended Jason's funeral. Had this been a TV show or novel, it would have been raining and everyone would be wearing perfectly coordinated black outfits, each holding the same black umbrella. It did not rain, and the attire, while still mostly black, was far from coordinated.

Elizabeth, Wyatt, and Harold attended along with Jason's family and friends. It was the first time since Jason's death that Elizabeth had seen his parents without lawyers. Elizabeth had always liked Jason's parents, and they'd even reached out to her after the split to let her know they were very disappointed in their son's choices.

Regardless of whose side they'd been on in the divorce, Jason was their son and they loved him. She knew they were hurting more than anyone at his loss. Briefly, between visits with her lawyer, his lawyer, and a club of paralegals, she'd been able to give them each a hug along with her condolences and a solemn promise that not only would they still see Wyatt, she would make an effort to increase his visits. This led to more crying and an immense gratitude that showed on their faces more than in their words.

Now she looked over the coffin where the man she'd married, had a son with, and had loved even in her hatred laid peacefully, and saw his parents standing strong in the warm, summer sun. Seeing them dressed in black attire in representation of their mourning brought it all home on a level it had not been before.

She looked at her son who was also not crying. At least, not now.

He had cried. He'd cried enough for the both of them as she sorted out her confused feelings. She'd lost someone she'd known and loved for many years. He'd lost someone he'd known and loved his entire life. Unlike her, he had no idea what life without Jason meant. Now he was forced to live without his father because a jealous, evil woman couldn't share.

That evil woman had seen that Jason truly loved Wyatt and could not bear to share that love with anyone, even his son. What a sick, psychotic, evil bitch.

As the coffin was lowered into the ground, Elizabeth couldn't help but wonder about Stacy's funeral. By now, the news had reported on the murder, and it was well known that she'd attacked Jason and they'd both died because of it. Was anyone at her funeral? She supposed her family; at least, the close ones. Elizabeth wondered if Stacy's sick grandmother who'd started this whole thing was well enough to sit graveside. She imagined a minister standing over the closed coffin. Looking around and seeing no one there, he shrugged, closed the Bible, and walked away. No need to read a scripture with no one there to hear it. She had to suppress a smile at the image. It would be unseemly to smile at a funeral.

Aside from Wyatt, there had been her dad, Rebecca, and Samuel.

Despite her wedding, still planned for the original date, Rebecca had made a point to be completely available to Elizabeth whenever she needed to have a total emotional breakdown, which she did multiple times. Elizabeth promised over and over that as soon as the funeral was over, she would be back to help put the finishing touches on what was shaping up to be the most beautiful wedding she could imagine.

Her dad had been a rock, stepping in to watch Wyatt while Elizabeth dealt with the fallout of losing a family member in such a unique way.

Finally, there had been Samuel. He was the only one of the three who was not at the funeral. He'd suggested — rightfully, despite her arguments — that it might not be appropriate for him to be with her at her ex-husband's funeral. He'd also made it perfectly clear that he would clear his schedule to be able to answer texts and closet phone calls as needed.

She thought she might sneak away to a closet and tell him about the thought she had about Stacy's funeral, then thought about how he might view that and decided against it. Her clutch vibrated in her hand. She had a guilty feeling Samuel had read her mind from the other end of the state and texted an admonishment. Obviously, that was not the case. But the inability to check her phone at that moment weighed on her, and she thought it might be time to get a smart watch.

Wyatt squeezed her hand, mistaking her stress over the unknown text as a more appropriate emotion to the task at hand, and she was filled with guilty embarrassment. She fought to clear her mind and refocus on what was taking place before her.

She thought again of the term "surreal." She'd never known someone who was murdered. People are murdered every day, so it wasn't specifically uncommon, but it was one of those things that happens to *other* people. In the game of seven degrees, she'd just become degree one.

She looked around at everyone present and used their reality to ground her own. Each person here was real, and each person here was really hurting over Jason's death. This was real, and she needed to be present in that reality. Afterward, though, she knew this would all blur into a nightmarish memory. Then she would have to find something else to anchor her reality and she already knew what that was.

Or, more appropriately, who that was.

Instead of running from the baggage that had been dropped on him, Samuel accepted it and agreed to help carry it for her.

She'd driven to Omaha the day she got the call. She went directly to the police station where they discussed the many aspects of Jason's life, specifically as it related to Stacy and Wyatt. Elizabeth felt strange as she recounted their recent fights. She felt guilty for speaking ill of the dead. Jason had died because he chose Wyatt over Stacy, and, here she was, portraying him as a terrible father. It made her sick and she'd, in fact, had to excuse herself to the restroom where she thankfully was able to keep her lunch down and pull herself together. After a lengthy foray through her negative memories, they listened to the voicemail exhaustively. Elizabeth lost count. She had started to zone out when Officer Dantez put his hand on her shoulder.

"You look exhausted. Let's take a break."

She'd been allowed to go to her house, which had its own feeling of surreality as she'd not stepped foot in it since going to Norton. She kept seeing memories in each room, floating into view like ghosts.

Jason putting up a Christmas tree in the living room. Jason cooking Valentine's Day bacon. She watched the specters as they acted out the life they'd enjoyed together, refraining from the less enjoyable scenes. She took a deep breath and realized the house had a musty, unlived smell to it, reminding her that the memories were not real. No one had set foot in the house for weeks.

So, she lit a candle, took a bath in the dark, and cried alone, receiving no comfort from any of the memories that flickered in the candlelight.

Verse 110

Council Bluffs, Iowa

GIDEON had spent the week diligently searching the internet for any information on Jason, Stacy, Elizabeth, and Wyatt. Bit by bit, with the information he gathered, he'd been able to get a general understanding of the relationships at play.

The story played out in court documents, newspaper announcements, addresses, and occupations.

Jason had been married to Elizabeth and, after having a child together, had run off with a nurse from a pediatrician's office, presumably the one where they took the kid, Wyatt. The information was interesting and full of drama, sure, but it didn't help him understand how Samuel was involved.

He knew from the short read of Jason's mind, before the man-in-the-mirror had stepped in, that there was a wedding and a singer, who was now all but confirmed to be Samuel. However, he could find no weddings in Omaha that had any ties to Elizabeth, Jason, Wyatt, or Stacy, or any relevance at all. He'd puzzled over where to go with the information he'd found.

One bit of information was the address of the only two surviving characters in this drama. He'd gone to the house, hoping to glean information from the mind of one of the residents that would further him along. He found out quickly, however, that their house was empty, and their neighborhood had an extremely diligent neighborhood watch. When a man in his late fifties knocked on his car window with a polite inquiry as to his business, Gideon had done a quick read of the man and realized that dealing with an ex-cop was not something he wanted to do. He gave a lame excuse before driving away.

His other plan was to attend the funeral, which felt perfect as men in black suits were chameleons at events like that. Even a weak story about how he knew the deceased would barely be considered, and he could use the funeral as one would use a library, flitting from mind to mind, each one hyper-focused on what he was looking for.

Those hopes were just as quickly dashed when it was announced it would be a closed funeral with only close friends and family allowed. While disappointed, Gideon was not surprised. An event like Jason's death was just that: an event. There would be news stations, journalists, and people who wanted nothing more than to see how well the mortician had been able to put Humpty Jason back together again.

Undeterred, he'd driven to the funeral anyway but rolled by when he saw the police presence outside the church, officers' heads slowly turning to track his progress. He reached out toward the church regardless, hoping for something, but only received a wave of grief that he had to cut off or risk drowning.

He returned to his hotel room, feeling defeated.

Then he had one last idea. It was weak, but, at this point, he was willing to try anything. He'd not been this close in so long. He got on his laptop and got to work.

Verse 111

Omaha, Nebraska

WHEN Elizabeth was finally able to sneak a peek at her phone to see what Samuel had said, she was shocked and touched to see it had actually been Bartholomew letting her know that he was praying for her and available if she needed him.

She considered her relationships with Bartholomew and Samuel; how quickly their friendships had bloomed and solidified into something akin to old friendship. Her friends in Omaha had been supportive, sending gifts and meals by the truckload, but it was the little texts and calls from the two new men in her life that had meant the most.

She felt that pang of fear and regret that always came when she started thinking about life after the wedding. There was so much undetermined. Would her rekindled friendship with Rebecca remain as strong as it was right now? Would Bartholomew still text her a month down the road?

Then there was Samuel. Her already complicated feelings for the singer always had the weight of the upcoming event hanging over them. Oh, and there was the death of her ex-husband to add to the pile. Despite everything, she'd loved Jason; more importantly, Wyatt had loved him. So, now she had to deal with those feelings while she had new feelings for another man, making her feel confused as to whether or not she should feel guilty while worrying whether the new baggage added to not unsubstantial baggage would and, by all accounts should, scare off Samuel. She felt like the world was spinning around her and uncertainty was her only anchor.

"Excuse me."

Elizabeth was very proud of the fact that a little squeaky noise and a quick shrug of her shoulders was the only response she had as the hand touched her arm, pulling her from her revelry. It was Jason's mother; a woman Elizabeth had thought of only as Wyatt's grandmother for years.

It was interesting how life events changed your identity completely. You were a baby, a high schooler, an employee, a wife, a mother. With each title change, those around you saw a different person. Maybe that was why she was enjoying her new relationships so much. All of the titles she'd collected meant nothing to the new people in her life. She was just Elizabeth.

"How are you doing, Joana?" Elizabeth had seen her crying at the church, standing over the open casket. Despite how Jason passed, the mortician had done exemplary work preserving the imitation of life. Now Joana's eyes were dry. She stood strong with the coffin closed, sealed, and placed six feet below ground.

"I am managing. How are you doing? We haven't had much of a chance to talk since . . ." She paused and swallowed hard. ". . . the event." She looked away from Elizabeth, searching her mind for the proper way to continue. "I know things were complicated between you toward the end, but you must understand that he loved you and that he loved Wyatt. I don't know why it's so important to me that you know that, but it is." She took a deep, steadying breath. Elizabeth recognized she was on the verge of tears again as her eyes gleamed with the as yet unfallen drops. "We never approved of what he did to you and were open about our feelings. He clearly made mistakes, and they cost him everything, but he was my son." The tears broke their hold and began to fall freely. "I loved him, despite his faults, and if there is one thing I am sure of, he still loved you and Wyatt."

Elizabeth was crying now as well. "I know he did. I loved him too." And she was relieved to find that was true. It simplified her confusion. She allowed herself to feel the pain tangled up in the complicated emotions wrapped around Jason. She loved him, and he was gone, and that hurt. Everything else was secondary.

She took Joana into her arms, and they cried together.

Verse 112

Norton, Kansas

THE next day, Harold, Wyatt, and Elizabeth somberly entered the quiet house in Norton. There was very little talking. Harold wondered to himself when talking would feel normal again.

Judy felt very close as his memories of returning to this same house after her funeral, also accompanied by her daughter and grandson, pulled him back to that day. Instead of pulling him deeper into his depression, however, it gave him hope as he realized that if talking had found normality after the loss of Judy, then conversation would return this time as well. It would just take time.

They ate delivered pizza that dripped grease after which Elizabeth leaned back in her chair, patting her belly. "Tell you what: After all that home-cooked casserole, this hit the spot."

Wyatt agreed with a loud belch, and Harold already felt the world settling back into place.

Yes, time fixes all wounds, but greasy pizza can speed up the process.

Verse 113

Alma, Nebraska

JACOB and Gary looked at Samuel with expressions of pure bewilderment. "You want us to do what now?" Jacob asked, his beer forgotten.

"Sing a song at the wedding." Samuel looked at them with an expression of pure mischievous glee. "No one here knows me aside from the wedding party, but you two are a fixture in this town. I think people would flip out if you two sang a song, and I can tell by the melodious way you discourse that you have musical talent that has been neglected for years, waiting for the right musician to coax it out of you."

Their expressions did not change, and neither did his.

"Just so we are clear here," Gary continued, "you want us two old fogies to get on a stage, with microphones, and sing in front of a crowd of people?" He picked up the beer and sipped it, not noticing that it was in fact Jacob's forgotten beer.

Jacob noticed and the beer was no longer forgotten. "Hey, that's mine."

"Sorry, sorry. My—what did he call it?—'melodious throat' was parched." He smiled, understanding this was a joke Samuel was pulling on them. Samuel's smile widened, but Gary saw only sincerity there. "You can't honestly be serious. You have never even heard us sing."

"Nor do you want to, I would say," Jacob cut back in. He sipped his shared beer.

Samuel replied, "A few things I would point out: One, it'll be toward the end so people will be drunk, and nothing sounds bad when people are drunk. Two, bad singing by people you know is better than good singing by people you don't, and that is a fact. Third, and finally, I want to dance with Elizabeth to something memorable, and I just don't see me playing a Sinatra song over the speakers as doing it. So, you see, you are the soundtrack playing over possibly the most important moment of my romantic life. Do you want to decline such an auspicious role?"

The look of pure bewilderment had returned to their faces. Jacob had opened his mouth to protest when the door opened. Silhouetted in the light of the afternoon sun was Elizabeth.

"Thank you, guys, so much. I will never forget this." Then Samuel was gone, taking Elizabeth by the arm, leading her out of the darkness into the summer light.

The door closed. Jacob and Gary were left alone, perplexed as to whether or not they'd agreed to anything. Gary absentmindedly took a sip of the beer in front of him. It was Jacob's.

Verse 114

Alma, Nebraska

THE time between the funeral and the wedding was an intangible blend of ups and downs, making Elizabeth feel as if she were on an unending rollercoaster operated by a maniacal carny.

She would spend a morning with Rebecca as they put the final touches on her upcoming wedding, giggling over coffee and old pictures of Rebecca and Patrick that would adorn the gifts table. Then she would receive a phone call from a long-forgotten friend who wanted to show their support at such a hard time by bringing up some also long-forgotten memory of Jason that would reopen the wound that had begun to heal. Then, in the afternoon, she would get to spend time with Samuel under the pretense of tying up any loose ends with regard to the music. This was obviously a joke as Samuel was a total professional and had taken care of everything, conveniently leaving them with plenty of time on their hands. These blissful hours, however, would take a turn if she ever opened her phone to the messages and well wishes of family and friends who'd heard the news.

Old friends from high school were even reaching out to her, sending friend requests years after ignoring her in the hallways of Norton Community High School. While she honestly didn't remember half the people reaching out to her, she had the odd sense that if she didn't accept the requests, she would be rude. These people were only trying to be kind in what was a hard time for her; the least she could do was let them be her Facebook friend. One bonus was that she would have more to talk about at the next reunion. She reasoned that she could always weed out those she added after the wedding when she was in a better headspace. However, each request was like a little cut.

"Sorry to hear about Jason."

"How are you doing?"

"I am here for you."

"Heard the news. Call me."

All she ever read was "Hey, remember that Jason is dead, and the last time you talked, you had a blow-up fight?"

"Thank you, friends and neighbors. I had forgotten all about it," she said sarcastically, not realizing she'd said it out loud.

Samuel looked up from the guitar he was tuning. Bartholomew poked his head out of his office.

She shook her head. "Sorry, it's just Facebook. You know."

Bartholomew gave her a compassionate, understanding smile and rolled his chair back out of view.

Samuel continued to look at her, then set down his guitar beside him.

"You wanna get outta here? You may have forgotten, but I have a special treatment for beating the blues. It is impossible to check your phone when you are going eighty miles per hour on a motorcycle."

She looked back at the current request she was on: her old student body president. She sighed, hit accept, and put away her phone.

"That sounds splendid, Samuel. But how about we keep it under seventy? While I am sure the bride could replace the maid of honor who has been her best friend since childhood, the singer is irreplaceable, and a motorcycle accident would ruin the wedding. I don't need that on my dying conscience." Her stomach rolled as she realized she'd been joking about a car accident, something that had taken her mother and her ex-husband. Well, she wasn't sure that Jason's death could technically be filed under car accident. Regardless, her flippant tone filled her with guilt, and had Samuel not taken her hand at that exact moment, she would have turned down his offer and left for home. However, his calloused fingers, still warm from racing the strings of his guitar, encircled her hand and she felt safe.

"I will protect you."

He pulled her close to him and, without thinking, she pressed her lips to his. She didn't think about Jason, she didn't think about Wyatt, she didn't think about what complications might arise after the wedding. She thought about Samuel, specifically how nice he felt against her.

"Jesus is watching, you know."

She jumped, successfully keeping away a blush. She'd been getting a lot of opportunities to practice that little skill.

Bartholomew was peeking out of his office again. "I meant that literally." He pointed with the pen he was holding, and their eyes followed to a giant picture of Jesus hanging on the wall near them. His expression was somber, hurt, and betrayed as if their kiss had put him on the cross. She supposed a kiss *had* put him on the cross, so it made sense that he wouldn't care for them too much.

"Maybe you should consider getting a picture of Jesus where he looks happy to be hanging in a church," Samuel said, never taking his eyes from those of Jesus. He moved one way then the other. "The eyes follow me wherever I go."

"I don't think Jesus is much of a smiler when it comes to hanging. You know, bad experiences and all." Bartholomew's statement was so similar to the thought Elizabeth had that, without warning, she burst into a fit of laughter that soon had them all bent over. Was it sacrilegious to laugh about Jesus in a church? Probably. But Elizabeth liked to think that Samuel was right about Jesus being a smiling God-man with a sense of humor. After all, he was one-third of the team that designed this world, and the world was a funny place, all things considered.

Soon, their laughter died down, and Samuel and Elizabeth bade Bartholomew farewell, headed toward a seventy mile per hour therapy session.

Verse 115

Council Bluffs, Iowa

GIDEON'S computer dinged with a notification. This was it; this was what he'd been waiting for.

The day of the funeral when he'd, yet again, been denied access into the minds of those who could help him, he'd returned to his hotel and had gotten to work on a new plan. First, he'd looked into the information he'd gleaned on Elizabeth, tracking down her high school in a little town in Kansas. Then he'd sifted through the records of that school until he'd found the student roster from the year she'd graduated, specifically the student body president, Heather Vincent. Bingo. He took a screenshot of the student pictures, lingering over the then-eighteen-year-old Elizabeth. She had no idea of the life coming in her direction outside of the relative safety of her lower education.

He shook his head. There was more work to be done. He established immediately that Heather did have a Facebook page but, bless the lord, she was rarely active. This worked well in his favor as he saw that she and Elizabeth were already friends, but Heather's name would not have popped up on her feed for some time. Heather did not lock her account, which was perfect as he went through her photos and copied them into his own new account, editing the profile info to match hers. Then, excluding Elizabeth, he sent friend requests to every other student that graduated that year. Half of them quickly responded by accepting the friend request; others said nothing. Some sent messages calling him a spam account.

He waited a few days, allowing more responses to trickle in. Most accepted the friend request, no questions asked. Eventually, the new Heather profile looked perfectly plain; nothing stood out to raise flags whatsoever.

He sent a new friend request with a message of condolence and waited. He hoped with everything going on, Elizabeth would be too distracted to thoroughly vet incoming requests. This was risky as it meant putting his faith in the hands of a woman who might have turned off social media altogether after such a traumatic event.

His computer's notification proclamation, however, meant he was in. Mission accomplished. He got back to work.

Verse 116

Norton, Kansas

HAROLD studied his grandson as he morosely looked at the book he was clearly not reading. He could almost see a dark cloud around him, and Harold's heart broke a little more. He wished he could explain loss, and grief, and acceptance in a way that would help. He also knew there was no explanation that could help—at least, none that had been shared with him.

Harold had lost his own parents years ago, but they'd lived full lives, each passing peacefully in their sleep. Yes, he had Judy's death to correlate to Wyatt's current situation, but how could he help there when he himself barely made it through the day without crying? He was surviving thanks only to the ghost-like replica his anguished mind made to keep him company.

He had opened his mouth, feeling like he had to say something compassionate, when Wyatt put down his book and turned toward the front window, head slightly cocked.

"What is it?" Then he heard it too. The unmistakable sound of a motorcycle.

Motorcycle engines were a common sound during the summer, making Harold wonder why this particular one had pulled their interest so completely. Then, in the back of his mind, he realized he could hear music within the deep bass growl. It was beautiful.

He was pondering the musicality of automobiles when he realized the motorcycle was slowing down outside his house. He watched as the single headlight slid across the windshield as it turned into his driveway. Suddenly, the music was gone as the engine cut out, and Harold gasped at the sudden loss of beauty. Wyatt turned to look at him and Harold realized Wyatt had heard it too. Before he could ask Wyatt what he thought about it, voices outside the window pulled him back to the present as two giggling teenagers made their way to the front door.

Harold began to get up, but Wyatt beat him to it and ran to the door, throwing it open with no hesitation. The two teenagers on the other side were actually two adults who jumped away from each other, startled.

Wyatt looked at them confused. "Mom?"

There was an awkward silence that no one seemed to know how to break.

Finally, the man Harold presumed was his daughter's new crush cleared his throat. "Hey, little man. I got something for you."

Wyatt's eyebrow slid up, and Harold saw the man he would grow up to be. The expression said, *I'm listening because I like to receive gifts, but don't think I forgot that little jump thing you and my mother did just now.*

"When I was a kid," said Samuel, "I moved around a lot with my brother. I was often scared of each new town, and music was the only thing that made me feel better. My brother told me it was a magical power against the forces of evil. So, he got me one of these, since we couldn't afford guitars or pianos, and had no room even if we could." He pulled out a small blue box and handed it to Wyatt.

Wyatt gingerly opened it. The light from the room behind him glistened off the shiny harmonica, lying in its tiny, fabric-lined coffin. It was beautiful.

"I can teach you how to play it properly, if you want."

Harold understood there was more in the request than simple harmonica lessons, but doubted Wyatt did.

Wyatt pulled out the harmonica and blew lightly into the rectangular holes. Without warning, he dashed forward and hugged Samuel around the waist.

Harold saw moisture glistening in Elizabeth's eyes and assumed his were equally damp. It had been hard recently, but something about the harmonica, like a musical totem, made him feel like everything would be okay.

Wyatt began to play noisily as Samuel and Elizabeth shut the door behind them. Despite the musicality leaving something to be desired, the joy was infectious, and the room felt a little brighter.

Verse 117

Norton, Kansas

HAROLD, Elizabeth, and Samuel sat on the back deck, enjoying the warm, summer evening. Harold and Samuel were each nursing glasses of scotch and Elizabeth had a Moscow mule, copper mug and all.

Wyatt had gone to bed early. Elizabeth knew he had been sleeping poorly. She assumed that was normal for a boy who'd lost his dad, specifically, in such a traumatic manner. She did her best as his mom to help, but she knew that until the wedding was done, her schedule was not helping. After the wedding, she would make a point to spend so much quality time with him that he would have to ask her to give him some space.

She sipped her drink, listening to the two other men in her life discuss sports in a way that clearly showed Samuel was making it up as he went along after briefly Googling the teams she'd told him might come up. *The rollercoaster that had been the past few days was finally leveling off, she thought, as the hills and valleys shrunk.* She realized that sitting here with her dad and Samuel, she felt contentment she hadn't felt in a long time. The drink helped as well as it was extra strong.

"Yeah, I would say the Shockers surprised everyone this year," Samuel said with real confidence. "We will have to see what the Huskers can do next year with the new coach."

Shoot. She should have explained to him that despite both being of interest in these states, they were in two different conferences. Harold nodded agreement and let it slide. She had a feeling that Samuel wasn't fooling her dad one bit, and she loved him even more for not pointing it out.

She felt that there was something important, something *special* here. The idea had started when she'd first been getting to know Samuel, but the fact that he'd been so supportive and stuck around after everything that had gone down gave her hope. She realized that hope was something she'd sworn off not long ago, but it was a hard habit to break. If he could outlast the horrendous death of her ex-husband, he could definitely outlast the wedding, right? She'd not been looking for anything during this trip or even considered she could find anything, but now that she had, she was reluctant to let it go.

For that matter, why should she? Didn't this relationship deserve a chance at life? Should it be prematurely aborted only because their mutual reason for being in this place at this time was coming to an end? Sticking with the analogy, she considered that it "takes two to tango," and she needed to discuss these thoughts with Samuel. For all she knew, she was planning out their future together while he was looking forward to seeing her in the rearview mirror—or whatever the mirrors on a motorcycle were called.

"Do you agree, Elizabeth?"

"Sorry, I was off in my own world." She paused. "I missed the question."

"There was no question," Samuel said, smiling that annoying, upper-hand smile he liked to wear. "I noticed you were, how did you put it, 'gathering wool'? And decided to bring you back into the conversation. You could help me dig myself out of the hole that is college athletics as I think I have adequately shown my lack of knowledge on the subject."

So, it would appear Samuel had not needed Harold to reveal that Samuel clearly knew nothing. She smiled and sipped her drink slowly, letting the silence drag out a little longer. She finished with a loud satisfied sigh.

"The Jayhawks could have done better, wouldn't you say, Samuel?" Harold choked on a laugh.

She decided to help the poor guy out and changed subjects. "So, Rebecca told me that Patrick invited you to the bachelor party tomorrow. Do you feel honored?"

"Honestly? I was starting to wonder what a guy had to do to get an invite. I was buying drinks, complimenting his looks, even dropping hints about how much I like bachelor parties. I've never had that much trouble getting a date." He stopped, then looked at Elizabeth, embarrassed. "Not that I date a lot."

She raised an accusatory eyebrow.

"I mean, I have gone on dates, but, you know, nothing serious."

Elizabeth was loving how uncomfortable Samuel had become. He kept darting looks at her dad, who was looking right back at him with an unreadable expression on his face. She was in heaven right now.

"Look, what I mean to say is I don't date, but I go on dates. Dating is hard when you travel. Not that I like to invite people to my hotel. I'm not saying that. I'm only trying to say that this is different."

Her smile faded. Her worries had been placed in front of her quite unexpectedly. He'd, quite unintentionally she was sure, arrived at the heart of the issue.

"Different, you say?"

Oh God. Right as Elizabeth had opened her mouth to change the subject, to continue letting future Elizabeth deal with the fallout, her dad had stepped up to the plate to take a swing.

"Different how?"

Her heart was racing. She wanted to scream. *Please don't answer; I'm not ready to deal with this. Future Elizabeth was supposed to handle this for me after the wedding.* At the same time, however, she was dying to know the answer. Now that her dad had taken the reins for her, she didn't want to waste this opportunity. Samuel's face grew very serious. Her heartbeat, which had been racing, seemed to stop, as did her breath, and time as well.

"Different in that I don't just want a date. I want to date. Your daughter is very important to me." He turned slowly, letting those brilliant blue eyes, caught in the light coming through the glass door behind them, catch hers. "You are worth changing my life, if you are willing to let me."

She saw something in those eyes, something that scared her a little. Of course, any talk about an uncertain future is scary. He'd taken every doubt she'd been feeling about their relationship and put them to bed. She felt tears form in her eyes as her emotions threatened to overwhelm her.

Again, her dad came to her rescue. "I think it is safe to say that she is willing. Now, back to more important issues at hand: How do we feel about the K-State lineup for next fall?"

They were back, the weight was gone, and Elizabeth knew that tonight was important. She was sure it would be a night she remembered for the rest of her life. A turning point.

She listened as Samuel made up players for the Kansas State football team, giving them fictitious stats, letting his eyes drift to her before darting back to her dad. She sat smiling, letting the joy of the moment wash over her. She sipped her drink and knew that everything was right in the world. Future Elizabeth would be sure to thank her dad for her. She smiled as Samuel's eyes met hers again. He smiled back at her. Yes, everything was right in the world.

Verse 118

Alma, Nebraska

WEDDING Eve had finally arrived. Elizabeth and Rebecca worked hard to put the final touches to decorations, dealt with a last-minute wedding party cancellation, and found housing for a last-minute aunt whose schedule miraculously opened up.

Patrick helped as best he could, but he was basically just a good-looking distracted statue that inconveniently kept finding himself in the way. With a kiss and words of affirmation, he was sent to get coffee at the coffee house they'd come to love. But he was made to swear that if the lovable, old men were there, he would have to explain that he had to get the coffee back while it was still hot or he would find out what a bridezilla was.

He showed up thirty minutes later, Jacob and Gary in tow, both of whom proved to be far more useful than Patrick in wedding prep.

Samuel was on stage, checking all the instruments, microphones, and song lists.

At one point, when Elizabeth was in the room where they would get dressed and wait 'til the big reveal, Gary and Jacob took to the stage and tentatively practiced singing a few bars into the mic while Samuel beamed up at them from below.

By the time she returned, they were sipping church coffee, as the good stuff had run out a while ago, and Bartholomew had made a fresh pot for everyone. Bartholomew, for his part, was preparing for the rehearsal later that night, making little changes here and there to the message and generally being a bucket of sunshine. When considering great mornings, most of them would have listed this one in their top five. It was perfect.

As more and more of the wedding party arrived, things broke down into chaotic fun, and the prep work was all but abandoned as old memories were shared, new life developments were explained, and everyone fell into a happy babble as they milled about.

Elizabeth mentally prepared to ward off questions and concerns about Jason. However, aside from furtive glances in her direction and a few awkward moments in conversations when someone would falter in their description of their happily wedded life, the topic was all but avoided. It was all reminiscent of when she'd been freshly divorced and acquaintances struggled to talk to her. For the most part, things were basically normal, and she could easily overlook the few occurrences of awkwardness.

The day passed quickly, as all days like this do, and they found themselves around a large table in the back lawn of Rebecca's parents' house.

Bartholomew sat between two bridesmaids who appeared to be fighting for his attention. Elizabeth watched with wry amusement, knowing that at least one of them was married. Awkward, faltered conversations were probably in her future, poor thing. Elizabeth gave a bitter smile. Rehearsal had gone great, and her bitter smile became one of pride as she recalled all the ladies looking lustfully at Samuel as he played the song to which they would walk in. Yet, his electric blue eyes had been for her alone, and she'd felt them on her all night.

Harold had agreed to watch Wyatt overnight so that she could stay in Alma for the bachelorette party. He would bring Wyatt up for the wedding the following day.

She had plenty of fun activities planned for the ladies that would keep them busy late into the night. However, after enduring hours of those eyes on her, when Samuel, upon leaving the church, had offered for her to maybe visit him at the hotel for a little while, it had taken all of her self-control not to hand off the party to someone else and go with him then. Instead, she had agreed that it might be nice to see him later, if she could find the time, and stepped into her car, shutting the door between them. This allowed her to take long, deep breaths in privacy as she forced the world around her to stop spinning. She stopped fighting it and let her face glow red as her mind filled with the possibilities the night held before her. She had plucked a penis whistle from the bag of bachelorette paraphernalia in the passenger seat and gave it a happy, little toot before pulling out of the church parking lot.

Now he sat beside her. Each time their arms brushed, she wanted to scream. God, she wasn't going to make it an hour if she didn't calm down. She knew that soon they would break into their two different gender-specific groups and go their different ways, and that would give her some reprieve from the torrent of sexual tension building between her legs. Deep breaths.

Finally, dinner was over. There were catcalls and jokes thrown between the two groups as the men piled into vehicles to head into town and the ladies stayed behind at the house.

Elizabeth sighed deeply. She already felt the tension easing. "All right, ladies, everything from here on out is penis-related, so let the envy begin."

The party was hilariously fun as they pinned a penis onto a scrotum, ate a penis-shaped cake that, impressively, had been made by the mother of the bride, and got more and more inebriated as they drank through penis-shaped straws. In short, it was the typical bachelorette party, and they enjoyed every moment of it. Elizabeth had gone all out, going so far as to have each lady apply a temporary penis tattoo somewhere that would be hidden by their dresses the following day.

For her part, Elizabeth drank less than everyone other than Rebecca. She didn't want to mess up the plans she had for later; plans she had to continuously distract herself from with phallic party favors and inappropriate games.

Verse 119

Alma, Nebraska

THE men had a normal bachelor party as well as they visited each bar the town had to offer, playing Keno, darts, and old school arcade games. There was one exchange that was forgettable to everyone aside from one. To that one, it was very memorable.

"Goddamn Patrick, fuckin' getting married. You sonofabitch."

"I know. Can you believe it? God. And she is perfect."

"Does she know about Veronica?"

"Fuck no!" Patrick exclaimed. "We were on a break, and it didn't mean anything. There is no reason to complicate something good with something that wasn't even a big deal. If anything, it was a good thing, because it was what convinced me I wanted to be with her for the rest of my life."

"Did she know you were on a break, Ross?"

This reference was followed by much laughing and merriment.

Samuel smiled. But had anyone noticed his eyes, they might have paused in their laughter to consider what was off there. The smile on his face had not reached his eyes; they were cold pools of ice. Soon after, however, he was hooting it up again with the rest, and the night continued ever on.

Verse 120

Norton, Kansas

HAROLD, who'd come to like Samuel quite a bit over the past few days and more so after their time the previous night, was finding a new hatred for the man tonight.

Wyatt had finally broken out of the fog of depression. For this, Harold was grateful. However, how Samuel had done so was through a little harmonica, given as a gift to the boy. Wyatt did not know how to play the harmonica. His lack of knowledge did not stop him from trying very hard, very frequently. Harold kept making up excuses to escape to other rooms, only to find Judy there, giving him a wry smile of amusement.

"Oh, like you could handle this any better."

Imaginary wives, by their nature, did not have to suffer such tortures as harmonica riffs.

Harold smiled. He'd been concerned that, after Randall's death, he might not see Judy again. If this were a novel, he supposed, her restless spirit would have been put to rest at that point, but as this was not a novel and she was not a ghost, but rather a figment of his imagination, she'd stuck around.

She gave him a knowing look and he sighed.

"Back into the trenches, I suppose." He picked up the book he'd claimed to be retrieving, the most recent excuse, and turned toward the brassy noise coming from his living room. "If this goes on much longer," he said over his shoulder, "I'll be joining you sooner than anticipated. There is no way I can survive this for long."

He left without looking back and was soon clapping along to the tune Wyatt was making up to show his support. All things considered, he was happy that Wyatt was happy, and that was enough for him.

Verse 121

Alma, Nebraska

IT had been a night to remember, but now people were dropping off. A combination of alcohol, travel, and simple exhaustion was finally taking its toll.

The women were not the only ones. Samuel had texted Elizabeth half an hour before that the party had moved to the hotel, and he'd already slipped away, preservation of his singing tools as his excuse. Elizabeth was starting to feel that stirring again as the realization of what lay before her became more solid with that text. Ever since, she'd been restless. As the first few ladies excused themselves to their rooms for bed, she knew the ending was within sight.

Now she sat, leaning her head on Rebecca's shoulder. She'd told Rebecca her plan for the evening as soon as she'd known there was a plan for the evening and had been greeted with exuberant support. However, she was still reluctant to leave her the night before the wedding. She felt like she was betraying her, dropping the ball in some way as the maid of honor.

"Shouldn't you go?" Rebecca cut into her thoughts. "Elizabeth."

Elizabeth sat up at Rebecca's use of her full name.

"I will be fine. You deserve tonight. No one I know deserves a night like tonight more than you." She smiled and placed a smooth palm on each of Elizabeth's cheeks, pulling her toward her to kiss her forehead. "Happiness is hard to find, so you should never pass on an opportunity to grab it, even if it feels fleeting." She moved back to look Elizabeth in the eyes again. "I love you. Now leave. Go find your happiness."

Elizabeth, tears welling in her eyes, threw her arms around Rebecca and held her close. It felt like a long time before she released her. She mouthed *thank you* before quietly sneaking past the few ladies still fighting sleep to escape out the front door.

The drive to the hotel was suffocating as the pressure in the car seemed overwhelming. She imagined a balloon airing up with her inside as the outside walls stopped expanding and the air, needing somewhere to go, began to press in on her.

"This is not a big deal," she said out loud, her voice sounding unusual to her own ears. "It's just one night, a night you deserve. It doesn't mean you'll end up with the house and the white picket fence. Let tomorrow worry about itself. Tonight you are just going to have sex." The declaration sounded so juvenile that she was embarrassed, even though she was alone in the car. Then, in a burst of confidence, she shouted into the empty car: "You are gonna have sex tonight!" It felt less juvenile this time. She decided to keep saying it until it broke down into giggles as she pulled into the hotel parking lot.

He was in room 19. He had slipped her a key earlier that day when leaving the church. She sat in her car, allowing her heart to slow down, worrying that if she got up too quickly, while it was beating as fast as it was, she would pass out. When she concluded it was safe to stand, she opened the car door and stepped out into the summer night.

She heard whooping and shouting coming through a window from one of the rooms further down and smiled.

Maybe her party hadn't been that great if the boys were still carrying on like this when her ladies had been dropping one by one. She shrugged in acceptance and grabbed her overnight bag from the trunk.

Soon she was standing in front of the door labeled "19," unsure of how to proceed. Should she knock or let herself in? He'd given her the key, but that could have been out of convenience, not out of a desire to be walked in on. The card bit into her hand as she squeezed it harder, trying to decide what the sexiest move would be, realizing too late how out of practice she was. She kicked herself for not texting him or giving him some warning before she headed in this direction. With a deep breath, she decided to quietly let herself in, hoping it was what he'd intended by giving her the pass key.

She eased open the door and was greeted with the most beautiful sound she could have heard: the shower.

"Perfect," she whispered in triumph and continued into the room.

Verse 122

Norton, Kansas

HAROLD sat where he'd sat the night before with Samuel and Elizabeth, enjoying the night air, his departed wife sitting next to him, waiting for him to talk.

"I'm nervous, you know," he said, a tear forming in the corner of his left eye. "I've never lived anywhere but here."

He turned to look at her and she looked back, smiling supportively.

"We met in this town, we dated, got married, had kids, lived in this very house." He gestured back toward the house he'd called home for the past forty years.

"Are you an old dog?" she asked.

He looked at her, honestly confused by the question.

"Can you not learn a few new tricks?"

Her smile now held a laugh, and he smiled back.

"New tricks are one thing. A new life is altogether something else."

"New life? You say that like you just became a grandfather. You've been one for these past five years."

The tear finally filled enough to make its trek down his cheek. "I was your husband for many years before that. I think . . ." He swallowed hard. "I am afraid that if I move to be closer to Elizabeth and Wyatt, you might not join me." He looked toward the backyard, unable to make eye contact with Judy, but he could feel her eyes on him. "I don't know if I am ready to give that up."

"But honey." She took his hand. Despite his mind trying to tell him it wasn't true, he could feel the little callouses from knitting as her fingers came to rest in his palm. "You will gain so much more. What is happening now can't last long; it shouldn't have lasted as long as it has." She squeezed his hand to emphasize her point. "They are more your family than I will ever be again. They will last. Don't throw away your future by holding too tightly to the past." She let go of his hand, stood, and stretched her back like she always did after getting up to go to bed. She leaned forward, kissed his cheek, and was gone.

He reached up to feel where her lips had pressed. At first, he believed he felt the moisture from her lips. When he pulled his fingers away, he realized it had only been his tear. He smiled, and he cried.

Verse 123

Alma, Nebraska

IN preparation for her honeymoon, Rebecca had bought an exuberant amount of lingerie. Upon hearing that Elizabeth would sleep with Samuel, she'd forced Elizabeth to look through the pieces and pick at least two for the event. Elizabeth had originally declined the offer, until she'd seen the sheer number of lacy offerings, each still adorned by a tag. She'd then reluctantly agreed to take a couple.

As she slipped into the hotel room, hearing the telltale signs of a person in the middle of a shower, she'd breathed a thank you toward Bex. She set down her overnight bag and pulled out the two offerings.

The first was a matching set: a light blue, see-through nightie with matching see-through panties. The other was a blazing red thing that looked like a tangle of ropes until it was on, at which point it still looked like ropes, only less tangled and very specifically placed to leave little to the imagination while still covering the important parts. As this was their first night together, she decided the light blue had the more innocent look, despite technically showing more. She reserved the red ropey thing for another night.

She took off her shirt, unclasped her bra, and let it fall to the floor. She popped open her belt, undid the button, unzipped her jeans, got a thumb into her old panties, and slid the whole assortment down to her ankles.

She was bent over, trying to pull her foot through the multiple garments, when she heard a throat clear behind her. She looked between her legs, realizing that her butt was facing the bathroom door which now stood open, water running in the background, completely exposed to a very pleased looking Samuel who infuriatingly wore a towel around his waist. The upper ground achieved by the lingerie had been lost.

She stood like that for a moment, him standing behind her, hair soaked, water running down his bare chest and torso, dampening the white towel around his waist with steam billowing out around him. Meanwhile, she was bent over, exposing herself in the lewdest way imaginable, one pair of cheeks parted, the other pair scarlet red. Neither said a word.

Finally, she said, "Who leaves the restroom with the shower still running?"

"Someone who hears another someone moving around in his hotel room while he is in the shower, I would presume."

They laughed and she straightened, feeling no need to be modest after the display he'd walked in on.

"I'll have you know this was meant for you." She threw the lacy blue top at him.

He caught it effortlessly and held it out in front of him. "I don't think it's my size, but thanks for thinking of me?"

She rolled her eyes.

"If you want, I could try it on. You know, if it'll make you feel better. Gift giving can be so tricky."

"The last thing I want at this moment is for you to be any more covered up." With decisive steps, she moved forward and removed his towel. They stood in front of each other, each now completely naked. Both had begun to breathe a little heavier. "There," she sighed, finding it hard to speak, "back on even ground."

He reached for her and pulled her to him. Their bodies met, and they kissed deeply. His wet body slid against hers as he ran his hands along her back, not hesitating to go where a belt line would have been. For her part, she moved so that her back was facing the bed. She pulled away, drawing her hand down his chest, down to his bellybutton, before following the light hair down. She grasped him there, pulled him toward the bed, and sat back on the mattress, all the while keeping a firm grip. His eyes had a glazed, pleading look as she shimmied further up the mattress, pulling him onto the bed where he knelt before her. She considered some form of foreplay, but decided there would be plenty of time for that later. He shimmied forward on his knees as she guided him into her. The tension she'd been feeling between her legs all day grew to a fever pitch. She was not sure she could hold on to her sanity before it blessedly broke apart and spilled out of her as she fell back onto the bed, joined by Samuel who fell beside her, draping an arm and a leg over her to keep her close. Again, they said nothing for a long time. Then she began to giggle.

"What?" he asked, with a little bit of concern in his voice. *The male ego is tied very closely to their prowess in bed*, she thought, and her giggle became more of a laugh.

"I was just thinking, if you do it after, it wouldn't be called foreplay; it'd have to be called post-play."

He nuzzled into her neck as he, too, laughed at her grammatical discovery. They stayed like that for what felt like an eternity, and all the concerns of what this relationship would look like the next day fell away.

Rebecca had been right. This had been worth it, no matter how fleeting it was. She turned to look at him, his blue eyes dazzling her as they always did. She searched her mind for something romantic to say that would fit the moment, but he was too quick for her.

"So, was that a penis tattoo on your right butt-cheek?"

Verse 124

Des Moines, Iowa

WHILE Elizabeth and Samuel discussed lewd temporary tattoos, Sally lay in bed, wide awake, thinking over the past few weeks.

Moving in with her sister had been the best decision she could have made. She and Boomer had been content, if not happy there. People didn't stop them as they walked down the street to offer condolences. They didn't see pity in every eye that turned their way. No, they lived their lives as normal people, and that normalcy had been a breath of fresh air. It's easy to take normal for granted when nothing is happening.

Boomer, who'd seemingly disappeared down a dark hole of depression no kid should have to deal with was finally opening up a little more. Amanda, Sally's sister, had even encouraged a smile on a few occasions. He'd delved into art recently and seemed oddly fixated on motorcycles, but Sally let that go as an average interest for a boy. She herself had loved motorcycles—a thought that, inevitably, like most things, led back to Samuel. He was like the chorus to a song stuck in her head; an earworm with brilliant blue eyes.

The trip to Amanda's had helped fix a lot of problems, but Samuel was the one problem it couldn't seem to do anything about. She'd thought putting some space between them—a state and a half, to be exact—would do the trick, but it had made things worse. At least while she was in Alma, she had a general idea of his comings and goings. In Iowa, she had no idea what he was doing and, more importantly, with whom he was doing it. She couldn't get that girl she'd met at the bar out of her mind. They'd been awfully close. Now with Sally completely out of the picture, at Samuel's request, the stranger was free to have him to herself. This was something Sally continuously reminded herself was okay, because she and Samuel had not been together. These were thoughts that did nothing to comfort her or, in the late hours of the night, let her sleep.

She knew the wedding was the next day, and Samuel would be moving on afterward. Out of Alma and out of her life. Again, this thought should have filled her with relief. Instead, her anxiety built around the idea that she was running out of time to tell Samuel how she felt.

A task that would be difficult as she couldn't distinguish that feeling for herself.

The fan on the guest bedroom ceiling spun lazily in the near dark. For a while, she tracked its revolutions. After watching the slow spin for what felt like an hour, she looked at the napkin she'd brought from Alma, sitting on the side table. The faded writing inspired her. She decided she had to seize the opportunity to see Samuel one last time.

She would run to Alma tomorrow, despite the long drive, and, hopefully, catch him before the wedding. She would confess something. She still wasn't sure what she would confess, but she figured she had a five- to six-hour drive to come up with something, and if she couldn't find the words by the time she rolled into Alma, then she didn't deserve to say them.

Satisfied with the plan, she rolled over and, within a few minutes, she was fast asleep. She slept a deep, dreamless sleep.

Verse 125

Des Moines, Iowa

IN the room beside Sally's, her son ran screaming from the motorcycle that pursued him through every nightmare, determined to finish the job it started with his dad. No matter how fast he ran, he always found himself in the circle of light cast by the single, searching eye of the mechanical demon. He tripped, falling into a pile of bones, one of which held tightly to a smoking pistol, blood dripping down the muzzle, bright red in the glare of the headlight. He heard the song now. It played from the motorcycle radio. It was terrifying and beautiful. He snatched the gun, aimed it at the bike, and screamed, "This is for my dad!" He pulled the trigger. Nothing happened. He realized too late, as the single front tire bore down on him, that he'd forgotten the very basics his dad had taught him. He flicked the safety off just as the bike reached him.

He shot up in bed, cold sweat drenching his shirt. The unfamiliar setting enhanced his terror as he tried desperately to remember where he was. By his second deep, gasping breath, he'd landed back in reality, recognizing the room at his aunt's house. The song from his dream drifted through his mind like a fog and dissipated in wakefulness. After a couple of deeper breaths, Boomer got up to pee, grateful that he hadn't gone in his bed. That would have been the cherry on top of a dream like that.

On his way back to his room, he stopped outside his mother's room. He considered crawling into bed with her. He dismissed the thought almost as quickly as it had come.

He knew he loved his mom, but the sentimentality needed to crawl in bed with her didn't exist anymore. Shortly after his dad died, she'd crawled into bed with him, and that had been nice, but, as time moved on, those visits had stopped and that, too, had been okay.

He whispered "I love you, Mom" to her mom before heading toward his room. It was true, and it warmed his insides to say it.

Before he crawled back into his bed, he changed pajamas to a pair that had less nightmare sweat soaked into them, then fell with a thump. As he drifted off to sleep, he heard his father's death song echoing in his mind like a lullaby, but he was too tired to be afraid as his consciousness went black.

Verse 126

Alma, Nebraska

THE morning of the wedding had arrived at last.

Elizabeth showed up at Rebecca's family house with coffee for herself and the bride-to-be from their favorite coffee shop. Rebecca's stated boldly "double shot espresso." In reality, it was half-caf, half decaf. They didn't want her passenger getting too excited today nor did they want the group of gossipy girls lounging around to question the lack of caffeine content.

Susannah understood the situation by now and had sketched the description on the cup without being asked. What a wonderful lady. Elizabeth waved goodbye on her way out, knowing she'd see Susannah and her little coffee cart shortly at the church.

At Rebecca's house, Elizabeth made her way around the ladies who were slowly rising like zombies, each a different level of hungover with a few still possibly intoxicated. She slipped into Rebecca's room, coffee in hand, to find her friend in an oversized shirt and panties. She sat down her cups, quietly made her way to the bed, and rubbed her hands together in preparation.

"For Narnia!" she yelled and brought her hand down on the exposed side of the left cheek, where the underwear had slid a little deeper into the crack.

Rebecca dove forward, unable to understand life as it existed around her, and almost fell out of bed before Elizabeth caught her.

Elizabeth laughed so hard at the writhing limbs beneath her that she almost dropped her friend as Rebecca looked around wildly for an explanation.

"Beth?" Rebecca rubbed the spot on her backside where a perfect handprint was forming. "What the hell?" She blinked a couple of times. "Did you scream 'For Narnia' at my ass?"

It was too much. They fell into each other's arms, laughing maniacally.

"I . . ." Elizabeth struggled to catch her breath. ". . . just wanted . . ." Still struggling. ". . . to make sure . . ." Dear lord, was she going to suffocate before finishing this sentence? ". . . . Patrick had a guide for hand placement." She breathed out in one exhalation.

Their eyes met and, for a second, there was silent contemplation. Then they were back into gales of laughter, and Elizabeth began to worry about suffocating. Finally, the laughter began to die down. They sat on the floor, backs against the bedspread, still giggling.

"You get married today," remarked Elizabeth.

"I do, don't I? Gosh, I should probably cancel my other plans."

They looked at each other, sharing a moment of pure joy before embracing tightly.

"Aaaannnddd?" asked Rebecca. "Did my outfits get the job done?"

"Let's just say they played a part, yes."

Rebecca beamed at her, nodding.

"I'll tell you all about it later. But today is your day. I got you coffee, a schedule, and a helpful heart." She smiled, pulled out her phone, and held it out to take a selfie.

"Wait. You can't post any pictures of me on my wedding day. It's bad luck." She looked around until she found a stuffed bear that she held in front of her face.

Elizabeth shrugged and held out the phone yet again.

"This is going to be a beary good day," Rebecca said.

Their selfie was of one woman in an oversized t-shirt holding a teddy bear in front of her face and another woman, fully dressed, mid-laugh. It was delightfully cute in the best kind of way.

Verse 127

Council Bluffs, Iowa

THE notification alert pinged on Gideon's phone. He ripped it out of his pocket.

It had been days since he'd been accepted as one of Elizabeth's friends and, yet, she'd not posted anything or checked in anywhere. She had, by all accounts, left social media after hitting the accept button. He'd been waiting ever since with no plan other than to see what she posted next. He'd checked her page religiously, worried that she would avoid posting anything and he would be left at square one.

The notification told him otherwise. He quickly opened the app to see an adorable picture of Elizabeth laughing next to someone holding up a teddy bear with a caption:

"The wait has been unBEARable, but today we finally marry off this beautiful Goldilocks to someone who is Just Right." Posted from Alma, NE.

Gideon grabbed his pre-packed bag and ran out of the hotel room.

Verse 128

Alma, Nebraska

BARTHOLOMEW and Samuel sat in Bartholomew's office, waiting for the wedding party to arrive and disrupt the peace. For the moment, however, they sat quietly, enjoying their morning coffees, each mentally preparing for the upcoming festivities.

"So," Bartholomew said, breaking the silence, "have you decided what you plan to do after the wedding?"

Samuel looked at him over his steaming cup and took another sip before setting it down on the table in front of him. "I do believe that this might be my last wedding." Samuel sighed heavily and fell back into the comfortable chair. "I think it might be time for me to find a more stationary career, but I haven't discussed it with pertinent parties at this present juncture."

"Have you told her anything about your feelings and/or considerations?"

Samuel looked at him sheepishly, brought up his hand, and seesawed it back and forth. "You have to realize, Bartholomew, that my whole life, from as early as I can remember, has been about the work I do. I have always known my purpose and my mission in life, and to give that up for a girl I just met seems . . . well . . . pretty crazy. But then I see her face, her eyes, and I think about how easy it is to laugh with her, and I feel joy like I have never known, and I have to consider that maybe chasing that joy is worth giving up on my perceived purpose." He sighed. "To tell her my thoughts in a straightforward, no-nonsense kind of way would be the first step in making them real, and once they are real, they have to be addressed."

Bartholomew nodded. "You do realize, though, that you have told me. Which means the thoughts have been put into words. They are real. I think it is high time you addressed them with the other person who might want a say." Bartholomew took a long breath. "So, are you ready for tonight?"

Samuel smiled at him with gratitude for the change of subject.

"My sermon is pretty kickass, so it would be a huge letdown if the music sucked."

"Don't you worry your holy, little head. All is fine on my side. Trust me when I say you haven't heard anything quite like it. I even have a surprise or two for—"

It was at that moment that they heard the front doors open. Within minutes, the sanctuary was filled with the laughing, joyous sounds of the wedding party. Samuel and Bartholomew walked to the door of his office and observed the commotion. Elizabeth walked in with Rebecca, and Bartholomew heard Samuel's sudden intake of breath beside him.

"She literally took your breath away, you big idiot."

Samuel smiled at him before returning his eyes to the two women. Rebecca, who'd been quite persuasive on the drive over, saw Samuel, then turned away from him and bent down to adjust her shoe, letting her jeans-clad rearend stand erect before him. She waggled it back and forth as Elizabeth's face turned scarlet. Samuel's jaw dropped. Bartholomew looked from one to the other, unsure of what was happening, but enjoying the reactions of all involved.

The moment passed quickly as the wedding preparation rolled ever onward like a monorail, full steam ahead with only one destination: marriage.

Soon, Bartholomew was giving instructions and reminding people about timeframes; Samuel was on stage tuning instruments for the millionth time; Elizabeth was busy helping with Rebecca's hair and makeup; and Patrick was enjoying cold beverages his groomsmen had brought and generally not doing much, as is customary for grooms. Time lost all meaning as the day went by both incredibly fast, with multiple curses at how little time they had, and incredibly slow, as the wedding loomed over everything still hours away.

If ever there were an equivalence to a time anomaly on Earth, it would be the day of a wedding.

Verse 129

Des Moines, Iowa

SALLY had thought, even hoped, that her crazy plan from last night would have been forgotten or, at least, faded by the time she woke up. Over breakfast, with each sip of coffee and bite of toast, she told herself to stay, enjoy the day, and let Samuel go.

However, after breakfast, she'd wandered into her room and the napkin had been there; a beacon, telling her to go. Telling her that she had to tell Samuel about her feelings. If he turned her away, so be it. She would be able to sleep knowing she'd tried. And if he didn't turn her away? Well, then, they could figure that out together.

Boomer was sitting in the living room watching TV, well within eavesdropping range of Sally's conversation with his aunt. "I have to run to Alma to grab a few more things and tie up a couple of loose ends. Could you watch Boomer? I will be back tomorrow."

Amanda said she had the weekend off and would be delighted to watch her nephew.

When the sisters walked out of the kitchen, Boomer was standing defiantly before them. "I want to go with you, Mom."

There was a brief argument where points were made, reasons were given, and tantrums were threatened, all of which led to Boomer sitting next to his mom, rolling down the interstate toward their hometown.

Sally was lost in thought as she went over different scenarios that might play out when she met Samuel, hoping to have contingencies in place for whatever reply he made. Her son sat beside her, muttering about motorcycles, but she barely noticed. Her thoughts dominated all senses not being used to keep the car on the road.

They traveled down the interstate, a long trip ahead of them, the feeling of time passing heavy in the car.

Verse 130

Somewhere Outside Lincoln, Nebraska

GIDEON sat next to his car on the side of the road, spewing every curse word he'd ever heard, filling in the spaces with new ones he made up on the spot.

His car, which had been nothing but reliable during his wanderings, decided that today of all days was when it would blow a tire in the construction that always existed on the interstate. In all the time he'd owned the car, he'd never once checked the spare under the trunk. He'd never had a need, so had never spared it a consideration, no pun intended. The car sat awkwardly on the new tire that was as flat as the one he'd replaced.

He'd called the nearest tow company, located in Lincoln. What that meant was the tow truck would have to drive past him in one direction until it came to the last exit he'd passed, then turn around to meet him headed in the correct direction.

Time, which had already been against him, now seemed to be toying with him. He had the distinct picture of an injured mouse and a cat; the cat letting the mouse think it was finally getting away when a paw would come down on its tail, pinning it in place.

He'd planned on confronting Samuel long before the wedding took place. Now he watched the clock on his phone screen, understanding that he would be lucky to catch him before the wedding at all. He kept reminding himself that

Samuel always waited until the end to finish his work. Gideon had plenty of time, as long as he made it before the end of the reception.

Granted, he hadn't even seen the tow truck pass him yet, and it had been what felt like a very long time since his call. So, he sat in the shade of his car, grabbing random thoughts from passers-by as they meandered around him, none of which were about helping him.

Verse 131

Norton, Kansas

HAROLD slid his hand through the sleeve of his suit jacket. He looked in the mirror as he adjusted his tie and saw Judy sitting on the bed behind him, smiling softly.

"This is the suit I wore to our anniversary dinner, you know. I remember joking that it was my wedding suit only to have the pictures from our wedding, prominently displayed in the party room at the bar, prove that I was a much slimmer man when we said, 'I do.'" He turned to look at her, wishing he could see her in her wedding gown or her anniversary dress.

Yet, she sat on the bed, wearing the sweater and jeans she'd worn the night when she'd left him here alone.

"Not alone," she said softly. "Not anymore."

They both turned toward the door and the sounds of Wyatt getting ready.

"Have you made a decision?"

He had, and she knew it. But there was power in saying an idea out loud, and it seemed she was hoping he would endow his secret considerations with that power now.

He looked at her, still beautiful after all the years.

She met his gaze. "I only look this good because you are wearing rose-colored glasses when you look at me, you old fool. You could just as easily imagine me as I looked fresh out of bed after a late shift." She smiled, however, clearly pleased with the compliment.

He wasn't sure he could have imagined that as he was unable to even change her outfit to fit the occasion. But he didn't say anything, and the moment passed.

"Grandpa? Could you do this for me?"

Harold turned to see Wyatt in the doorway, holding his little tie in front of him. He turned back to the empty bed. Not even an impression remained where Judy had been sitting. He turned back to his grandson.

"Sure, I can. I'll have you know I am a bit of an expert at tying ties."

Wyatt looked at him impressed.

As Harold stepped forward to take the tie, he heard a whispered voice behind him, like the wind through a cracked door:

"Not alone. Not anymore."

Verse 132

Alma, Nebraska

THE wedding was closer than ever.

The women were in their room, putting final touches to makeup and helping Rebecca with her dress and veil. And the men, in their room, were sipping beers and making hypersexualized comments in regard to Patrick's upcoming night.

Coffee was constantly being passed around from the little cart Susannah and Johanna wheeled between the rooms. Guests had begun to arrive, milling into the church little by little. They commented on the decorations, left gifts at the designated table, signed the guest book, and were ushered to their seats.

Bartholomew made the rounds, checking both the women's and men's rooms through the shut doors, keeping everyone up to date on the time and inquiring whether anything was needed. Upon confirmation that all was well, he returned to the sanctuary to continue chatting with the guests. Two guests he was thrilled to meet were Harold and Wyatt, the family of Elizabeth whom he'd grown quite close to over the past weeks. They chatted for a short time. Bartholomew made a mental note, as he moved on to another couple, that he would find them after the wedding and get to know them better.

Samuel was on the stage, sitting on a stool, plucking beautifully on an acoustic guitar amplified through the sound system. He effortlessly added a romantic ambiance to the room, occasionally humming along with the guitar. Everyone in the room felt the song reach into them and uplift their hearts, making them feel as if they were a part of the great romance they'd come to witness. Samuel's eyes, blue crystals, looked out toward the crowd as he crooned. Ladies—and not a small number of men—felt their knees weaken with the combination of music and gaze.

At one point, Elizabeth, after running to grab emergency tissues to hide in her dress, stopped in the door to the sanctuary and watched him in his element, doing what he loved and being loved by all for doing it.

Two old men, looking awkward in nice suits, shuffled in together. Samuel, still playing background music, saw them. His face lit up in a beautiful smile, followed by a conspiratorial wink. Despite both men having deep tans, their faces noticeably blanched.

"Are you okay? Do you need to sit down? If you are anemic, we can get you something to eat."

Their heads turned quickly to see the young man who'd come forward ready to lead them to their seats. They looked at him incredulously.

"Sorry. It's, just, I'm a nurse, and the way your faces paled concerned me."

"Look, son, thank you for the concern, but we will be fine." Gary patted the young man's shoulder. "Now, if you could kindly lead us to our chairs, I think I feel a heart attack coming on, and I would like to be comfortable when it hits."

It was the boy's turn to go a little pale.

"He's kidding. After his last three, you think he would have learned to not make light of it."

The boy's face went even paler. They ended up leading him to their seats as he trailed behind, unsure how to proceed. After they sat, they gave him innocent smiles that left him feeling a little better as he returned to the back to help a young man waiting to be seated. They turned toward Samuel, still beaming at them. Jacob looked around, saw the coast was clear, and gave him the middle finger.

Bartholomew, who'd appeared from behind the pulpit, let his jaw drop at the obscene gesture. Had the nurse been around, he might have been alarmed as Jacob's face turned bright scarlet. He hid his finger quickly, going so far as to shove his hand into his jacket pocket.

Verse 133

Somewhere Outside Lincoln, Nebraska

GIDEON shot to his feet, eyes blazing, scanning all the cars flying by in both directions. It had been over an hour since his initial call to the towing company, and still he had not seen any sign of a tow truck.

They had the decency to call him after thirty minutes to apologize for the long wait time and explain that the job before his had taken longer than anticipated. He'd considered then finding a different tow company, but figured the callback meant he was prioritized. Thirty minutes later, he was in the position of having waited so long, it wasn't worth starting over. He had not received a second callback. He'd been in his car, out of his car, and had even walked a little ways off the interstate to relieve himself.

He'd been sitting next to his car, leaning back against the warm metal, when the thought entered and exited his mind, going roughly 80 miles per hour:

Samuel, I drove all the way to Alma, because I knew after this wedding you would . . . No, that seems too forced . . .

Gideon fully understood that whoever had that thought was going to the exact same wedding he was trying to get to and having a much better go of it. Had he been expecting it, maybe he could have flagged the car and rode along. Gideon stood by his car, baffled by the strange overlap in two people headed to the same wedding to confront the same person who wasn't even one of the people getting married.

As he stood there, still fruitlessly watching vehicles, knowing that the car carrying Samuel's other confronter was long gone, he saw a tow truck lumber by in the lane going the opposite direction, and he listened in to confirm that it was in fact his tow truck coming at last. He watched it drive out of sight on its way to the exit ramp behind him only to get right back on to meet him.

He turned to look toward the direction the voice had been heading and marveled at it all.

Verse 134

Alma, Nebraska

BARTHOLOMEW stood at the front of the church with Patrick
next to him, trying hard to contain his nerves. Bartholomew put
a calming hand on his shoulder. It seemed to help a little. The
wedding party advanced slowly toward them as Samuel sat off
to the side, strumming an old love song. When Elizabeth
entered, Samuel looked up, and, when their eyes met, Elizabeth
could see in his eyes that today wasn't the end for them. She
smiled back at him quickly, then turned her attention toward
Bartholomew, still smiling. When their eyes met, she felt the
compassion that comes from old friendship and had to mentally
remind herself that they'd only met a month ago. She filed in
next to the other ladies where she made a conscious effort to not
look over at Samuel, whom she knew was looking at her every
chance he got.

Samuel's learned hands seamlessly moved from the
wedding party's entrance melody to that of the bride's. The
mother of the bride stood, causing a ripple effect, as everyone
stood to look at the back doors of the sanctuary. Patrick began
to cry before the doors even opened. Elizabeth joined him
shortly after. It was like finally understanding what the word
"beauty" meant and wondering how it had ever been used to
describe inferior moments. Natural, white light poured in
around Elizabeth and her father as the sunlight through the

stained-glass windows that adorned the sides of the sanctuary colored those in the pews, giving the bride an angelic, ethereal look.

Verse 135

Kearney, Nebraska

SALLY sat exasperated in her car, parked outside a gas station in Kearney. She was so close to Alma, she could almost smell the bar she'd worked in for so long.

Boomer, being the young boy he was, had the bladder size of a young boy. They'd stopped at every rest stop from Des Moines to Kearney to allow the little tagalong to scamper in to void a liquid that seemed to magically appear. Sally had limited his liquid intake to avoid this very scenario. At one of these potty breaks, Boomer had convinced her to purchase Subway sandwiches as they were going to be on the road over the lunch hour and he was already hungry.

She began wondering about her own sanity as she could hear, quite clearly, the tick-tocking of a giant cosmic clock, counting down the minutes until Samuel would pack up his musical equipment and leave Alma and Sally forever.

Tick.

"I gotta pee."

Tock.

"I'm hungry."

Tick.

"I don't feel so good."

Tock.

"Can I get a candy bar?"

Now, as she sat in the parking lot, she took deep breaths and prayed to a God she didn't believe in that Boomer's bladder would fully empty, and that Samuel would still be there when she got to town.

Through the store window, she saw Boomer looking at a rack of magazines, and she said many words she would not have felt comfortable saying had he been in the car. He nodded at the rack as if it had imparted on him some necessary wisdom for his trek, and he walked out the door, plodding maddingly slow toward the car. Sally let one more adult word slip past her lips as he grabbed the handle and opened the door.

Tick.

"I saw a comic about . . ."

Tock.

"Um, never mind."

Neither said another word as Sally guided the car back onto the interstate.

Verse 136

Alma, Nebraska

ELIZABETH stood in the foyer with her dad and Wyatt as guests filed out, hugging the recently married couple.

It had been a beautiful service. Bartholomew had been exceptional, and, of course, Samuel's music enhanced the mood in a way Elizabeth had never quite experienced. Toward the end of the ceremony, as she reminded herself to bend a knee slightly to keep from passing out, she found herself wondering if it was because the music was that good or because she had feelings for the musician.

She couldn't remember what the music had been like at her wedding. She had a faint memory of Jason paying a friend twenty bucks to run an iPod through the sound system. Regardless, she'd been to other weddings with singers, and she was unable to recall feeling anything in regard to the music. It had always been background noise.

Today, however, Samuel's light touch on the guitar and the song he sang during the sand ceremony had woven through everything. Elizabeth was not alone in the feeling. She could tell by the expressions on the faces of those attending. At one point during the ceremony, she'd noticed the guitar he played was the same he'd borrowed for the audition, but the thought had been fleeting, blown away on Samuel's melody.

Samuel was still back in the sanctuary, playing softly as the seats slowly emptied, and Elizabeth had an urge to push her way through those exiting to watch him play. Instead, she led Wyatt and her dad with the slowly progressing line toward the church's dining room. She knew that there would be pictures for which she would need to return, but she also knew that her shoes were eating her feet like two vivacious piranha and a moment in a chair would do her a world of good.

She sat, sighing loudly as Wyatt and Harold found chairs next to her.

"What a beautiful wedding," Harold commented.

Elizabeth grunted agreement as she massaged her right foot, her shoe abandoned on the floor beneath her.

"Did Samuel . . . ?" He paused.

Elizabeth looked at him cautiously, an image of her rear-end above her head flashing into her mind.

"Did Samuel bring something to this wedding that most musicians don't?"

Another sigh escaped Elizabeth and her mind turned back to her feet.

"I mean, I guess I don't know what I mean, but the music made me feel something I haven't felt in years."

"No, I agree," Elizabeth said, begrudgingly buckling the shoe back on before turning to the other foot. "It was like Rebecca and Patrick's love was a secret, and Samuel was sharing it with us. It was like being a part of their love story, not just someone in attendance. I must say, whatever it was, I, as the one who chose him for the job, made a damn good choice."

"You dare to speak such words in the house of the Lord?" chided Bartholomew, standing behind her.

She had the urge to hit him with the recently removed shoe. She probably would have had it not been for all the other guests who would find it strange if the maid of honor began beating the minister.

"They are ready to start taking pictures, if you want to head back to the sanctuary."

She sighed one last deep exhalation and returned her shoe to her foot. She stood, winced, then turned to follow Bartholomew.

"If it's any consolation," he said conspiratorially, "I agree. You did make a damn good choice."

This time, she did hit him, not caring what those around them thought. He looked at her in fake astonishment and pointed toward another picture of Jesus. In this portrait, too, Jesus did not look happy.

Verse 137

Lincoln, Nebraska

HOURS. It had been hours between when his tire blew on I-80 to when he finally pulled out the lot of Husker's Car Repair. Gideon could feel time passing as a physical thing, like a current flowing in the opposite direction, making every movement feel slow.

His plan had been to catch Samuel before the wedding, then beg him to not go through with it or stop him some other way. Gideon turned to look at the glove compartment, knowing that "some other way" was stashed with his driver's license and registration. Now, however, his plans had changed to catch him after the upcoming massacre to prevent him from moving on to the next one. Even that option looked like it might not happen. If he believed in some overarching power in the universe, he would have had some real questions about which side it was on.

He turned up the music to drown out the passing voices. He was stressed enough without hearing about failing marriages, late periods, and terrible children. He drove as fast as he dared, knowing a stop by Nebraska's finest could bring the whole endeavor to a crashing stop. Still, time pulled at him as it flowed ever onward.

Verse 138

Alma, Nebraska

THE dance was in full swing. If Samuel's music touched people during the wedding, it moved them now.

It was arguably the most entertaining event Elizabeth had ever attended. She danced with Rebecca, Patrick, Bartholomew, and even Wyatt and her dad. She was filled with energy, joy, and love for everyone involved, going so far as to kiss Bartholomew on the cheek, catching a little bit of his lips. He blushed bright red, and Elizabeth was grateful that, for once, it wasn't her blushing.

Samuel was like a god overseeing his creations as he manipulated everyone in attendance, working them like marionettes, everyone a willing slave to the beat. It was intoxicating. It felt like each drink Elizabeth took had a little extra shot of melody that gave her a high unlike anything she'd known, including those brownies she'd tried in college one night.

When she wasn't dancing, she found herself staring at Samuel. He was clearly in his element, doing what he'd been born to do.

Her father and son had left a few songs before, citing their ages as the reason. She'd hugged them both, promising to see them tomorrow. She was staying overnight at Rebecca's family house to allow herself the leisure of intoxication if she felt like indulging. Like the night before, however, she drank only socially, making sure to never get past a little buzz. Tension was finding its way back between her legs as she kept remembering the night before, imaging what the night ahead might hold in store.

Samuel didn't help. He was almost always looking in her direction as she danced as if he were in a gallery in front of the Mona Lisa with plans to take her to bed. When she'd first had that thought, she'd laughed out loud and her dance partner, Bartholomew, asked what she was laughing about. Predictably, her face tried to redden, but she fought back the flush, explaining that Samuel had made a face. Bartholomew looked at Samuel and the two shared a friendly nod. Crisis averted; Mona Lisa's pale face remained colorless.

Elizabeth, now shoeless, sat at a table enjoying a glass of white wine. Bartholomew joined her.

"I'm gonna head out. Unlike the rest of you heathens, I don't get to skip church tomorrow." He stood and she stood as well. "I want you to know, in case we don't get to talk much after the wedding, that I am truly grateful to have met you and see you as a real friend." He looked at her and smiled awkwardly, clearly not used to addressing people so formally.

Without thinking about it and without warning, she took him in her arms and held him in a firm embrace. Despite having every intention of staying in contact with the young minister, it all felt so final that she had to fight back an urge to cry. When they separated, she could see in his eyes that he shared the emotion.

He brought the back of her hand to his lips and kissed it. "Goodnight, Elizabeth." Then he turned and walked out of the dance.

Verse 139

Hastings, Nebraska

IT was taking every ounce of patience Sally possessed to not scream at the top of her lungs. Boomer was again in a bathroom; this time, at a Sonic.

She recalled their trip to Des Moines only a few weeks ago when they'd stopped once for lunch. Somehow, he'd been able to hold it for both halves of that journey. But he must have been drowning in his own saliva on this trip as he continuously found reserves of liquid to eject, despite not having anything to drink since lunch.

Tick.

They were less than an hour outside Alma.

Tock.

But he'd been in tears, squirming all over his chair, threatening the upholstery with an unavoidable accident unless they stopped. So, begrudgingly, she'd pulled into Sonic. She looked at the menu as she waited, scanning the beverages, seeing only refills for her son's bladder. Samuel was so close, she could almost hear him singing.

Tick.

Boomer came back around the corner, smiling absently, oblivious to the rush in which Sally found herself.

Tock.

"Mom, can I get a slush?"

She answered by backing the car out of the slot as he grabbed for his seatbelt.

Verse 140

Alma, Nebraska

THE night was nearing the end when Samuel surprised Elizabeth with a dance. She was standing by the refreshments, chatting with one of the bridesmaids named Bridgett, when she felt the tap on the shoulder. Apologizing, she turned to see who was behind her and was both confused and delighted to see Samuel.

"If you're not flying this ship, then who is?"

He nodded his head toward the stage where Elizabeth saw with delight the two older men from the bar and the coffee shop. Gary and Jacob, both looking as though they wished the floor would open up and swallow them, stood next to each other on the stage, awkwardly waiting for the music to begin. Samuel took out his phone, pressed the screen, and a piano began to play through the speakers. "May I have this dance?"

She took his outstretched hand and followed him back onto the dance floor. When the retired farmers began to sing, they took away Elizabeth's breath. Their voices were deep, rich, and beautiful. Every head turned to look at them as they began. Every head but from Samuel's. His eyes never left Elizabeth as he pulled her close, wrapping his hands around her waist. As she turned back to him, reaching around his neck to complete the high school dance position, their eyes met and held. His blue bombardier eyes recaptured her as they had the first time they met.

"I was wondering if you had any plans later tonight," said Samuel.

"I hadn't committed to anything, one way or the other." She instantly regretted the word "commit" as it clearly held much more meaning than she was hoping to convey in her flirtatious reply. However, she did not let her face show the doubt, and his face didn't reveal if he took any deeper meaning. "I was thinking I might grab a room, take a shower . . ." She paused. "Do some toe touches. You know, to stretch my legs after wearing those high heels."

He laughed openly. She was amazed to hear it blend into the music perfectly, melding into the already encapsulating melody coming from the two older men.

"I can honestly say that your plan puts all of mine to shame." He glanced up at the stage before returning his blue eyes to hers. "Can I ask you a favor?"

She nodded, feeling that knot of tension twist a little tighter.

"I have a song or two left after this one before calling it a night. I was wondering if you would be willing to leave a little early and . . ." He trailed off, looking back at the stage where the two men continued to sing beautifully while looking completely out of place. "I was hoping you could be waiting for me at the hotel." She saw red begin to color his face and it thrilled her. "I was hoping to give you a little more time to get dressed." At this suggestion, his face bloomed scarlet, even as he bounced his eyebrows toward her.

Elizabeth considered this and saw no reason not to head over early. All the teardown was scheduled for the day after, and Rebecca would honestly be thrilled at the idea of Elizabeth sneaking away to prepare for a night of wild lovemaking. She looked back at Samuel, bit her lower lip in a hopefully sensual way, and nodded.

His face filled with relief. This surprised her. She'd not realized how important his request had been. According to his own count, she would only miss the last couple of songs. Would it have been so bad had she declined to leave early and wait for the finale? She decided to let it go, understanding that walking into a hotel room with a woman clad in lingerie was possibly the epitome of sexual fantasy for most men, and Samuel was no exception. The knot tightened a little more at the image of her lying in the bed on her back in one of the pieces she'd kept from Rebecca. After this conversation, she realized it honestly would have been hard to keep her there.

She leaned forward and kissed Samuel deeply as the song came to an end around them. The room erupted in applause as the two men bowed awkwardly before dashing off the stage.

"Oh, look at the time," Elizabeth said, looking at her empty wrist. "I forgot that I have somewhere to be." She winked at Samuel who smiled back before energetically bounding toward the stage.

Elizabeth found Rebecca and Patrick, and wished them a good night, answering Rebecca's questions with an overly dramatic wink that left her giggling, while Patrick did his best to feign ignorance. Elizabeth then sought out the two still disheveled men to thank them for the best sung song of the night. Lastly, she walked up to the stage, blew a kiss to the DJ, who beamed back at her as he pretended to catch it, kissing his palm. With the goodbyes sorted, Elizabeth found her heels and walked barefoot into the summer night.

Verse 141

Alma, Nebraska

SAMUEL sang a couple more songs after Elizabeth left to give her plenty of time to get to the hotel and make sure she didn't forget anything important enough to return.

While he sang the last few songs, he contemplated how his life had changed since meeting her. This would be his last time. He was retiring from the game and would settle down. This was something he'd never considered. Even when his older brother had tried to convince him to hang up his coat, he'd refused. Elizabeth, however, had done something to him; she had rewritten his story. Spending the rest of his life with her was too important to risk for his self-declared mission.

Not that there was much risk in getting caught. No one would believe that a man sang people to death. But even the small risk made him nervous.

He'd considered calling off tonight. But after all the work he'd put into his list, he couldn't walk away. Not to mention when he quit, he wanted to end with a show.

He went over the list in his head as he sang one of the last songs of the night, again pleased with how short it was. This had been a nice little town, so cleaning it up was not nearly as big a job as some of his others had been.

He watched Patrick spin Rebecca out away from him only to curl her back up into his arms. Patrick was the only name on the list he regretted and had gone back and forth on. In the end, he'd reasoned that leopards don't change their spots, and he was doing Rebecca a favor. If he allowed their relationship to continue, years from now, it would end in tragic betrayal. Better to nip it in the bud now. Wouldn't Elizabeth have been happier if her last marriage ended in the height of love rather than the depths of hatred?

He scanned the room. None of those on his list had left early. This was not surprising as he'd compelled them to stay with each song he sang.

As the second to last song came to an end, he quickly reviewed the tale he was about to spin.

He'd lucked out when an old boyfriend of Rebecca's, with whom she'd maintained a friendship, had come to the bachelor party and now the wedding. Samuel was able to add him to this list, based solely on the terrible life he bragged about to the other men. He would use him for the main event. The classic old lover who can't let go, shows up to the wedding, and goes on a killing spree before taking his own life. The story was simple, clean, and would give Patrick a heroic ending that Rebecca could be proud of in her grief. Murder always made for a better story than suicide. And it allowed the innocent to reap the benefits, a real win-win scenario for everyone involved.

He brought the song to an end and took a deep breath. "Tonight has been amazing. Do we all agree?"

The crowd, despite the hour, let out a roar of approval. Patrick squeezed Rebecca close to him, kissing her head.

"I have one last song for you."

Sounds of disapproval arose.

He raised his hands in surrender. "I know, I know. I wish we could go all night, but, alas, all good things must come to an end. In light of this, I have saved the very best song for last."

A cheer arose from the leftover crowd as Samuel took the microphone off the stand. He began to sing. As he did, he walked toward the front of the stage where he first sat, then dropped onto the dance floor. His song wove around them like a snake slithering into one ear and out the other on its way to the next auditory cave.

Every eye that had, moments ago, blazed with the energy of the night took on a glazed look as a general understanding took hold. Samuel walked through the throng of people who parted like the Red Sea toward the door. Everything had been planned to the last detail, including his leaving before the action took place. After he broke through the crowd, every head turning to track his progress, he turned to his little flock. His melody changed octaves, and the little crowd began to move into position, setting the stage for his final finale.

"Samuel."

He whirled around, shocked by the unexpected voice behind him. He was completely thrown off by the presence of the bartender who shouldn't have been in town. In his confusion, something happened that had never happened before: he lost his concentration.

All the murderous intent he'd been wrapping around those on his list focused on Sally, standing expectantly in the open door. Without a second thought, she reached up, dug her nails into her neck, and tore out her throat, spraying Samuel with her blood. She stood in front of him for a moment as everything went silent, her hopeful smile never leaving her face. Then, she fell to her knees, the bloody mess in her hand dropping beside her.

The stunned silence held a moment longer until a hand fell onto his shoulder.

"Samuel, what in the—?"

Gary was unable to finish the thought as Samuel's unfocused mind lashed out at the man beside him. Samuel watched in horror as the old man, who had not even been on his list, shattered the bottle of fancy wheat beer he was holding and used the shattered remains to slice cleanly through the soft flesh under his jaw.

The room fell into disarray then as no one understood what was happening; only that they were in danger and the wedding singer was somehow involved.

Blood dripped from Samuel's chin as he turned toward them and began to sing a new ballad.

Verse 142

Alma, Nebraska

BOOMER had been told to wait in the car. This suited him fine as he'd heard his mother rehearsing and rehearsing over and over what she planned to say to the man from the bar and, frankly, he did not want to witness it in real life.

He watched her walk into the church. Then his eyes fell on something that grabbed his heart, squeezing painfully as fear froze the blood in his veins. There stood the motorcycle, propped on its stand, facing the open door his mother had entered. He was suddenly filled with understanding. His mother's last-minute trip had not been a spur-of-the-moment decision, but a plan set in place by this evil machine to bring her back to this town.

But the motorcycle had not planned on Boomer.

He took the Swiss army knife his dad had given him out of his pocket, flipped out the longest blade, and stepped into the summer night. This was why he'd come. He had to stand strong to protect his mother and to end this nightmare once and for all.

He walked bravely toward the machine. It stood motionless, playing dead, when he knew it was anything but. Then he heard screams from within the church and knew the motorcycle had begun its lethal work. It had, after all, taken his dad while outside their house.

There was no time to lose. He ran the last few steps to the metal death machine. "This is for my dad, you son of a bitch!" he screamed before burying the knife into the front tire.

Verse 143

Alma, Nebraska

SAMUEL was rewriting the narrative as he went, the narrative now being "no survivors means no witnesses." He was heartbroken by this outcome as he'd truly come to like a good number of the people there, but he loved Elizabeth and could not risk anything messing with their future. He thought about how real his relationship with her had become. For the first time in his life, he was free to be himself; no tricks, no songs, no manipulation. That was something he was not willing to give up.

That was something he was willing to kill every single remaining wedding guest to protect.

After Gary had, unfortunately, taken his life and before Samuel could refocus and resume singing, Patrick started shoving everyone around him through a nearby door.

Samuel's melody reached out. Patrick's best man, presumably the next person Patrick would shove through the door, pulled out a commemorative pen he'd bought specifically to sign the marriage license and shoved it into Patrick's right eye, pushing him back against the wall. Patrick reached up to feel the pen, his remaining eye staring in disbelief. He watched as his oldest friend in the world threw his weight into the pen and it slid further in. Patrick's searching eye stopped moving, glazed over, and he slid down the wall, the pen pulling free, held tightly in the hand that killed him. Singing happily,

Patrick's best man gave an encore performance. This time, it was a solo act.

Samuel, still singing, turned toward a small cluster of wedding guests on the other side of the room, sending a few bars of melody in that direction before a scream brought his attention back to Patrick's door.

Rebecca, the first one Patrick sent through the door, had returned and now stood over her husband's body.

Samuel paused a moment, understanding that he was about to end the life of Elizabeth's best friend. Their eyes met. He realized that there was no future with Elizabeth as long as Rebecca survived.

But before he could act, he heard a shrieking from the parking lot. Through one of the stained-glass windows, he saw a child tearing into his bike's tires with a knife. Samuel stopped singing altogether as his mind tried to process this new information. He glanced back toward Patrick's body, but Rebecca was gone.

"Shit."

He turned back to the boy destroying his motorcycle.

Verse 144

Alma, Nebraska

ELIZABETH stretched out in the bed, then rolled over, trying different positions that she considered enticing. After the previous night's awkward introduction, she was determined to stun Samuel with an unforgettable image that would wipe that from of his mind. Tonight, she wore the red ropey outfit, the complexity of which had left her grateful for the extra time Samuel had given.

Now, as she rolled over again, flexing up on her elbows to boost her chest, she wondered if Samuel would struggle as much taking it off as she had struggled getting it on. She raised one leg, then the other, then raised her hips off the bed. She was posed in this position when her phone started buzzing on the side table.

She rolled over, adjusted a strap that was biting into her hip, and picked up the vibrating machine. The call was from Rebecca.

"Bex?" she said aloud. There were two places her friend should be: dancing to the last few songs of Samuel's or being ravished by her new husband, neither of which should require a phone call to Elizabeth. "Hello?"

"Run. Elizabeth, run now. Get out of town. Hide."

Elizabeth's heart began to race. Adrenaline poured into her veins as confusion mixed with fear. "What? I—what?" She was unable to articulate her confusion in a way that would lead to answers.

"Elizabeth, Patrick is dead. Everyone is dead. Samuel killed them."

Elizabeth's heart suddenly stopped. Everything stopped. Her breathing. Time. Her life.

"Elizabeth? Did you hear me? Get in your car right now. Run!"

Elizabeth dropped her phone, grabbed her keys, and ran to her car. Her mind struggled to land on a single thought as it flitted to each word Rebecca said.

Samuel killed? Patrick is dead? Run?

She was struggling to take full breaths. Instead, she took quick, little breaths. She felt lightheaded. This didn't seem real. She found herself wondering if maybe she'd messed up one of the straps and passed out on the bed from lack of oxygen. Was she dying right now, lying in a hotel room strapped up in lingerie? Unable to focus, she ran on autopilot, following the last command she'd been given:

"Run."

Barefoot, and basically naked, she did just that. Once in her car, she threw it in reverse, pulled out of the parking lot, and sped onto the highway.

Verse 145

Alma, Nebraska

SAMUEL looked down at the boy who looked back up at him with only the barest recognition in his eyes. The blood that dripped down Samuel's face and splattered across his suit, however, held Boomer's attention.

"Did the motorcycle do that?" he asked.

Samuel looked at the frightened child for a second, completely baffled by the turn of events that had brought him to this moment. Then, all the rage at having the night go off the rails and the realization that everything had been ruined struck him. He reached forward, needing to release his anger physically for once and grasped the boy's wrist with the knife. With a quick motion, he snapped Boomer's brittle bones, causing the weapon to fall uselessly to the ground.

The boy screamed in pain, but Samuel put a stop to that as he wrapped his other hand around the boy's throat, cutting off the sound.

The wind blew and dust surrounded them as the boy struggled with his free hand to pry off Samuel's hands. Then the wind died down and Boomer's grasping hand began to lose its strength. It fell to his side as his eyes rolled up into his head. Samuel was about to give a final squeeze, to guarantee an end to this distraction, when the dust settled back on the parking lot. Out of the corner of his eye, he recognized a car speeding madly down the highway toward the bridge out of town.

He dropped the kid to the ground and began to run down the hill toward the street. He started to sing at the top of his lungs. It sounded anything but beautiful.

Verse 146

Alma, Nebraska

TEARS streamed down Elizabeth's face as her car bumped up onto the bridge. She wondered if she should call the police or her dad or the FBI, then, just as quickly, realized that in her panic, she'd dropped her phone in the hotel. Her only option was to keep going.

The darkness waiting at the far end of the bridge represented safety. Once she crossed the bridge, she could hide in that darkness and finally catch her breath.

She began to sing. It was a hysterical song. She took her foot off the pedal, letting her car drift to a stop.

The darkness was so far away, it felt unattainable.

She looked in her rearview mirror and saw a man walking in her direction, a silhouette against the streetlights of Alma. She continued to sing, more quietly now, almost a whisper as she opened her car door, stepping barefoot onto the pavement of the bridge. Samuel continued to walk toward her, singing to her, and now it was beautiful.

She felt the urge to forget everything, to run to him, to escape the bad dream in which she found herself. Somewhere in the recesses of her mind, she registered the heat of the pavement on her feet. She felt the warm wind on her tear-streaked face, the straps of the lingerie shifting uncomfortably. She heard a wailing from nearby and understood that she was no longer in control. Her feet began to walk toward Samuel, her fear evaporating into the melody.

"Elizabeth." Although he spoke the word, they fit into the song as if he were singing them. The world had become a musical, and she was acting the part, directed to play a role in a drama she didn't understand. "Please listen to me. I know you are confused, and you are scared, but believe me when I say it is all going to be all right."

The words carried in the song reached into her, and she did believe, and she was filled with a relief so immense, she would have fallen to her knees had she been in control of her own body.

"I would never hurt you, never do anything to cause you grief." He smiled.

She was close enough now to see the blue diamonds of his eyes.

"I have been working very hard to remove any source of grief from your life."

Samuel's declaration found the melodically buried memory of Rebecca's tortured screams and through the euphoric cloud of the music, a dawning horror fought its way from her subconscious mind.

How had she not seen it before? Three deaths, all related to her, happening so close together, and she'd taken them as coincidence?

Her mind fought to focus on one aspect of that thought: *Samuel* had killed Jason, not Stacy as all the evidence seemed to say. He had, in fact, gone out of his way to make sure Jason's death had looked like a lover's murder.

Why?

Because life insurance policies don't pay for suicides.

This man, with whom she'd been ready to fall in love, ready to mold her future, had killed her son's father.

Her son.

Her mind was torn in two as the grief of realization fought desperately against the joy of singing with Samuel.

Wyatt. She had to focus on him, on what Samuel had taken from him. Wyatt, the greatest love in her life.

"Just let me explain. I can start from the beginning, and you will understand. I'll tell you everything."

She was close enough now that she could see him clearer, and she saw the blood smeared across his face, splattered across his suit. But his blue eyes shone out above the red. When their eyes met, she was unable to look away. In that moment standing on the bridge, his music surrounding them, they looked into each other's eyes and time came to a stop.

Trapped in his serenade, she was uncontrollably in love and happy to be so. She was ready to let everything else go to be with him. Even her son could not stand in the way of her desire as she stared into those eyes.

The details of his face suddenly disappeared. He again became a silhouette; this time in the bright glare of headlights.

Instinctively, they both turned to look at the newest cast member of their little drama. The door opened. As a young man stepped out, Elizabeth felt the song recede from her as Samuel's focus yanked toward the newcomer.

"Hello, Samuel. Based on the blood, I assume I am too late."

Samuel's mouth hung open as he stared at the man.

"This has to end, Samuel. I am here to make sure it does."

"You, Gideon?" Samuel choked on a laugh.

Elizabeth felt the song recede a little more.

"You are here to make sure it ends?" Samuel took a step forward. "The ironic thing, brother, is I had planned on making this my last night."

Elizabeth, who'd been all but forgotten, found clarity as Samuel confronted the newcomer. Her subconscious finally gained a foothold.

With the weight of the song lifting, her mind filled the vacant space by flashing through the past few months. Their night together. Jason's casket. Their first kiss. The blood dripping down Samuel's face. Wyatt. Randall. Her diary.

She saw her hand moving as she wrote her name followed by his. With great effort, she looked at the hand that had written the name. She tried to move it, testing how much will she had over her body.

It was like moving through sludge, but she was able to lift the hand slightly. Regaining that small amount of ownership gave her clarity over the racing of her mind.

No matter what else happened, Samuel had taken away her freedom. That was the only fact she knew definitively. That, and the fact that she was taking it back.

She felt a flare of hope. It flamed brighter as she felt the song continue to shift away.

Verse 147

Alma, Nebraska

"YOU show up here like a knight in shining armor, ready to save the day, when it was you who used to write the list." Samuel spat the words at Gideon. "So don't give me that holier than thou bullshit, you who used to assign death for a living." Samuel began to cry.

"Samuel, please. I know there is goodness in you," said Gideon. "I understand that you have a need to fix the world. You want to save those who cannot, or will not, save themselves. It's one of the things I love about you."

"Love?" Samuel gasped between sobs.

"But you have to know that this has gone too far. You've lost sight of those you are trying to help." Gideon felt his own tears now. "Come with me. We can figure this out together. There doesn't have to be any more death."

"Love. Everything I have ever done has been out of love. Every name on my list was written to show love: for the beaten child, the betrayed wife, the widowed husband, the unheard victims of crimes who would never find justice. I sacrificed *everything* for the *love* of others." Samuel's eyes pierced into Gideon. "I even lost you. I loved you, Gideon. I would have died for you." The music that had been flowing through every word Samuel said shifted in tone. "I am done sacrificing for others. My own love has become too important. And I will sacrifice everything to protect it."

Gideon heard the thoughts before Samuel fully formed them. Gideon read Samuel's intent and understood that his time was up.

As fast as he could, he reached back, grabbed the gun he'd lodged in his waistband, and pulled it free. His heart breaking, he brought it around.

He watched as the barrel passed harmlessly past Samuel and continued its arch, wrapped in melody, to his own head. Gideon sang "I love you" into Samuel's song and heard Samuel return the thought. As the bullet tore through his skull, he found peace in the fact that there would be no more voices in death.

Verse 148

Alma, Nebraska

SAMUEL screamed at the night sky.

Elizabeth had a moment to muse that even his scream sounded musical. She tore herself from the remaining hold the song had on her and threw herself at Samuel, who stood over the crumpled form of the stranger. She shoved him as hard as she could.

His scream of grief turned into a shriek of surprise as his legs caught the guardrail. His arms flew out, reaching for something to grab on to, finding nothing.

Elizabeth stumbled to her knees as his body shifted, and she carried him out and over the safety of the rail where gravity took hold of him.

Many years before, the bridge had traveled over a lake where Elizabeth herself went camping many times, swimming and boating with Rebecca in childhood. The water, however, had long dried up, taken for use in the fields without sufficient rain to replenish.

Samuel fell, his songs of no use to him now as the dry lake bed came to meet him.

Elizabeth sat on the bridge, completely wrapped in silence. Beautiful silence.

Bridge

Omaha, Nebraska

ELIZABETH set down the box she was carrying and, with the back of her arm, wiped away the sweat threatening to drip into her left eye. Even though the fall semester was only a few weeks away, the air still felt very summery.

Her dad shuffled into the room, set down his much heavier box, straightened, and sighed as his back let out a firecracker pop.

"You know, I could help out with the bigger boxes. I'm not an invalid," Elizabeth said as they left the room that had once been Jason's mancave, then Elizabeth's craft room before becoming what would be Grandpa's room.

"I would not hear of it. Wyatt and I are more than strong enough to carry the big stuff. Right, Wyatt?"

Wyatt, who was carrying his grandpa's pillow, nodded vigorously.

Elizabeth smiled her support until her son was out of sight, then rolled her eyes. "Yep. A lot of help there. Okay, I will keep my lifting within the doctor-recommended twenty pounds, but you had better believe I will push that limit to the line. You didn't raise a slacker."

Her dad gave her a knowing look. "And I assume you have plans today, and the quicker we get done, the sooner you can go. Does all the staff at the hospital know you by name yet?"

She laughed as if it were a joke. But actually, most of the staff did and would often bring her a decaf coffee, even when she didn't ask. "I told you: Today is a simple call-and-check. Moving an old hoarder from a full house into a bedroom is a full-day kind of job. This is essentially the opposite of when we moved Rebecca from her one-bedroom apartment to her parents' house."

This thought reminded Elizabeth that, after she called the hospital, she needed to call Rebecca. Even though things were better for her best friend since she'd moved back to Alma, Elizabeth still liked checking in. Recently, Rebecca had sent her a bump picture and Elizabeth had been shocked at how much bigger she had grown. It was safe to say she'd "popped." Absentmindedly, Elizabeth gently ran her fingers above her own beltline.

"Okay, I take it back. You can lift heavier boxes if it means you'll get back to work," Harold said, pulling her from her revelries.

She blinked, smiled, and did just that, heading back into the late summer heat.

As she picked up a roughly twenty-pound box, she began to hum. The song was always in her mind because it was the soundtrack of her nightmares. In time, though, she believed she could mold the tune into something different. The first step would be claiming it as her own.

So, she hummed as she lifted, she hummed as she organized, and she hummed as she took a well-earned bath. That night, when the two men left in her life were asleep in their rooms, she fell asleep humming the melody of her dreams.

Coda

Omaha, Nebraska

GIDEON swam in and out of a thick, dark unconsciousness. There were moments when he would brush the surface, when he could make out distant voices.

"... he may be the only one with answers ..."

He started to sink again, fought back, trying desperately to break the surface.

"... Yeah, Dad is watching him while I'm here ..."

There were times he almost gave up, almost allowed the abyss to claim him. But that voice ...

"... I know it's been months, but ..."

Like a lighthouse in the mist, the voice gave him a beacon toward which to swim.

When he finally broke through the surface of his consciousness and opened his eyes for the first time, what he noticed first was the quiet.

That isn't to say he didn't hear sounds. There were the muffled sounds of voices nearby, the beeping of machinery, and someone humming a song off to his left. Gideon, however, had spent his entire life hearing the thoughts, emotions, loves, hates, muses, and mental notes of everyone around him, and now he heard only his own confused thoughts. The world, despite all its noise, was incredibly quiet.

With monumental effort, he forced his eyes to focus. The beeping immediately made sense as he saw an IV pole. Without moving his body, he scanned the small hospital room, his eyes momentarily settling on a young woman sitting in a chair near his bed, humming to herself as she read a paperback. Her heavy sweater did little to hide the fact that she was clearly pregnant.

Then, as his mind came fully awake, his blood ran cold. He recognized the song she was humming.

It was Samuel's song.

He stared at the unknown woman who'd not yet noticed his awakened state. She absentmindedly stroked the swell of her stomach, humming the lullaby to her unborn child.

Out of the corner of his eye, Gideon saw movement. He allowed his eyes to leave his guest and watched in amazed dread as a pen that had been carelessly left on the side table floated a couple of inches into the air.

He slowly turned back toward the woman whose baby was very much enjoying the song.

FINALE

Acknowledgements

There were innumerable people involved in the creation of this book who deserve my thanks. Sadly, the list would dwarf the novel, so I will only shine a light on a specific few. For those not mentioned, know I love you and appreciate your help and encouragement.

First and foremost, I must thank my wife Karlynn, I sometimes believe you have loftier dreams for my writing than I do. You've done more research on the world of writing and publishing than most agents and publishers and continue to work diligently to make this book a success. I am, as always, humbled to be your partner. That joke you made on that long ago night on the road to Norton birthed Serenade. Keep joking, my life as a writer depends on it.

I would like to thank my family, both by blood and marriage, who have always cultivated an environment of creativity from the start. Your pride in every artistic endeavor is something I don't take for granted. I wonder how many great works of art were never created because the first one was met with indifference. Specifically, I want to thank my brother Aaron, a fellow author, you are always willing to spend hours editing and helping me with something I wrote in thirty minutes. Your patience at those times is appreciated. Also, sorry, I bet that's pretty annoying. Two of my best friends from childhood, Travis and Andrew, you will always be family and know that the stories we came up with in our youth continue to play in my mind.

I have to thank my editor, Priscilla. Thanks for that skillful way you bluntly tell me when something I write is terrible, but shower me with praise when you love something as well. It's that combination that keeps me writing and reaching out to you for your opinions on everything. I don't think I could ever express how important your influence on this book was. Without you, there is no Serenade.

Pace, you have taken every idea from my mind and beautifully recreated it as physical art. I know I can be a lot and it is often hard to hold back once I let the ideas start flowing. Your willingness and eagerness to listen and create those images is nothing short of miraculous.

Josh, remember when you tricked me into reading Stephen King via The Dark Tower, despite my claim to not like horror? My entire identity has been remodeled due to that recommendation. For that, I will always be immeasurably thankful. You've also read every version of Serenade from the rough draft to the final draft. Thanks for coming along for the journey.

Other readers worth mentioning. Chelsea you literally got down on your hands and knees to act out a scene solely to help me write it believably. That's greater dedication than even I have. Ben when you edited the draft I sent to you to show me what it could look like published, that was possibly the first time it felt like a reality. My BEENS book club, Beth, Elaine, Emily, and Nichol, I rely on our monthly get-togethers not only for great book discussion but for my sanity and your support. You guys are the best thing to come out of the COVID era. Thanks, Beth, for bringing us together. May we continue to read great literature together for many years to come. Jonathan Janz, you are my hero. I will forever sing your praises, both for your exceptional writing and your incredible kindness.

Julie from JD Drama. You were the first to publish my writing. I don't think you know how big of an impact that had on my life. I framed that first script along with the contract and whenever I doubt my writing all I have to do is look at the wall where it hangs.

Finally, Amanda with Line by Lion Publications. Thank you so much for opening the door to me when I knocked. That has changed my life. Let's sit by the fire and tell great stories.